PROMETHEUS
REBOUND

OAK RIDGE PUBLIC LIBRARY
Civic Center
Oak Ridge, TN 37830

Copyright © 2008-2013 The Orbital Defense Corps, LLC. All rights reserved. Except as permitted under the Copyright Act of 1976, no part of this book may be reproduced in any form or by any electronic or mechanical means, including the use of information storage and retrieval systems, without express written permission from the copyright owner.

Certain stock imagery © iStockphoto.

Cover design and internal design © 2013 The Orbital Defense Corps, LLC.

The ODC Roundel circle/star design is trademark and service mark of The Orbital Defense Corps, LLC.

All Art of War quotations come from the 1910 translation by Lionel Giles, which is public domain in the United States and other applicable countries and/or territories.

All Ronald Reagan quotations come from transcripts of public speeches.

This book is a work of fiction. Names, characters, institutions, establishments, places, events, and incidents are the product of the author's imagination and/or are used fictitiously. Events or situations described in this book with reference to real locations, institutions, establishments, and/or actual living persons are historical, merely coincidental, and/or fictionalized with the intent to provide the reader with a sense of reality and authenticity.

Because of the dynamic nature of the Internet, any web addresses or links contained in this book may have changed since publication and may no longer be valid, without knowledge of the author or publisher. The author and publisher claim no rights in, and expressly disclaim any liability potentially arising from, the accessing and/or use of any referenced websites. Neither the author nor the publisher guarantees, approves, or endorses the information, products, and/or services available on such websites, nor does any reference to any website indicate any association with, or endorsement by, the author or publisher.

First Printing, October 2013

ISBN-13: 978-1492701439
ISBN-10: 1492701432

To all those who have sacrificed
in service to their nation.

Many of us dream of being heroes.
You *are* heroes.

Acknowledgments

This project has been so long in the making that I despair of acknowledging everyone who has contributed to its success. I will, however, do my best.

Near the top of the list have to be my readers: beta testers Dr. Ruth Akers, Beth Paul, Jeremy Hunt, Mason Matthews, Brian Tripp, Stuart Bauman, Monica Robinson, Sarah Ogle, Alicia Platz; gamma testers Les Akers, Brian McCann, Matt Santen; and of course others who prefer anonymity. Your responses and suggestions for improvement were often in direct contradiction with each other's, and that proved a great encouragement to craft a more broadly accessible finished product. Jeremy, some of your feedback was the hardest to hear, but you forced me to acknowledge things that desperately needed fixing, and I wouldn't trade that for anything.

Mason Matthews was also my science advisor from the very beginning, and I appreciate the dozens of snatches of conversation we've had over these years. From designing spacecraft to discussing some of the more esoteric concepts of general relativity, your input has been absolutely critical.

My friends in the Army, Navy, Air Force, and Marine Corps provided insight that was integral to the story I wanted to create. Though I set out to write the most authentic story possible given my premise, I ultimately accepted that verisimilitude does not always a good story make. Nevertheless, I have these men and women to thank for what credibility I did achieve in the military aspects of this narrative (despite never serving in the military myself). Any gaffes that remain are entirely my own fault. (Note: these individuals asked to remain nameless for professional reasons, *not* because they violated national security by providing me with sensitive intelligence about actual alien encounters! All aspects of this story relating to alien encounters, Area 51, etc. are either my own fabrication or else based upon popular conspiracy theories.)

I couldn't have written the climactic end to this volume without the unique perspective of a certain deepwater drilling engineer, one of just five hundred people in the world who does what he does. Also invaluable was the assistance of Matt Rothgeb, an engineer working for NASA, who made some recommendations about the best way to transport 800+ people into orbit within a short time frame, and who helped me wrap my mind around the topic of hypergolics and bi-propellants. I appreciated Dr. Jennifer Burg's aid in answering a specific question regarding historical software development, one that was far outside my experience. Other professors at my alma mater assisted me in crafting the ODC's Latin motto, which appears in the Gryphen crest (*Ultima spes hominum*). Entertainment lawyer Kevin Levine helped me avoid the pitfalls inherent in publishing a book set within a very litigious real world. And of course Dr. Rob Johnston was generous with his medical expertise, though it applies more to the second volume of this story (don't worry, Rob, I wrote you into the story as requested... with a twist!). Outside the book itself, Bob and Pat Weiford and Steve McConihay helped make the cinematic launch trailer a reality, selflessly offering their time and expertise at no expense.

I would be remiss not to thank the countless contributors to Wikipedia. I cannot imagine the difficulty of writing this book without so much of the info I needed at my fingertips. I have contributed financially to that meaningful initiative, and I hope to do more in the future. I also have to recognize National Novel Writing Month and my local NaNoWriMo group for challenging me to stop procrastinating and actually produce a manuscript during the month of November 2008. I can say for a fact that this book would never have happened if I had never started writing it! Finally, I owe gratitude to my friend Greg Auerbach for enabling my transition to freelance software development, which also opened up the time I needed to finish this project.

In addition to being a reader and editor, my mother has been an unending sense of encouragement on this and, truly, *all* of the big undertakings I have tackled in my life. She never expressed any doubt that I could and would someday publish. My father is responsible for getting me interested in science fiction in the first place, and I appreciate the many hours I have shared with him and my brother over the years, enjoying (and often critiquing) others' submissions to the genre. I am also grateful to my sister and brother-in-law—him for his service in our nation's military, and her for the sacrifice she has made while he is overseas.

Finally but most importantly, I want to recognize my Lord, Savior, and most faithful friend for… well, for everything. For making my life worth living. For giving me a never-ending desire for good story, and now for the opportunity to craft my own. For being patient and forgiving when, too often, I let this project (and others) take precedence over our relationship. I hope and pray that this novel honors You. Matthew 6:33.

PROMETHEUS
REBOUND

Day 1,529 of Incarceration
Med Bay 5, Bunker 18-B, Groom Lake Facility
37°15'04" N, 115°49'26" W – Elev. 4,284 feet
(178 feet below ground)

The room is stark, sterile. Row upon row of 4-inch white tiles cover each wall, stretching from floor to ceiling. The floor itself is waxed to a high shine. Medical machines line the periphery, beeping, whirring, blinking, and an analog clock reads 10:27. Everything is white.

The patient perches at the center of the room.

Stock-still, sitting on the very edge of the small bed, the patient stares at the floor... then explodes into motion.

Immediately, alarms begin blaring. The figure rips a device from the wall, pauses, then drops it before speeding towards the entrance in an ungainly lope. Throwing up spindly arms, the patient crashes into the door at speed and bursts through into the hallway beyond.

The alarms continue, unabated.

The patient yells, incoherent. One long white hallway leads to another, and a sharp right turn reveals still another. But this hallway is occupied.

Two burly forms collide with the fleeing figure, clamping hands around arms to prevent struggle. But struggle persists as the patient is marched back to that stark, sterile room. Struggle continues even as the thrashing form is ultimately strapped to the bed with wide leather cuffs.

Then all falls motionless as the patient espies the needle: a long silvery hypodermic joined to a glass syringe, brimming with some cloudy substance. The contents of that syringe spell death.

The patient's effort intensifies then, head jerking back and forth, even as the needle is forcibly injected. Slowly but surely, the effects become obvious. Eyelids droop, motions become jerky. But with one final, monumental exertion, the creature rips one arm free of the band encircling it.

Pausing just out of reach, the attendant leans over the supine form, momentarily transfixed by startling blue eyes set in an ashen face. Even as those lids tremble, the piercing eye contact is maintained, and the patient manages to raise a three-fingered hand.

"The Nymph." *The words come out as a croak, barely decipherable.* "Tell him it's the Nymph." *Then the eyes roll up, and the fingers slacken. A wadded ball of paper drops from their grip. The doctor arrives, and the procedure begins under the observation of two military officers. Twenty minutes later, the one known as* KLINE *stops breathing.*

Standing to the side in that stark, sterile room, the older of the two uniformed figures smoothes out the wadded paper... and nearly stops breathing as well.

This paper contains the key to everything.

BOOK ONE
CULTIVATION

nk7 Nomad short-range, heat-seeking, rocket-propelled "air-to-air" missile, better known as "Rambler"

dynamic directional thrusters emit random bursts to create distinctive erratic flight pattern

- Ramblers
- Double-Hull Design
- Outer Hull
- Inner Hull
- Weapons Cradle with customizable ordnance hardpoints
- Rate of Fire in excess of 100 rounds per second
- 1,000-round capacity per gun
- Acceleration couch
- Manual releases
- Hatch
- Underseat sidearm holster
- Electromagnetic cradle anchors
- 37mm chain guns
- Paired Emitter Nozzles for spin cancelation/reversal
- Fuel & Oxidizer Tanks integrated into outer hull
- Transversal Axis Maneuvering
- Vertical Axis Maneuvering
- Lateral Axis Maneuvering
- Main Propulsion
- Electromagnetic Docking Grapple
- Ball-Bearing & Ratchet System for smooth, independent movement of hulls

The V-Series DESTRIER

Revision 1.42a
Logged 6-20-84
by Callista G.

All warfare is based on deception

> ~ Sun Tzu, *The Art of War*,
> sometime between the
> 4th and 6th centuries B.C.

I couldn't help but say to [General Secretary Gorbachev], just think how easy his task and mine might be in these meetings that we held if suddenly there was a threat to this world from some other species, from another planet, outside in the universe. We'd forget all the little local differences that we have between our countries, and we would find out once and for all that we really are all human beings here on this Earth together.

> ~ Ronald Reagan
> Fallston, Maryland
> December 4, 1985

[Chapter 00]

Friday morning
February 7, 2014

"They're going to kill you."

Kara almost misses a step. In disbelief, she pulls the cell phone away from her ear, double-checks that she doesn't recognize the number. "Who is this?"

"This is a friend," the earnest voice says. *"You have to listen—"*

"I'm hanging up now." Kara doesn't mind a good prank, but this is just tasteless.

"No wait! This is Kara Dunn, right? Project lead on Rampant?"

"Who is this?" she demands again. Obviously this isn't just a random prank; the caller knows her.

"You and your friend are in terrible danger. They're all around you, they could—"

"Goodbye," she says firmly and ends the call.

"Who was that?" Viviane asks.

Kara shrugs uneasily. "Prank call."

The two women are in the midst of their morning run, on a wooded trail in a park not far from the townhouse they share. Usually Kara revels in being outdoors, but suddenly the trees all around seem ominous in the predawn light.

A branch snaps and she jumps, glancing behind her. Oh. Just another runner, about thirty yards back. Bright green warmup jacket—same guy they overtook a few minutes ago.

Viviane gives her an odd look. "What's got into you? Something about that call?"

Kara brushes it off. "It's nothing." She loves Viviane like a sister, but the younger woman can be a bit of a drama queen. The last thing she needs is to think they're in some sort of danger.

Shoving the phone back in her pocket, Kara retrieves a hair elastic and tries to put it to good use. She'd recently started wearing her dark hair short, and she's mostly happy with that decision, except that it's so much harder to keep out of her face now.

Her phone rings, and she barely stops herself from jumping again. Same number. With a grimace, she cancels the call unanswered.

"Paul?" Viviane guesses, angling for a look at the phone, which Kara turns away.

"What makes you say that?"

Viviane shrugs. "I don't know. You always frown like that when Paul calls. Ever since you broke up, I mean."

Kara snorts a laugh. Yes, Paul had been annoyingly insistent in the weeks since she ended things, hoping to patch things up with her. All he'd accomplished was to blow rapidly through what goodwill she still felt for him.

The obvious question occurs to her: Could her ex be the one behind this stupid prank call? It must be *someone* who knows her, and Paul's taste in movies certainly evidenced a love for the cloak-and-dagger stuff.

"Well anyway," Viviane says conversationally, launching back into the monologue she'd been in the midst of when the strange call came. "Taylor and Dane are back at it again. You'd think they were salesmen working on commission, not fundraisers on the same team. But Jenny was telling me last week…"

Try as she might, Kara can't stay focused on Viviane. Usually she appreciates the mostly one-side exchange while they run. Great exercise or not, running is torture; having Viviane along, with her never-ending store of the latest gossip, keeps that torture bearable. But at the moment, that strange call continues to occupy her thoughts.

As if on cue, the phone tweedles, this time indicating receipt of a text message. With a sigh, she pulls it up. Same number. *itll happen today. u wont leave park alive*

A chill runs through her. This prankster actually knows where she is right now? That's creepy.

Another tweedle: *tall man, green jacket. hes one of them. killer. waiting for the right place to do it*

This time Kara *does* miss a step, stumbling forward until she catches her balance again.

Viviane stares at her. "You sure you're okay?"

"Yeah, fine," she lies, pulling herself together. Again, there's no question of whether to tell Viviane what's going on. The girl would freak.

Viviane takes her reassurance at face value and picks up again in midsentence, while Kara slowly turns to glance over her shoulder. The man in the green jacket is still there, about the same distance behind. Unintentionally, she catches the man's eye and, not knowing what else to do, gives him an uncertain smile and wave over her shoulder. For the longest moment, he doesn't react, but then he waves back, just as uncertainly.

This is ridiculous. It's gotta be some sort of elaborate prank. *I don't believe you*, she texts back at her unknown caller, finding the little buttons difficult to hit while running. Disbelieving or not, she anxiously awaits his response, even as Viviane transitions into a tirade about her supervisor's lack of managerial talent.

Tweedle. *try to loose him. green jacket. youll see. blue shirt will take his place*

Kara thinks about it for a moment. The whole thing is absurd, and yet… a new suspicion takes root. *If* this isn't a prank, *if* this isn't Paul or one of his friends, then maybe it's not about Kara at all. Maybe this is about Viviane.

She gazes surreptitiously at her closest friend. Shorter and slimmer than Kara, but with the same coloring—fair skin, blue eyes, chestnut hair worn long—Viviane has sometimes been confused for her younger sister. Her far *prettier* younger sister.

Then again, maybe it's about Viviane's dad. Although Kara's never met the man—Viviane's relationship with him is very strained—Kara knows that her friend's father is a very important, very powerful figure in the military. Is it possible someone might attack or kidnap Viviane to get to him?

The hair slowly stands up on the back of Kara's neck. Yes, that sounds quite plausible, much more likely than Kara being targeted herself.

Coming to a decision, she stops abruptly, dropping to one knee and pulling loose her left shoe's laces in a fairly smooth motion. "Hold up a second," she says to her friend, impressed at her own level tone. She repositions herself a little as she begins retying, so she can keep Green Jacket in her peripheral vision.

Her tension grows steadily as he approaches, and there's no need to pretend to have trouble with the laces—the fumbling comes quite naturally. The man draws level with them...

And tosses them a friendly smile on his way past. Kara stares after the guy, momentarily forgetting her shoelaces.

"Um, Kara?" Viviane says from where she jogs in place, keeping up her rhythm.

"Huh? Oh. Right." She returns to her laces, remembering belatedly what that last text had said: *blue shirt will take his place.* Of course. Even if Green Jacket was stalking them, he couldn't simply have stopped, not unless he wanted to attack them here; it would have been too suspicious.

Making a frustrated sound, Kara pulls out her knot again and restarts, taking painstaking care as she glances back the way she came. Nothing. She looks left and then right again. Green Jacket is almost out of sight around the bend, but no one new has come up behind them. Kara finishes the one shoe, then goes ahead and re-ties the other, taking plenty of time to double-knot, giving the universe plenty of time to produce someone in a blue shirt. Viviane makes impatient noises all the while, but in the end, Kara is satisfied—and relieved. This is just someone messing with them. As she returns to her feet and the women set off again, she strings together a few choice words for Paul and his games. Just in case it's him.

But almost immediately, she hears the sound of footfalls behind her. Her dread returns in an instant as she turns to glance over her shoulder. Short guy, muscular build. Blue shirt.

Kara gulps.

Tweedle: *told u so*

Kara struggles to think. This whole thing is outlandish. *Surely* someone is just having fun at her expense. Someone here in the park with her; he's watching her... he can see Green Jacket and Blue Shirt running near her... that doesn't make them killers.

She fumbles out a return text: *They don't look like killers.*

The phone tweedles back almost instantly: *guns in fanny packs*

Kara blinks, glances back over her shoulder. Sure enough, the guy's wearing a big honking fanny pack. Large, unstylish, and obviously heavy, judging by the lack of bounce. And as she thinks about it, she realizes Green Jacket had one too.

What do I do? she texts, then jerks away as she realizes Viviane is trying to read her screen.

"Please," Viviane begs her sincerely, "*please* tell me you're not getting back together with Paul."

"Huh? Why do you say that?"

"That's like a dozen texts in a minute. You never talk to anyone else that way."

"Yeah. No. I mean—" Kara makes a sound of frustration. "Just... sorry, I can't text and talk at the same time."

Viviane seems to accept this explanation, even though she herself never has difficulty doing exactly that.

Tweedle: *u know the old stone bridg?*

Yes, Kara texts back.

loose blue shirt and meet me there. they wont make a move not yet

Ok, she texts back.

The old stone bridge, one of her favorite places in the park. The path splits maybe half a mile ahead, the main trail continuing on while the branching trail meets a small stream soon after. Considering the low volume of water involved, the bridge is extreme overkill, but it's quaint and fun. The sort of place couples go to get their pictures taken.

Half a mile to the branch... that means Kara has about five minutes to decide whether to go through with this.

"Viviane..." she says slowly, interrupting her friend's characterization of the new grantwriter her agency just hired. "When was the last time you talked with your dad?"

The non-sequiter obviously surprises the other woman, and she's a moment responding. "Um. Yesterday."

Kara blinks. "Yesterday?" It's so rare that they talk, after all.

"Yeah. Twice." She adopts a hurt look—the one that usually arises when her father comes up in conversation. "He called to say he'd be in town today. Wanted to take me to dinner, meet Gregoire finally."

Despite the scary uncertainty of the present situation, this stokes Kara's curiosity. "You finally told him about Gregoire?"

Viviane scowls. "*No.* But Daddy doesn't need to talk to me to find out whatever he wants. Super spy Air Force general has other ways of getting info. He already knew about Greg." She pauses. "Seemed hurt I hadn't told him myself, though."

"Well, you guys *have* been dating... what, six months now?" Viviane doesn't answer. "You say you talked twice?"

"Yeah, he called back last night. To *cancel*," she spits out the word. "I could've told you that would happen. But he was 'so sorry.' Turned into another *long* apology about all the times he wasn't there for me," she says bitterly. "Another *long* explanation about how everything he does, it's really about me. How I'm the center of his world. How his purpose in life is to protect me."

Kara frowns. She's heard all this before, and it really does sound like the excuses of a man who failed spectacularly as a father... but what if there *is* something to it? Something more than 'making the world a better place,' something more along the lines of trying to protect Viviane specifically?

The turnoff to the bridge isn't far. If Viviane really is at some risk, following the instructions of this strange caller might save her friend's life. And if it really is just a joke? At worst, it'll mean some laughs at Kara's expense. Boiled down like that, it really isn't a difficult choice.

As they approach the fork, Kara refreshes herself on the lay of the land and plans her move. The bridge path branches off to the right, after which the main path takes a rise and bends shortly thereafter into a thick copse of trees. Yes, this will be perfect.

Kara deliberately bypasses the branch and runs a dozen yards before stumbling, clutching at her calf. Viviane catches her arm and helps her a few steps further, lowering her to the ground. Blue Shirt is on them almost instantly. "Everything okay?" he asks with apparent concern.

Swallowing hard, Kara forces a smile. "Sure, fine. Just a cramp."

The man wavers. "Anything I can do for you? It'd be no trouble."

"Nope!" Kara says brightly. "I just need a couple minutes. We'll be fine, thanks."

"Okay, he says," and continues along the main path.

Kara waits until the man takes the turn out of sight, then waits another two seconds before leaping to her feet. "C'mon!" she says to her friend with quiet, forced enthusiasm. "Let's go this way." She drags her friend back to the branch, as quietly as possible, ignoring Viviane's blessedly silent bewilderment. Taking the turn, she goes into an all-out sprint, and Viviane is forced to do the same. And there, finally, is the bridge.

With a finger to her lips, Kara grabs Viviane and guides her off the path, down to the stream, and then under the bridge. They settle onto the dry leaves, backs to the underside of the arch, Viviane automatically mimicking Kara's quiet movements.

"What the heck are we doing?" Viviane hisses, uncertain whether to be amused or confused.

"Hiding!" Kara hisses back even softer. She casts around for an explanation, a story, anything she can say to make this make sense. "We're... playing hide and seek. With a friend of mine."

Viviane just stares at her like she's crazy, but then her lip twitches, and Kara knows the other woman is amused enough to play along for a while.

A thought occurs to her, and she pulls out her phone to mute it, motioning for Viviane to do the same. And then there's the sound of footfalls approaching quickly, someone else in an all-out sprint. They pound down the path the women just left, then onto the bridge above them before coming to a sudden stop. Silence then, followed by short bursts of stomping—Kara guesses the person must be running back and forth on the bridge above them, using it as a good vantage to search the woods all around.

A voice speaks, so softly she can't make out the words. The sound comes and goes, intermittently, and it takes her a few moments to realize she's just barely hearing one side of a hushed phone conversation. Then the footsteps are pounding again, back the direction they came, eventually fading away to nothing.

Heart thudding, Kara turns to look at Viviane. The other girl gives her a questioning look, as if asking how much longer they need to huddle in this uncomfortable position.

"A little longer," Kara replies softly. She's about to say more, but then the dry leaves are rustling nearby, almost right on top of them. Eyes wide, Kara looks around for something, anything to defend herself with—

And a man steps casually into view—someone new, not either of the men who may or may not have been following her. He takes in the sight of the two women, scrunched up beneath the bridge, and smiles. "Kara Dunn?" he asks.

Kara moves out where there's more room and straightens, approaching the man cautiously. "Yes..." she says slowly. "Are you the person who called me?"

The man gives her a warm smile, and she can't help but smile back, a little of the tension easing out of her shoulders. And then there's a gun in his hand, rising up to point at her.

Everything happens quickly after that. Viviane gives a bloodcurdling scream, jumps up and cracks her skull into the bridge above her, and collapses without another sound. The gun comes level with Kara's head, letting her look straight down its barrel. And the man's finger tightens on the trigger, even as his smile turns decidedly ugly.

Then his body is spinning, to the left, to the right, back to the left again, before he finally crumples, his prone form coming to rest near Viviane's.

And through it all, Kara remains frozen in place, unable to move or speak.

The bicycle cop finishes reading through the text messages on Kara's phone, then chews his lip thoughtfully for a moment. Raising a radio to his lips, he contacts a colleague elsewhere in the park. "Check back along the main path, maybe in the parking lot. We're looking for a male suspect, Caucasian, bright green warm-up jacket." He eyes Kara as he says this, catches her confirming nod. "Also another male Caucasian, blue t-shirt. Short—you'd say, what five-six? Five-seven?" Another nod. "That match anyone there?"

The radio isn't silent for long. *"I see them, both suspects."*

"Understood. Over." Kara's cop returns the radio to a clip on his chest. "They'll take the men into custody and bring them here, if possible." He pauses, giving her a measuring look. "You sure you're okay?"

Kara, trembling beneath a blanket, is most definitely *not* okay. But at least she's doing better than Viviane; true to form, the younger woman had outshone Kara from the moment she awoke. Even now, she has all three of the EMTs looking after her. Of course, she'd actually sustained a real injury—unlike Kara who, despite years of martial arts training, froze up completely.

Unbidden, her eyes turn yet again to the still form beneath the sheet. Looking down the barrel of that gun, she'd thought it was all over. It was only the greatest stroke of luck that this cop had come biking past at that exact moment and, seeing a woman about to be shot, had responded with instant, lethal force.

Not that she'd believed it at first. The timing was a little too coincidental, and the situation had already driven Kara to the edge of paranoia. But she'd called 911 and they'd confirmed he was a real cop. Only then had her heart rate begun to slow a little… and that was when the trembling started. The ambulance hadn't been long in arriving after that. They'd provided the blanket and set to work on reviving Viviane.

"I'm fine," Kara tells the cop unconvincingly, forcing a smile.

"Can you think of any reason someone would want to hurt you or your friend?" he asks. "Do you have any enemies?"

She shakes her head. "No. Of course not—enemies?" She laughs weakly. "Who actually has enemies in the real world?"

"Tell me about that first phone call again," he says, handing the phone back to her. "Walk through what he said, and what you said, step by step."

To the best of her ability, she does so.

"What's this about 'rampant'?" he asks. "What's that?"

"It's a video game. Released last year."

He shows no sign of recognition. Of course. "So you're a video game developer?"

She sighs. "I was. It was just a short thing. I'm back here now, teaching at the university. Finishing up my PhD."

"And you can't think of anything—something connected with your work or any projects you've been on—a reason for someone to attack you."

She shakes her head yet again, at a loss.

"Well, I'll be interested to hear what your alleged stalkers have to say for themselves."

Interestingly, the two men—when they arrive handcuffed and escorted by two more cops—exhibit nothing but shock at the suggestion they were involved in an attack. A search of their fanny packs reveals nothing suspicious; Blue Shirt has a nice camera with telephoto lens, while Green Jacket is carrying a veritable pantry of snacks to keep his blood sugar within acceptable ranges. The two are such unlikely criminals that even Kara begins to doubt they were anything more than fellow runners. The cops eventually cut them loose.

And then sit her down to explain the great unlikelihood of an elaborate conspiracy against her.

"But you read the texts!" Kara says, lowering her voice. Viviane is absorbed with the ministrations of the EMTs, and Kara doesn't want to draw her attention. "So maybe those guys weren't involved. But someone *did* attack us, just like this guy warned me!" She shakes her phone to indicate the mysterious caller.

The cop exchanges a look with his fellows, then smiles apologetically at her. As if embarrassed that she's missing the obvious. "Miss Dunn... if you would, try calling your anonymous friend back."

Frowning, she does as she's told. A moment later, a phone starts ringing—from beneath the sheet where the dead body hides. She can't help but turn crimson from embarrassment.

"See?" The cop says gently. "No conspiracy. Just one guy. He convinced you to leave the main path—which gets a lot more traffic—and meet him here, where he could attack you without anyone around."

Kara buries her face in her hands. "How could I be so stupid?" There's an awkward silence. "But why? Why would he attack me?"

"I think we've established there's no reason why anyone would want to attack you. Some people are just sick. But Miss Dunn..." He waits until she looks up. "The important thing to remember is that you're safe now. As terrible as it is, this man can't hurt you anymore. And since he was acting alone, you can go back to your normal life without any fear."

She swallows past the lump in her throat. And this time, she succeeds in keeping her gaze away from the body. "You're right."

The cop gives her a brilliant smile. "But I *do* hope you've learned your lesson. There's safety in numbers. If you ever have any concern that someone is following you or wants to hurt you, get to a public place and stay there. Call the police if need be. That's what we're here for."

"Of course. And..." She abruptly feels like an even bigger fool. Here this man saved her life, coming out of nowhere at exactly the right moment and taking an incredible shot, and she has yet to even thank him. "Officer, thank you *so much*." Her lip trembles.

"My pleasure," he says, his smile growing. "Again, it's what we're here for."

One of the other cops returns, a reserved Viviane trailing after him. "Ma'am, if you'll come with me, I'll give you a ride home."

Kara nods her appreciation, throwing a blanketed arm over Viviane as they follow him to his cruiser. It's only as she's climbing into the back of the car that a discordant thought strikes her. If her attacker truly had been working alone, then who was it that had come chasing after her, stomping around on the bridge trying to figure out where she and Viviane had gone? Or did that have nothing to do with their adventure today?

The bike cop helps muscle the body into the back of the ambulance, then climbs inside with two of the EMTs before pulling the doors closed. For a long moment, no one speaks. Then:

"That was close."

"Way too close," the ersatz cop agrees.

More silence. All three men give a start when the door opens of its own accord, admitting the short man in the blue shirt, who closes the door behind him. He eyes them for a moment. "Guess I'm off the team now." He grimaces. "Sorry, guys."

Ignoring the newcomer, one of the EMTs growls, "How long is he gonna let this go on?"

The cop can only shake his head. "He puts way too much faith in her ability to protect herself. Obviously."

"No," Blue Shirt disagrees, taking a deep breath and letting some of his frustration bleed out as he exhales. "He's protecting her, not just from this kind of thing"—he indicates the body—"but from the truth of what's going on. He'll keep her in the dark as long as possible, for her own good."

"But what *is* the truth?" the other EMT demands. "Why is this one woman so important?"

The cop sighs. "I wish I knew. But that's the old man for you. Always plays it close to the vest." He clears his throat, then leans forward to unzip the bag and reveal the assassin. "Come on, let's get to work."

[Chapter 01]

Friday evening
February 7, 2014

"Can I sit here?"

Skylar McClinic looks up from the window with an amused frown. "I don't know, can you?"

The man standing in the aisle—a major, according to his lapel insignia—flashes a big grin. "Yes, ma'am. Seating assignments don't mean much on the Dreamland Express—it's more like riding the school bus than the commercial flights you're used to."

Which makes sense. This *isn't* a commercial flight. More of a commuter trip, though she still can't believe a single Air Force installation has the personnel to fill up an entire 737 for a daily commute between here and Vegas.

Of course, Skylar's response had been as much a commentary on the man's poor grammar as a question of seating assignment, but she lets it go, waving him toward the seat next to her.

"*So*," he says, eyes dancing with humor and energy. "First week here? Whaddya think so far?"

Skylar gives the man a closer look, only belatedly recognizing him as one of the other pilots she met this week—one of maybe fifty. "Sorry… remind me…?"

"Barrett Williams, ma'am." He grows suddenly solemn. "I'm the chief morale officer for this unit. Whether you're looking for a good laugh, or maybe some of the good stuff smuggled on-base, I'm your—"

"You're so full of crap, Twix." This from a petite blonde woman as she collapses into the seat on Barrett's other side. The newcomer doesn't even look over, just slumps down and eyes the other passengers as they file aboard.

Barrett hooks a thumb at his new neighbor. "And that's Anna Haynes—Sweeps—my better half." Haynes snorts, but offers no confirmation or denial.

Skylar has no trouble remembering Haynes. She's already had half a dozen encounters with the pilot, whose attitude consistently teetered on the knife's edge of disrespect. "Better half?" Skylar questions.

"Nah, not really," Barrett assures her. After all, there are regulations against that sort of thing. "She keeps trying, though." He lowers his voice confidentially. "Been chasin' me for years—" He breaks off with a grunt, no doubt the result of his better half's elbow inserted into his ribs.

Skylar gives them a noncommittal smile and pulls out a paperback novel.

"Well?" the dark-skinned man persists, giving no indication that his chattiness will soon abate. "What do you think of our operation, Colonel?"

Skylar isn't a full-bird colonel, of course, just a lieutenant colonel. But considering what a mouthful that rank is, a simple 'colonel' is considered appropriate address. "I don't know..." she says, glancing around at all the other people filing onto the plane. "I hardly think this is something we should be discussing here."

Barrett shrugs but plows right on, though he *does* lower his voice. "Let me see if I can guess. You were personally recruited by one Carl Grant, brigadier general, who said you'd have the chance to change the world. He was skimpy on the details, but when you found out the posting was *here*, you figured you'd be a test pilot. You'd be flyin' stuff like the SR-71, the Stealth fighter, 'cept *better*—stuff no one's heard of yet. The newest, top secret-est tech. And you thought, heck *yeah*, baby, sign me up!"

Skylar can't help but crack a smile. "I take it that was your experience?"

He shrugs. "Somethin' like that. Then we get here"—he seems to encompass Haynes in this—"and it's all simulators. Then more simulators. And I betcha next week is gonna be..." He turns to his friend. "Did you hear what they've got scheduled for next week? Oh, simulators? Oh, okay." He turns back to Skylar. "More simulators."

"Well, it's a space combat sim—unless they ship you to orbit, simulator's about your only option."

"Hey, space is cool," Barrett insists. "I don't mind shippin' to space."

"But I'm sure they've got other stuff in development here," Skylar continues. "One way or another, they'll get us into a real cockpit soon enough."

Barrett's brows rise. "They tell you that? 'Cause I'm just sayin', four years of doin' this now, I'm ready for somethin' diff'rent."

Skylar's eyes pop a little. "Four years?"

"Yep. Same project, the whole time." He shrugs. "Changed simulators a couple years ago—this one's much better—but even that's pretty dull by now."

"Plus," Haynes breaks in, "Peterson can't script missions worth—" This time she's the one that grunts as Barrett's elbow digs into *her* ribs. Which is just as well. Everything about this project—about this whole military installation—may be unorthodox, but Skylar can't sit by and listen to her subordinates badmouth general officers without taking disciplinary action.

"You know the crazy thing?" Barrett says hurriedly. He drops his voice further. "It's not even secret."

"What's not?"

"What we're doing, these simulators we spend so much time on? It's just a video game."

"I know it seems that way—" Skylar begins.

"No, I mean *really*. An actual commercial video game. You can pick it up for fifty bucks at any gaming shop. Or online. Tompkins' mom actually bought him a copy for Christmas."

"I don't understand."

"Our hardware's better," Barrett admits. "*Much* better. But the *software* is exactly the same. Even the mission editor Peterson uses—*General* Peterson," he amends. "He uses the same mission editor that was packaged with the game." He turns to Haynes, snapping his fingers impatiently. "What's it called again? The game?"

"*Rampant*," she replies disinterestedly.

Skylar feels a sinking sensation. "That doesn't make any sense."

"No, ma'am, it doesn't." Despite the tone of Barrett's complaint, his eyes are still dancing; he obviously enjoys sharing gossip with someone new. "Commercially available video game, released in the last year—but we had it at least a year *before* that.

A full squadron of pilots drilling on this software, every day since then—that ain't cheap. People cost, equipment, facilities usage, the fact that we're based *here* of all places… Air Force is *pourin'* money on this thing. So what gives?"

Skylar wishes she knew. Barrett's description of Skylar's recruitment was pretty much spot-on, except that she and her long-time associate—Col. John McLaughlin—had come as a package deal. But Barrett was right about her excitement, her sense of anticipation. In some people's minds, the words "test pilot" might equate with "crash test dummy," but for her it meant flying the latest and greatest in cutting edge tech. Of course, her first week here had been nothing but sims—that and introductions to the pilots she and John would be working with—but that hadn't fazed her. Obviously the real work would be coming.

But now she wonders.

At the nose of the plane, John comes into view, one of the last passengers to board. Maybe John knows more. After all, as a full colonel himself, John is now the top-ranking pilot in Grant and Peterson's outfit. And though he probably *shouldn't* share what he knows, he and Skylar have been flying together for years. Skylar was in the man's wedding, for crying out loud; he'd better share what he knows.

Skylar exhales and leans back, trying to expunge this sudden concern that she's made a terrible career move. Trying to remember to relax, that this commute marks the beginning of her weekend leave, a chance to relax after a very long week.

"I think it's safe to say something's coming," Haynes pipes up. "Drills may be same as ever, but the number of pilots has doubled this year. I'd say someone's ramping up for something."

"Maybe they *will* ship us out to space," Barrett adds wistfully. "Wouldn't that be somethin'."

[Chapter 02]

Monday morning
February 10, 2014

"Wednesday's assignment is in your syllabus," Kara says, wrapping up the lecture. "At the very least, the program you turn in has to compile and provide the specified output. But feel free to get creative—that's a great way to bring your grade up."

A hand goes up. "You mean like extra credit?"

She gives a wry smile. "No. As I explained in our first session, when you meet the minimum requirements, I will award you the minimum satisfactory grade—a C." There are the usual groans, but she pushes through. "If that's what you want to shoot for, that's fine. For most of you, this class is just a requirement; only a few of you will choose to major, so I won't expect you to prioritize this class. But if you want an A, you'll have to impress me."

"Seriously?" someone calls. "I have to do *extra* work just to get an A?"

"You're not in high school anymore."

"But—"

"You still have a week to drop my class, but I'm not going to argue this with you."

"Dr. Dunn," someone calls from the back of the lecture hall, waving another hand. "I have a question."

Kara sighs. "Remember, just 'Kara' is fine. I'm a grad student, not a professor. As I've already explained." It always amazes her, the frequency with which she has to repeat certain things during the first few weeks of a new class.

"Oh," her questioner says, momentarily diverted. "I just added the class." He pauses, confused. "So... you don't have a PhD?"

"Nope. I'm about three-quarters done with two different doctorates—one in CS, one in Physics—but unfortunately that doesn't add up to a full degree." This draws a few overly-enthusiastic laughs. "What was your question?"

"Well, I've been all the way through your syllabus—"

"Oh, so someone *did* read it," she says with a grin. More overly-enthusiastic laughs.

"—and it doesn't say anything about video games."

Kara frowns. "Why would it?"

The student seems surprised. "Well, um, this is a programming class. Eventually you'll be teaching us to make games, right? You know, flight simulators, 3D shooters, that sorta thing."

Kara can't help but laugh. "No, that 'sorta thing' is outside the scope of an intro programming class. And it's not the kind of programming most developers do anyway."

A different hand goes up. "But isn't that what *you* do for a living? I mean, that's the whole reason I chose to take this class, because you're teaching it."

Kara's smile fades. "You're talking about *Rampant*?" The kid nods, and a number of other students perk up. "Yes, I was project lead on the team that developed *Rampant* for DactiSoft. After the game released last summer, I returned here to finish up my degree. Degrees," she amends. "At the moment, I teach for a living." And, fortunately, collect on scholarships, since the pay offered to grad assistants is hardly stellar.

A student on the front row gives her a winning smile. "So maybe this class isn't about gaming, but you could still show us some stuff, right?"

She'd gone through this same thing with her intro class last fall, right after she'd returned. She never anticipated becoming famous making video games—especially a quasi-educational one that did poorly in the marketplace—but somehow word had gotten out on campus all the same. At least it had enrollment figures up for the intro class, but as far as her department chair was concerned, that was the only positive to come out of Kara's stint with DactiSoft.

She sighs. "When I said video game programming was outside the scope of this class, I meant that it requires a skillset far beyond what you'll develop here. If you choose to major, some of the upper level classes might introduce you to the concepts you'd need, but even then, you're not going to take on any large-scale video game projects. Maybe some card games, board games. Probably nothing 3D."

"Why not?" Smiley asks.

"Because of the sheer amount of effort involved in creating that kind of game. Not just programming, but testing as well. I managed a team of forty at DactiSoft, and it took us three years to put out *Rampant*."

"Then what's the point of this class?"

"To give you a foundation for software development. Upper-level courses will build on that foundation. And if you graduate with a comp sci degree, you can apply for programming jobs. Yes"—she staves off the predictable questions—"maybe you get hired by a game developer, though competition is stiff. But there are plenty of other rewarding careers out there. Like I said, most programmers do *not* write video games for a living."

A girl in the second row asks, "When you finish your doctorate, are you going back to game development?"

Kara's wry smile returns. "I think it's safe to say that I'm done with video games."

Judging by the number of disappointed faces, Kara's guessing she'll be getting ten or fifteen drop notifications before Wednesday's session rolls around.

"I think that's all for today," she concludes. "Remember that I keep office hours from now until 11:30, so feel free to drop by. That's Matthews 328, upstairs."

The students file out, except for that girl from the second row. Kara wracks her brain for a moment, eventually coming up the girl's name: Calin. Calin Tennison. This is now the third week of class, but Calin had already followed her back to her office twice before, peppering her with questions about programming and, well, anything else she could come up with. Each time, Calin had clearly struggled to keep the conversation afloat, which tells Kara the girl's attention is probably less about interest in the subject and more about making an impression; out of a class of a hundred, she's hoping Kara will specifically remember her, and perhaps, reward her interest with a better grade.

Kara stifles a smile as she finishes packing up. These students arrive from high school, and they think they've got the game all figured out; they have no idea just how transparent they are.

Of course, after what Kara survived over the weekend, student antics don't bother her nearly as much today as usual; though Calin follows her all the way back to the third floor, jabbering the whole way and then another half hour after reaching Kara's office, Kara manages to avoid rolling her eyes. Much.

Eventually, though, she has to kick the girl out, office hours or not. She has far too much work to do on her dissertation as it is, and conversation had long since turned from software development to other matters.

"No, it's okay! The girl says brightly. I completely understand. I'll just be here in the lab." She points, as if Kara doesn't know that the glass-enclosed undergraduate computer lab is situated across the hall from her tiny office. "You know, working on my program for Wednesday."

Kara drops wearily into her chair. Finally. No students, no distractions, no gun-toting maniacs—she puts that last thought firmly out of her mind. Just her and her laptop, and a few hours to make progress on her long-neglected dissertation... the dissertation she keeps finding reasons to avoid, even after five months back on campus.

She calls up her abstract and reads through it, trying to decide where to focus her efforts today. Trying to push past the complete lack of interest she feels at the moment.

In her mind, she'd never left academia on a lark to develop a video game. Rather, she'd been working on concepts relating to space age personal transportation, and the gaming industry had sought *her* out; her research had only continued during her years of game development, culminating with *Rampant*'s release, which had garnered hundreds of thousands of data points she needed. After all, what better, *broader* way to simulate and test space age concepts than under the guise of entertainment?

Unfortunately, her department chair had never seen it that way, nor had her advisor or most of the other faculty whose opinions she generally respected. Some academics are only willing to go so far in their definition of serious research, and certainly Kara's methodology fell outside those bounds. "UFOs and Ray Guns," that's what one colleague had called her work. Which was rich, considering that academics in both her fields—comp sci and physics—tend to be some of the biggest geeks around. If she had a dollar for every time she'd heard peers arguing vehemently over whether Kirk was a better captain than Picard, she wouldn't have needed all those loans and scholarships in the first place.

With a start, Kara realizes an hour has passed, during which she has done little more than stare at her screen and think bitter thoughts. With a groan, she pushes the laptop back and lays her head down on her crossed arms. She has half a mind to jettison the entire project and start fresh on something new… which is just plain discouraging.

Her phone rings. "Hello?"

"*Hello, Kara? It is Gregoire.*"

A genuine smile spreads across her face at the sound of that cultured French accent. "Hey Greg, what's up?"

"*I have a question I must ask you. In person,*" he adds, sounding nervous.

Kara's forehead creases. "Okay… You're coming up to the house tonight, right?"

"*No-no. I mean yes! I am coming, but I must talk to you without Viviane. Please, I will come to you.*"

Feeling a little concerned, Kara says, "Well sure, okay. Can we talk over lunch?"

"*Status report.*"

"Subject is at the food court."

"*Still?*"

"She's finished eating, but yessir, she's still talking with the roommate's boyfriend. Hard to tell how long she'll be."

"*I see. Be advised, we may have a situation along subject's typical egress route.*"

"Need backup?"

"*No, remain in position unless you hear otherwise. Could be a feint.*" Long pause. "*Either way, I think the old man is finally ready to make a move.*"

"Copy."

With a laugh, Kara pushes back from the table and crosses her legs. She watches Gregoire as his own smile slowly fades; he'd been sharing a story of his early days adjusting to culture in the U.S. The events really weren't that funny, but the man has such a way with words, he could retell MacBeth and have his audience howling with laughter.

The silence lingers, and he begins fiddling with his wadded napkin.

"Greg," Kara begins, "I appreciate lunch. You really know how to treat a girl." They share another laugh at that. Campus food isn't that bad, but the selection does tend to be limited and overpriced. "But what's going on? What do you need to ask me without Viviane around?"

He nibbles his lip thoughtfully for a moment.

"I mean," she adds, "if word gets back to her that I'm seeing her boyfriend on the side, you know how she'll get." She says the words playfully, though of course Viviane *is* prone to overreaction.

"Not with you, Kara," the Frenchman says with a more sober smile. "You, she trusts." He sighs. "Kara, I want to marry Viviane."

"Oh," she says stupidly.

"Oh?" he repeats uncertainly.

"No, sorry," Kara hastens to say. "You just surprised me." She takes a moment to process this. "Have you talked to her about this?" No, Kara realizes immediately, of course he hasn't; if he had, Viviane would've already told Kara all about it. "Why are you telling *me*?"

A smile flickers across the man's face. "I ask for your advice. And your permission."

Kara blinks at this. "My permission? I... don't know how it is in France, but here, the guys usually ask the father..." She trails off.

"Exactly." Greg sighs. "But he is not in her life. I do not think he even knows I exist."

"You'd be surprised."

"Besides, if I ask him, it might make Viviane cross with me. But you... you are like family to her."

Kara allows a look of dismay to cross her face. "Well sure, we talk about being like family, like sisters. But Greg, this is different."

"No, hear me out. Her father, he comes, he goes. You have been constant for her. How long, you have lived together? Nine years? Ten?"

"We met... almost eight years ago," Kara says thoughtfully.

"And even when you move to Utah, still you talk, still you are best friends. More than that. You watch out for her, like parents should." He gazes absently out the window. "I know Viviane. She will be happy, me asking *your* permission."

Kara drops the argument, saddened as ever by her friend's tough upbringing, her lack of family.

"So?" Greg asks leadingly. "Do I have your permission?"

She thinks about it, though she doesn't really need to. For herself, personally, marriage doesn't hold much allure. But for Viviane, it would be a good thing, and Gregoire really is perfect for her. "Yes..." she says slowly. "But be careful."

This surprises him. "Careful? How do you mean?"

"I mean, don't just pop the question on her. Ease her into the idea, give her time to think about it. Sound her out."

"But... that will ruin the surprise." He frowns. "You American women, I thought you *like* big surprise proposals."

Kara smiles. "Yes, in general. But Viviane... " Her smile fades. "Greg, Viviane has commitment issues." She raises a hand, staving off his automatic defense of the girl. "I'm not being negative, just honest. She has a heart of gold, and she lives to help other people. That's why she can't seem to leave the nonprofit sector, even for better pay—but look how many different charities she's jumped around between. Plus, as good as she is to her friends, you know how she lets stupid little things end good friendships." Kara sighs. "She just... she sabotages things sometimes. I don't know if that's a result of her upbringing, or just something about her, or what."

"You're saying she won't want to commit?"

Kara frowns. "No... I'm just saying she's scared of being locked in—to *anything*, even stuff a lot less scary than marriage.

Which is why you shouldn't surprise her with the idea, then expect her to make an immediate decision." Kara shakes her head. "Instead, make sure she knows *you* feel that kind of commitment to her. Sooner or later, the M word will come up naturally, and if she's not ready yet, you can still back away from the conversation." Kara gives a wry smile. "Honestly, you pop the question now, out of the blue, and Viviane's likely to bolt. And then things would be weird between you."

Gregoire nods slowly. "Not the answer I hoped for."

"Sorry."

"But it does prove you are the right person to ask. Her father, he never could have said all this."

A few minutes later, having made excuses about returning to her work, Kara is passing through a little known exit of the student life center, within which the food court resides. It's really more of a service entrance, letting out onto a back alley as it does, but she long since learned it was the quickest way back to Matthews Hall.

The gap between the building and its neighbor, the library, is less than six feet, and there are no facing windows. In short, it's the perfect setting for a mugging. Usually that thought makes her smile; this is a very safe campus, after all, and it's broad daylight. But after last week's near-death experience with the mugger—or murderer, or rapist, or whatever he was—she finds herself less comfortable with these surroundings than normal. Which is why she experiences a sense of relief as she approaches the end of the alley.

Just as a van comes squealing out of nowhere.

It slams to a stop, neatly blocking the opening, its side door already sliding open. And in her shock, Kara freezes. *Again*, she freezes, staring in disbelief as two masked men reach out and grab her, pulling her roughly into the back of the van, which is already in motion once more.

By the time she starts screaming, there's a hand over her mouth, tight enough that she can't get any purchase to bite. Her hands are pinned too, which leaves her legs. She lashes out with a wild kick, and she's rewarded with a curse.

"Enough," a firm voice commands.

The hands holding Kara seem to slacken for a moment, and she renews her thrashing.

"Miss Dunn!" that voice comes again. "You will not be harmed. Unlike the man you met last week, we only want to talk to you." As an aside, he adds, "Sit her up."

As Kara comes to a sitting position, she sees there are at least two other people in the wide-open back of the van, a young woman and an elderly man—probably the one who had been speaking. The man's appearance is striking, full of vitality despite sagging jowls and a head full of snowy hair. She subsides warily under his intense gaze, and at his sharp nod, the other hands release her.

Licking her lips nervously, Kara glances around. The men who grabbed her are now removing their masks, giving her some space... though one of them remains between her and the door. At the rear of the van, the door is similarly blocked by the young woman, who—

"*Calin?*" she demands.

"Yes, ma'am," Kara's student replies crisply, nodding.

"But—"

"Really, Miss Dunn," the older man says, "you have nothing to fear. We simply needed some privacy to talk, and there are too many prying eyes and ears on campus. For that matter, there are eyes and ears *everywhere* you normally spend time, your home especially." He straightens up, as much as possible in the back of a utility van. "You have my word of honor you will not be harmed in any way. But you need to hear me out."

"Who *are* you?" Kara finally manages. "Why should I believe you?"

The man's smile is so sudden, so high-intensity, Kara almost flinches. "Allow me to introduce myself," he says. "I'm Brigadier General Carl Grant of the United States Air Force." He pauses. "But you would know me better as Viviane's father."

[Chapter 03]

**Monday afternoon
February 10, 2014**

They park the van at a fast food place not far from campus, at which point Gen. Grant's team starts filing out. Through the window, she watches the two men head into the restaurant, even as the driver takes up a casual position on a nearby sidewalk bench. Kara levels a glare at Calin Tennison as the girl sidles past, but it has no noticeable effect. She hops out, gives Kara an unreadable look of her own, then slides the door closed.

Leaving Kara alone with Grant.

At this point, most of Kara's fear has fled, replaced by anger. Mostly anger about being forced into the van and finding out one of her students was part of it, but it doesn't help knowing that the man in charge is also Viviane's father. Kara has picked up plenty of vicarious anger at this man over the years, even though she's never met him.

But despite her best intentions, she's a little curious too.

"We should be safe here for a while," Grant says.

This takes Kara aback. "Safe?"

"Certainly. You don't frequent this establishment, so there's no reason for anyone to expect you here. We can speak at length without being observed."

"Why would anyone care about me?"

"Well, your attacker last week is hardly the only one interested in kidnapping or killing you."

"*What?*"

Grant sighs. "Indeed. My team has been providing your security for more than a year now." He waves a hand dismissively. "We trade out personnel frequently, of course, so that you and others wouldn't notice. But in that time, there have been three abduction attempts that we caught before you knew anything was amiss. Not counting last week, obviously."

"*What?*" she demands a second time, with perhaps even more intensity than before. What Grant says is so absurd, and for so many different reasons, Kara's not even sure where to begin. "Assuming that's even true," she finally manages to say, "*why?*"

The corner of the man's lip rises. "Because you possess very specialized knowledge, knowledge that will prove very valuable in the coming months."

Kara bites back another inane, kneejerk response, angrily squeezing the bridge of her nose instead. "I don't have a *clue* what you're talking about. What knowledge?"

"Why, the knowledge you developed while working on *Rampant*, of course."

"This is about a *video game?*" she demands.

"Absolutely. Or rather, the very real science behind the game. Your work in the area of space combat weapons conceptualization. Your theories with regard to feasible, maintainable propulsion systems. All together, it's nothing short of groundbreaking."

"It's just a *game.*"

"Even you don't believe that," the general counters. "If *Rampant* was primarily about entertainment, you would have taken it to one of the big firms instead of a tiny outfit barely acknowledged in the industry, known only for its educational software products." He leans forward, his eyes bright with excitement. "Miss Dunn, what you accomplished with *Rampant* was inspirational! A so-called game that taught basic concepts of matter, energy, force, thermodynamics, mechanics... all in the guise of flight training and mission briefings. And you explored more theoretical concepts within the gameplay engine itself... you truly presented space combat and exploration as it *would* be, unlike so much of the farcical science fiction we've been subjected to in the last few decades."

He pauses. "It's a shame the title wasn't more successful. I suspect that in the next few years, colleges would have seen a surge in applicants with a stronger grasp of the physical sciences. But the failing wasn't the product—quite simply, I don't think DactiSoft was equipped to handle the marketing and distribution."

Kara stares at the man. "What I meant was, why does the Air Force care about a video game? And why in the *world* would anyone want to hurt me because of it?"

Gen. Grant ponders the question for a long moment, eyes on her as his excitement ebbs. "I'm afraid I'm not in a position to answer that question at the moment."

"Seriously?" Kara bites back her anger. "Let me see if I've got this straight. You just kidnapped me—"

"Only temporarily," he interjects.

"—to tell me that my life is in danger, all because of knowledge I acquired while developing a *video game*, but you can't be any more specific than that?"

"The video game is secondary, Kara; you of all people know that. It's the science behind it that's so valuable. And the knowledge you've acquired—not just the data you've collected, but your personal knowledge and experience—will soon be in high demand. At this point, only a few nations are aware of the situation, but they're scrambling to secure the people with your specific kind of knowledge." His lip quirks again. "You just happen to be more famous than most, thanks to *Rampant*."

Kara feels a cube of ice settling in her stomach. "But the only reason the military would care about my research—you're saying we're gearing up for a war in *space?* That doesn't make any sense!"

"I'm not saying anything of the kind," he responds with a sly smile. "I'm afraid I can't comment on matters of national security at the present time. You don't have the proper clearance."

"So... what? This is a warning? Just a friendly 'hi, hello, try not to get kidnapped or killed'?"

"Why, no. This is a job offer."

"*What?*" she demands yet again.

Grant tries—and fails—to completely stifle a smile. "The U.S. Government would like to hire you as a contractor on a sensitive project for which you are uniquely suited. I cannot say more until you've completed reams of nondisclosure forms and acquired the proper clearances. But I'm sure you can fill in the blanks."

Despite herself, Kara barks a laugh. "You want to hire me for a job, but you won't tell me anything about it."

"In essence, yes."

"Viviane's right. You're crazy."

Grant's jaw tightens, his mirth disappearing. "On a more administrative level, the job pays well and would require an initial six month commitment. We're prepared to offer $93,000 as the annual starting salary, along with full hospitalization and coverage for dental and vision as well." His expression gives no further indication of humor.

"And if I refuse? You'll just take me anyway?"

"No. That would hardly encourage you to give our project your best effort." He pauses, grimaces. "Though… eventually, we *would* need to place you in productive custody. We can't afford to let the enemy or any rival nations get their hands on you."

"Well isn't *that* convenient," Kara says bitterly. "So I might as well go with you willingly, is that it?"

Grant falls silent for a long minute, alternately watching her and gazing absently out the windshield. During that time, he slowly sags, his age becoming more apparent. "I don't know if I can convince you of this, Kara," he says sincerely, "but I *do* want what's best for you. I… I know how much Viviane cares about you, and I would never intentionally do anything to hurt her, no matter my unintentional failings in the past." He sighs. "The fact is, no matter how important you are to Viviane, your continued involvement in her life is putting her at the same risk you face."

He gives Kara a chance to think about that. Assuming he's not just blowing smoke about the danger Kara's in—and the attack last week suggests he's not—then Kara has to grudgingly admit it's true: she herself is putting Viviane in danger by continuing to live with her. But this is all so sudden, it's kinda hard to process as quickly as Grant seems to expect her to.

"So…" he continues. "We can take you into custody, hide you away, place you in a program like witness protection where you can go mad with boredom. *Or*," he adds with a smile, "you can accept my offer, continue your research in a real-world setting—complete with a real-world budget—and get your student loans paid off in the process." He sobers again. "Kara, you *do* need to know… this is your opportunity to change the world. I cannot exaggerate this: you are in a unique position to affect the life of every person on this planet—and for the better," he hastens to add. "Please. Do not be precipitant in your decision."

"Look." Kara tries to draw her thoughts into a semblance of order. "Aside from what happened last Friday, you're asking me to take a lot on faith. And for all I know, that guy *was* just a mugger, working alone. Which, by the way, is exactly what the cops said."

Grant's smile returns. "Those police officers you spoke with were all men in my employ." Kara blinks as he continues. "As were the emergency medical personnel, and even the two joggers. Part of what your 'mugger' told you was true, after all. Those men *were* keeping tabs on you, though only for your protection. That was the very reason he needed to draw you away from them before he approached."

Kara massages her head, still struggling with a whole host of objections. "If I'm really in so much danger, and there have been so many attempts to kidnap or kill me already, why haven't we had this conversation before now?" She thinks for a moment. "Just the cost of personnel to keep me under surveillance, without me knowing, that has to be expensive. Plus the risk that I would get hurt anyway... This just isn't adding up for me."

"I'm sorry to hear that," he says, sounding genuine. "To your first point, you are well worth the cost involved, and I wanted to preserve your blissful ignorance as long as possible. To your second point, this security detail is the best, and I have the greatest confidence in their abilities. That said... now that you know what's going on, I would prefer not to continue tempting fate."

"I'm not sure what to tell you," Kara says. "But I'm not about to just accept your offer on blind faith."

"Nor would I expect you to, my dear." He sighs. "My team will return you to your home or office—whichever you prefer—and give you a chance to think things over. We will continue our surveillance. When you decide to accept my offer, as I have every confidence you will, you can reach me at this number." He hands her a rather generic-looking business card.

"*If* I accept," she asks, making very clear that she does not share his confidence, "what then?"

"You'll have a few days to pack up and say your goodbyes. Like I said, powerful people are interested in you right now, so it would be best to keep up appearances. We'll make it look like you got a job offer you couldn't refuse. Certainly the other people watching you will wonder what's going on, but hopefully they won't be spooked into doing anything drastic. Which should help keep Viviane safe until you're gone."

"Yeah, speaking of Viviane," Kara says, seizing on something that's bothered her since Grant first started this crazy pitch. "It seems awfully coincidental that you desperately want to recruit me for your project *and* I just happen to be your daughter's roommate."

"There's no such thing as coincidence, my dear," Grant offers with an enigmatic smile. "How do you think I became aware of your research in the first place?"

Kara stares at him for a long time, but the elderly man doesn't say anything more. "Can I go now?" she asks finally.

"Absolutely. Promise to think on my offer."

"I would have a hard time thinking of anything else at the moment," Kara says bitterly.

[Chapter 04]

Four Years Earlier

**Sunday evening
November 29, 2009**

Kara pulled her long dark hair into a ponytail as the taxi pulled to a stop in front of her apartment complex. She paid, retrieved her rolling suitcase from the trunk, and headed inside.

She heard the sobs as soon as she'd unlocked and opened the hall door. "Viviane?" Kara hadn't expected her roommate back until later that week. Moving to the younger woman's open bedroom door, she poked her head in. "Hey."

The pretty brunette had swaddled herself in blankets and was watching TV, surrounded by spent tissues. Judging by the number of wads and the state of Viviane's eyes, it had either been a weekend-long romance extravaganza or her friend was hurting from something major. Even for Viviane, who had a talent for bursting into tears at the slightest provocation, this looked serious.

"Hey," Kara repeated, more softly.

Viviane sniffled and switched off the television by remote. She cracked an unconvincing smile and patted the bed next to her.

Kara settled gingerly onto the corner of the tissue-strewn comforter. She'd come to love Viviane in the three years she'd known her, but that regard didn't extend to snotty tissues. "Thanksgiving not go so well?" she prompted.

Viviane's voice caught before she could get out more than a syllable, and her response turned into a sobbing moan. It was clear, however, that her tear ducts had already run dry. Eventually, she managed to gain control. "I don't ever want to see him again."

Kara had hoped it wasn't this bad. "Your dad? What happened?"

"I don't want to talk about it." Viviane had never shared much about her background, but Kara knew the woman's relationship with her father—her only surviving relative—was strained. Over the previous year, the man had made a special effort to reconnect with his daughter, however; Thanksgiving was to have been the first real test of their reconciliation. "I want to tell you."

"Okay…" Kara responded slowly, confused at the sudden reversal.

"No, not about Thanksgiving!" She sniffled. "I mean everything. The other stuff. I'm not supposed to, but I didn't agree to that, it was forced on me, and I want to, so I'm gonna."

"Okay…" Kara responded at length, no less confused.

"Yeah, I've decided." The woman straightened into a sitting position and very deliberately rubbed at her face, clearing her eyes. "I've never told anybody."

Kara nodded, casually folding the comforter over the mess of tissues and sliding it off the bed; a few more snotty wads came to light, but she felt more comfortable settling onto the mattress for what was likely to be a long story.

"So you know I'm from Nevada, right?" Kara nodded. "Well, the truth is…" Viviane leaned forward conspiratorially, and Kara couldn't help but smile at her friend. "The truth is, I was born at Area 51." The younger woman leaned back against the headboard, allowing that to sink in.

"You mean… the military base?"

"Yeah. The one with the aliens. Um… supposedly."

"Wow" was all Kara could think to offer.

Viviane nodded seriously. "Daddy's, like, this big muck-a-muck with the Air Force. *Very* important. And Mom… she, you know… she died when I was born."

"I'm sorry, I didn't know."

Viviane heaved a sigh. "I don't know how old I was when we moved off base. Daddy never paid any attention to me, but I always told myself there was something special about me—that they were doing experiments on me or something, and that's why we'd lived at Area 51. But when I got old enough I realized we wouldn't have moved off base if that was true." For a moment, the emotion threatened to return. "Daddy's work didn't have anything to do with me. It was other stuff, more important than me. That's how it always was." She paused. "I thought that was changing recently, but… I was wrong."

"So…" Kara searched for a reasonable response to this strange revelation. "Your dad's a pilot?"

Viviane laughed. "Hardly." For a moment, her face registered sudden uncertainty. "At least, I don't..." She relaxed and shook her head with confidence. "No."

"Well, what does he do?"

The younger woman shrugged. "Heck if I know—that's the thing. It's all secrets. Spy stuff. All I know is..." She paused. "Well, he always had guns. In the house, I mean."

Kara nodded slowly. This whole conversation was bizarre.

"I'm just sick of him coming in and out of my life, trying to control me. Like when I was fifteen. He was this big drinker—I think because of Mom, dying and all—and then one day he just goes to church and gets 'saved.'" She mimes the quotation marks one-handed. "And bang, he just stops drinking. And suddenly he cares all about me and wants me to be saved too, wants me to ask Jesus in my heart. I told him it was a little late to decide he cared." She shrugged. "Anyway, I'm just tired of keeping my whole life secret. That's all." She reached for the remote.

Kara scrambled for something to say, to stave off a return to the stupor she'd found Viviane in. She'd already known about Viviane's dad's pushiness with religion, at least, which Kara herself didn't have much use for. But as much as she'd like to share her opinion of the matter, it wouldn't help Viviane feel any better. "Tell me about your mom."

Viviane shrugged again, eyes glued to the tube. "I don't really know anything. My dad would just start crying sometimes when I asked about her—or start drinking—and he never told me much. A few stupid stories." She sniffled. "But he never answered any questions about her, so I finally stopped asking. Never saw any pictures either—they couldn't even own a camera on base." She brightened suddenly and looked at Kara. "But there's that." She pointed.

At the foot of her bed, where it always sat, was Viviane's beautiful hand-painted chest—a large wooden locker with a hinged lid, much like a treasure chest. Kara reached for the key protruding from the antiquated brass lock.

"No!" Viviane squealed.

Kara's eyes popped wide. "What? I'm—"

Viviane settled. "Sorry. It's just... that's all I have from her. It's called a hope chest. She was putting stuff in for me for when I get married—I'm not supposed to open it until then. She woulda kept putting stuff in, but she died... anyway, yeah."

Kara had always wondered, but this was the first Viviane had opened up about the handsome piece. "It's beautiful, Viviane," she offered in a hushed voice. "Even if there wasn't anything in it, it's wonderful." She ran her fingers lightly over the hand-painted filigree. "Look at the detail... it's amazing anyone can do that —I know I wouldn't have the patience. I bet your mom spent a lot of time on it."

Viviane nodded again, absently. Muting the television, she grabbed Kara's hands in hers as her eyes began filling with fresh tears after all. "I'm serious, Kara. I know you don't take me serious, but I'm serious—I don't ever want to see him again."

Kara's eyes filled too. "I know when you're serious. I'm so sorry."

"I don't need him anyway. You're better family than he ever was."

Kara looked at the other woman in surprise, then thought about her words. Kara's own upbringing had hardly been idyllic, but it was nothing like Viviane's. Kara had never experienced doubts about her parents' love for her, even though she and her mother clashed frequently, mostly due to differences in personality. And as for Kara's father, well, he was the person who understood her best, the one she traditionally called first when she needed to vent. And yet Kara realized now that she thought of Viviane as family too—she was like the little sister she'd never had, and a best friend, all rolled into one.

It was amazing, really. They were so different, and yet they'd bonded completely since that day they'd met randomly through a roommate-matching service. Viviane had been a 21-year-old party girl coming out of a bad relationship and struggling with alcohol abuse. Kara had been a shy, aloof grad student of 27, struggling in her own way with a lack of supportive friendships locally. They'd simply accepted each other the way they were, often easier to do with someone you don't know at all. Since that time, Kara had grown to thrive on Viviane's vitality and drama, just as Viviane came to depend upon Kara's stability.

The women broke into smiles almost simultaneously, and Kara could almost believe the tears were done for now.

[Chapter 05]

Monday evening
February 10, 2014

Kara finds Viviane entangled with Gregoire on the sofa when she arrives home that night. She'd had Grant's team drop her off on campus, but she'd accomplished little after returning to her office—little more than examine and re-examine Grant's story and offer from every conceivable angle. And ultimately, she decided she needs Viviane's opinion.

On certain elements, at least. She's not about to share the whole story with the girl.

Greg glances up and smiles at Kara's entrance, but Viviane is so fixed on the TV that Kara wonders what the news piece is about; the other woman is paying the kind of attention usually reserved for major disasters or tragedies. But oddly, Kara realizes after watching for a moment, this is mostly old news.

"*...announced that Out of this World Tours will be making its initial public offering in the next two months. In an interview today, CEO Jeff Donnegan shared that capital raised from the IPO will finance the initial test flight phase of its Longship orbiter...*"

Watching her friend, Kara can't help but smile. "Viviane," she calls.

"*—otherwise known as OWT—made news last month with their announcement of the Longship prototype, the first spacecraft capable of carrying more than two hundred passengers into orbit, and also the first of its kind to enter development by a space tourism concern. Although early investors have been buying their tickets for years at a million dollars per seat, this is the first time...*"

"Viviane!"

The girl gives a start, then scrambles for the remote, quickly muting the television. "Sorry," she says. "I just... this whole thing sounds so familiar. The company name, the logo..."

"It has been on the news much lately," Greg offers, by way of explanation.

"No, it's not that. Even this guy, Donnegan. I could swear I know him." She keeps staring at the screen for a moment, then wrenches her attention over to Kara. "Sorry. How was your day?"

Kara opens her mouth to respond, realizes she has no idea what to say. "It was... different."

"Make any progress on your paper?"

"The dissertation? Um, no. Not really." Kara purses her lips. "Listen... weird question, I know, but can I go look through some of your old photo albums?"

Viviane's forehead bunches, but she shrugs. "Yeah, sure."

Kara hears the TV unmute as she climbs the stairs to the bedrooms. Viviane's room is packed full of girly items, like jewelry and keepsakes and lots and lots of pink, but she also has several dozen photo albums and scrapbooks. Kara locates the oldest one and begins flipping through. Carl Grant doesn't appear frequently in those photos, but he's definitely there—enough for Kara to confirm the man she met today really was Viviane's father.

Dang. That would have made this decision a lot easier. No less scary, but definitely easier.

She rejoins the lovebirds downstairs, manages to convince Viviane to shut off the TV. "Viviane... I have another weird question for you."

The girl's face lights up. "This sounds like fun."

"Well actually... I was wondering if you could tell me a little about your father again."

That takes her by surprise—Greg too. In fact, by the look on his face, it's clear he's wondering if this is related to his conversation with Kara earlier today. "Why?" Viviane asks.

"Just... trust me."

The girl does an admirable job of not scowling. "He's in the Air Force. That's probably the most important fact about him. He turned 80 last year, and he's *still* active duty, as far as I know. Which is supposedly against the rules, but apparently the rules don't apply to him."

Kara had been wondering at Grant's age. "I never realized your dad was so..."

"Old? Yeah. He was pushing 50 when I was born. Mom was younger, but not much. Maybe 40, I think. They say that's why..." She swallows and falls silent.

"Viviane, I know you've had your problems with your dad—he's terrible at keeping promises. But... would you say he's an honest person?"

It's clear the other woman wants to ask why she's being questioned like this, but mercifully, she holds off. "I guess. No, not always. But after he got religious, yeah. At least, I can't think of any times he wasn't." She licks her lips. "I don't know. Mostly, he wouldn't tell me stuff. There's a lot I just don't know about him."

"So you don't know anything about his work?"

"Not really, no. Just that it's important."

Kara gives her friend a sympathetic smile. "I'm sorry, Viviane."

"No, I didn't mean that sarcastically." She smiles a little. "I mean, it *is* important. He took me to the White House one time, introduced me to the President."

Kara blinks. "Really?"

"Yeah. I was seven. It was just the three of us in his office—"

"You mean the *Oval* Office?"

"Right. And the President put me in his lap and told me how proud I should be of my daddy, that he was doing really important work."

"You never told me that story."

Viviane shrugs. "It meant a lot to me at the time. Later—I mean like, as an adult—it just made me angry. I get it, okay? Daddy's important, his work is important. It's just *me* that's not important." Kara fears a histrionic episode, but Viviane maintains control. "Kara, why are you asking me all this?"

The moment of truth. "Well... Viviane, I sorta met your dad today."

"*What?*"

"Yeah, that's exactly what I said."

Viviane stares at her for a long time, thinking it all through. "He's trying to recruit you, isn't he? Because of your research."

Kara blanches. "Why do you say that?"

"Because he's been trying to get me to introduce you for years. He always mentions you, even though we barely talk. He wants to know about you, how you're doing, what's up with your research." Her tone is definitely turning bitter now. "As if he couldn't just call up his spy buddies and find out everything there is to know about you *without* my help." With a sob, Viviane turns and buries her face in Greg's chest. Greg, in turn, looks at Kara uncertainly.

Kara finds herself unsure what to say. That was typical in her early association with Viviane, but not lately. "Yes," she admits belatedly. "Your dad came to recruit me. Offer me a job."

There's a pause. "You're going to take it," her friend's voice comes, muffled by Greg's shirt. "Aren't you." There's no question in the girl's tone.

Kara stares out the window. Is she? As ridiculous and shocking as the whole thing is, as angry as Carl Grant makes her, Kara's objections are steadily eroding. Whatever else he may be, Grant is apparently not a liar, and she believes he loves his daughter. So it's probably true that Viviane is in danger as long as Kara is around. Maybe Kara should just move away. But a cross-country move would mean upturning her whole life, trying to transfer to a different university; because if she stayed local, it would defeat the purpose unless she cut herself completely off from Viviane, which would be hard. And even then, what would it accomplish? It might protect Viviane, but it would also hurt her, and Kara herself would likely still be in danger. And no matter what she chose, if she didn't join Grant's team, they'd eventually take her into custody anyway.

Feeling trapped, she whispers, "Yeah. I think I have to take the job."

"Why?"

"It's… it's a chance to do something real with my work," she stumbles through the first rationalization that comes to mind. "Not a game. Not just research. Something… real," she finishes lamely.

Viviane pulls back and meets her gaze. Looking vulnerable, with the tears pooling in her eyes, Viviane is nevertheless as beautiful as ever—a sight that would cause any man's breath to catch, as Greg immediately demonstrates. But when she speaks, Viviane sounds as old and tired as Kara has ever heard her. "Don't you see, it's happening again. The military, duty"—usually Viviane spits this word out spitefully, but today it comes out sadly—"again, they're stealing away someone I love, someone I need."

"Don't you think you're being just a bit melodramatic? It's not like I'd be abandoning you entirely. I mean, yes, I'd be moving out, but we'd keep in touch, *better* than just 'in touch.' We'd burn up the airwaves like last time, when I was with DactiSoft. It may not be ideal, but it works."

Viviane just shakes her head sadly. "No, Kara, it doesn't. If you're following dear Daddy into one of his projects, you might as well be entering a black hole. It's not just that you won't be allowed to talk about *it*. You actually won't be allowed to talk about *anything*. Maybe, *maybe*, they'll let you mail or email back and forth, but there will be people poring over every message, removing anything that might possibly convey info that's supposed to be secret." She suddenly giggles at Kara's shocked expression. "What, Daddy didn't mention that?"

"Um, no." And with that admission, all is apparently forgiven. Viviane is now convinced that Kara is also a victim in this situation. She throws open her arms to draw her into a hug.

"Did you already accept the job?" comes Viviane's voice from behind her back.

"Yes," Kara lies after just a momentary hesitation. Her rationale for making this decision probably sounds shaky as it is; if she admits the truth, that'll require more explanation, and she's not about to tell Viviane of the danger they both face.

"Do you know where you'll be working?"

"No, not really."

"I can take a guess. He didn't tell you much of anything, did he?"

"No," Kara whispers. The question now repeating in Kara's mind is *What have I gotten myself into?*

She doesn't realize she'd spoken the thought aloud until Viviane's voice answers. "You *don't* know what you've gotten yourself into. That's the whole point, isn't it?"

[Chapter 06]

Mid-February 2014

The week that follows is a blur of activity. Kara calls Grant the very next morning to inform him of her decision, and the man sounds pleased, if not overly surprised. But he's very firm regarding how quickly he wants her relocated. Next Monday, less than a week away, will mark her departure—the end of her current life and the beginning of something new and unknown.

One week to extricate herself from departmental responsibilities at the university, transferring her classes to another grad student. One week to put her doctoral studies on hold—again—and do damage control with the scholarship committee. One week to explain to all of her loved ones, including her father, that she's taking a new job that she can't tell them anything about. In short, one week to rearrange her entire life. It's madness.

Viviane proves surprisingly supportive, helping with packing and offering an encouraging word from time to time—which is a good thing, considering the overwhelming uncertainty that continues to plague Kara about this whole situation. The more she thinks about it, the more questions occur to her. Fortunately, when she called to accept, Grant provided the number of an associate who, supposedly, would answer any questions Kara might have. The first call she places to the number proves interesting.

"*Hello.*" Not a question, a statement.

"Yes, hi, this is Kara Dunn, I'll be working with… actually, I don't know what I'll be doing. I'm with General Grant's… group."

"*Yes, I know.*"

"Okay, um…" Kara waits for a moment, not sure if she's about to be transferred, but feeling at the very least that the rules of polite conversation dictate some further comment from the other party. An introduction, perhaps. After a moment, she begins to wonder if they've been disconnected. "Um, hello?"

"*Yes, Ms. Dunn.*" Again, not a question.

Kara forges ahead. "I had a few questions regarding my upcoming work with... well, General Grant's group. Are you the person I should speak with?"

"*Yes, Ms. Dunn, I am the only individual at this number.*"

"Oh. Right." And so Kara proceeds to ask her questions and receive her responses. The woman on the other end of the line is never *rude*, per se, but neither is she personable. Every question is answered in terse, economical language, each word feeling as though it's been carefully weighed before transmission over the phone line.

It's during this conversation that Kara's flight arrangements are made. "Okay, so just to verify, my flight departs LAX at 7:00 Monday morning bound for McCarran in Las Vegas. I can pick up my ticket from the ticketing desk two hours before departure."

"*Correct.*"

Just to get the woman's reaction, Kara adds, "And how much time do I have before my connection to Area 51?" It was Viviane who insisted that's where she's ultimately going. Kara allows the answering silence to go on long enough that she again wonders after the status of their connection. "Okay then. So I'll just call you if I have any more questions?"

"*Yes, ma'am.*"

"Okay. Thank you."

Several more short conversations take place over the ensuing days. The third time Kara calls and identifies herself, the other woman—who never does offer her own name—responds with the only other bit of unnecessary information she would share: "*Yes, I know, Ms. Dunn. You are the only individual with this number.*"

And it turns out Viviane was right about correspondence with the outside world. In answer to her question about a forwarding address, Kara's contact responds, "*It is best to assume you will not be permitted contact with the outside world during your engagement. However, you may use the following address if you so choose,*" after which she relays an address in Hoboken, New Jersey. In the end, Kara chooses to forgo mail forwarding and just allow Viviane to send along anything that seems urgent but not *too* urgent.

Kara never does experience much in the way of excitement or anticipation about the move, but she reminds herself frequently that this situation is apparently her best choice from among limited options. And it will keep her friend safe.

By the time Monday finally dawns, Kara's anxiety has mostly worn itself out. She's just ready for some answers.

**Monday morning
February 17, 2014**

Kara looks over the ticket quickly before thanking the attendant and stepping away from the desk.

"Everything taken care of?" Viviane asks.

"Yep. Departing here 7 o'clock, arriving LAS at 8:23. No connecting flight."

Viviane smirks. "Right. Don't worry, they'll be waiting for you."

"I still can't believe they took all my luggage." She had checked four large bags, in essence bringing all of her wardrobe with her on the flight. The agent had seemed a bit surprised at something that popped up on her screen, but then she'd waived the normal $125 per bag fee.

"Hey, you're part of a privileged elite now." Viviane's smirk fades, and Kara catches just a glimpse of a worried expression as the other woman envelops her in a hug.

Eventually they pull away, and Kara says, "Take care of yourself, okay?"

"I will. I'll miss you, you know."

"Oh, I know. I'll miss you too. Terribly." They smile tearfully, then Kara turns to Gregoire, who is carefully loitering far enough away to give them privacy but close enough to be easily beckoned. Viviane has trained him well. "Greg!"

He smiles as he hurries up to them.

"Thank you so much for carrying the bags." After all, it wouldn't have been possible had he not accompanied them. She begins digging in her purse. Notepad, pens, sunglasses, mints, inhaler, wallet… "I have your tip here somewhere…"

He looks horrified for a moment and tries to wave her off, but she finds what she's looking for and thrusts it into his hands: a scrap of yellow legal paper bearing the handwritten note, "Live life to the fullest. When going to the bathroom, make sure you grab the newspaper."

They all laugh. She offers her hand, and he leans in to peck her on both cheeks, amidst protestations from Viviane. More laughter. It's a ritual with them, but it's comforting nonetheless.

Kara squeezes one last hug out of Viviane before grabbing her carry-ons and heading through security. She turns one last time and calls back, "I'll see if I can't get a message to you when I arrive. So you know I'm there safe!"

Kara's flight arrives twenty minutes late, which seems almost like arriving early. She is met at the gate by a suited man holding a sign with her name on it. This is quite the curiosity for most of the passengers as they pass around him; Kara vaguely remembers the time before 9/11 when just anyone could trounce into an airport and meet a passenger at the gate.

The man, who naturally remains nameless—Kara is no longer surprised by this sort of thing—walks with her to the baggage claim where he commandeers a cart for her duffels. After that they board a commuter vehicle to what is apparently a private corporate terminal, judging from the signage. She queries the man about this, and he smiles. "Defense contractor." Other than that, Kara's pretty sure nothing substantive is said by any of the commuters during the entire five-minute trip aboard the people mover. Clearly many of these people know each other, as there are numerous greetings and smiles; everyone is friendly, but they are ultimately reserved. For that matter, so is her guide. No one offers information, and no one solicits it.

It occurs to Kara that she could grow to like this.

Whatever Kara was expecting for the final leg of her flight to Area 51, a packed Boeing 737 was definitely not on her radar. And yet it's at just such a vehicle—a pristine white jet with red striping, otherwise unmarked, with mobile staircase pulled alongside—that her guide leaves her after gamely adding her bags to an otherwise empty cart for "checked" luggage.

The flight proves mostly uneventful, though there are some small differences from the norm. To start with, the safety presentation put on by the attendants is a bit truncated; in fact, it seems to Kara as though the eyes of one stewardess fall on her unusually frequently. Clearly most of these travelers are regulars, whereas Kara's name was probably flagged as a newbie on the passenger manifest. But since she's well practiced in fastening a seat belt, she's not given any trouble. Following the safety demo, a voice comes over the intercom and introduces itself as the captain, sans name, and announces that flight time will be a short twenty-eight minutes; Kara cannot remember having ever taken such a short flight in such a large plane before, but the size of their jetliner certainly makes sense considering the number of passengers. She's been assigned a window seat near the front of the plane, so she's able to look outside periodically. There's not much to see, however: mostly just desert, although towards the end she thinks they fly over a few ranks of fences; come to think of it, if she's making out chain link fences, they must not be flying very high. When the attendant comes on to announce their imminent landing, complete with an injunction to "return seats and tray tables to their upright and locked position," there is an unexpected addition: "and remove all hands, faces, and other obstructions from the windows in preparation for landing." This she does, and after a moment the plastic window shade slides smoothly into place, all by itself. So much for a first look at her new home.

The landing is smooth, though the taxiing following the landing is a bit bumpy. No one seems disturbed by this. It's not until she steps out of the plane that she realizes why. As she comes through the hatch, her eyes are assaulted with light, and she stumbles slightly. The man behind her grabs her shoulder to steady her; with a smile, he asks, "Sunglasses?" She digs hers out and slaps them on once they reach the bottom, and finally she's able to process the alien landscape she's been dropped into.

A vast flat surface stretches out before her, at least a square mile in area, and the entire expanse is glitteringly, blindingly white. She crouches down and runs her hand across the ground; it comes back dusted with a fine powder. Salt, she realizes. Hard-packed salt. Sure enough, as she straightens and looks about, she realizes that the area is ringed by low hills, exactly as a lake would be. Almost certainly this very surface once *was* a lake, a terminal lake fed by rivers and streams but with no outlets of its own. The only way for water to escape would be through evaporation, thus leaving behind impurities and salt. And just like the Great Salt Lake in Utah or the Dead Sea in Israel, the salinity would continue to climb until the body of water was far saltier than seawater. Except that in this case, *all* of the water had eventually evaporated, probably at the same time the surrounding land had turned to desert. "Which would make it a saltpan," she mutters.

"Precisely," comes a cultured voice from right behind her.

She jerks around so fast she ends up with a crick in her neck. Her pained expression runs counterpoint to Gen. Grant's huge smile.

"Welcome to your new home."

"You know, that sort of thing may seem dramatic in the movies..." Kara begins while rubbing her neck, then stops.

Grant's smile falters, then returns apologetically. "Oh... I'm sorry. I just—"

He reaches down to grab her carry-on, giving Kara a chance to study his uniform unobtrusively. 'Fatigues' is how she would have described the camouflage outfit, except that her rather cursory research on the Air Force this last week showed that term to be outdated. 'Airman battle uniform' or 'ABUs' is apparently preferred, though she can't see why it matters.

In any case, the only distinctive feature of Grant's attire is a single black star embroidered on his lapel—he doesn't even have a name patch. Despite his advanced age, he shoulders her admittedly-heavy carryon with no apparent effort and begins striding across the saltpan. Kara looks around for some indication of where to collect her checked baggage, then gives up and hurries after the older man. Eighty years old—amazing. As part of her research, Kara had followed up on Viviane's comment about "the rules," and confirmed her friend was quite right—the mandatory retirement age for an Air Force officer is sixty-four. Which makes the elder Grant even more of an enigma.

"Well, then, should we start the tour?" he asks when she joins him.

"Sure," she responds, forcing herself to relax and smile. She may hate everything about the situation that brought her here, but she's here now, and she needs to make the best of it. That means a good working relationship with the new boss. Besides, her natural curiosity is already surfacing. "So what's this place called? Area 51, right?"

Her boss chuckles as he leads her across the flat towards a distant SUV. She notices that no one else is moving in the same direction. "This place doesn't actually have a name, per se. The facility we work out of belongs to the Air Force and was built in the early 1950s; unlike our other domestic installations—like Eglin or Peterson or Nellis, which is right next door—this base was never given a name. It made for better operational security in the early days; names can be dropped accidentally, but no civilian takes note when a serviceman says, 'Gotta head back to base,' especially with Nellis so near.

"You may certainly call this base Area 51, as I am sure many of our contractors do. However, even that is a bit of a misnomer perpetrated by Hollywood and novelists. Area 51 actually refers to this plot of land, and the designation predates construction of the base. This entire area of desert, for a thousand square miles around, was set aside for nuclear weapons testing in the 1940s, during World War II. There were twenty-seven other plots just like this one. And I'm sure," he adds with a smile and a sidelong glance, "you can guess what they were called."

"Areas... 1, 2, 3, and so on?" She frowns. "If there are only twenty-eight, how did we get to Area 51?"

"Oh, Kara, my dear, I can see you're going to take some work." He shakes his head in mock disappointment as they arrive at the SUV, and Kara can see that her checked bags have been magically transported to the cargo rack. "See," he continues, "you're still thinking like a scientist. The point of scientific research is to increase knowledge, and so you take copious notes and make sure that everything you do is logical. You're always laying the groundwork for the ones who will someday follow in your footsteps."

He swings into the driver's seat, incredibly spry, and flashes her an easy smile. "But this is the military, and we work just the opposite. Our goal isn't to increase knowledge so much as to hoard it and prevent its spread. And so when they slicked up the Nevada Test Site, it was second nature to number the plots in as confusing a manner as possible. Suffice it to say that we probably do not share a border with Area 52. In fact," he pauses and squints off in the distance a moment, as if accessing a very old memory file, "I seem to recall a rumor that some of the plots weren't even designated with regular numbers. They say there's an Area Pi out there. They say it's *circular*, which I am sure was quite a treat for the surveyors."

He puts the vehicle into gear and chooses a seemingly random direction before continuing his narrative. "In any case, this base was established within Area 51 because of Groom Lake, this salt pan we're driving upon. You can imagine how many millions of dollars it would have cost the taxpayers to reproduce so much tarmac using asphalt, and the government is a sucker for a good deal." He chuckles. "Incidentally, that's another name used for this place—Groom Lake. Groom Lake, Home Base, Paradise Ranch, even Dreamland—I've heard them all used in reference to this facility. But no official name... nor is one needed. This isn't a single military base so much as it's a highly secure location within which dozens of unconnected projects are pursued, with very little overlap or communication between personnel of differing projects."

Grant checks his mirrors, as if he's changing lanes, even though there are no stripes or even other cars anywhere nearby. Kara finds herself confused by the man's demeanor. At the moment, he hardly seems like a tough-as-nails military man, or even like someone wrapped up in a cloak-and-dagger lifestyle. He's quite personable and grandfatherly—and she realizes she glimpsed some of that same personality last week, but only when his subordinates were elsewhere.

She seizes an opening in the conversation. "Why are you telling me all this? I thought everything here was top secret, don't share info unnecessarily, that kind of thing. Your 'job offer,'"—she manages to say this evenly—"every conversation I had with my contact, every encounter I've had since I arrived in Vegas—none of you have volunteered info."

"True." He's driving them toward the perimeter of the salt flat, where Kara can begin to make out numerous roads cut into the surrounding hills. Unsurprisingly, many of the routes are unlabeled, and even the few signs are a mishmash of codes and symbols she cannot comprehend. Grant speaks up, "Secrecy is the culture of this place. I've struggled with it all my life, because... well, I used to be something of a practical joker, and if the military has a sense of humor, it's located somewhere other than this facility. It's a wonder I ever joined the military, much less stayed so long in a post like this, but there were good reasons. Of course," he shoots her a wink, "if I told you anything more, I'd have to kill you.

"In all seriousness, nothing I've told you is secret—the reason we volunteered so little intel this last week was so that you'd have very little to accidentally divulge about your destination. But now you're here, and everything I've told you can be found on the Internet, even just on that free encyclopedia everyone talks about. Much of the information was declassified in 2003. Not that the government is going to spell it out for the world... the conspiracy theorists still have to draw their own conclusions." He smiles. In fact, the smile seems an almost constant thing for him at the moment.

Grant turns off onto one of the many perimeter roads, and they follow it for perhaps a half mile without speaking. Another question occurs to Kara as she watches his deft handling of the vehicle. According to her research, there are barely two hundred Air Force officers of his rank at any given time, so... "Don't you rate your own driver?"

He glances at her with another smile. "Certainly." He's silent long enough that Kara wonders whether he'll say more, then he adds, "But I like to do as much for myself as I can. When you reach my age, you'll understand." Inexplicably, his face clouds momentarily before he forces another smile.

Three curves later, they come across what appears to be an impromptu parking area, just six or seven cars parked haphazardly beside a low bluff. Grant pulls his alongside and kills the engine.

Once she looks more closely, Kara realizes there's a door built into the face of the bluff. No, not a door, she revises her first impression as they approach it—more of a hatch, like something one would see in a submarine, or at least in a movie about submarines. The wheel begins spinning of its own accord, the hatch swings open, and they step inside. She has to crouch slightly for the first several steps of the entranceway until she can step down into the room proper. Stepping down beside her, Grant hands off the car keys to another ABU-clad man, who immediately exits without a word exchanged between them.

There's not really much exciting to be seen; with her back to the hatch, Kara observes nothing unique to separate this hallway from that of any office building in the country. No windows, of course, but it certainly doesn't have the feel of a subterranean cavern; all walls have been finished with drywall, and there are drop ceilings and fluorescent lights. She tucks her hair over her ear as she takes it all in.

Despite the bland familiarity of her surroundings, Kara feels the low-level tension of being outside her comfort zone. Grant is speaking softly with a severe-looking woman at a desk to the right. Kara does a double-take, because Grant's entire bearing has changed. Gone is the smile playing constantly about his lips; gone is the relaxed posture. He is indeed a military man now, every inch the commanding officer.

Exchange complete, he turns to her and says, "Miss Dunn, welcome to the barracks for Project Prometheus. This will be your home for the next several months. Please note that you are not to exit these premises under any circumstances without my express written approval; and note that the door behind you is the only exit." He steps closer and drops his voice, just a hint of his former levity returning. "Being a secret government operation has some perks. We don't really have to worry about fire code."

"Ms. Dunn," the woman speaks up, "please follow me to the conference room. We have some paperwork for you to sign. And," she holds up a hand as Kara begins to speak, "don't worry, your bags are being seen to."

[Chapter 07]

Monday afternoon
February 17, 2014

As it happens, "some paperwork for you to sign" is a bit misleading. A *mountain* of paperwork is more like it. What's more, these pages serve an entirely different purpose from most of the fine print Kara has read in the past. Usually waivers or warnings are about providing protection against consumers who may pursue litigation; though officially the consumer is supposed to read them, it doesn't really matter to anyone except that consumer if she does.

In this case, however, it is made clear beyond doubt that she is to read and understand every word before leaving the room. If she has questions, she is to ask them. Since much of the documentation outlines penalties for divulging classified information—starting with forty-year federal prison sentences and going all the way up to capital punishment—Kara can understand why. She reads it all twice, feeling very, very small as she does so.

Beyond the obvious—that she is never to reveal any information about her involvement with Prometheus, no matter how generalized—Kara is also introduced to the more mundane policies and procedures that will govern her life for the upcoming months. She will be issued a security clearance badge which is to be clipped at all times on the front of her torso, within six inches of her collar. The badge must remain in place even within her own quarters, to be removed only while in the shower, at which time it is to be clipped to the outside of the shower stall. The badge will feature her photo, and it will include radio frequency and barcode technology for monitoring her movements; the badge will not, however, display her name or any other distinguishing information.

In fact, her name itself is to remain a closely guarded secret, as is the name of every other project participant. Only when introductions are made by the project manager—in this case, Gen. Grant—are names to be acknowledged or shared. As an allowance for practical communication and division of duties, each project participant is issued a code name and a serial number.

No use of electronics is permitted except when those electronics are issued to the participant. There is almost an entire page outlining and prohibiting, in 10-point font, every possible connotation and permutation of the word "electronics." Amazingly, the prohibition extends to the use of scratch paper or any form of paper notebook without permission.

Reading and signing finally complete, Kara presses the intercom button in the center of the conference table.

"Yes?" the front desk minder answers.

"I'm finished."

No answer comes until a minute later, when the door opens and Grant enters. He seems a bit more relaxed than when they arrived, but then, there's no one else present.

"No questions?"

"None that you're going to answer unless you're already planning to answer them," she responds dryly.

"Excellent. Now you're getting the hang of it. Your code name is to be HERACLES. Mine is PANDORA, although you are welcome to address me as General Grant. As project lead, my name is known to all participants."

"I'm Heracles and you're Pandora? I don't suppose you wanted to leave our genders intact?"

He just looks at her blankly. "Codenames are supposed to be meaningless, otherwise it would defeat the purpose," he says finally. "Perhaps someone in the back office is on a Greek tragedy kick."

"Well, don't go opening any boxes."

He can't help but smile at this.

"Actually, General, just one question. About being secretive with our names, and with details about our own personal lives. I'm no extrovert, but some of that kind of thing can't help but slip out occasionally."

"Best rule of thumb: just don't talk to other people unless it's necessary."

"Oh."

"Don't worry, I'll draw your thoughts from you when it's appropriate."

"Okay."

"So, are you ready to finally hear what Prometheus is all about?"

Kara just smiles, finding herself unexpectedly excited.

"Well, I can't really tell you what it's *all* about, but I can show you a bigger slice of the pie than most people get. We're the R&D team for developing manned space combat vehicles."

"Yes, but why?" Kara asks. "What combat are you expecting us to fight in space?"

"I can divulge no details, of course, but the short version is this: there is a risk of orbital attack by a foreign power."

"But why?" Kara repeats. "Why would anyone attack from space?" He doesn't answer immediately, and she offers up the logic she'd been thinking through over the last week, ever since he'd first dropped his hints about orbital combat. "Not that I would know, but... wouldn't it be cheaper to attack by air or ground? What kind of attack are we talking about?" Pause. "Nuclear? It would have to be something small and quick like that if they're coming from that direction."

Grant's lip quirks briefly. "As I said, it's not for me to divulge details, even if I had all of them, which I don't. It's certainly not within my mandate to hypothesize the rationale behind our aggressor's choice of attack vector."

"What country is it?"

Grant just keeps smiling. "What I *can* tell you is that the U.S. Government is privy to information that an orbital attack will occur within the year. What we need to do is place versatile and intelligently responsive craft—that is, manned craft—into orbit in that time frame."

"Manned craft...? But again, wouldn't that be..." She stops herself. No reason to question Grant's decisions first thing off the bat. "Putting people in space is expensive, right?"

He sighs. "Yes, it is. But remember, we need reliability and responsiveness. We simply cannot afford even a second's delay, and there's always a communication delay when using remote operators—a delay that grows with distance."

"Okay, so manned craft." She bobs her head in acknowledgment. "So... how close are we? What is it you need me to do?"

"Oh, we've come quite a ways, but you have a unique perspective on what we're trying to do. Take a look." He swivels his chair around and she mirrors the movement, as the wall they now face slides silently into the ceiling. Through the window that remains, the inside of a small warehouse facility is revealed. And in the center, surrounded by perhaps a dozen men and women in jumpsuits, a large silvery sphere—

Kara gasps, unconsciously rising to her feet. "The Destrier! But how—" She glances back at Grant, who smiles broadly.

"Like I said, we've come quite a ways, 'standing on the shoulders of giants,' as it were. The starfighter designs you developed as part of *Rampant* provided the perfect foundation for what we needed to create in a relatively short time period. The degree of practical consideration you gave to the whole project is astounding. You could easily have cut corners in your game—after all, it's 'just a game,'" he repeats again, with a sly smile. "But instead you made sure it all made sense.

"Just consider the guidance system. Well-situated maneuvering jets, with fuel lines running concentrically to six evenly spaced tanks. The need for range balanced against redundancy and space constraints. You allowed for how the recoil of weapon fire influences and confuses the trajectory of a moving craft, and you even programmed a tertiary fire mode that could be used to deliberately realign or accelerate the craft if the pilot were to 'run out of gas.'

"Not that I have to tell you any of this, but the virtual yoke all by itself is brilliant. Human movement is generally constrained to two dimensions, and even though pilots have some control over altitude, they are constrained by gravity on the one hand and atmospheric pressure on the other. Space is totally different. Speed doesn't matter, acceleration does. Rather than banking or rolling into course corrections, a craft has to be capable of literally jumping in any direction at a moment's notice, because the physics of space allows for that—and even if *your* craft can't do it, chances are your enemy's can.

"You not only recognized the differences, you came up with elegant solutions for them. As I've said before, I applaud you."

Kara listens with only half an ear. Her eyes are glued to the small craft parked before her. In a very real sense, it had never been more than a pipe dream—a dream long before *Rampant*, long before the video game industry strapped guns onto it. And though Kara could draw every square inch of it from memory, and though her people had built scale models of it while developing *Rampant*, it's a different matter entirely to see her creation in the real-world, full-size, up close. It brings up a whole mix of emotions, all of them pleasant. In a word, this Destrier prototype is *validation*, validation for the last several years of her life.

Swallowing past the lump in her throat, Kara asks, "Can I go down and see it?"

Human movement is generally constrained to two dimensions, as Gen. Grant had stated. A person on foot can walk forward, backward, sideways, or something in between, but all of that movement is limited to a relatively flat plane. Actions such as jumping, climbing stairs, or riding elevators can open up a degree of motion into the third dimension—altitude—but even that is heavily limited by gravity. In fact, most humans tend to *think* in only two dimensions, and anyone who disagrees with this statement should consider just how many three-dimensional maps are published each year. They're all flat, and even most globes aren't anything more than spheres with flat maps wrapped around them.

The advent of flying vehicles opened up a bit more flexibility in terms of movement; however, in one sense, flying humans remain just as dimensionally limited in their outlook as ground movers. Because most vehicles cannot maintain any position above ground—that is, they can't just float—they require constant propulsion in one direction or another to keep them aloft. But constant propulsion in any one direction essentially limits the pilot's available range of motion within that dimension. For example, a jet fighter cannot simply come to a complete stop in midair and begin moving in the opposite direction; it must cut a sharp turn or loop around.

Naturally, there have been many innovations that serve to open up that elusive third dimension. Helicopters have been around quite a while, and VTOLs— jets with Vertical Take-Off and Landing capability—have seen quite a bit of action in recent decades. And yet, neither of these flying machines is capable of equally unrestricted motion in all three dimensions. It seems that, within a planet's atmosphere, not all dimensions are created equal.

It's an entirely different ball game outside a planet's atmosphere, however. Gravity still exists, but it's not nearly as influential. Just as importantly, the air and pressure that exist in such strength within any atmosphere are missing in the cold vacuum of space; without friction from wind resistance, objects in motion continue in motion, carried by inertia. Thus, absent the presence of significant gravity or friction, it is theoretically possible to create a craft capable of unfettered three-dimensional motion.

It was upon this precept that the *Rampant* team assembled the software engine behind the Destrier space combat craft. They weren't the first to do what they did, but their practical consideration for addressing the real-world laws of physics set their efforts apart from most of their forebears. The vast majority of space combat simulators published before that time, fun though they were, failed to take full advantage of the freedom of movement possible in vacuum. Spacecraft in games generally moved just like aircraft, which is to say they were capable of moving forward at varying speeds, and directional control was attained by turning and banking.

There was one notable exception, an early precursor of *Rampant* developed in the late 1990s which later spawned several sequels. In that game, pilots had much more freedom to move in three dimensions, and they were also bound by the laws of inertia; however, certain constraints were still imposed upon how well a pilot could control his movement—constraints enacted not by the game developers so much as by the limitations of existing input devices.

And so it was that the very first goal Kara set before her team was this: to develop an input device that would allow free movement in any direction, to make it highly intuitive, and to make it highly responsive. The virtual yoke was what resulted.

Unlike a traditional aircraft yoke—or "joystick," in gamer parlance—the virtual yoke was not attached at any point to an immobile surface, which was, of course, what dictated that it must be virtual. The team's concept called for a small sphere that would, in essence, float before the pilot, who would then control the spacecraft by exerting force on the sphere. A burst of speed along any trajectory could be accomplished by grabbing the sphere and punching in that direction or, in the case of moving backward relative to the pilot, by jerking the sphere back towards oneself. Reorientation of the craft could be accomplished by simply taking sphere between thumb and forefinger and turning it; swiping a hand quickly across one side of the sphere would result in spin. By combining a punching motion with a spin, complex trajectories could be achieved, in much the same way a baseball pitcher produces a curveball.

The team implemented the control sphere using virtual reality technology, which in itself was nothing new. Special VR goggles, connected by USB to the gamer's computer, represented the sphere by projecting slightly different images onto the retina of each eye, simulating depth. The real trick was the accompanying gloves. Also plugged into the computer, they tracked the user's hand movement and simulated pressure on the inside of the fingers. For example, when the user reached his hand toward where the goggles told him the control sphere floated, the gloves would cause the user to, in a sense, *feel* the sphere as well as see it. If the user wrapped a hand around the sphere—which was, after all, the point—the gloves would become rigid to prevent him from crushing it. And naturally, from that point on, any movement of the hand was transmitted back through the glove to the computer, thus exerting the same movement upon the spacecraft itself. The virtual yoke was nothing less than a groundbreaking concept.

Not that it solved all of their problems. After all, once a pitcher lobs his curveball, he has lost the ability to exert further influence on it, at least until the catcher returns the ball to him. What the team had to do was create a way to return the control sphere to a point right in front of the user without sacrificing the perception of movement. In the end, this was accomplished by placing the sphere within a translucent 3D grid that faded to nothing within a few inches of the sphere. Whenever the user moved the sphere away from its normal position, the grid would remain static in relation to the user while the sphere moved; after a moment, however, the software would smoothly transition the sphere back to its place front and center, and the grid would begin moving to reflect all the movement. The faster the grid moved, the faster the sphere was perceived to move, much as a race car on a television screen is perceived as speeding quickly along, even though it remains centered on the screen while its *surroundings* blur past on the periphery. In *Rampant*, perception of spinning motion was made possible by placing a few distinguishing marks upon the sphere itself, thus designating an apparent front and back of the craft.

Meanwhile, the use of the gloves opened up a whole vista of other opportunities. No longer was a user limited to using the keys on a keyboard. With two gloves, he could use one for the virtual yoke and one for a virtual control board—a board that he himself could layout however he desired. The pressure pads within the gloves' fingers even gave the sensation of resistance whenever a button was pressed or a switch flipped. When the game was released, a cleverly developed software utility for laying out the control surface was included, as well as several templates and default configurations.

It was the technology behind *Rampant*, so well thought-out and implemented, that led one industry publication to name it game of the year for 2013. Ironically, it was that same technology that led, at least in part, to the game's failure in the marketplace. Even at a relatively low price point of $39.99 brand new, *Rampant* wasn't much fun without the goggles and gloves, easily an additional investment of $50—even more for wireless models. In the end, the team provided support for traditional joysticks, but the concession invalidated everything they'd been trying to accomplish. It was like trying to use a hammer or even a screwdriver when what was needed was a hammer drill; the game required a complexity of input the joystick just wasn't capable of.

The team's sense of discouragement was intense when it became clear that the game would not sell as well as they had hoped, and far from what the reviews had seemed to suggest.

That discouragement is far from Kara's mind now, replaced by something akin to awe. She strolls around the prototype, crawls beneath it, traverses the catwalk above it, viewing it from every angle. She pokes her head within every access hatch, climbs inside, sits down, stands up. She questions the technicians on every little detail. She is in seventh heaven.

Notwithstanding all the work her team did, the many little details researched and simulated *ad nauseam*, designing a virtual spacecraft for a video game is still a far cry from building one in real life. A *far* cry.

Take the double hull for example. The craft's exterior is exactly like what they used in the game, a simple sphere, just like the representational virtual yoke. Since the pilot's orientation—the direction he's facing—is not always the same as the craft's orientation, the team needed a way of moving the cockpit interior independent of the craft's exterior. This led to a double hull design, such that a heavily armored exterior shell encased a smaller sphere, in which resided the cockpit with its seat, displays, and control apparatuses, not to mention life support equipment. What the programming team never had to consider was what materials to use to allow for frictionless, easy movement of the inner sphere within the outer shell. The solution that Prometheus came up with turns out to be both simple and rather boring: a ball bearing and ratcheting system.

Similarly, the guidance system, while simple in theory, apparently proved a beast to implement in the real world. Kara's design called for eight emission nozzles or "jets"—the two largest used for main propulsion and situated at the "back" of the craft's outer hull; the other six mounted on swivels around the craft's circumference and used for reorienting or spinning the craft on its axis. When it came to actual testing in an underwater environment, the Prometheus team found that responsiveness wasn't good enough with six vectoring jets, so the number was doubled and the jets locked down; at each position where Kara's design called for a single nozzle on a swivel, the prototype features a pair of *fixed* nozzles aimed in opposite directions, a configuration that also eliminates the extra risk associated with moving parts.

Further inspection reveals that all eight nozzles are linked by two independent networks of feeder lines leading to fuel and oxidizer tanks situated at intervals around the craft, the reservoirs apparently integrated into the hull itself.

"Hypergolics?" she asks one of the technicians, referring to the class of bi-propellant materials historically used by NASA for this purpose.

"Cryogenic, actually," the man responds. "We're using liquid oxygen and methane for both propulsion and guidance. There's lots of options, of course, but we think LOX-methane at 3-to-1 offers the best balance between velocity of emission and storage density; other combinations might give pilots slightly better maneuverability, but they'll run out of fuel faster. Also, non-hypergolics are safer to handle."

Of course, the most exciting and most obvious feature of this Destrier—not to mention the most frightening—is the weapons system. It is here where the prototype most significantly diverges from her design. "Ah yes," comes Grant's voice from behind her, as he notices her eyeing the three-inch rotary chain guns. "We've made some modifications there. You see, we've got some experience with weaponry."

"These are based on a design used by the Soviets in their MiG-15 and -17 fighters." Grant runs his hand along the three-foot length of one weapon, which looks like six bamboo sticks tied together at intervals. "Six barrels, which fire in rotation, after the fashion of the original weapon developed by Richard Gatling in the Civil War. Each barrel is 37mm in diameter. And as you can see, we've designed an entirely new weapons cradle—rather than affix the weapons directly to the outer hull, which slaves them to shoot in the same direction the craft is oriented."

"Yeah, we struggled with that one," Kara admits. "We wanted to have complete flexibility of weapons usage no matter whether the main jets were firing, but we couldn't come up with any ideas that didn't seem absurd." She laughs. "We talked at one point about mounting them *inside* the cockpit, and then timing them to fire through holes in the outer hull, kinda like the way guns on some World War Two-era fighters were timed to fire between the propeller blades. But none of us wanted to figure out the math, and besides, it would have undermined the integrity of the outer hull, not to mention resulted in a lot of smoke inside the cockpit."

Grant laughs. "Well, what we've done with this cradle," he continues, "is essentially create a third shell capable of independent movement around the outer hull. Although, for purposes of simplicity, it is indeed slaved to match movement of the cockpit pod. The beauty of it is that it's imminently customizable. Say heavier ordnance is needed—just weld it onto one of the cradle's free hardpoints. And if you get into a spot of trouble, the whole thing can be jettisoned."

"How is it connected?" Kara leans over the edge of the catwalk, trying to get a look at how the cradle joins to the outer hull. "I'm not sure I understand how you can accomplish that complete freedom of movement without crisscrossing the outer hull with dozens of tracks."

"Actually, it's not connected at all." Grant waves at a man sitting by a computer desk across the room. Everyone moves back a step, and the man flips a switch. A deep hum fills the large room and the cradle lifts a few inches into the air. "Electromagnets, placed on the inside of the inner hull. Each one paired to one of the main struts you see here on the cradle. As long as the cradle maintains its form, the dozen magnets pulling it with equal force in conflicting directions keep the Destrier perfectly centered within the cradle's arc. Unless something goes wrong, the cradle never comes into physical contact with the main body of the craft."

Kara blows out her breath. "That," she smiles, "is amazing." Shaking her head, she climbs down from the gantry. "You're still communicating with the external systems via radio?"

Grant nods towards one of the techs. "That's right," the man says. "Propulsion, guidance, weapons, and radar systems—all are linked to the pilot's control board by very short range, heavily-encrypted radio. The only perforation between the two hulls is the hatch itself, which remains sealed during flight.

She nods. "And what about ammo?"

Another tech fields this one. "We've fitted each gun with a thousand rounds each, but it presents a problem. Although 2,000 rounds is far more than any of our aircraft would carry for a gun like this, it's still not that much. Rule of thumb is that each squeeze of the trigger releases a burst of a hundred. So what you've got here is enough for twenty shots.

"The problem is the weight." Grant interjects, handing her a shell roughly four inches long and more than an inch in diameter. It isn't heavy, but it certainly has substance to it. "That single round," Grant says, "weighs in at over five ounces."

"Multiply that by two thousand rounds," pipes in another tech, "and you've got yourself... well, that's our problem. Six hundred pounds of ammo swinging around on that cradle."

Grant leans in and says, *sotto voce*, "I've been tempted to add a few rounds just so we could accurately refer to it as the 800-pound gorilla."

Kara bites her lip, thinking. "What's the overall weight of the craft?"

"Two and a half tons, if you count the ammo."

"So that's... okay, the ammo makes up roughly a sixth of the total weight of the craft. Except that the weight's not distributed, which makes for unusual inertial movement in vacuum. Swinging," she adds, looking at the tech.

"Yes..." he says, prompting her to continue.

"But on top of that, munitions weight is variable. With each burst fired, the whole equation changes."

"Indeed." The general agrees approvingly.

"But what about distributing the weight? Like wrapping it around the craft somehow?"

"Bad idea."

"Yes, of course." Kara has already leapt to the next conclusion. "Explosive shells are already a danger. If detonated in combat, they'd damage the craft. Distributing them across the hull would negate the value of the armor."

"Exactly."

"Well, whatever the solution, I'm probably not the one who will come up with it," Kara reasons. "So, what exactly *do* you need me here for? It looks like you're making incredible progress." Even as she says this, she can't keep the smile from returning to her face. The revelation that this, the Destrier—*her* Destrier—is the project she was recruited for… it's finally sinking in. And it suddenly cancels out a *lot* of her frustration towards Grant and the situation she finds herself in.

"The project is certainly… coming along," Grant says carefully as he waves away the techs, who return to their other duties. "Though not as quickly as I would prefer. What we need you for is the software. You wrote all of what we're using anyway, though some of it has been heavily modified. Where we're running into problems is the radio communications with the externals."

"Okay. When do you want me to get started?" she asks, still struggling with that smile.

Grant mirrors the expression, his own grin decidedly mischievous. "Oh, I think you've got time to change into a lab coat."

[Chapter 08]

**Tuesday afternoon
March 4, 2014**

    Lt. Col. Kevin Smith, Air Force Special Operations Command, stalks the narrow corridors of the dirty concrete building assigned to his people by the government of Lumbawi. He acknowledges the salutes of subordinates as he passes, but he waves off attempts to thrust paperwork into his hands. He couldn't focus on it right now if his life depended on it.
    He does stop to clasp the shoulder of Anthony Reed, a distracted young UAV operator who belatedly salutes. Kevin forces a gentler expression onto his face. "You did good, Reed. You saved innocent lives."
    Reed is making a good showing of it, but this morning's incident has clearly shaken him. "Yessir. I know, sir."
    Kevin glances up and down the hall, then pulls Reed into a vacant room. "It's not like in the video games, is it?"
    Reed winces, looking every bit the college-aged kid he is. "No, sir. I… I killed someone today." He swallows. "I…"
    "You took a human life, and that's not easy. I know." Kevin sighs. "The emotions you're feeling right now are good, normal. If you *didn't* feel this way, it would prove you're not the kind of man I want under my command."
    Something like relief flickers across the boy's face. "Thank you, sir."
    "If you feel the guilt starting to overwhelm you, just remember: you killed the enemy. A human being, yes, but someone who was trying to hurt innocent people. And *they* owe their lives to you."
    The kid thanks him again, salutes again, and departs. Continuing down the hall, Kevin stops briefly in the doorway to his operations center, looking over the people at work there. Great people, exactly the sort any officer wants under his command: loyal, efficient, but also conscientious, just like Reed. He moves on, making for the stairwell before anyone notices him standing there.

Kevin's hand is trembling by the time he reaches the third floor, but he remains composed long enough to reach his small private room. With a last nod to a passing serviceman, he closes and locks the door—then crosses the room and buries his face in a pillow just as the first sobs erupt.

USSOCOM had sent Kevin's people to Lumbawi two months prior, a quiet and unofficial attempt to restore stability to the region, which had been in turmoil since the recent national elections. Kevin's mission was to provide aerial support and reconnaissance, for which he'd been granted a small fleet of choppers and UAVs—unmanned aerial vehicles.

Today's op was simple. Recon the route to be used by a Lumbawese military convoy, guiding the vehicles around potential ambushes. In essence, provide the sort of up-to-the-second intel which only a birds-eye view can provide. Reed had been remote-piloting one of the unit's drones, and he'd been the one to see the insurgent popping up on the roof of a nearby building as the convoy passed—apparently holding some variant of grenade launcher.

There'd been only moments in which to act. The UAV cam footage was grainy, and it was impossible to confirm the threat as bona fide before the shooter had a chance to fire. But this stretch of road was through an abandoned factory district, meaning there was no good reason for anyone to be on that roof.

So Kevin Smith gave the order, and Anthony Reed rained a precision anti-armor ASM onto that rooftop. And as designed, that warhead fragmented on impact, shredding the target and causing the roof to collapse. The convoy arrived safely at its destination. Mission accomplished.

Eight hours later, the report came in. Lumbawese authorities had found not one but *three* bodies in the collapsed building. Small bodies—children, not even teenagers. What the investigators had *not* found was any weapons.

Face buried, Kevin's sobs make no noise. There's no need for his people to know. His superiors, yes—he'd already forwarded the report up the chain of command. But Kevin's people don't need this on their consciences, Reed least of all. It had been Kevin's call. Kevin had given the order.

Sitting up finally, he lets the pillow fall away. The hell of it is, even in retrospect, it was *still* the right call. Maybe some innocent kids were in that building playing, and one of them climbed to the roof and just pointed a stick at the passing convoy—simply pretending at war in the way of innocent kids the world round. But maybe they weren't just playing. In this place, youth doesn't presuppose innocence. They could just as easily have been insurgents themselves. Nor does the missing weapon mean anything; another rebel could easily have recovered the weapon before authorities arrived.

But enemy or not, innocent or not, these were *kids*. Kevin wraps his arms around his roiling belly, swallowing back acid. *Children.*

It's not the first time he's seen death, certainly not the first time he's questioned his own decisions. After fifteen years of this kind of action off-and-on, sent to half the dark corners in the Middle East and Africa, Kevin is well accustomed to both death and self-doubt. But *children?*

Abruptly, he decides he's had enough

[Chapter 09]

March – June 2014

Despite the heavy security and limitations on her movement, Kara quickly grows accustomed to her new environment. She is assigned spacious quarters a mere two-minute walk from the lab. The accommodations are top-notch, including a fully-stocked kitchenette, queen-sized bed, and old-fashioned oversized tub in the bathroom. After the first week, Kara barely notices any of it.

Her every waking moment, or very near to it, is spent in the lab. The development bug has bitten her once more, and she knows she won't slow down until they've worked out all the kinks. Days run together, and food and sleep become needs she addresses whenever her body's signals become so urgent she can't ignore them any longer. In so many ways, life has returned to the way it was when her team was developing *Rampant*, with the exception that there's very little camaraderie among her and the techs.

All five of these men, plus the one woman, are military personnel. It doesn't take her long to realize this. Nevertheless, despite the fact that Kara herself is merely a consultant on the project, holding no rank of her own, the six of them frequently consult her when questions arise. When she herself has questions, they always afford her priority treatment. Kara feels both flattered and empowered by this deference.

Most of the work involves cleaning up the code that runs the interactions between the pilot's control boards and the exterior weapons, guidance nozzles, and radar emitters. In fact, only a small portion of the techs' time is spent working on the equipment itself, and that is mostly repair and maintenance, or adjustment when needed to meet the specifications of Kara's improved software.

Reading through the project journal, Kara begins to realize that fabrication has long since been complete. As far back as summer 2012, there are indications that the majority of the work involved software compliance. This strikes her as very odd, since the *Rampant* team had barely finished conceptualizing the spacecraft for their game prior to Christmas 2011. She distinctly remembers discussing several as-yet-unfinalized details with Mark Lawson over cups of eggnog; since he left the project in January 2012, she knows she's not confused on the timing. As far as the journal goes, there appears to be nothing significant prior to the mid-2012 entries.

Increasingly curious, Kara begins dropping innocuous questions to the members of her team. She's never obvious; after all, the warnings were clear about discussing past lives with other project participants. But she's curious how long these individuals have been involved with the project. She hits pay dirt when she manages to draw one man, codenamed Io, into a discussion on the merits of the Chrono Killer movies. He mentions a particularly violent scene from the sixth, most recent movie in which he felt the need to cover his son's eyes. Since no one has been allowed to leave the premises since she arrived, a restriction which has probably always been Prometheus policy, Kara concludes that this man had not joined the team until May 2013 at the earliest—the month that movie was released. Given the amount of code she recognizes as his, she would hazard the further guess that none of the other techs has been around much longer than he.

So, there appears to have been a complete turnover of personnel at least once, which conveniently precludes her finding out more about the early timing of the project. In and of itself, that's not suspicious; after all, every scrap of paper she signed indicated that compartmentalization of information is a priority. Still, the timing bothers her.

Not as much as the code bothers her, however. It's rife with inconsistencies, and extremely redundant in places—redundant in a bad way, not in a helpful military backup sort of way. She indeed recognizes much of it as the C++ code developed by the *Rampant* team, and she wonders idly how it was acquired. Although she authored much of it, legal ownership fell to DactiSoft as the publisher and sole financial backer; while it's certainly possible Grant's people licensed the code properly, they would probably commit industrial espionage in the name of national security without a twinge of conscience. Regardless, the code has been heavily modified in places, and there are hundreds of new references to independent compiled modules—in essence, library files that allow the programmer to draw on functionality developed for other projects without having to reproduce it. What's crazy is that, looking at what source code is available for these modules, Kara sees that many of the object models are written in Simula of all things, a language positively ancient by modern standards. Simula was one of the first object-oriented programming languages, from which followed the C++ that Kara's team used. Unlike C++, however, Simula is so limited in capability that it's seldom used outside the classroom in modern times.

What makes the use of Simula especially unusual is that so much of it appears to reproduce the code that came from her team, yet without making any apparent improvement. Why would someone go to the trouble of using such an arcane language to describe lateral nozzle firing procedures, when what was written in the C++ already worked so well?

She shares these and many other questions with Grant one day when no one else is around the lab. He waves her queries off. "There have been a lot of fits and starts on this project. Fortunately, you're now here to bring it all together."

"What happened to the previous team?" she asks, almost without thinking.

"The previous team?"

Kara grimaces. "Yeah. I know none of these people have been here more than a year."

Grant's eyes widen slightly. "You were expressly forbidden from discussing that sort of thing!" The volume of his speech does not modulate, but the new edge in his voice is unmistakable.

This is the first time Kara's felt any of his quiet steel directed towards her, and she finds herself simultaneously angry and embarrassed in response. "I haven't!" she blurts, flushing beneath her freckles. "I haven't discussed anything with anyone. It's just obvious, that's all. They weren't working on the project long before I arrived, and it's clear that they weren't involved in a lot of the modifications on my software. I can read the journal as well as anyone."

"Never mind," Grant says, and some of the tension seems to evaporate as he prepares to leave. "Just don't forget those forms you signed."

"General?"

Looking incredibly tired all of a sudden, he doesn't respond during the moment it takes to shuffle for the door. Then: "Yes, my dear?"

"Exactly how long *has* this project been going? It's not just the turnover. The journal entries seem to suggest that you started on all this long before we ever developed *Rampant*."

He chuckles, though it sounds forced. "Oh, we started the project a long, long time ago, when information first became available about the, um, attack. But regardless of how things may appear, your work has been the foundation for all our most important efforts. The rest of us are just helping round out the edges." And before Kara has a chance to reply, he changes the subject completely. "By the way, I took the liberty of arranging a personal trainer for you."

That pulls her up short. "You—I'm sorry, what?" Without meaning to, she glances down at herself, wondering if this is a commentary on the fact that she's put on weight since arriving here.

"A trainer. I thought it would be good to refresh you on your hand-to-hand combat training."

This leaves Kara even more bewildered. "You lost me."

"You were active in *tae kwon do* for a time, yes?" Grant asks with a small smile. "Earned your brown belt, if I recall. Wouldn't hurt for you to get back into training, what with your current situation."

Kara can feel the color creeping onto her face. "You're thinking about that day in the park. The guy pulled a gun on me, and I froze up." Not to mention the following week, when Grant's people snatched her in broad daylight, and she froze up again.

Grant shrugs politely. "It's one thing to develop fighting skills. It's something else to turn them into reflexes—that requires constant practice." His smile brightens. "That's why I've scheduled your trainer for daily one-hour sessions. You'll meet him at six tonight." And with that, he completes his escape, Kara's dismayed objection notwithstanding.

Brigadier General Carl Grant is perhaps the greatest enigma Kara faces. The man is by turns charming and gruff, usually depending on whether any of his military subordinates are around. But that's not always it—sometimes he closes down suddenly, becoming inexplicably more guarded in the middle of a conversation. Despite her acceptance of the secrecy of their work, Kara can't rid herself of that nugget of suspicion towards Grant. In direct contradiction to Viviane's characterization of her father, Kara gets the feeling that Grant is sometimes deliberately misleading in his explanations; rather than simply hide behind military secrecy, it's as though he sometimes spins superfluous explanations. Why he would need to do so is beyond her.

And then there's the growing creepiness factor. The man's genteel charm is one thing. It's something else entirely when she looks up suddenly to find him watching her closely from across the room, especially at times when she isn't even aware he's present. On the several occasions she's caught him doing this, he immediately finds something else to focus on, but she still catches the look on his face. It's something like... longing. And coming from an 81-year old man, half a century her senior, that's just plain gross.

All of this taken together means that when Kara and her team complete their upgrades to the software, she's not terribly sad to see this phase of the project behind her... even though she's clueless about what comes next.

Carl Grant fingers the remote to the widescreen flat panel display hanging on his office wall. He squeezes his eyes shut, and when he looks up again his eyes are moist. Motioning with the controller, he activates the screen.

On screen, a woman in a bathrobe moves about a room, apparently making preparations for bed. For a moment, she stops and turns in the direction of the camera, which is apparently hidden in the corner of the room, where the walls meet the ceiling. The woman is Kara Dunn.

Grant sighs heavily. His eyes follow her around the room until she steps to the bathroom and reaches towards the sash at her waist. Quickly, he kills the screen.

The remote control drops from his hand and clatters on the floor as Carl Grant buries his face in his hands and weeps.

[Chapter 10]

Twenty-nine Years Earlier

**Saturday morning
October 12, 1985**

The little girl scraped the trowel carefully across the surface of the large glass mixing bowl, doing a respectable job of smoothing the concrete despite her unfamiliarity with the implement. Beaded sweat stood out on her furrowed brow, despite the chill air wafting into the open garage where she worked. She looked up momentarily as a few particularly crunchy-looking fall leaves blew in and settled beneath her father's sedan. The temptation to go check them out as possible specimens for her leaf collection—or, failing that, victims for stomping—was strong, but for once she overcame the distraction and turned back to her experiment with a look of intense concentration.

"Kara?" Her father's voice sounded from somewhere within the house.

"I'm in my lab, Dad!" she shouted in response, very distractedly.

Kara rotated the glass bowl carefully, looking for pockets of air the concrete had not filled. Finding one, she worked at the wet concrete some more with her mother's now-ruined wooden spoon.

"Kara?"

She glanced up to see her father standing just inside the door, an unfamiliar man beside him. She flashed them a big smile, characteristic of a sweet seven-year-old kid, and returned to her work with an intensity not the least characteristic of a child that age.

Mr. Dunn took in the state of his wife's kitchenware with only the mildest exasperation. His companion, a fit, fifty-ish man with graying hair, showed considerably more interest. He made a quiet comment about Kara's child-sized workbench, strewn with various science-themed magazines for kids, and Kara's father broke into a proud smile.

"Kara, this is Carl Janus from that important college I was telling you about. You may call him Dr. Janus."

"Oh no," the man objected. "It's just Mister."

Kara spared them a quick glance and a perfunctory smile. "Hello, Mr. Janus," she intoned dutifully.

"Sweetie," her dad continued, "Why don't you go wash up—"

"I can't, Dad!" she objected, abruptly animated. "This is the most *crucial* step of my experiment! If I mess up now, it would be *disaster*-ous!"

Their visitor chuckled, but Mr. Dunn frowned. "I asked you not to start anything this morning."

"I *know*, Daddy, but I can't stop now. If I do this wrong, Mr. Wizard might die!" Her eyes were wide with conviction.

Again the visitor chuckled, though in uncertain confusion this time, but Kara's father leapt forward in alarm. "Mr. Wizard? Where—" He grabbed the mixing bowl from Kara and began turning it, peering within. "Kara," he said, with dawning comprehension, "What did you do?"

Her eyes began swimming in response to her father's alarm; one fat tear broke free and cut an interesting track through the gray dust caked on her face. "It was just an experiment! He'll be okay!" However confident she may have been before, she's obviously not so sure now.

Quickly unbuttoning and rolling up his sleeve, her father plunged his hand into the gritty morass and began feeling around. A moment later he pulled a dripping lump from the bowl. To the visitor's surprise, the lump appeared to shiver and cough before letting out an unmistakable *Ribbit!*

Bending down to eye level, Mr. Dunn gave his daughter a severe look. "Kara Anne, what have I told you about experimenting on living creatures?"

Beneath the dust and tears, beneath the smattering of faint freckles across her cheeks and nose, Kara's face turned beet red.

"You take Mr. Wizard out to the hose, and don't come back until you're both washed up."

"Yes, sir," she whispered miserably, then spun on her heel and fled the garage.

The Dunns lived on a hill in a small two-story with white siding and navy shutters, not terribly removed from civilization, but definitely out of sight of the neighboring houses. The spigot and hose were just around the corner from the garage, and Kara began washing the wet concrete mix from her pet horned frog. The tears continued. It wasn't that she was afraid of punishment—she just didn't disappoint her father often, and she hated the look he gave her when she did. They were best buddies. Straining her ears, she tried to make out the voices of the adults, wondering how angry her dad really was. With some relief, she heard him chuckle.

"No, it was some documentary we watched the other night," he said. "One of those unexplained phenomena segments. Talked about animals encased in stone or concrete, discovered still alive after years. Usually amphibians..." Another chuckle. "Guess I should've expected this."

"You let her watch such programs frequently? She's, what, six?"

"Just turned seven. And... well, yes. We're careful, of course. But the girl's curiosity is insatiable."

Kara frowned, her task temporarily forgotten. She sounded out the word: *in-say-sha bull*. Was that a good thing or a bad thing? Mr. Wizard croaked miserably beneath the streaming spigot, and Kara got back to work. She couldn't make out the next few words.

Then: "I have to say I'm surprised you're here," her father's voice came again, a bit louder.

"Well, as I said on the phone, the university's program exists for the sole purpose of identifying exceptional children and ensuring they're given every opportunity to develop to their full potential." It sounded like Mr. Janus had said these words many times before.

"Yes, but I asked Frank Sims at the school—he said the talent search is for fourth and fifth graders."

"Oh, um, well, yes." Mr. Janus cleared his throat. "But sometimes we do home visits for, well, *truly* exceptional children."

"But how did you find out about Kara?"

"Her school begins standardized testing in first grade. Her scores were remarkable."

"Oh," her father sounded surprised. "I was a little disappointed in her scores. We really expected she would—" He broke off suddenly, perhaps realizing—belatedly—that Kara was in earshot.

Kara was stung at the revelation, and almost immediately her tears began anew. Then the wind picked up, and goose pimples stood out on her wet arms. Feeling suddenly motivated, she redoubled her cleaning efforts amidst continued sniffles. Returning to the now empty-garage, she deposited Mr. Wizard in his tank and changed into a t-shirt of dubious cleanliness, which she found amongst her things. By the time she found the two men sitting in the dining room, she'd dried even her face.

Her father offered a gentle smile that made Kara feel a little bit better. "Have a seat, sweetie. Remember when I told you Mr. Janus would be coming, that he wanted to ask you some questions?"

She nodded seriously.

"Okay then." He glanced at Mr. Janus. "If you don't mind, I'll just stay here."

For a moment, Mr. Janus looked like he might object, but then he thought better of it. "Of course." He turned to Kara and gave her a big smile. "Miss Dunn, I am going to administer a very special kind of test for you. There will be some things on this test you don't understand, and that is perfectly alright. Some of these questions were designed for people much older than you. I just want you to answer each question to the best of your ability, and not get discouraged if you're not sure of the answer. For some questions, there *is* no right answer."

Kara nodded again, but she ignored the man's reassurance. She wanted to impress the man and she wanted Daddy to be proud of her, and she would do whatever it took to make those things happen. Concentrating as hard as she could against the constant distractions of the world around her, Kara began answering Mr. Janus's questions.

Even had she not been so committed, Kara would have found concentration at least a little easier than usual. The test was fascinating, even more so than the special achievement tests her first-grade teacher had given the class recently. There were boring vocab and spelling questions, of course, and history and geography questions. She didn't like those, because even when she knew the answer, she sometimes couldn't find the right words to say what she wanted to say. But there were also story puzzles in which she got to guess at the answer. And then there were questions with pictures, and questions with math problems—but unlike any math she'd ever done—and memory-testing games.

The best part of all was the block-building test. Mr. Janus would show her cards with pictures of block structures, and she got to build what she saw in the picture using the red and white wooden blocks he provided. Every time he showed a new card, Mr. Janus would push a button on his wristwatch, and he would press it again whenever Kara finished. The first pictures were too easy, and not very much fun, but the block structures got crazier and crazier the more she did, until Kara completely forgot this was supposed to be a test. It was just like building Legos, except that Lego manuals showed you how to do it step-by-step, and Mr. Janus just showed the finished building. The only problem Kara had with the block building test was that sometimes she wanted to improve the structure, make it better than the picture—like she sometimes did with Legos. But she forced herself to match the picture perfectly. She wanted the adults to be pleased.

Mr. Janus offered her frequent breaks and opportunities to get a snack or drink, but with only one exception (to use the bathroom), she insisted on continuing immediately to the next portion of the test. Two hours passed in this manner before the test was concluded, and although her father appeared surprised at her staying power, her test administrator just smiled approvingly.

"Okay, that's it," Mr. Janus announced finally, not looking up until he'd finished writing in his notebook. "Miss Dunn, I am very pleased with how you did on your test. You are a *very* smart little girl."

Kara smiled uncertainly, turning immediately to meet her father's eyes questioningly. "I'm very proud of you too, sweetie," her father added, and indeed, she could hear the pride in his voice. She flushed bright red again, this time in pleasure rather than shame.

"Why don't you go get that snack now," Mr. Janus suggested. "I'd like to talk with your father for a few minutes."

"Yes, sir," she said, the image of politeness, and excused herself gravely from the table. As she entered the kitchen, she considered grabbing her gummy bears and rushing back so she could listen with her dad to whatever Mr. Janus had to say. But then she realized Mr. Janus wanted to talk to her dad without her around. In *that* case...

Kara turned on her heel and crept stealthily back down the hall, stopping shy of the doorway, just out of sight of the adults.

"... absolutely astounding!" came the hushed but excited voice of Mr. Janus.

"You really think so?" came the equally hushed voice of Kara's father, sounding surprised but nonetheless thrilled.

"Here, take a look. This is her Performance IQ—notice her Processing Speed Index is in the 98th percentile for her age? Girl's sharp as a tack."

"Wow," said Mr. Dunn, sounding suitably impressed.

"But look at her Perceptual Organization Index." There sounded the rustling of papers.

"Oh." Her father sounded disappointed. "Only 86th?"

The smile in Mr. Janus's voice was obvious even from the hallway. "Right... 86th percentile for kids age 16."

"I don't understand."

"The POI measures a person's visio-spatial perception, among other things. Performance on the block design problems is one of the measures that contribute to POI. Mr. Dunn, your daughter... she blew through those cards so fast, I'm sure she broke a few records. The children's test simply wasn't capable of measuring your daughter's potential—so I started her on the block design problems from the adult test."

"You're telling me Kara's as smart as a 16-year-old?"

"I'm telling you that she is an unusually perceptive child whose innate understanding of the physical world is *superior* to 86% of 16-year-olds in this country."

"Wow." A long pause followed. "Um, what exactly does that mean? That she's a genius?"

Mr. Janus chuckled. "It means she has a very special mind that is capable of thinking in three dimensions. Remember how quickly she was able to build those block buildings? Even though the pictures were two-dimensional, her mind was able to absorb the patterns from what was visible and extrapolate what the hidden parts of each structure looked like—without much conscious thought. The ability to conceptualize models in '3D,' as they call it, is highly prized in many advanced scientific disciplines. Your daughter's ability in this regard is, again, absolutely astounding. It's not the highest score recorded for a child of her age, but I suspect she's the most highly functioning child to have scored that well."

"Highly functioning...?"

"Most 7-year-olds with that sort of perceptual cognition are savants." Kara sounded out the word, *suh-vawn-tt*, wondering what it meant.

"Oh," her father replied, taken aback.

"Exactly," Mr. Janus continued. "We've been discussing Kara's Performance quotient. But what about her Verbal IQ?" Papers rustled. "Here you'll see she's much closer to the middle of the pack for her age. But don't be disappointed—her peers on the PIQ are in the tenth percentile or lower when it comes to Verbal. Kara has some offsetting factors that put her in the 50s. On the one hand, her vocabulary is excellent."

"She reads entirely on her own, has for almost a year. And the stuff she reads—especially those science magazines—is probably a little old for her."

"That's good; it stretches her. She's also got a good memory. But all of that is offset by her tendency to drift, to lose interest. Have you ever noticed that about her? I thought so. But overall"—again, the smile in Mr. Janus's voice was obvious—"Kara is a *very* intelligent girl. She's definitely in the top one-hundredth of children her age when it comes to overall or 'full-scale' IQ."

"That's great," said her father, sounding equally pleased. "So... what does that mean about the university's talent program?"

Mr. Janus cleared his throat. "Well, um, as you discovered, our program doesn't really officially work with children until they're older. I've come here today as a courtesy to you, and because we feel a commitment toward encouraging the development of our nation's most exceptional children. What I'd really like to do is just give you some advice before I leave."

"Oh. Um, okay."

"Your daughter is naturally exceptional, but I suspect she has also developed well because of a healthy home environment. You and your wife surround her with love and encouragement here, don't you?"

"We try. I mean, she makes it easy."

"That's great—keep it up. Obviously she's interested in maths and sciences, and you should continue to indulge that, but not at the expense of her other education. She will probably never care as much for soft subjects, like languages or social studies, but she can't ignore them. And outside of the classroom, your daughter is likely to struggle in social settings. It's absolutely imperative that you help her learn to cope with these tendencies."

"You make it sound... urgent."

"Well... the world expects much of a child like Kara. The way she's wired, she can accomplish things for humanity that would be impossible for most of us. Mark my words, she will be a leader some day. I can't say in what arena, but you can be sure that leadership will require her to be not just brilliant but well-rounded."

Mr. Dunn laughed nervously. "Carl, she's only seven!"

"Raise your daughter with an eye to the future, Mr. Dunn."

"I do, it's just—"

"One last thing, very important. Your daughter is incredibly eager to please. I know, all kids are to some degree. But Kara—I suspect she will struggle with insecurity to a degree proportionate with her exceptional abilities. The approval and appreciation of other people will fuel her for days, but disapproval can be debilitating."

Pause. "You got that from just two hours with her."

"I have a great deal of experience in this matter. It also fits the model, connected to the social awkwardness I mentioned earlier. Because of this, it is vitally important that your daughter develop a strong moral compass, otherwise her desire to please others will erode her potential to become a strong leader. Not to mention it will probably get her into trouble as a teenager. Moral compass, Mr. Dunn," he emphasized.

Another pause. "My wife and I..." Her dad hesitated again. "We're not religious people, you understand."

"Well, yes, I'm—I understand."

"But we'll raise her right." His sigh was audible. "Wow. Carl—Mr. Janus—I have to say this is a lot to take in. Certainly more than I expected when I first got your call."

"Oh, well, I'm sorry" came Mr. Janus's voice, suddenly sounding much lighter. "I do come on very strong sometimes, I suppose. I just place a lot of importance in building tomorrow's leaders today."

"I can see that."

"In any case..." Pause. "I suppose I really should be going." He sounded almost sad. "Is it possible I might say goodbye to your daughter first?"

"Oh, sure. In fact... Hmm, I'm surprised she's kept herself busy this long. She might be out in her 'lab' again..."

Swiftly, and as silently as possible, Kara dashed down the hall and out into the garage. When her dad appeared a moment later, she was breathing hard through her nose, trying and failing to look casual as she chipped half-dry concrete from the mixing bowl.

Back inside, at the front door, Mr. Janus squatted down and placed his hands on Kara's shoulders. Looking her in the eye with all the sincerity of a peer, he said, "You are a very special girl. Keep up all your hard work, my dear. I look forward to following your career someday." Rising, he turned to her father and added, "We'll touch base with you periodically, see if there's anything we can offer."

"Thank you very much," he answered sincerely, as he let the visitor out the front door.

Returning to the lab yet again, Kara and her father worked at cleaning up the mess. From Mr. Dunn's smile and the tune he kept humming, Kara could tell just how happy and proud he was, despite her abortive and illicit experiment earlier. Before she knew it, she'd dropped her guard entirely.

"Daddy," she asked, "what's a savant?"

He frowned. "Well, sweetie, a savant is a..." The frown deepened, and then became a look of horror. "Kara! Were you—?"

And so Kara Dunn was sent to her room in punishment that Saturday after all. But although the details grew fuzzy over the years, she never forgot that day… and despite what Mr. Janus said upon leaving, to Kara's knowledge, her father never heard from the man again.

[Chapter 11]

Wednesday afternoon
July 2, 2014

Kara watches through the observation window in the conference room as the techs finish tightening everything down in preparation for the Destrier's transportation. Grant enters behind her and joins her at the window.

"What's next?" she asks.

"Well, the Destrier will be carried into space next month. Ostensibly, it goes as a new satellite put into orbit by a telecom, but the Air Force has an arrangement with the company. The test pilot will follow the month after as part of a commercial shuttle mission—this is a different company, an approved government contractor who can be trusted to keep our involvement under wraps, but the mission itself is a legitimate look into space tourism possibilities."

He quirks a smile. "Though I don't imagine they'll pursue the tourism venture, not since OWT went public. You heard about OWT—Out of this World Tours? With their first Longship launch scheduled this fall, OWT is so far ahead of the competition, it's ceased to *be* a competition." He seems inordinately pleased by this. "Regardless, if all goes well with our launch and testing, you should have a whole new list of Destrier bugs to work out by September."

"You know," Kara says tentatively, "R&D would be a lot more effective if the people designing the spaceship were actually allowed to talk to the people *flying* the spaceship."

A ghost of a smile passes over Grant's face. "Yes, my dear, I understand. But that's the military for you. Compartmentalization of knowledge."

Kara lets out a frustrated sigh. "So, what's next for *me*? Am I supposed to sit here for two months? If I had something to do, that would be one thing, but if not—and if I'm not allowed to leave—I'll go crazy."

Grant leans over the table and depresses the button to drop the section of wall back over the observation window, hiding it.

"Well, I have Corporal Skewrs scheduled for three-hour daily sessions starting next week."

Kara groans at this, though she has to admit the one-on-one training has done wonders, not just for her form and fitness, but also for her confidence. Still... even three hours of training each day leaves ten of boredom. "What about the pilots—the people who will eventually fly the Destrier?"

Grant frowns. "What about them?"

"I assume you've got them running drills?"

"Yes. Quite actively."

"They're using the game, aren't they?"

Grant smiles in understanding, inclines his head.

"Then why not let me get involved?"

"Oh, but Kara, compartmentalization. You know." He's playing with her. His smile is evidence of that.

"Oh, come on, General. I designed the game. I designed the interface. At the moment, I'm a wasted resource, especially if I have to sit around here doing nothing. At least let me advise on tactics or something."

Grant holds her eyes for a long time. Finally, he says, "I'll see if I can work something out."

Two weeks pass, during which time there is no contact from Grant. Meanwhile, she has the run of the place, the only person who continues to live there after the techs are transferred.

She spends a lot of time working out, even when Skewrs isn't there to force her. She also spends some time exploring. There's not much to her corner of the world, and most of it she's seen before, though until now she'd not spent any time just wandering around. The R&D wing in which Project Prometheus is housed takes up two levels, with little more than thirty thousand square feet of floor space. Her security badge automatically grants entry to all areas she's cleared for, and that turns out to be most of them.

Nearly the whole upper level, aside from the conference room and a small lobby, is living quarters. She walks through some of them and finds that they're all as spacious and nearly as well appointed as hers. She had rather expected the techs were put up in barracks-style quarters, but this way, she knows, they were less likely to communicate on topics other than the project. She notes that all of the rooms across the hall from hers have narrow windows overlooking the lab, just as the conference room has.

The lower level is taken up largely by the lab in which the team worked on the Destrier, although there are also several offices, Gen. Grant's being one of these. The back wall of the lab is one large sliding door, the portal through which the Destrier was moved on its journey towards space. Grant's office shares this wall, granting him access also to the facility beyond. What that facility is used for is anybody's guess; Kara had gotten the feeling that, other than their project leader, none of the individuals she worked with had any idea what lay beyond that wall. Naturally, Kara's badge does not allow her past that point or into Grant's office, which includes his living quarters.

She spends a few days going over some of her code in the lab. By way of mental exercise—or, more importantly, to pass the time—she chooses a few subroutines and reprograms them from scratch, thus discovering a few small efficiency boosts. However, her boredom is not yet so great that she feels the need to code in Simula. She certainly could if she wanted to, given her nonstop exposure to the language in recent months, but that prospect is just too much like torture in her mind. Regardless, when her reprogramming no longer excites even the mildest interest, she turns to outside-the-box brainstorming: if she were to start from scratch with the Destrier project, knowing what she knows now, what changes might she make to the framework of the craft? Her conclusions prove interesting, and she promises herself to share them with Grant if she ever sees him again.

By the end of that two-week period, she's ready to go stir-crazy, but Grant finally returns to tell her the news: "Your security clearance has just been upgraded. Please come with me."

**Friday morning
July 18, 2014**

Kara follows him into his office and through his private entry into the facility beyond. Wonder upon wonders, it looks exactly like the area she just left. They walk down a long hallway and enter a conference room at the end, a room which also looks quite familiar. Just before entering, he pulls her aside and whispers, "I'm about to introduce you to other members of the top brass on this project. Don't expect them to introduce themselves in turn."

To a man, each of the room's half dozen occupants stands chivalrously as she enters, though for one man at the end of the table, the gesture appears a bit forced. They show a great deal of interest in meeting her. One particularly elderly man, perhaps older than Grant himself, shakes his head and smiles, glancing at Grant.

"Let's get to it." This comes from Brigadier General Jerome Peterson, the only individual whom Grant introduced by name, the same one who seemed so disinterested in her arrival. He is a fit man in his mid-40s, blond crew cut graying at the temples, military all the way. "All due respect to General Grant—and the rest of you who were persuaded by him—I still think bringing this woman more fully into our confidence is a mistake."

"Your disagreement is duly noted," says the elderly man dryly. "Again. And let me say—again—that there are, um, *aspects* of this project that even you are unaware of."

"And let us not forget the chain of command here either," adds Grant, with a longsuffering look at Peterson.

"Very well. Before you, you will find reports on the performance of my pilots in simulated trials. As you can see, mission completion times are down across the board, in total an 18% improvement since my last report three months ago. Also improved is the average death-to-kill ratio, which has jumped from 1:7.2 to 1:8.9. Unaggregated data is available pilot by pilot starting on page 13. Are there any questions?"

Kara glances around the table, where everyone seems absorbed by the numbers. She raises her hand to speak.

"Very well then," Peterson continues, as if not noticing her. "If you will turn your attention to the video screens—"

"Excuse me," Kara pipes up. She feels the blood rush to her face but maintains a blank expression, hoping the color itself is not too telling.

Peterson stops his movement but does not look up. Instead he locks eyes with Grant, who is seated to his right. Neither moves for a long moment, then Peterson breaks the tension of the moment by turning to Kara. "Yes?" he asks between tight lips.

"I understand you're using *Rampant* to run these trials, is that right?"

Peterson's eyes flick briefly to Grant, then back to Kara. "That's right." He appears somewhat ashamed at having to make this admission, though no one in the room seems to treat it as a revelation.

"Are you focusing on the training missions alone, or the combat missions as well?"

"We have made extensive use of all the applicable missions designed for the game. I had to adapt most of the campaigns to use actual weapons, of course—not the *harpoons* your writers seemed to favor." His lips purse. "In addition, I've developed numerous scenarios using the mission editor software. And I have downloaded missions from several... fan sites." The words are clearly distasteful.

Kara lets the comment about harpoons slide. "Where do these numbers come from? Are they straight from the pilot statistics screen in-game? Or did you compile them based on other data?"

"In-game."

Kara makes a face. "Have the pilots tested against other live pilots? I don't mean cooperative flying, I mean head to head."

"Look, miss, I understand that you're out of the loop and struggling to tread water here. Our pilots have undergone an intensive training regimen, part of which is your game, all of it overseen by the men here. You have been allowed into this room as a courtesy to General Grant"—he all but spits this name—"but I am under no compulsion to hold your hand until you feel comfortable with every aspect of this project." Peterson's not just being rude; he's clearly angry as he says this.

For her part, Kara can't deny the flush that creeps across her face, equal parts embarrassment and anger.

"Answer her question, Jerry." There is quiet steel in Grant's voice.

Peterson makes a noise of disgust. "Fine." He pauses, then with mock politeness: "What was the question again?"

"Have your pilots flown against other live pilots?"

"Of course. They fly against each other every day."

"Yes, but what about other opponents? Pilots outside this facility, I mean. The game allows for combat with others over the Internet, you know."

"Oh, I know. But I'm not about to endanger national security by exposing our network to the world, just so my men can play video games on the Internet. We have some of the finest pilots in the world here. There's no benefit to be gained by pitting them against teenagers playing on daddy's computer."

Kara's anger overcomes her embarrassment. "I don't know the details of how your network is set up, or what the security considerations are. That's not my area of expertise. But I *can* hazard a guess that your training regimen is not as strong as you think it is."

Peterson glares daggers at her. For their part, the rest of the room's occupants seem to be watching a silent tennis match, swinging their heads back and forth between the two combatants.

"May I see some of these pilots in action?" Kara asks.

"Funny you should mention that," Peterson returns sarcastically, "since that's actually the next item on the agenda." He taps a button on the panel built into the table, then picks up a remote control. "Please turn your attention to the video screens. The scenario you are about to observe involved an attack on an enemy weapons platform. I chose this mission because it showcases pilot preparedness for all three aspects of our mandate: not only must the pilots defeat the platform, they must also interdict craft intent on escaping the area, all while defending themselves against personal attackers."

Kara narrows her eyes. Interdiction makes sense in terms of what the Air Force is trying to do, namely defend against missile launches towards Earth, and the need for in-close dogfighting skills is obvious. But why would attacking capital craft be a part of their mandate? It's one thing for a nation to launch a few missiles or other small craft into space, but surely no foreign power could possibly build something of *that* size without drawing attention. Across the table, the elderly man catches her eye and winks. "There are *certainly* many aspects of this project that *you* are unaware of, at least so far," he whispers.

The recording plays out on a dozen large flat panel displays mounted about the room. Most of the displays shift frequently from pilot to pilot, either showing their cockpit perspective or some third-party angle calculated to reveal the significance of how they are maneuvering. Three screens give unique, stationary perspectives on the weapons platform, making it possible to follow all aspects of each multi-prong attack. One screen keeps track of the stats. The room's occupants watch silently as events unfold, and in just under twenty minutes, the pilots achieve all of their win conditions and the mission ends.

"And there you have it," says Peterson as the lights come up. "So tell me," he continues, spearing Kara with a look, "are my boys up to snuff?"

Kara catches herself before grinding her teeth. She's already the weakest of the assembled individuals: the youngest, the civilian, the woman. She forces herself not to give any outward sign of how this man is getting under her skin. "Up to snuff?" she repeats. She makes a show of considering the question. "No, I'd have to say they're not. They're good," she hastens to add, "there's no doubt about it, but they're not fantastic." She looks around the room. "I don't know the details of what we're facing, just the broad strokes, but my guess is we won't have many shots at this. When the attack comes, we need to have the most talented and best-prepared pilots ready to respond. These pilots could use a lot of work."

She's pleased to see that *Peterson* is actually grinding his teeth now. But since he can't seem to string a sentence together quickly enough, Kara goes on to answer the questions he's no doubt trying to formulate.

"For one thing, they have orientation issues." She takes a deep breath and studies the wood grain of the conference table as she collects her thoughts. The floor is hers now, so she needs to make her case carefully, despite all those distracting eyes. "Your pilots think in terms of up and down. And that's a good thing if you're in a supersonic jet traveling at hundreds of miles an hour, because losing track of where the ground is can get you into trouble." The handful of chuckles is reassuring. "In a spacecraft, however, there *is* no up and down. And yet I watched 'your boys' wasting precious seconds reorienting their craft following a tight maneuver, probably because they envision that weapons platform as having a top and a bottom. They need to become comfortable with continuing their mission, even if they feel like they're lying on their side in relation to another ship. When they're flying close-in to Earth, they can't be wasting time spinning their craft around so Earth is always at their feet.

"For another thing, your pilots don't transition smoothly from vector to vector. When they make drastic direction changes, they're doing so in a way that kills their momentum, leaving them as sitting ducks for a few moments before their speed is restored.

"Let me show you." Her confidence growing, she rises and grabs a marker, drawing a line across an otherwise unused dry-erase board. "This point," she indicates a spot just above the middle of the line, "is an enemy spacecraft. Our fighter is moving along this trajectory as he attacks the enemy craft." She traces the line again. "As he passes the other craft, 'our boy' spins around so he continues to face and fire at the enemy. Meanwhile, he gooses his main propulsion jets to throttle back towards the enemy for another close-in pass. The problem is that his acceleration is now working directly against his inertia, which is what you want to do *when you're trying to slow down.* His craft steadily decelerates until it comes to a complete stop for just a moment at this point," she indicates the end of the traced line, "after which it begins accelerating in the opposite direction, back up the line.

"The reason this is a problem is that maneuverability and defensibility decrease exponentially the slower a craft is moving. Your pilots need to learn to accomplish their tactical goals through maneuvers that never leave them without momentum. And believe me," she says with a smile, "it's possible. One solution would be something like this." She changes from black marker to red and draws a line that passes the enemy point and loops back around in a curve. "When the pilot passes the target, he still flips around and begins fighting his inertia with main propulsion; however, he *also* fires his lateral and diagonal maneuvering jets, which serves to produce a sliding spiral maneuver. In the end, he finds himself throttling back towards the target just as quickly as in the previous maneuver, but without ever stopping dead in space. And just as before, he's able to maintain uninterrupted fire on the target."

Heads are nodding around the table, though Peterson's isn't one of them.

"Most importantly," she continues, "the most damning evidence I see of their unpreparedness is a general lack of tactical cooperation. Sure, they cover each other in dogfights, but there are some rather sophisticated maneuvers available that would serve them much better.

"The fact is that your pilots have not been stretched. The game's AI is just a start. They need to fly against real pilots, and not"—she jabs a finger to emphasize her point—"*not* just against each other. After a while, flying against each other will strengthen them as much as inbreeding strengthens a bloodline." This draws an outright laugh. "If you're not careful, your pilots will grow so used to the tactics they themselves use that they're more likely to be surprised by something new. And as we all know, surprise can get a person killed in combat.

"What you need is fresh blood. At the very least, these pilots need to train against a wider, more unpredictable array of opponents, even if some of these opponents are far inferior pilots. However, I would also suggest you consider bringing in additional pilots from outside the military. Judging by what I've seen here," she nods at the screens, "and what I've read just glancing over this," she taps the report, "I bet I could find you at least two dozen pilots who are far more capable than your current pilots, without further training, that is. And that's only counting the ones I know personally—there are hundreds more out there that I *don't* know."

Kara can tell Peterson is furious; he sits tight-lipped and straight-backed at the end of the table, hands grasped firmly before him. She doesn't say anything more, though; as victorious as she's now feeling, she doesn't want to push things.

"Tell me, Ms. Dunn," says a man who has previously remained silent. "Would you be one of these exceptional pilots?"

Her breath catches and she pauses, momentarily caught between her characteristic false modesty and the desire to prove herself right. Then: "I would."

He smiles in return. "Peterson!" he barks, turning toward the man. "In the interest of national security, why don't we set up a bit of an exhibition, just to gauge the validity of Dunn's claims before we make any drastic adjustments to our training or recruitment methodologies. Would that be acceptable for you?"

Peterson nods slowly, baleful eyes still on Kara.

"Ms. Dunn? Any thoughts on the scenario?"

She thinks. "How about a simple six-on-one furball, standard historical weapons loadout—just to get things started? We can always increase the odds from there, and it should definitely help to reveal what I'm talking about." Unbeknownst to the others in the room, her heart speeds up a little. Six against one? Maybe that was a little cocky to start...

"General Peterson, how much time do you require?"

Peterson checks his watch. "Let's say three hours, so I can prep my men and have an extra station prepared for Ms. Dunn."

"Very well. Three hours."

The room empties fairly quickly following adjournment. Other than Kara, who wouldn't know where to go if she left, only Grant and another man remain. Grant is gazing at her openly, a smile playing about his lips. The other individual is absorbed with something displayed on the screen of his cellular device.

Grant stands up and moves to take the seat next to Kara. "Well, *that* was fun!" he exclaims, punctuating the comment by slapping his hand loudly on the table. This draws a wry smile from the man at the other end of the room.

Kara beams, flush with victory, feeling an unexpected camaraderie with Grant. He lowers his voice conspiratorially. "Peterson's been asking for a dressing down for some time. I suspect you're about to administer it."

"You're his boss? Or... commanding officer?"

"I am. But we all have our own responsibilities here. Seeing as I'm not a pilot, the training of other pilots must necessarily be a duty I delegate."

"I thought in the Air Force, all the officers were pilots?" Even as she formulates the question, she does vaguely recall Viviane telling her otherwise.

Grant eyes her and thinks for a moment, probably considering whether he's about to violate national security by telling her more about himself. "No, I was never a pilot. There are some Air Force officers that fly the skies only as passengers. But even among them, my career path has been... unusual."

Kara nods at this, sobering. "I guess it's required a lot of sacrifices?"

His eyes take on a wistful look, and he sighs. "Yes, my dear, it has."

The silence grows long, and Kara toys with raising the issue that has bothered her throughout the length of her association with Grant. She realizes this is probably the best segue she will find, so she plunges ahead.

Only to find it impossible to form a sentence that doesn't come across as insulting. "You know..." she begins tentatively, "I've known Viviane for a while, and... well..."

"Yes?"

"Well, we've been through a lot with each other. For each other. And... well, her relationship with you has always been... strained..."

Grant smiles sadly, looking down.

She forges ahead. "I just, I always had this impression of you as... as a... well, gruff, impersonal..." she struggles for words, "well, just a stereotypical military guy." Already, Kara's wishing she'd never brought this up. "But you're not what I expected. At least... I mean, sometimes you're... intimidating. But you've got a personality too, and I think you care about people." She sighs, frustrated as usual by her inability to form words for her thoughts—and belatedly grateful that this didn't happen twenty minutes ago, when she shanghaied Peterson's presentation.

Grant looks amused, in a sad way. "Was that a question?"

"I just don't understand," she persists. "You " She breaks off, deciding to stop filtering her words. "You were just never there, okay? For Viviane, I mean, as she was growing up. You were this absentee dad—you weren't even there the day she was born. Work was more important to you than your only daughter. And all the time I've known Viviane, it was easy for me to envision you as this... emotionless robot, who doesn't care about anybody. The stereotype from the movies. Someone like..."

"...like Peterson?" he supplies helpfully.

She lets all her breath out in a rush, looking away. "Yeah, like that. But you're not. You're... considerate. So how could you hurt your daughter so much? Why weren't you ever there for her?"

"First of all," Grant drops his voice low, so only she can hear him; the other man seems to take this as a cue and exits the room. Kara had forgotten about the other guy, and she feels suddenly guilty for bringing all this up in earshot of him. "First of all," Grant repeats, "I may seem like a normal person to you, but I'm not. My psychiatrist has told me several times that I'm 'not very well-adjusted,' that I'm 'emotionally unhealthy.'" He catches her look. "Yes, the U.S. Government now requires periodic psychiatric evaluations of those of us in command of these ultra-secret projects. I suppose they've finally wised up to the fact that burying us in caves in the desert for most of our natural lives isn't the healthiest thing for us."

He sighs and continues. "I've never been good with people, though I've been better since—" He breaks off and eyes her appraisingly for a moment, before slowly finishing the thought with: "better since I started going to church." He shakes his head. "It's helped me see the value in other people, to care about people I don't even know."

Kara feels the stirrings of anger. "But your own daughter—" *What good is caring about people you don't know when you're shirking your duty to your own daughter?*

Grant slams his hand down on the table suddenly. "I love my daughter! She's my entire world, all I have left—" He swivels in his chair abruptly, turning his face away. After a few moments of silence, he produces a cloth handkerchief to blot his eyes, then reverently refolds and pockets it; Kara can make out the hand-embroidered initials CKG as he does so. Looking up again finally, Grant repeats himself, more calmly: "I love my daughter. Very, very much."

Kara's not sure what to say, so she says nothing.

Grant sighs. "You obviously think I'm a bad father. Well... I am. I hate it. I despise myself for it. I didn't decide to be a bad father, but... it was a thousand little decisions... late nights, unexpected trips... And yet... my motives were pure. It was all about making the world safe for her. Making sure the world survived long enough for her to marry and have children of her own." He looks up. "That's what Callie wanted. For Viviane to live a long and fulfilling life. A normal life, a normal family." He snorts. "That's stupid—of course she wanted that for Viviane... what parent doesn't? It's just... that's the other thing." His eyes flit to hers and away. "She died giving birth to Viviane, you know. There was no warning, and I wasn't there. I never got to say goodbye. And..."

Kara waits. "And... what?"

"I was simply wondering if maybe I had ever held that against Viviane... the fact that she took my wife away from me. But it's not that... there was just so much pain for me, all of it associated with Viviane's birth. It *wasn't* Viviane's fault. But..." His voice drops and his eyes seem to mist over again. "... it *was* hard for me to look at her sometimes. She just looked more and more like her mom, the older she got. Her hair, her eyes, even the way she would smile, which is silly since she never knew her mother growing up."

He heaves a sigh, his shoulders actually bunching and releasing. "I miss her horribly. Callie, I mean... but I miss Viviane as well. I imagine Callie would be disappointed in me right now, if she were here." He chuckles sadly.

This has officially become the most awkward conversation Kara has ever endured. If you can even call it a conversation. More like a lonely verbal progression into suicidal despair, with her providing the occasional poke to keep things moving. Despite herself, she finds herself drawn in by Grant's pain. She's actually... empathetic... even though she still can't comprehend his failure to prioritize his daughter.

Grant speaks up suddenly. "I don't want to talk about my wife anymore," he declares.

Kara ponders just how patently obvious it would be if she asked where the bathroom is. Two and a half hours to go, no escape in sight. "So then," she begins, "after your wife—after

Callie—died, you…" She trails off, suddenly unsure of the proper terminology. Found Jesus? Got saved? Were born again? She's not sure she can say any of those things without sounding pejorative—which, after all, is exactly how she can't help feeling.

He smiles genuinely, apparently not needing to hear the rest of her question. "Yes, I decided to follow Jesus."

Follow Jesus. She tucks that away into her lexicon of religious phrases and resists the urge to roll her eyes. Follow Jesus? Follow him where? Or does Grant mean he decided to *live* like Jesus? She tries to ignore the sudden mental image of Carl Grant dressed in robes, carrying around a staff. What possible bearing can the life and death of a man two thousand years gone have on the present?

Grant watches her as these thoughts run through her mind, as if trying to gauge the sincerity of her interest. No, as if he sees through her, knows that his religious conversion means nothing to her beyond the detrimental effect it may have had on his relationship with his daughter.

He leans forward suddenly and grasps her hands, one in each of his, with a intensity that sends a chill straight up her spine. "I don't expect you to understand this, Kara, maybe not ever, because you're an intellectual. I used to take pride in my intellect too. I didn't need God. The concept of God was a crutch for people who didn't have the strength to lead their own lives.

"Well, it turns out I was right. God *is* a crutch. And I do need him, because I *don't* have the strength to lead my own life." He expels his breath. "Just look at how badly I messed up with Viviane. I wish I could do it over. But I know now that she was God's child long before she was mine, and that he loves her far more than I ever could. He's taking care of her. And if you see that as a psychological crutch, or as shirking responsibility, so be it. I call it faith. I call it casting all of my concerns on the only one capable of handling them."

He holds her eyes and her hands for another uncomfortable moment… then releases them and stands abruptly. "Thank you for listening to this tired old man, and good luck with your mission. I have no doubt as to the outcome." He walks to the door and opens it, then pauses. "I hope," he says without turning, "that you'll consider accepting that crutch someday. When you find yourself without enough strength to continue." He turns then and meets her eye, then disappears.

Great, Kara thinks, breathing out her tension with a weak attempt at levity. *I still don't know where the bathroom is.*

[Chapter 12]

Friday afternoon
July 18, 2014

  The monitors begin winking on around her as Kara settles into her "acceleration couch"—which, when you're playing a video game, is really just a fancy word for "chair." There isn't, in fact, anything fancy about the chair, but everything else that surrounds her is quite fancy—expensively so.
  The eight screens are 26-inch liquid crystal displays, positioned at each directional and sub-directional point of the compass, just above head height. Not everyone plays the game this way, of course, as the display is the most expensive part of the personal computer. But for those individuals who are either hard-core gamers or terminally rich, Kara's team provided multi-display functionality. The screens connect via DVI-to-USB adaptors to a USB hub, which is how the computer is made to support multiple screens without additional video cards. With any other game, extra vid cards would be necessary to render all of the graphics, but *Rampant* doesn't require this—other than what is occasionally shown on the primary monitor, the graphics are kept intentionally simple.
  Kara dons the goggles and gloves, which turn out to be wireless models. Again, expensive, but very nice if you're not a fan of inadvertently garroting yourself when the game gets exciting. Each hand on the opposite wrist, she squeezes an activation switch for three seconds to initiate the gloves, then flips a switch on her goggles. She leans back in her chair as the game's calibration routine launches.
  The control sphere materializes bright green in front of her, semi-transparent and a bit ghostly looking. Following the instructions of an ethereal female voice, she grasps the yoke with her right hand, spins it a few times in varying directions, then throws her arms out in a sequence of test maneuvers. What the system is doing is determining her arm's range of movement, saving this data for future use in determining how sensitive the craft's controls will be. As she does this, all eight monitors display

an identical warning—something about being careful to avoid striking the screens and other objects, and how DactiSoft and its partners, vendors, etc. will not be held responsible for injury or damage, etc. etc. It's a lot of text, and Kara only read it once.

Yoke calibration complete, Kara's virtual control board appears just below the sphere, not quite the same shade of green. She grabs the board with her left glove, pulling it to a comfortable position near her left hip. It's an unusual position, but she knows the controls well enough that she doesn't really need it in direct line of sight. She taps the far corner of the board repeatedly until she finds the control layout she prefers, then locks it into place. Reaching over and waving her right hand through the board satisfies her that the game's VR intersection matrices are set properly. The mechanics of the programming are such that she can grab the yoke with either right or left hand, though she will use her right primarily; however, only her left hand can access the board, which means that in the heat of battle, her maneuverability will not be limited by an inability to jerk the yoke through the position inhabited by the board.

Okay, quick mental review. Standard weapons loadout in *Rampant* would be harpoons and grapples for the fighter craft, trebuchets for military bases—certainly *not* the sort of weapons applicable to modern warfare, but consistent with *Rampant*'s main story arc, that of a dystopian feudal society engaged in medieval-esque warfare in space. So it's understandable that Peterson had adapted most missions to use "actual" weapons. That would mean the historical loadout, the one used in some of the backstory missions—engagements that, within the fictional timeline of the game, occurred in Earth's near future. *That* loadout translated to a pair of chain guns, 5,000 rounds per, and eight guided missiles, with the optional addition of the electromagnet grapple.

Kara exhales and rolls her head to get the kinks out. A quick punch of the proper key on her board signals her readiness to the server. The mission countdown appears, and when it reaches zero, the screens transition to in-game mode.

What they now display is a simple representation of a hangar, little more than a wire frame model with uniform skin, no textures or images to give the impression of realism. In fact, the image is rather distorted; although Kara has a complete lateral 360-degree view across the middle of the screens, the imagery is actually warped to include visibility above and below as well. It takes some getting used to, but the monitors aren't really what the game's all about anyway.

Kara recognizes the hangar immediately; it's part of a military base positioned in the midst of a tight asteroid field. Peterson has chosen well if he wants to embarrass her, since the presence of so many small bodies will make detecting other craft difficult. Not only that, but she's a bit limited in terms of her first move; there's only one way out of the hangar, and there's a good chance her opponents have already taken up position around the entrance.

Firing her maneuvering jets, Kara pushes her craft gently into the back corner of the hangar. *Might as well get a running start.* She slams hard on the main thrusters and leans forward, hands wide open on either side of the yoke, feeling it lightly upon her upper palms. The calm blue grid lines fly past in her visualization, and then she's blasting out of the hangar, two bright orange tendrils of weapons fire burning past immediately on either side.

As soon as she's out, Kara jerks her hands off the yoke in opposite directions, twisting as she goes and throwing the sphere hard in the direction of her feet. As the yoke returns to keel in front of her, the perspective shifts to show a crazily spinning and bucking grid. What the other pilots see makes a lot more sense, even if they can't follow it—her craft is whipping about in an unpredictably widening spiral, gaining speed and distance from their ambush.

Kara adjusts her orientation with a small thumb-and-forefinger twist of the yoke, which has no effect on her inertial drift. She shakes her head at what she sees. *Amateurs.* So sure were they in their ambush, her opponents parked their craft in stationary positions. She pumps the nearest full of lead but fails to complete the kill before a large asteroid passes between their craft. No matter—now that she's out of the kill zone, she shouldn't have any trouble turning the match to her advantage.

As far as the graphics go, Kara's team had never made an attempt to render the in-game environment in anything approaching "realistic" imagery. In the real world—or rather, in real outer space—there's really not that much exciting to see. If you're close enough to a star to have light, everything is a study in extreme contrast. In Earth's atmosphere, the presence of air diffuses light and bounces it around behind objects so that even shadows are softly lit; in space, with no air, the lighted sides of objects tend to be blindingly white, whereas the shadowed sides are so dark as to appear featureless. And of course, if your closest star is more than, say, four or five million miles away, pretty much everything is featureless darkness. Either way, reality doesn't leave much room for stunning visuals; even telling the difference between spacecraft and other natural bodies, such as asteroids, would be nearly impossible with the naked eye at any great distance. Thus the game's use of simple, shaded wireframe models to represent other bodies in space. In fact, the player's spacecraft supposedly does not even have viewports or external cameras; all visual data fed to the pilot is acquired by radar array, just like in the Destrier prototype Kara spent the last several months working on.

By default, the software renders most solid bodies in a shade of red. Being in an asteroid field, Kara is closely surrounded by dozens of constructs in varying shapes, sizes, and shades of crimson. Keeping one hand on the yoke, she taps out a simple sequence on the control board, prioritizing target acquisition on objects whose speed is above a certain threshold relative to their surroundings. Several dozen results appear on her primary display, and Kara dials up the threshold until four obvious matches remain. She assigns these bodies a blink rhythm, then releases them to her display.

She continues her defensive flight pattern for a moment, but no more than those four objects appear. That leaves two craft unaccounted for—hiding, perhaps, or stationary. Kara catches herself, smiling; there may be even more than two unaccounted foes. Considering the welcome awaiting her near the hangar, she knows Peterson isn't going out of his way to make this a fair fight.

With a twist of her wrist, Kara propels her craft back towards the engagement. She dodges around a small asteroid with a spastic move of her arm, then goes on the offensive against the target designated H-002—hostile #2. She doesn't move straight in, but rather puts a subtle spin and a strong slew on it, in essence swinging around in a circular strafing motion as she squeezes off a steady stream of fire with her left hand. Ammo's cheap, after all, at least in *Rampant*. After just a few hits, H-002 goes dead in space, which is to say that all course corrections cease and he continues flying along the same vector until he collides with another body. Either she hit something vital, or Two was the hostile she capped coming out of the chute. She glances at her weapons system display.

Whoops. Cannon ammunition is already down by 29%. It seems ammo's not so cheap after all. With a sick feeling in her belly, Kara looks to see what's been loaded in her launcher tubes. Four GXF-8s—unguided missiles. In other words, dummy torps that keep going in the direction you fire until they hit something. She berates herself for not checking her craft configuration first thing out of the hangar. She'd let Peterson pull another fast one on her.

She blows out her breath as she jerks out of the way of three converging orange fire trails. *Not even 1,500 rounds left,* she thinks, *and five or more hostiles remaining. It's doable... maybe.* At least her craft has a magnetic grapple—assuming Peterson doesn't decide to simulate equipment failure on her.

Three streams of gunfire again stitch across empty space towards her craft, and she again slips out of the way. These three bozos are working together in that they're all firing at her simultaneously, but fortunately they're not really cooperating. With a minimum of three fighter craft, a commander who knew what she was doing in space would come up with a firing solution to corral Kara into an ever-shrinking pocket, where the crossfire stands a better than even chance of ultimately shredding her to pieces. At this point, Kara's thankful for small favors and doesn't even take the opportunity to gloat.

Her craft slips around another small body, and she throws the yoke hard forward. She stops its spin once it returns, orienting herself back towards the battle she just left. A blinking red construct labeled H-003 drops over the floating rock in a mimicry of her maneuver and lines up straight on her tail. At least, he clearly *thinks* of it as her tail since inertia is carrying her craft directly away from him. He's still carefully lining up his shot when she opens up point blank with the main gun. Sparingly. A wrist twitch shifts her trajectory, which Three fails to match, continuing on his merry way right out of the asteroid field. Even in the real world, if she could look on his craft with the naked eye, there would be no good way to verify a kill short of tearing the craft into pieces—after all, the fiery explosions so common in sci-fi movies can't actually happen without pressurized cockpits full of combustible air. That's why standard game tactics call for a few POMs or "piece of mind" shots, but ammo is unfortunately scarce today. Now only 54% remaining.

The remaining two hostiles—the two she's identified—have re-formed into a wing pair and are maintaining their distance. Now that she's got a little room to breathe, Kara focuses on programming a more sophisticated pattern match on her surroundings while keeping up an erratic flight pattern. To the uninitiated outside observer, it might appear as though she's punching randomly into the air, her attention wholly absorbed with the control board. That's clearly not the case, however, as the landscape is so densely packed with moving bodies that two wrong moves in a row could prove fatal.

She completes her algorithm and assigns the results to her northwest monitor. Low, one-second whistles begin sounding from around her, more than she can count, as softly glowing orbs appear on her displays. A quick glance at the northwest display reveals twenty-three search results, twenty-three bodies of the appropriate size and shape to be enemy starfighters, but none of them are moving. Yet.

Her focus returns to H-001 and H-004, which have been steadily leap-frogging their way closer, keeping some of the bulkier rocks between them and her. Each time they disappear for seconds at a time, her targeting reticules leap out to track possible trajectories and highlight the most likely. The longer the craft remain invisible, the more extrapolations appear. Kara smiles. *These two are a bit more talented*, she thinks, not without some apprehension.

She jumps into the fray, matching their tactics, really just stalling for time in hopes of a hit on her search. She avoids getting too close to any of the large rocks, as doing so destroys her predictive tracking suite's effectiveness. Unfortunately, that also leaves her without as much cover as her hunters. A line of fire flashes across her bow, a line she would have passed straight through, but she throws the yoke straight back through her belly, flipping her fingers around on the release to give it some roll. She's not attempting to kill her forward momentum entirely, as that would leave her dead in space. Instead she's bleeding it off even as she pushes back in a new direction—just inside her attacker's line of fire. Even so, the other player stitches a few rounds up the leading face of her craft.

A curse slips through her lips, but then a new sound grabs her attention. A screaming whistle coming from the monitor over her right shoulder. She doesn't try to turn, she just shoves back across the stream of fire even as it stops. She loops behind a nearby asteroid, reversing her orientation and building inertia back up before reappearing.

There they are, two blinking red blips representing H-001 and H-004, nearly half a mile away across a surprisingly large clearing. And not fifty yards from her, almost dead ahead, is a glowing purple orb, the source of the screaming alarm. A body that's the right size to be another fighter craft. It still hasn't changed position, but it's given itself away regardless.

Dummy torps aren't good against anything but stationary targets, so this seems like a perfect opportunity to use one. She sidesteps hard left, just in case the immobile fighter is about to fire, then re-sights the target quickly before dropping the torpedo and jumping above the plane of the asteroid field. By now, the target knows she's on to him—there's no other excuse for such fancy flying, unless she's aware of a close-in threat. She sidesteps again just as he opens up on her, but that's when the torpedo hits. The firing stops.

Kara lines up on the pair, who are now less than a mile away and closing fast, flying in tight formation. Actually flying side-by-side and coming straight on, as if challenging her to a game of chicken. In atmosphere, it would be a sure win for them—there'd be no way for her to take them both before they got her, and so she would have to break off, leaving them on her tail. But in space, it's a different story.

She doesn't bother firing back as they light up the sky around her; she just focuses on dodging their spray while still coming on fast. A thousand feet out, she throws her arm out but doesn't let go, actually willing her craft to a stop in midair. As the craft whip by her, side-by-side, they present their profile—the both of them now in her line of fire, which she lets loose in a long sustained burst. The first craft actually fragments, pieces flying every direction, while the other loses control and speeds headlong into a nearby asteroid.

Kara punches the main jets before even checking her scope again, nervous at moving so slowly. She becomes aware of another screaming signal. Ah yes, H-006. It's almost anticlimactic when she slips around the slow moving craft and squeezes off a burst from the main gun. It threatens to become a bit more climactic when she hears the ammo depleted warble, but after a moment it's clear that the other craft is dead in space.

She checks her scope. One and Four came apart, and Two is nowhere to be seen. Three is still blinking steadily, but he's now seventy miles out, without a course adjustment since she shot him up. Five and Six, which started the engagement sitting still, never even picked up enough speed to key the blink pattern on her display. A quick entry on the board, and their icons disappear from her displays.

A few moments pass, but nothing happens. She's waiting to hear a message over her comm, or perhaps for the server to shut the game down. Instead, nothing. Which makes no sense unless the game isn't over yet... which means Peterson *does* have more ships lurking around. She bats aside the yoke, putting so much spin on it that it looks like she's trying to rip the ball in two different directions, a maneuver which launches her into a senseless and dizzying spin—just as a pink streak passes through where she would otherwise have been.

Keying up the search preset confirms it. Two new moving bodies, one matching the profile of a Stiletto assassin fighter, the other that of a Double-Z, a kind of guided missile. They both arc around to follow her unexpected maneuver.

What follows is nearly ten minutes of the fanciest flying of Kara's life. The Stiletto is the quickest, most agile craft in the game, with nearly twice the acceleration of her own craft. That should actually prove an advantage to her in such tight quarters, as an inexperienced pilot is likely to accelerate over-quick into a large floating boulder. But no matter what she tries, she can neither get the drop on her pursuer nor incite him to make a stupid move. Meanwhile, she is out of ammunition for her artillery. All she has left are dummy torpedoes, and two of the three are non-responsive thanks to the damage she took earlier. *On the bright side,* she thinks, *if I make it out of this alive it'll be* really *impressive!*

Since her only real hope is to provoke a mistake on the part of her adversary, she begins pulling even closer to the large moving rocks as she slaloms about amidst them. But he's too good, and on two occasions he manages to clip her with a few rounds. By now he surely knows she's out of ammo, and he does seem to grow bolder, but she's impressed by his restraint; he refuses to do anything stupid.

It's when she dodges the torpedo for the last time and it detonates into a nearby rock that Kara has her bright idea. Coming around a particularly large asteroid, she breaks far wide rather than hugging the turn, then whips about and fires her last good torp directly into the rock face. A moment later, the Stiletto screams around the corner at high speed—directly into an expanding cloud of sharp pebbles.

It's not every development team that will go to the trouble of programming such an obscure feature into a game, especially when they haven't developed the graphics to show it off, but Kara's suddenly glad Marty insisted on realistic physics for explosive disintegrations.

It's not yet clear if the other ship is in any shape to recover, but Kara doesn't give it a chance. Now completely out of ammunition, she has only one more trick up her sleeve. She swoops down and locks onto the other craft's slim profile with her magnetic grapple, then accelerates at full power towards the next large rock, letting go and side-stepping even as her opponent's ship is pulverized against the unyielding surface.

And *now* the screens dim as Gen. Grant's voice comes through the speakers. "I think we've seen enough." Kara can hear his smile even through the radio. "Kara, please unstrap and rejoin us in the conference room."

Grant gazes in at Kara through the one-way glass while the rest of the officers watch the various displays spread about the room. She has just succeeded in defeating two of her six adversaries, not counting Peterson's ace in the hole. Although Grant feels a stake in the proceedings, he also knows that, in a sense, it really doesn't matter how Kara performs. There's only one way all this can end, and that's with Kara joining the team as the first of a new class of military pilot. The idea fills him with dread, but also with anticipation.

"*What?* What's *that?*" Peterson is all but shouting. "That's not a standard feature. How did she identify Eagle Three? He's not even moving! She must have some sort of backdoor in the software!"

Nobody responds. Everyone is too absorbed. Each one of them a career military man, they appreciate the grim beauty of this dance of death, recognizing Kara's talent even though she's using a video game to display it. Grant just watches her lithe form amid the displays, twisting this way and that, whipping one arm back and forth while the other hand enters commands on an imaginary keyboard. *No, not imaginary,* he corrects himself, *invisible.* He suddenly feels very, very old, staring at this beautiful woman as she operates technology so advanced he can't even see it. *Technology has come a long way since all of this started*, he thinks.

Grant shakes himself out of nostalgic memories when he sees Kara's whole body jerk spastically. "Ah!" Peterson exclaims behind him, followed by excited tittering from the other brass. Grant turns to see Peterson is now seated quietly at the table, wearing an unreadable expression. By the time the Stiletto has met its fate, Peterson's head has begun wagging back and forth.

"She's good, eh, Petey?" This from one of the other men.

It's a nickname he hates, but Peterson doesn't appear to notice. "Yeah. She is," he responds quietly.

Leaning over the table with a grin, Grant punches the intercom button and beckons Kara to rejoin them. Releasing the connection, he sits down and looks around the table, making sure to meet each man's eyes. "Gentlemen, I have a recommendation."

Kara's escort holds the door for her, then closes himself out.

"Ms. Dunn," Peterson says, "please take a seat." He waits for her to comply before continuing. "Welcome to your first debriefing. Would you please explain to us," he gestures about the room, "how you managed to identify a stationary, motionless target in the midst of such a motion-rich environment?"

She takes a moment to collect her thoughts. "At the start of the mission, I initiated a standard threat ID procedure, one of the presets on the board. It identifies potential threats based on movement—how fast an object is moving, how frequently it changes direction, whether it's demonstrating hostile intent. It's not a sophisticated algorithm, so it can't tell the difference between a craft changing course under its own power and a rock changing course because it's bounced off another rock. But by dialing down its sensitivity, I can pick out those nearby bodies that are most likely piloted ships.

"In this way I identified the first four enemy ships, which my system designated H-001 through H-004. Knowing there were additional ships out there, I initiated a more complicated pattern match when I had the chance—this time I had the computer ignore movement, looking instead for bodies within a certain size and shape range. I also narrowed the scope of the search to a much smaller radius around my craft. Two dozen possibles were ID'd, and I ran another standard analysis to capture additional data on each. In particular, I was curious how quickly each body was rotating on its axis."

"That's not possible," one man interjects, "at least not with the ships in your game. They're spheres, almost perfectly smooth. The radar signature is identical whether it spins or not."

"Almost," Kara agrees. "But on a smooth surface, a radar ping cannot help but slip in the direction of rotation if the body is, in fact, rotating. This results in a nearly infinitesimal delay in the return of the signal. It's recognizable, at least to the computer, if you've told it what to look for. I did.

"In any case, I had realized the two missing craft were probably sitting out in the open. This may seem like an obvious tactic to you, but it took me a moment to catch on; when you spend the majority of your time flying against kids who don't even have a driver's license, you grow used to a certain impatience that doesn't lend itself to such tactics. But yeah, I realized that they would wait for me to close in, then they would try to target me—and to keep me targeted, they would have to continue spinning on their axes to keep me within their targeting brackets. The alarm that went off was a notification of exactly that behavior from one of the bodies I had tagged as a possible ship. I went evasive to prevent his firing on me, which allowed me to maintain the illusion that I was unaware of him, at least for a few more moments."

"These advanced pattern searches." Peterson says. "Are they a documented feature of the game?"

Kara smiles. "They're documented, though not in the printed version of the manual. We had to cut a lot of the tactical info from the game manual, since it was way too long. But it's available in the full version, which is available for download from the website. Of course," she adds, "it's still not very commonly used. The pilot has to feel pretty comfortable with operating the board half-blind while flying, and of course it's very helpful to have a multi-display setup."

Peterson nods. "And your final... kill? Was that another seldom-used tactic?"

"No, I actually dreamed that one up on the spot. When his torpedo detonated, I was so close to the debris cloud that my radar array actually lagged sorting it all out. I've always known how accurately the software determines the effects of such a detonation, but I'd never thought about taking advantage of it. Since I didn't have a chance of actually hitting the other ship, I created a minefield in his path, which probably punched a hundred tiny holes in his ship. Or rather *he* punched the holes in his ship by flying so fast through a cloud of stationary particles."

Peterson nods again. "Very well. What is your assessment of the pilots you flew against?"

Kara considers. "Confusion about orientation killed the first two, just like I warned you before. The two that started off stationary died because... well, because they started off stationary. The other two worked together, but it was the wrong tactic;

formational flying is a bad idea if you don't understand the physics of your environment.

"Your flyers had their best chance to kill me that first moment I shot out of the gate. Three or more pilots with the right placement and firing solutions could have used their weapons fire to corral me and shred my ship. I shouldn't have had a chance."

"And what about the last pilot, Ms. Dunn?" This from one of the mostly quiet men in the group. "What killed him?"

Her lip quirks at the question. "A bit of creative flying and a whole lot of luck. He's good," she says, shaking her head, "Very good."

"Well, so were you," says Peterson, to Kara's surprise. To his credit, it doesn't appear as though the admission cost Peterson anything. For a moment, Kara even wonders if she doesn't see a ghostly smile flit across the man's hard face.

"Ms. Dunn." Kara focuses on the elderly man who had winked at her earlier. "This may seem rather sudden, but we'd like you to become more involved in our project. We'd like to offer you a commission."

"A commission?"

Grant explains. "We'd like you to join the Air Force as one of the pilots assigned to Prometheus, more specifically as one of the officers in charge of developing the training regimen. We'd like to bring you in as a full colonel."

Kara blinks several times, stunned. "Uh, well... um, that isn't... That isn't quite what I had in mind." Ironically, the invitation brings back all her feelings of uncertainty sharing this room with these men—even though it indicates their confidence in her ability.

"I know it's not where you saw your career moving," Grant continues, "but you have some idea what we're facing, and you yourself convinced us that you're needed in more of leadership role here. And the military's not such a bad choice. Certainly the take-home pay isn't much, even as an O-6—nothing like what you've earned these last few months as a consultant—but I think we can put together a signing bonus you'll find satisfactory. Besides, I believe the GI Bill includes a condition for paying off outstanding educational expenses, even if they're incurred before joining the service."

Kara struggles to sort out her thoughts. "Isn't that a little... unusual? Starting someone at a... an advanced rank like that, skipping the... lower ranks?" She feels stupid, not knowing the terminology.

"It's not common," the elderly man responds in his reedy voice. "But it certainly happens. When the military has need of specialized experience or knowledge, it makes sense to bring it in from outside, and to award the individual a rank commensurate to his—or her—value. This is especially true in wartime. When World War II broke out, quite a few doctors were recruited and commissioned at elevated ranks."

"You would know about World War II," the elderly general's neighbor offers with a sly smile, and there are chuckles around the room. It breaks some of Kara's tension. These men aren't emotionless robots any more than Grant is. They're just human beings with a great deal of responsibility.

"You're the SME," Peterson adds quietly, as if that explains everything.

"SME?" Kara asks in confusion. Peterson pronounces it 'smee,' but it has the sound of another military acronym.

Grant chuckles. "Yes, you're the systems matter expert." He nods appreciatively at his cohort. "I believe General Peterson is acknowledging your legitimacy as an expert in the field of space combat—not just in terms of weapons design, but also in terms of waging war." He laughs. "You certainly flew circles around his pilots."

Kara meets Peterson's eyes, and the man's intense gaze seems to drill straight through her. Silence falls upon the assembled officers.

"So...?" Grant prompts her finally.

"Well..." Kara begins, unable to avoid the feeling that every individual in the room is hanging on the word. "It's a bit of a commitment, isn't it? I can't just get out later if I feel like it."

"Kara," Grant says, looking down abruptly to inspect a sheet of paper lying in front of him. "When this crisis has passed, you may resign your commission and accept honorable discharge, no questions asked." He casts a sidelong glance at his fellow octogenarian, and they share an inscrutable look, smiles gone. "Your country still has need of your unique skills... and when it comes right down to it, your situation outside this base hasn't changed in the last five months." Translation: there are still people hoping to kidnap or murder you.

"Okay," she says finally, still feeling very small and uncertain. "I'll do it." Amazingly, there seems to be a collective sigh of relief from certain individuals around the table—as if it really is vitally important to these powerful men that Kara take on this role, after she had to push and shove to even gain admittance to this briefing.

"Very good," Grant says with a smile, though there's a more complex emotion hiding there somewhere. "You'll start by working the tactical angle with Colonel McLaughlin, and while you're training with the pilots, put together recommendations on which pilots make the cut and which do not."

Kara nods slowly.

"McLaughlin's the pilot you met at the end," Peterson adds.

She smiles. "As long as he's not God's gift to the world, I shouldn't have any trouble working with him, then."

"And lastly," Grant concludes, "we'll set you up with someone from military intelligence. You point out who, and he'll start working up dossiers on potential additions to this merry band."

[Chapter 13]

Friday afternoon
July 18, 2014

Col. John McLaughlin stares at his main display with something akin to shock, even as the screens around him dim. Shaking himself, he taps a sequence into his virtual board, bringing up a replay of the last minute of the mission. He watches as his Stilleto pursues the enemy Destrier through the asteroid field, catching it here and there with rounds of fire, slowly wearing it down.

And then his ship whips around another rock body—directly into an expanding cloud of debris. John pauses playback, rewinds a bit, and uses both gloved hands to rotate the vantage point. He restarts playback, and this time he sees the enemy pilot fire a torpedo into the asteroid to create the sudden minefield.

A rueful smile steals across his face.

"That's total crap!" Will Hicks complains.

John glances over at the younger pilot, who's crouched inside John's ring of monitors, watching. "Why do you say that?" Hicks had been one of the first casualties of the engagement, thanks to the fact that he'd foolishly parked himself in stationary orbit around the hangar asteroid.

"Why?" Hicks waves a hand at the display. "He cheated! You didn't know that would happen if he shot up an asteroid. No one knew that!" He continues grumbling, "And how did he ID our ships that weren't even moving? He's got some backdoor into the software, I'll bet you ten to one."

Three hours ago, none of John's pilots had known this little exercise was coming. Then Gen. Peterson had blown through their barracks, rustling up the best pilots who hadn't yet escaped for weekend leave. Apparently the top brass had decided to change things up a bit, pitting John's pilots against someone experienced with the *Rampant* video game. Not even a *real* pilot, just a gamer. It was an affront to their pride, and John's people had been tripping over themselves to volunteer.

"Maybe you just suck, Redneck," Anna Haynes suggests. She and the rest of John's pilots have clustered around his carrel, those that are still on base at least.

"Shut it, Sweeps."

John sighs. Air Force pilots… so much like little kids. "It only seems like cheating because you insist on thinking of this as a video game. It's *not*." He initiates shutdown of his sim carrel, then pulls at his gloves. "This kind of tactic makes perfect sense in the real world. And there's no such thing as cheating in real warfare, you know that."

In truth, John is perversely pleased at the way the op played out. Even at seven-to-one odds, this mysterious pilot had schooled them, and his people need that kind of enforced humility from time to time. John would have preferred a little less personal humiliation, of course—he'd barely lasted longer than Hicks—but he can't summon any real anger at the enemy pilot. He'd hated the disingenuous role Peterson assigned him for this op, notwithstanding what John just told Hicks about cheating and real-world warfare.

Clint Jackson speaks up. "Think we'll fly against this guy again?"

John nods slowly. "I hope so. I think we could learn a lot from him."

His opinion is met by groans, along with a gleeful cackle from Haynes. Of course, she hadn't been one of the pilots humiliated today.

[Chapter 14]

**Friday evening
July 18, 2014**

Kara is exhausted by the time she returns to her quarters above the Prometheus lab. Exhausted, with head spinning at the speed of today's life-altering decisions.

Even as a kid graduating high school, she'd never considered military service. It wasn't that she thought she was too good for it—she knew the military served a vital role... but at the time, the idea of joining simply never occurred to her as an option. All through her childhood, she had looked forward to attending college (and probably grad school) without consciously considering that there were other options, in the same way that she had attended elementary, middle, and high school without question. College was a given.

Certainly she'd never considered joining since. Her ex-boyfriend Paul obviously idolized the military—not that he'd ever admit it, and definitely not in those terms. But from his preference in movies and games, she always suspected he fantasized about somehow becoming a war hero. Maybe that's something lots of men do.

But Kara had never once entertained such a thought, much less a desire. Which is what makes her present situation so incredibly ironic. Not only is she now an Air Force officer (she'll apparently undergo Commissioned Officer Training at some point in the future, after the fact), she's been granted a fairly *elevated* rank. Even more, part of her new responsibility is to recruit other civilians into unexpected military commissions. It's too bad—for Paul's sake—that his piloting skills never impressed her on the occasions they gamed together.

She realizes that despite her exhaustion, she's actually a little *giddy*. Giddy... and humbled... and proud... and scared, all at once. The recognition of Grant's "top brass" feels good. To be granted this rank so suddenly, without the two decades of service and hard work they said it usually costs... yes, "giddy" describes that feeling of having gotten something valuable at no cost. But it's also humbling to know she'll be compared to men and women who actually earned the honor... and unsettling to know she'll probably be resented by them too.

She blinks at a new thought. Grant said she could accept discharge after the crisis passes... Surely that doesn't mean she, herself, would actually be *deployed* into orbit... right? It probably would've been a good idea to confirm that before accepting the job, and she berates herself for being too stunned at the time to think critically. But no. Of course they wouldn't expect her to fly in combat. They're bringing her onboard strictly to oversee training—that's certainly a full-time job all by itself. It would have to continue even after the first batches of pilots were deployed. Although... the idea of *really* flying her Destrier, and of visiting outer space...

The thoughts and emotions continue to run circles in Kara's mind. It's unfortunate, because what her body really needs right now is sleep. But maybe a nice hot soak in the tub would unwind her, preferably with head mostly submerged.

She's stepping toward the bathroom when she notices a white rectangle on the floor. It's a letter, she realizes as she stoops to retrieve it—no, a *stack* of letters—slipped under the door while she was away.

Letters. The first she's received since arriving here.

She flips through them, sees her old return address in Viviane's lovely script; actually, *every* envelope in the stack is from Viviane, sent to that bogus address in Hoboken. Eagerly, she slips a finger under the flap to tear the first one open, noticing belatedly that it's already been slit. Undoubtedly read by some person she'll never meet. Oh well, that's no surprise. She withdraws two sheets of thick stationery, unfolds them, and begins reading:

February 21

Dear Kara,

I know it's only been a few days since you left, but I miss you terribly. The place is just so lonely without you around.

> *Well, okay, that's not entirely true. The phone has been ringing off the hook with people trying to get ahold of you. And Paul is pouting that you didn't tell him before you left, but that's just Paul...*

There's little of substance, but Kara soaks up every word just the same. Coming to the end of that first letter, she tears greedily into the next.

> *March 1*
>
> *Dear Kara,*
>
> *Lots of people still wanting to know where you went. People I don't even know. Right after I mailed my last letter, two different men came to the door asking for you. (And one of them was <u>really</u> scary looking!) I just told them how you'd moved, and I gave them your new address. Even though the one guy looked like a stalker, I thought you would probably be safe even if he had your address (wink wink, nudge nudge).*
>
> *Gregoire has been an absolute doll, of course. He's been going out of his way to make me feel special...*

She reads through several more letters—Viviane had been writing faithfully, usually once or twice a week—before coming across the one with the big news.

> *May 21*
>
> *Dear Kara,*
>
> *Guess what? He proposed! You know we've been talking around the subject for weeks now. The more I've thought about it, the more sure I've been. He's the one! So we made it official this weekend.*

> *We've already been talking wedding details, but first, a request: Will you be my maid of honor?*
>
> *It's not all good news. Greg's worried about his mom... he just found out she's been sick, and she was always in poor health. He's talking about flying back to France to see her. I wish I could go with him, but things are strained with Jenny right now. Even if I could afford to quit working for a few weeks, I don't think she would hold my job for me...*

Most of the recent letters continue in a similar vein: details about the upcoming wedding (no date set), and other bits and pieces of the latest gossip. The final letter is dated June 3rd and includes a snapshot of a beautiful diamond ring, along with an apology that she hadn't sent the photo earlier. Altogether, it's classic Viviane: sterile facts related in high drama, personality just screaming off the pages. When Kara's finished reading the stack, she returns to reread some of the passages a second time, more carefully. Simply tracing the strokes of the familiar handwriting gives her a sense of physical closeness to her dearest friend.

So it all worked out. Gregoire proposed, and Viviane didn't flip. And maid of honor? It's hardly a surprise, but even so, it *is* an honor.

Kara realizes her head is no longer spinning from the day's events. Tentatively, she sets down the last letter and ponders the reality of her present situation. She sighs—yep, it's still surreal. And yet Viviane's ramblings have restored her confidence in what she's doing. It's as Grant said earlier: nothing has changed in Kara's circumstances since she left home in February... and Kara's most immediate reason for joining Grant was to protect Viviane. To now take a more active role in training these pilots, well... that's ultimately about protecting Viviane too, isn't it? Viviane and hundreds of millions of other Americans.

She flips through the stack yet again, smiling in appreciation for her distant friend. Her eye settles on a paragraph in one of the earliest letters, and her smile slips. This bit about unknown, scary visitors could be significant, in light of the situation when Kara was first recruited. She'll make sure to mention it to Grant tomorrow.

Oh. Except that he's probably already read these letters for himself. And even before that, he probably had security people hiding in the trees watching those very visitors when they approached Viviane's door in the first place.

Kara shakes her head at the reminder of how much she has still to learn about her new life. But as for right now, even if her head's no longer spinning, that soak in the tub still sounds like a great idea.

[Chapter 15]

Late July – September 2014

The weeks that follow find Kara almost as busy as she was during her involvement with the R&D side of the project; unlike that period, however, she finds that now, at least, she maintains relatively consistent work hours—usually up by 4, not often up later than 11.

She quickly becomes comfortable with Col. John McLaughlin, an affable and surprisingly humble man, considering how talented he is with the yoke. As if to compensate for his lack of ego, the man is a startling 6'5", the tallest pilot Kara will meet. For his part, McLaughlin seems to accept Kara as his new commanding officer with little trouble, despite the fact that they share the same rank of "full bird" colonel—a rank he earned through twenty-three years of service, she by the momentary whim of their higher-ups.

McLaughlin's support seems to be enough for the other members of the squad—*most* of the them, at least. Not all of Kara's new subordinates accept her leadership at first, McLaughlin's backing or not. In particular, one of the more talented pilots—a woman by the name of Anna Haynes—seems hell-bent on bucking Kara's authority whenever possible. She never goes so far as to be openly rude, and it happens less when McLaughlin is around, but her words usually serve to undermine what Kara is trying to accomplish. Until one day, when Kara's frustration gets the better of her and she lashes back—calling Anna out in front of everyone, then enumerating some of the woman's bad habits without any attempt at diplomacy. For a wonder, this appears to impress Anna; not only does she seem to target Kara less from that day forward, she redoubles her efforts at correcting the failings Kara had called her on.

"I don't get it," Kara complains to McLaughlin, whose opinion she's coming to trust. "I mean, Anna's good, but I didn't think I could put up with her crap much longer. And suddenly the crap stops."

McLaughlin chuckles. "Haynes struggles with the blind obedience thing. You had to earn her respect."

"By embarrassing her in front of everyone? I thought for sure I'd have to cut her after that. Thought I'd made an enemy for life."

"That's just it—you *didn't* cut her, before or after. You treated her more like a peer than someone you expected blind obedience from. Most officers would have booted that kind of subordinate first chance they had, which is probably what she expected."

Kara can only shake her head at this. She's having a hard time adjusting to military culture—the hierarchy is so different from the meritocracy she knew in the academic world. She can't seem to accept the idea that her opinions are automatically more important than others, just because of the little black bird insignia embroidered on her newly-issued airman battle uniform. Even if most of the pilots seem to accept Kara's authority on the surface, they've got to be questioning it in private. And now McLaughlin is saying Anna Haynes respects her *because* her management style is completely different? The whole thing is so messed up, Kara's not sure how she feels about it.

Of course, the other pilots' opinions are becoming increasingly less important, as their representation in the unit dwindles. The fresh training regimen Kara develops stretches them in ways the standard gameplay never did, allowing Kara a modicum of objectivity in evaluating the fifty-plus pilots Peterson had intended to use as the backbone of Grant's new fighting force. As she had so boldly informed the brass, most of them simply aren't capable of adapting to a whole different paradigm of combat flying... which makes sense, after years of being trained to fly reactively and instinctively within atmosphere. Peterson is none too pleased at the rapidity with which she cuts his pilots loose, but he did, after all, delegate the responsibility to her, and McLaughlin backs her up on most such decisions. In fact, she has the distinct impression McLaughlin raised some of the very same concerns with Peterson in the past, to no avail.

Meanwhile, testing of the prototype Destrier goes well in orbit. Although Kara has never met Lt. Jim Marks—who was delivered to the ship via commercial shuttle, and whom her new role now permits her to speak with—she is nonetheless impressed by his attitude and the insight he displays in putting the Destrier through its paces. All in all, testing goes very well, which is to say that only about three dozen issues are revealed. Most of these are software glitches, though a few are integration issues between the software and the physical equipment. A couple of the former are so minor that Kara is able to write quick fixes and upload them via encrypted radio signal to the craft, which passes over Nevada roughly once every hour and a half. After almost eight hours, Marks goes extravehicular once more and spacewalks the two dozen yards to the shuttle for his flight back home. The Destrier remains, it being somewhat infeasible to bring it back to the surface.

Lt. Marks' time in the saddle does convince the brass of one practical design flaw. Upon booting up the ship's systems for the first time, Marks discovers that two of the craft's eight LCD displays had been damaged in transit; although not a major issue, at least not during the testing phase, it hearkens back to one of Kara's recent out-of-the-box questions: Why use monitors at all? Why not use the VR function to display *all* constructs holographically? It was never feasible when she was developing *Rampant*, because distinguishing a large number of VR constructs is difficult for the eye if there's any ambient light in the room. But for their purposes now, Kara realizes, using the goggles as the primary display device is perfect since the pilot certainly doesn't need to worry about ambient light while locked in a vacuum-sealed pod without any windows.

Kara immediately retasks half of her technicians, who have been assigned back to Prometheus now that there's more work, to modify the display programming; the others she leaves to take care of the glitches discovered during testing. Kara herself does very little coding, providing oversight as she now does for both the pilots and the technicians, not to mention still spending an hour with Skewrs every day. The pilots and the techs remain segregated from one another, and though Kara travels back and forth between wings through the door outside Grant's office, she maintains her quarters in the techs' area.

Grant himself is once again conspicuously absent, popping up only occasionally, their most significant conversation being his denial of her request to end training with Skewrs—as much as she's come to enjoy it, she simply can't conscience stealing that time away from more urgent responsibilities. But apparently that's no longer her decision, assuming it ever was. As for the other general officers Kara recently met, she little expected to see much of them, and that instinct bears out.

The only member of Grant's top brass who spends most of his time here at Prometheus HQ is Peterson, and though he remains highly visible, he allows Kara free rein. His involvement in the daily grind with the pilots is so minor, in fact, that Kara almost wonders if she has completely replaced him; every time she appears at his office door with a report, however, she finds him deeply engrossed in something. She recalls the octogenarian's allusion to "aspects of the project that you are unaware of," as well as Grant's love of compartmentalization. Most definitely there is still much that Kara is not privy to, although she finally feels like she has something approaching a full picture of the situation.

In fact, after two months working with the pilots, Kara begins to feel almost comfortable with them—but that's because she's established a rapport. The idea of actually ordering them around, of sending anyone into danger, is terrifying. It's a good thing she only has to prepare them for combat rather than lead them into it.

Peterson himself seems pleased with the progress Kara has made… except for one admittedly significant problem.

Thursday afternoon
October 2, 2014

"Four." Peterson rubs the bridge of his nose with a pained expression. Kara and McLaughlin glance at each other uncomfortably while Stephens, the plainclothes officer on loan from military intelligence, pretends to flip obliviously through his notes. The three of them are seated before Peterson's large oak desk. "We only have four pilots now?"

"Yes," Kara responds. "In addition to John here, there's Skylar McClinic, Barrett Williams, and Anna Haynes."

John McLaughlin clears his throat. "In all fairness, sir, we have five—counting Colonel Dunn."

Kara looks up sharply at this, but Peterson growls, a low rumble in his throat. "And what's the holdup with Dunn's long list of appropriate replacements?"

She takes a moment to shift mental gears, then waves a hand in the general direction of the dossiers in Stephens' lap. "Well, we've identified most of the gamers I've flown with, and I can vouch for their talent behind the controls. The problem is, well…"

"The problem," Stephens takes up where Kara left off, "is that the majority of these individuals are not suitable candidates for top secret security clearance. In fact, many of them do not even meet minimum standards for military service." He pushes his glasses back up his nose as he flips open a folder. "Some of these folks are not American citizens, a great many of them are underage, and we have a number with past felony convictions. Out of forty-six, fifteen remain candidates, and I'm still uneasy with a few of those.

"Take for example Miss Shannon Dembry, who turns eighteen this month. Multiple shoplifting charges as a minor, though, admittedly, most of them were dropped. Then there's Mr. William Cobb, night manager at a convenience store—he's quite obese. And of course Jeremiah Blankenship, whose sole occupation is sitting out front of a supermarket… panhandling."

Peterson drills Kara with an unpleasant look and she scratches her ear uncomfortably, mostly for something to do. "I've never actually *met* any of these people," she says dismissively. "How was I supposed to know? And who would've ever guessed Brewtus is homeless? Honestly? How does a homeless man play an online video game three nights a week?"

Stephens flips a page. "Apparently he breaks into the chaplain's office at the shelter where he stays." How Stephens' people found this out, he doesn't say.

Peterson blows out his breath and leans back in his swivel chair. "Fifteen."

"Well," Stephens says, referring to his notes once more, "plus another two." He turns to McLaughlin. "I ran down that other list you gave me."

Both Kara and Peterson turn to the tall pilot in surprise, and he clears his throat uncomfortably. "Sorry, I meant to tell you... I worked up a list of my own, pilots I've flown with over the years that I knew would meet Kara's criteria. They already have top clearances too."

"Great idea," Kara interjects before Peterson can say anything.

"So," Stephens continues, "of *those* seven, only two are available for transfer in the near future." He shakes his head. "I don't know what sort of stuff you've been into, John, but the officers you run with are buried in so many layers of secrecy even I had trouble cutting through." He sighs. "Anyway, there should be no problem with transferring Jameson Faulk and Daniel Smith, assuming you approve, General."

Peterson waves a hand, and McLaughlin relaxes. "It's actually J.T. Faulk. And the other pilot is *Kevin* Smith... no one uses his first name."

"So..." Peterson muses, bringing them all back on track. "Even assuming all fifteen of these nerds join our club—including the panhandler, the pudge-bucket, and the shoplifter—that only brings us to twenty-two if you count Faulk and Smith." Kara runs the math in her own head, brow beetling; again, the others seem to be counting her among the final total. She raises a hand to object, but Peterson waves her off distractedly. "It's still barely a tenth of what we'll eventually need," he continues. "Do you understand the problem this presents?"

"I know we're not where we want to be," Kara responds, "but your training regimen just wasn't up to snuff."

"That's all well and good, but it still leaves us a couple hundred pilots short. I can appreciate your high standards, but we can't simply audition pilots for these roles—for every five pilots you train, you'll end up rejecting three, and that's three more potential security leaks. Doesn't matter how little we tell them, word will get out." He shakes his head, his tone now accusatory. "You were supposed to offer us a long list of pilots you *knew* would make the cut, so it was simply a matter of Stephens vetting them. But instead, not only did you fail to deliver these pilots, you fired the ranking pilots who would've filled most of the command roles in our new outfit."

Kara looks at her feet, face flush, but says nothing.

"You're pretty much telling me there's no way to recruit the pilots we need."

Kara feels a stirring of anger. "Only because you insist on an absurd level of secrecy."

"Well, that's not going to change!"

Silence reigns long and awkward until McLaughlin speaks up unexpectedly. "We could run a competition."

"A competition?" Kara repeats stupidly.

"Yeah," he leans forward, hands on knees, tentatively excited. We go through your publisher, um…"

"My pub—you mean DactiSoft?" Kara asks after a momentary pause.

"DactiSoft, right. We go through them, keep our name out of it—no whiff of Air Force or the U.S. Government, that is. Invite fans of the game to compete and offer major prizes. Give it lots of publicity, so that no one can miss it. Between that and the prizes, we should draw a crowd."

Kara can tell Peterson's not going for it, so she jumps in before he can object. "I like it. And it makes sense. DactiSoft actually… well, they lost money on the game. This could be seen as a way to recoup their expenses."

"What were your sales on the game?" McLaughlin asks. "I mean, how many copies were purchased?"

"Only thirty-two thousand," she responds wryly.

"Only thirty-two thousand," he repeats, but with more enthusiasm. "Thirty-two *thousand*. Surely we can find at least 200 good pilots out of that group—we'd only need one out of every… what, 150? And a big competition with prizes is the best way to attract a large pool to choose from."

It's obvious Peterson would very much like to crush the suggestion, but it really isn't a bad idea. With a look like he's sucking lemon, he says, "You're talking, in essence, about handing out commissions for being good at a video game." He seems to shiver. "I can't believe I'm even listening to this. If our backs weren't against the wall here…" He exhales noisily. "*Well*, how exactly would you market something like this? It's one thing to say 'lots of publicity'; it's another to make it happen. Do either of you have public relations experience?"

"We could hire someone…" Kara says after a moment.

"No," Peterson shakes his head. "I keep telling you—I don't want anyone else brought into the loop unnecessarily. And that includes other Air Force personnel."

It seems for a moment as though Peterson has found his objection, but then help comes from an unexpected direction. "How about Gene Jenkins?" asks Stephens.

Peterson and McLaughlin draw a blank, but Kara says, "You mean Jinx?"

"Right. He's one of the few people on your list that I have no objection to." Stephens flips to the right dossier and whips it open. "Gene Jenkins, aged 45, almost twenty years experience in public relations in various industries." He flips another page. "Looks like he's worked with some very high visibility clients." Glancing up at Peterson, he adds, "You'd have to bring him up to speed, but he's one of the ones you'll be recruiting for your squad anyway."

Peterson stares off into the distance for a moment, then nods definitively. "Fine. We'll run with this, and I'll have my people work with you on securing his participation," he nods at Stephens. "Looks like we're in business."

"Assuming Jenkins signs on," Kara says.

"Oh, that won't be a problem," Peterson responds with a wicked smile. "McLaughlin, Dunn, dismissed."

Kara opens her mouth to object—this issue of whether she herself will be deployed needs to be addressed—but Peterson is already moving onto the next item with Stephens. "What's this I hear about an attack on our Jersey mail center?" he demands, ignoring her.

Kara sighs and turns to follow McLaughlin out the door. Stephens shrugs as she passes. "What do you want me to say?"

"It was a whole month ago, and only now am I—"

Kara misses the rest of what's said as the door clicks shut. She heaves another sigh. "John…?" she begins, and the tall pilot turns in response.

"Yes?"

She tries to formulate the question but slowly realizes just how absurd it would sound. Of course they would be counting her among the pilots who will ultimately face this threat. They granted her a command rank and put her in charge of training. It's not like she's got any physical conditions keeping her from active duty, and pilots are at a premium right now. If anything, it's her own fault—*she*'s the one who cut so many pilots, and *she*'s the one who was so adamant about recruiting from outside the Air Force. *What was I thinking?*

Her mind flits back to that day in the conference room. When they offered that commission, were they thinking even then that she would be deployed? *Probably*, she realizes now, but that possibility never even occurred to her until later. And even if that hadn't been their intention, what difference does it make? When she signed that dotted line, she gave up control of her own life.

McLaughlin is eyeing her with some concern, but Kara is oblivious. She sways slightly, and he catches her. "Kara?"

"Wow... oh, wow." She blinks and focuses on his face. "What have I gotten myself into?"

He laughs, but kindly. "I know how you feel."

[Chapter 16]

**Monday morning
October 6, 2014**

    The aide ushers Gen. Carl Grant into the office, then closes the door as he exits. The man at the desk barely glances up from his writing. Grant removes a device from his jacket and asks, "May I?"
    Grant's boss doesn't respond for the long moment it takes to finish his work, then he flips the expensive fountain pen onto the desk in an annoyed manner and sits back in his chair. The gaze he levels at Grant is skeptical, bordering on suspicious. Finally he responds, "Sure." He shows almost sarcastic interest as the other man moves about the circular room, waving his electronic wand in wide arcs across the walls and over different pieces of furniture. "You know," he says mock-conversationally, "in the twenty months since I moved in here, you have been the only visitor to doubt the security of this room."
    "It pays to be paranoid, Mr. President."
    "Fine, be paranoid. Please just be quick about it." The President of the United States returns to the notes he was taking when Grant arrived.
    After a moment, Grant completes his search for electronic surveillance devices and tucks the detector into his pocket. "The room's clean."
    "What a surprise." The President doesn't even look up.
    "I think I prefer the personality you show to the public."
    The most powerful man in the world again throws his pen back onto the desk and sits back, his gaze frank and evaluating. Finally he barks a laugh. "You know, you are one of the most difficult people I have ever met, but to your credit, you're not a simpering fool, and you're not just another divisive politico. I appreciate that." Almost under his breath, but clearly audible, he adds, "But it doesn't make you or your project any less annoying. And for your information," he looks back up at Grant, "you're the only one that consistently sees my cranky side."
    "Sir," Grant cuts to the chase, "it's October."

The President shakes his head at the inanity of this statement, then cradles his forehead in his palms, elbows on the desk.

"Next month is November," Grant continues.

The only response is a raised hand, gesturing weakly as if to say, *Of course, how could I have forgotten?*

"*Sir.*" Now Grant is growing exasperated as well.

"General, do you have any new information you're ready to share with me?"

Grant is silent.

"Then I'm sorry, my answer remains the same."

"Mr. President, it's already too late to defend ourselves. All we can do is get those people out and work to be better prepared for the next attack. You need to approve the evacuation and give us the funding we need."

"As before, you ask me to accept a lot on faith."

"Sometimes faith is all we have available to us. That doesn't make the object of one's faith any less real."

"Oh, cut the crap. I wasn't talking religion." He picks up his pen, dismissively. "Until something changes, my answer remains the same. And might I point out that you're in danger of losing your already limited funding. So get your act together."

"Mr. President," Grant says heatedly, "we have been preparing for next month for thirty years. Now, in the last ten years, when we should have been ramping up to meet this threat, we've done exactly the opposite—cut the funding we so desperately need."

"Now hold on, it was my predecessors that reined you in, Grant, not me. Your R&D wasn't paying dividends in the war effort."

"So fix it now. Give us our funding."

"No. We're already in the middle of a domestic crisis, trying to reduce government spending, and you want me to create another funding black hole? Just last week, the minority leader was in here asking probing questions about that special line item we have just for you. I was tempted to refer him to the Secretary of the Air Force and be done with it."

"The Secretary would have just sent him back to you. He doesn't know anything—no one does. The chain of command between me and this office has been deliberately left out of the loop since the very beginning."

"Well, I'm hardly *in* the loop, am I?"

"Sir, it was one of your predecessors who set up Project Prometheus in '83 by special executive order, and he gave us direct access to this office for a reason. Is that not enough for you?"

Now it's the President's turn to sit silently, expectantly.

"Very well," Grant almost snarls. He digs into his attaché case and pulls out a slim folder. "Mr. President, this is eyes-only. I cannot stress enough how vitally important it is that this remain absolutely secret. Even a vague reference to your wife or one of your staff could have devastating consequences." They lock gazes for a long moment before he finally hands the file over. "Here's your proof. The KLINE Document."

So the President begins to read. He does so slowly, giving the paper his undivided attention, even re-reading several sections. And as he does so, he becomes increasingly agitated. Finally he slams the folder down on his desk—not in annoyance, as before, but now in real anger... and not just a little fear. He stands and paces quickly back and forth behind his desk a few times, twice starting to speak, and each time cutting himself off, casting Grant frequent angry and suspicious glares.

Finally he whirls on the other man, index finger outstretched. "This whole thing is ridiculous." Grant doesn't respond, and the President relaxes slightly. "Your source, this... KLINE. Still alive?"

"No, KLINE... KLINE expired a long time ago." He seems pained by this. "But surely now you see why an evacuation is vital."

The President is incredulous. "What, based on a... a... a *prophecy* from thirty years ago?" He sputters. *"Thirty years?* We've fought how many wars since then? Any number of factors could have changed! There's no reason to believe they're still on the same timetable."

"There's been no change, sir. You read what it says!" He grabs the document from the desk and holds it out to the other man, but the President stares at it as he would a poisonous snake, refusing to take it in hand again. Finally, Grant shoves it back into his case. "There's no doubt," he continues, calmer. "The attack will come in November."

The President, also calmer, simply shakes his head. "November is a wide window. No specific date. Just like a horoscope, vague and open to interpretation."

Grant speaks through his teeth. "There's nothing vague about this threat. We know almost every detail, all except for the exact date."

"I'm sorry, Carl. You've... you've definitely given me a lot to think about. But my answer is the same. No evacuation, no additional funding. I will, however" —he holds up a hand to forestall Grant's angry response—"order an upgrade to the terror threat level, and we'll ensure that emergency response units are ready just in case. Beyond that, I'll need to see evidence. *Current* evidence."

Grant just shakes his head tiredly. "You'll have your evidence. Next month. Should I just set an appointment with your secretary on my way out the door?"

Grant pulls out his cell phone as he climbs into the back of the town car. Flipping through his saved numbers, he selects the one labeled "Mom" and puts a call through.

"Hello?"

"We're on for the Halloween party."

"Okay."

Grant terminates the call and looks out the window at the passing sakura trees, shaking his head sadly.

[Chapter 17]

**Tuesday afternoon
October 14, 2014**

Gene Jenkins steps out of the 737 onto the rollaway stairs and almost trips, so bright is the sunlight off the salt pan; fortunately, he grabs the railing in time. The similarity to her own memorable arrival at Groom Lake is so great that Kara can't help but laugh. She grabs his arm as he reaches the ground and pulls him out of the main flow of commuters.

Squinting, he asks, "Kara?" He eyes her ABUs dubiously.

"That's right, Gene."

He breaks into a wide, easy smile, his pristine white teeth glittering in stark contrast to his dark skin. He shakes her hand enthusiastically. "It's great to finally meet you. In person, I mean."

"Definitely. I'm glad you were willing to join us here."

Gene's expression darkens momentarily, but he says, "I was between contracts, so the timing was good."

"How was your flight?" she asks him as they carry his luggage to the SUV she requisitioned.

"Oh, not bad. This whole thing"—he waves his hand to encompass the jet, the hundreds of passengers, the facility in the distance—"it's far more… matter-of-fact—you know, ho-hum—than I expected." He shuffles quietly for a moment. "Actually, the most exciting thing that happened to me today was being accosted by a cultist while on layover in Denver. He kept grabbing everyone and screaming into their faces, 'Flee! Flee! Destruction is upon us!' and things like that." He chuckles at the memory.

"Well," she responds, "you've definitely escaped the cultural mainstream out here. Come on," she adds as she hops into the driver's seat, "I'll show you around."

"So you see," Kara sums up, "we need to identify this country's most top notch vacuum flyers, and quickly." She glances in turn at Peterson and McLaughlin, to make sure they have nothing to add. So far, Peterson has allowed them to bring Gene up to speed; from the very first moment, there appeared to be an unexpected tension between him and the newcomer.

Gene's brow furrows. "I'm not sure I follow. Who exactly is supposed to be attacking us?"

Kara and McLaughlin share a look, then turn back to Gene. "That's need-to-know," McLaughlin intones.

"I really don't know," Kara admits at the same moment. She blushes as McLaughlin turns to her with a raised eyebrow. She doesn't look Peterson's way. "Sorry, I'm... uh... still getting used to this."

"Okay, I guess," Gene responds. "So *someone*'s gonna launch missiles and we need pilots in Destriers out in space to stop them. I guess I can accept that," he concludes, unconvincingly.

Peterson's grip on his ballpoint pen tightens, and Kara can only imagine how he feels hearing such top secret info so casually summarized. She clears her throat. "Right."

"And how many pilots do we need?"

"Well," Kara begins. "Right now, we're thinking of structuring our defense around four points in orbit, with each—"

"Plan for two hundred," Peterson breaks in, his eyes warning Kara to go easy on the intel.

"Right, but... um. Well, we can't recruit openly, and we're not sure who to approach anyway. So... McLaughlin here dreamed up the idea of a competition, to draw the talent out of the woodwork. But beyond liking the idea, we don't know where to go. With your expertise in PR and event promotion, you seemed like a perfect choice to help us put something together on short notice."

That unreadable look again flits across Gene's face, same as when Kara met him at the jet, but he responds before she can comment on it. "Of course. Like I said, I'm between contracts right now, and this should be a fun one to work on.

"And I'm glad you've chosen to call in a professional on this," he adds, addressing Kara specifically. "After the fiasco with *Rampant*—" He waves his hand suddenly as if to obviate the effrontery of this remark. "What I mean is that you had a great product, obviously; your people just didn't position it properly. In fact, I've got some thoughts on things you could try even now, perhaps resurrect the franchise. I know, I know," he interrupts himself, again waving his hand, "that's not what we're here to talk about, but depending on how we structure this competition, a comeback may make sense."

"So... how do we start?" McLaughlin asks.

"Well, we need to get DactiSoft on board, since they hold the rights to the software. How's your relationship with their leadership, Kara?"

"I was friendly with all of them, especially the CEO, Jamie Miles. He's a former college professor, and we had some common background. Of course, *Rampant* lost them a lot of money, so things were a little strained at the end."

"Would he see you if called for an appointment?"

"Sure. I think so, at least."

"So we meet with him and sell him on the idea of the competition. He'll ask why, or more importantly, why *now*. You and I can talk about the continuing strong support we see in the gaming community—even though it's a small niche, it's a committed niche."

"It won't be enough," Kara says, and Peterson looks up in surprise. "Yeah, I know what I said at the last meeting, but I've had time to give it some more thought. Jamie... he's a very conservative businessman. He doesn't commit to anything without checking every fact and figure first, and when it comes right down to it, I doubt the facts will support the idea of a competition—not unless DactiSoft is willing to lose a bunch more money on it. And sure, you could call it an investment towards a second wave of game sales, but again, I doubt Jamie will go for it."

Gene has been shaking his head. "No-no, this isn't about the cash. We're not looking for any outlay from DactiSoft, just their permission to do preliminary research on a competition. Even that research won't cost anything, since you and I'll be volunteering our time, as members of the gaming community. You'll be doing the logistics planning, while I work on securing the corporate sponsorships to pay for the whole thing."

Peterson speaks up. "So what makes you think you can convince someone else to part with that kind of money?"

Gene just smiles. "Selling a few major corporations on the event is easy. It's all advertising dollars to them, so we just have to convince them that slapping their logo on our event will get them as good or better visibility as other options available to them. And when was the last time they had a publicity opportunity like this? It's totally unique. Besides, I think we could secure one of the big sports networks to provide coverage; that'll go a long way towards convincing potential sponsors."

"A big sports network? You mean like…?" Peterson actually looks impressed. "Um…" He refocuses. "About these sponsorships—you know who to talk to at these companies?" he asks.

"Well…" Gene appears slightly less sure of himself. "I have a few contacts. Finding the right person, the decision maker, that's really where the challenge is." He brightens. "But that's where you government types come in. You know everything about everyone, right? So if I give you a list of people, can you just get me their private phone numbers? Direct lines, cell numbers?"

Peterson shakes his head. "Fine, not an issue—we can put Stephens on it. But let's back up. We need to get DactiSoft's approval."

"Right," Gene says, then adds in an uncharacteristically sarcastic tone, "unless you want to horn in on their operation and take control. Because the U.S. Government can take whatever it wants from the private sector in the name of national security, right?"

Kara's eyes flick between Peterson and Gene in confusion.

"No," Peterson replies—belatedly, but in a tone that brooks no argument. "This thing needs to avoid the appearance of any federal involvement. That means keeping DactiSoft out of the loop. Your arguments are sound, so you shouldn't have any problem getting them on board."

"Okay, then," Kara pipes in. "So I'll call over and see if I can't set up an appointment with Jamie, and we'll go from there. Fortunately his office isn't far—just over the border into Utah. Town of Ashland." Peterson's eyes narrow, probably at the idea of Kara leaving the base; she raises her eyebrows in silent challenge, ready to throw a fit if he makes an issue of security for such a short trip. He remains silent, and she continues: "I haven't checked, but I bet we could drive there in four or five hours."

That does it. "*Drive* there?" Peterson clarifies. "Out of the question. You'll take air transport."

"I thought you wanted to avoid even the hint of government involvement—being dropped off in Ashland by a helicopter bristling with machine guns would scream just the opposite. You don't understand," she continues, "Ashland is tiny. Just a sleepy, middle-America town. It's not a commercial magnet; it just happens to be where Miles and his partners lived before they started the company."

By now, Peterson is getting used to how frequently circumstances overrule his desires. He blows out his frustration noisily. "Fine. You can take a sedan from the motor pool. Just make sure it's topped off—you won't find many gas stations between here and there. But you'll take McLaughlin and someone from SF, both armed."

Kara frowns. "SF?"

"Our Security Forces."

"Ah..." She thinks about it, decides it's probably the best deal she'll get. "Okay," she finally agrees. "I'll also need a phone. Gene too, if he's going to be coordinating sponsorships."

"I'll put someone on it," Peterson nods. "And just one more thing," he adds, pinning Gene Jenkins with his most impressive military stare. "It's obvious you don't take this threat to national security very seriously, but let me be very clear: you *will* respect the secrecy of this operation. If I get even a whiff from Dunn or McLaughlin or anyone else that you've let anything slip, I'll have you up on a treason charge. Am I understood?"

Gene looks simultaneously terrified and furious, if that's even possible. "Y-yes," he stammers.

"Fine," Peterson responds, leaning back in his chair and shutting off the force of his glare as if flipping a switch. "You might just make a good military man yet."

It takes Gene a long moment to register the import of this comment. "Huh? Wait, you mean me? A pi—"

"Dunn, Jenkins, dismissed. McLaughlin, stick around—we need to discuss something."

**Friday morning
October 17, 2014**

    Kara pulls the sedan out of the subterranean parking garage and heads out into the open desert, the road they drive upon the only artificial construct in sight. Gene sits beside her, fiddling with his new cell phone, while McLaughlin and a member of the Air Force Security Forces sit quietly in the rear.

    "I don't get it," Gene complains. "All those thousand-dollar hammers I've helped pay for, and the best the military can give me is a $10 disposable jobbie. Why can't I have one of those new eighth-gen smartphones?"

    No one responds. Gene had adapted remarkably well—and quickly—to the idea that he himself might be one of the pilots ultimately deployed to defend the country. He definitely exhibited some panic that first day, right after he and Kara left Peterson's office, and Kara had no trouble identifying. But he seemed to recover much more quickly. For Kara, it had taken the last two weeks to come to grips—mostly, at least—with the idea of actually fighting in a war; ultimately, she'd had to bow to inevitability. She had, after all, accepted the commission; her life was no longer hers to direct. But Gene… well, maybe Gene thinks he'll be off the hook if his recruitment efforts succeed. Only time will tell.

    Kara glances in the rear view mirror and blinks. They've gone barely a mile, and she's astonished to realize she can't even make out the facility behind them, so carefully has it been built into the hills. She shakes her head. It's a good thing she's not alone in the car, because otherwise the undulating terrain would undoubtedly lull her to sleep. She checks the clock and calculates an ETA; as it had turned out, the drive should only require about three hours.

    Gene finally sets his phone down and looks out over the desert. "You never told me, Kara. How did we get an appointment with Miles this quickly?"

"I called and told him you and I and some other gamers were in Vegas for the week, and we wanted to drop in and talk with him about a business proposition we had."

Gene looks alarmed. "You didn't! Kara, it's a wonder he's seeing us. Considering *Rampant*'s sales record, I wouldn't think he'd want to hear another idea from you." After a moment, he adds, "No offense."

Kara finds herself taking offense anyway. "Well, he seemed pleased to hear from me. Didn't even sound surprised to get my call. When I mentioned meeting, he just asked what was convenient for us, and that was that."

Gene just shakes his head. In the back, McLaughlin and the other man, whose name Kara has not been given, remain silent, each looking out his respective window. The 'cop,' as McLaughlin had referred to him—formerly referred to as an MP, though that's apparently yet another outdated term—looks particularly uncomfortable in street clothes. Between his ramrod bearing and distinctive crew cut, Kara had insisted the man don a ball cap before leaving base.

By now, Gene has resumed discussion of how *Rampant* might have performed better had it been marketed differently, a topic which seems to be among his new favorites. The subject is closely related to their competition plans, so he transitions frequently between analyzing past failures and pointing out future possibilities. Kara joins the backseaters in their stoic silence for as long as possible, but eventually she can't help breaking in.

"You know, Gene, the issue wasn't just the marketing. I'm not sure the game itself would have been that popular even if it'd been pushed better."

Gene looks perplexed. "What do you mean? It's a great game." He starts ticking off points on his fingers: "Fun gameplay, great story. And best yet," he extends a third finger, "it's *intelligent* entertainment. Educational, whether you realize it or not."

"Don't forget the incredible graphics, Gene."

He looks at her blankly. "Well, I don't know if I'd say 'incredible'...."

"That's my point." She sighs. "I've read a lot of game reviews since then—user reviews, not critics—and it seems like the most important factor is always graphics. Gamers want to be wowed by gorgeous visuals. It's not the only factor, but it seems to be the first prerequisite. And *Rampant*... with its use of basic wireframes and polygons, it probably seemed 10 or 15 years behind the times."

"Yes, but... it's still fun, great graphics or not." Gene struggles to resurrect his argument. "The gameplay is addicting—"

"You're not much of a video gamer, are you, Gene?"

"No, not really," he admits. "I try to get into them as something to do with my boy. *Rampant* became something we could do together."

"But you're not a mainstream gamer. Neither am I... and neither was most of our devel team. We built something we would enjoy, and we were excited about merging education and entertainment. We thought we were being subtle. But *Rampant*, the way we made it at least... I just don't think it would appeal to everyone. Only to a small—what did you call it?"

He looks at her. "A niche, you mean?" He sighs too. "Okay, I see your point. And maybe that's part of why we're so committed to the game, those of us who play it. It's what you call a cult following—some people like it probably *because* it never reached mainstream popularity. And they tell themselves part of the appeal is the intelligent gameplay, which in turn compliments them on their taste in entertainment." Gene is clearly just thinking out loud now. "If the game were to be redeveloped—not just re-released, but actually rebuilt, the visuals would be the first thing to look at. But if you 'fixed' the graphics, and if that led to more widespread appeal, would it mean the death of the core fan base?" He lets that question hang, lapsing into silence.

Kara can't help but smile. Here they are talking about a video game comeback, while the whole point of this trip—and Gene's involvement—is preparing for a devastating real-life attack. She wonders what the backseaters are thinking now. About twenty minutes into their journey, they reach the guard shack along the outer perimeter of Area 51. The guard waves them through without making them stop.

The shack is just barely out of sight when a big SUV swerves onto the road in front of them, clipping their left front quarter panel. Kara fishtails around him, regains control of the wheel, and brings the car to a stop. She's reaching to shift the car into park when McLaughlin shouts, "Go, go, go! Get us out of here!"

She obeys without thinking, all but standing on the gas pedal as the car squeals from stationary to sixty in ten seconds. Under different circumstances, Kara would probably note that this car has clearly seen some aftermarket modification, but at the moment her heart is thumping so loudly she can barely think. She glances in the rearview, only to see that the SUV is already back on their tail. McLaughlin is twisted around in his seat, looking out the back window and speaking quietly into a large phone of some kind. The SF cop is completely turned around, seated cross-legged with his back to Kara's seatback. Both men have handguns drawn.

"What is it?" she asks shakily. "Why are they chasing us? Why are we running?" Despite her fear—or because of it—she has a sudden mental image of Peterson saying 'I told you so,' even though he hadn't actually made an issue of security.

"They're armed," the man beside McLaughlin responds simply. It takes Gene a moment to process this, but when he does, he suddenly turns to face forward and sinks low in his seat.

Kara tries to speed up even more, but the road is far too curvy, which allows the bulkier vehicle behind them to keep pace. The other driver, far more aggressive, forces his vehicle into the inside of a turn and manages to pull partly alongside them. Amidst all the bumping and swaying, Kara catches sight of a rifle barrel leveled in their direction from a lowered rear window. She screams and puts the pedal all the way to the floor. Gene shouts, "Shoot their tires out! Shoot their tires out!"

The man from Security Forces turns to him, his expression incredulous. "Shoot their tires out? From a moving vehicle?" He turns back to face the window.

"Well, you've got to do *something*," Gene says in a panicky voice.

"We are," comes McLaughlin's calm reply. "We're keeping the windows up until the cavalry arrives. This car *is* bulletproofed, you know," he adds dryly. "Just sit tight and stay silent."

After what seems like an hour, Kara detects the thundering sound of rapidly approaching rotors. There are several loud cracks and the SUV spins out of control, nosing into the ditch. Kara gets her sedan another fifty yards down the road before she coasts to a stop and turns around to look. By now, a half dozen soldiers in ABUs have rappelled from the hovering chopper, ripped open the doors of the SUV, and thrown its occupants down face first in the road. McLaughlin's phone bleeps.

"Come on," he says, and jumps out of the car. Kara and Gene follow more slowly, preceded by the cop who, having holstered his gun beneath his jacket, is nonetheless keeping one hand ready for a quick draw.

McLaughlin is met halfway by one of the soldiers, who pulls his combat goggles up from his eyes to the fore of his helmet. "Sir." He salutes, and McLaughlin answers in kind. "It's not quite as bad as you initially thought."

"Right," McLaughlin smiles tightly. "I realized that when they pulled back alongside."

"What do you mean?" Kara interrupts as the three of them catch up.

"Your pursuers weren't actually armed," the soldier responds.

"What I thought was a rifle turned out to be a shotgun mike," McLaughlin explains. "A long cylindrical microphone specifically designed for picking up sound at a distance or, in our case, through a car window. They're used in surveillance work," he pauses and smiles, then adds, "and in sports coverage, too."

"They were just spying on us?" Kara asks. "They nearly ran us off the road."

"Probably not their intention," the soldier says. "These guys are just cranks, UFO fanatics. See that guy?" he points out the wildest-looking of the SUV's three occupants. "We've picked him up a half dozen times for breaking through the fence line. You wouldn't believe how many wackos patrol our border hoping for a glimpse of something crazy. They've got cameras, microphones, you name it. We slap 'em with fines, throw 'em in jail, and they still come back. Of course, Intelligence checks up on them, makes sure they're not tied in with any terrorist groups or foreign powers, but that almost never happens." The crazy-looking man is shouting and spitting, his long raven hair flying about, as two soldiers carry his shackled form to the chopper, which has now landed. "The only thing that sets these guys apart is their budget." Kara cringes as she watches several thousand dollars-worth of equipment being systematically destroyed, the tapes wiped with magnets. "In any case," the man concludes, "we don't have a whole lot of ground traffic out of the base, which explains why they zeroed in on you. Pretty exciting, huh?" And he laughs.

"Well, thanks for the assist," McLaughlin replies with a smile.

Gene is clearly not sharing their amusement at the situation. "We could've been killed!"

"Doubtful," the soldier responds. "You folks are in good hands." He might have said more, but McLaughlin raises a hand.

Kara furrows her brows, suddenly suspicious. She tries to decipher the rank insignia on the soldier's uniform. "Um, Captain?"

The man blanches and clears his throat. "Um, no ma'am. Just Corporal."

"Oh, right." She's very glad she's not in uniform herself at the moment; it wouldn't have been very convincing. "Corporal, exactly how long did it take you to, um, rescue us?"

He glances at McLaughlin, who nods. "Exactly forty-seven seconds from the moment they appeared," he announces proudly.

"And thank you again for that," McLaughlin interjects smoothly. "We'd better be going. Timetable to keep."

As they make their way back to the car, Kara falls back until it's just her and McLaughlin. "That was no lucky accident. They're pacing us, aren't they?"

The other pilot smiles sheepishly. "You're a valuable national resource, Kara. Just because Peterson let you drive out of here on your own doesn't mean he's not keeping an eye on you."

The rest of the drive is uneventful, and after the terror of being pursued by that huge SUV, Kara almost welcomes the banal annoyance of Gene's compulsive talking. Almost. This time around, he's criticizing anyone silly enough to believe in extraterrestrial life, which seems like a natural enough direction for Gene's tongue to turn following their close encounter with the UFO enthusiasts.

"I just don't see how anyone can believe in aliens," he opines fervently. "I mean, I like science fiction as much as the next guy, but the idea is just silly. Besides," he offers, almost as an afterthought, "aliens are never mentioned in the Bible." And that, apparently, settles the matter for Gene. "Something that big, I think God would have made some mention."

Kara immediately thinks of a dozen other "big" things she doubts are mentioned in the Bible: cars, helicopters, computers, and so on. She phrases her retort in her mind, but doesn't actually deliver it. She mostly feels a little embarrassed on Gene's behalf, and the silence that follows his statement feels heavy to her.

Ironically, Kara's no more a believer in aliens than Gene, but she can name more scientific reasons for her stance. She knows that life was only possible on Earth because of a rare combination of factors—the sun being just the right size, the Earth being just the right distance from the sun, rotation and revolution speeds being just so; it was unlikely enough that it happened once, but in Kara's opinion, it's improbable in the extreme that life could exist on another planet anywhere nearby. The odds are simply against it.

Gene's nonstop commentary transitions somehow from aliens to his family—a segue she suddenly wishes she hadn't missed—and Kara forces herself to pay more attention.

"I married June in '91; happiest day of my life. Get this," he adds, turning in his seat to face Kara directly. "We tied the knot on June 19, 1991. You know men are always forgetting their anniversaries? Not me. The month matches her name, and the date and year are all the same digits—ones and nines. Impossible to forget!" he declares, obviously pleased with himself. "So what if it was a Wednesday!" More quietly, he adds, "It's too bad I didn't have any control over the day she was born… Anyway, she's a good woman. My shirts are always ironed and dinner's always ready when I get home, and she's still a looker. I won't be trading her in anytime soon!" He laughs loudly, and Kara's not sure whether he's serious, joking, or getting his kicks by being honest jokingly so that no one will take him seriously.

"My boy was born in '97," he continues. "John's a class act, I tell you. Good-looking, smart, athletic. He's a senior this year, quarterback on the varsity team, going for state championship third year running. Near the top of his class, too. I couldn't be prouder of him.

"And Jen's just as wonderful. She's fifteen now, studying for her permit. Safest driver that age I've ever seen! Always using her signals properly and stopping far enough back that she can see the tires of the car in front of her. She's captain of the JV cheerleading squad, *and* she takes advanced ballet three nights a week." He slaps the dash in front of him. "My Jen even won the role of Clara in the local *Nutcracker* this year!

"Like I said, it's the kids that got me into *Rampant*—John mostly, but Jen got into it too. We wanted something we could do as a family, and so we networked three PCs in the rec room and started playing together. I tell you, the maneuvers we developed! It's not like finding random people online to play the game with. When you fly with someone you trust, someone you know..." And on it goes, *ad nauseum*. Kara usually enjoys hearing a person's story, because the unique details of a person's life gives him or her a certain distinct flavor. Gene's family, on the other hand... they're so picture-perfect, so sickly sweet, it really does make her want to vomit.

They arrive in Ashland not a moment too soon, even if they are still twenty minutes ahead of schedule when she pulls the dented sedan into DactiSoft's parking lot.

The four of them pile out of the car and head inside, where Kara introduces the others to the receptionist as hardcore fans of the game, hoping the bulges beneath the servicemen's sports coats aren't obvious. The friendly middle-aged woman, who remembers Kara from her time with the company, takes them on a quick but boring tour of the facilities while they await their meeting with Miles. At 11 a.m. sharp, Kara and Gene manage to leave McLaughlin and the Air Force cop reading magazines in the CEO's outer office.

For whatever reason, Gene—who has already proven himself disgustingly chivalrous—actually precedes Kara into Jamie Miles' inner sanctum. Following him, Kara catches just a glimpse of her former boss before colliding full force with Gene's suddenly stationary form. She sidles around him to discover the room has another occupant; a man she does not recognize is rising from one of the chairs before Jamie's desk. It's clear, however, that Gene *does* recognize this man.

Miles clears his throat and speaks up. "Uh, Mr. Williams, this is Kara Dunn; Kara, may I introduce Nate Williams?"

Nate... Williams? "Axmatik?" she says out loud.

"That's right, Ms. Dunn," Williams responds with an easy, expensive smile. "I'm pleased to finally meet you."

Kara now feels as stunned as Gene, and rightly so. Nathan James Williams is chairman of Axmatik Ltd, a software development powerhouse with operations on a global scale. And the man, Williams, is just as well known as the company he created. If Kara got more of her news through the television, she might have recognized him; as it is, the name triggers a large file of information she's learned about the man just in the course of checking the daily headlines online. He's a controversial character, well known for his strong arm business tactics, and yet also for his generosity to charitable causes. That this man is standing in front of her, enthusiastically shaking her hand, leaves Kara slightly breathless. Now it's Gene's turn to clear his throat, and Kara snaps out of it, effecting introductions among the three men she shares the room with.

Gene seems particularly pleased with the unexpected addition to their meeting. Kara, meanwhile, resets automatically to her default mode in awkward social situations: silent, uncomfortable with speaking unless spoken to. And she can't help feeling a certain amount of deference toward Nate Williams. The conversation therefore lags, despite the questions that she and Gene clearly have; Williams' presence at the meeting is obviously not coincidental.

Finally, Miles speaks up. "Please, everyone, have a seat." They obey, pulling three leather chairs closer to the desk behind which Miles has seated himself. "Kara, I'm pleased you finally called me back. Would you explain again what your involvement with Mr. Jenkins is?"

Gene holds up a hand, saying magnanimously, "Please, it's just Gene. Really."

"Gene and I fly together sometimes," Kara says, adding quickly: "online, that is." She gives a nervous laugh, but the significance of her clarification is naturally lost on Williams and

Miles. "We got together with some of the other gamers, a 'meet each other in person' sort of thing." She's feeling off-kilter, and her carefully-crafted story is coming out disjointed.

"In Vegas?" Miles responds, skeptically. "I thought you hated Vegas." He turns to Williams in explanation, "Every few weeks, some of our employees arrange a trip down to the city. Most of Kara's team were out-of-towners, and so almost all of them would participate. Kara, though…" He chuckles and turns to her. "I remember you saying you wouldn't be caught dead in a place like that."

The cat has again stolen Kara's tongue, so Gene jumps to the rescue. "Um, actually, it was my idea. I love Las Vegas. If I was gonna come out West, Vegas had to be the place." He says it with all the sincerity he can muster, though a sickly look crosses his face when he stops to consider what he's just said. *No doubt*, Kara muses, *gambling is one of the seven deadly sins.*

Before they can push any harder against her story, which is suddenly feeling rather flimsy, Kara forces herself onto the offensive. "Gene and I had something to discuss with you Jamie, but I'm surprised Mr. Williams is here."

"Please, it's just Nate," he breaks in, also magnanimously, but not quite as pompously as Gene.

"Okay," she responds dumbly. "So… why are you here?"

There's a moment's uncomfortable silence. "Kara," Miles begins tentatively, "you haven't been checking your email, have you?"

Well, no, she thinks, *I've been buried beneath a hundred feet of rock in a top secret military base in the middle of the desert. No email.* She reddens slightly. "No, I—"

"I mean," Miles continues, "you hadn't gotten any of my messages when you called me? You really called me about something totally unrelated?"

Her embarrassment comes into full bloom. "I guess so." She hadn't banked on the fact that Miles was apparently trying to reach her while she was incommunicado. It raised uncomfortable questions about what she'd been up to in recent months. And she hadn't really developed a story to explain that period of her life. Belatedly, Kara realizes that top secret military work is difficult in ways she'd never considered.

"I don't get it!" Miles complains, abruptly exasperated. "Half my old programmers seem to have dropped off the planet—you, Harris, Cameron... even Ghee. It's like my emails and voice messages are disappearing into some black hole! The only one I ever heard back from was Mark Lawson, and that was just his wife calling to tell me he'd disappeared."

"What?" Kara asks in alarm, a horrible suspicion having formed as Miles ticked off the names of her erstwhile teammates.

"Yeah, he ran off with some floozy. Left Jeannie with the kids."

"Oh," Kara responds, feeling relieved. "Um... yeah, nothing crazy like that for me. I just..."

Gene pipes in again, never one for keeping quiet. "Kara, didn't you say some marketers got ahold of your email address, that you were covered up in junk?"

"Oh." She blinks. "Yeah. And then I got nailed by that new Chrysalis virus," she adds tentatively.

"Ouch," Williams grimaces. "That one was bad. You really should check into some of our antiviral packages—you could've immunized your machine months ago. Did you lose everything?"

"Oh, yeah. Everything." She finally feels she's reestablishing her balance. "Sorry, Jamie, I didn't even know you were trying to get ahold of me."

Jamie Miles' brows furrow, as if her explanation doesn't hold water; but of course—he was probably leaving voicemails also. Before Miles can say anything more, however, Williams finally begins to explain his involvement. "Kara, the reason Jamie was trying to reach you, not to mention your teammates—well, Axmatik has purchased a controlling interest in DactiSoft. One of my reasons behind the acquisition was so I could get my hands on you and your code." He chuckles, as if realizing how sinister his words might sound. "What I mean is that I have a great deal of interest in what you and your team accomplished with *Rampant*. Handled differently—in terms of sales and marketing, that is—it could have been a big deal. I'm even thinking there's room for a sequel."

Gene can no longer control himself. "That's what I keep telling her!" he blurts, rising halfway out of his chair.

Williams seems not to notice the interruption. "I've been so eager to talk with you, I'm afraid I've pestered Dr. Miles here half to death."

Miles waves this away, but not very energetically.

"Wow" is all Kara can think to say for a moment. "I'm... honored. But you've got the code now. What do you want to talk to me about?"

"I've got some ideas for how to revive the franchise, and we're working on those—we need to spiff up the graphics, for one thing. But if we're going to look at a sequel, we want you involved... say, co-project manager? I really wanted to reunite more of your old development team too, but it's not looking like that's possible right now."

"Oh. What's your timeframe?" *Crap,* she thinks, *I'm not exactly available for hire just now.*

"Pretty much as soon as possible."

Kara pulls a face, pretty convincingly if she does say so herself. "I can't get into something new anytime soon, I'm afraid. I just took a contract doing some... multi-discipline research with a... a large corporation. Really boring, but they made me sign all sorts of non-disclosures. They probably wouldn't let me just walk out of my contract. Even if it would be a lot of fun," she adds wistfully.

Williams also makes a face. Clearly this isn't the answer he was expecting, nor the answer he's used to receiving. "Well... perhaps we could put you on retainer? If you can't lead the project, you could at least be available by phone certain hours of the day. We could pay you, what, four hours minimum a week? And anything above that, you could cap if it interferes with your other work?"

Eager to be through with this conversation, Kara says, "Sure, that might work. I'll have to check with my employer, of course. Can I get back to you?"

"Fine," Williams smiles. "I'll have my people go ahead and draw up a contract and send it to you. What's your email address?"

"Oh." *Here we go again.* "I've actually been without one since, you know, the virus thing. I've been meaning to set up a new one. Maybe I could just call you when it's ready?"

Williams pulls out his billfold and withdraws a business card, upon which he scribbles his cell phone number. Gene is all but drooling, his eyes locked on the card as it passes from Williams' hand to Kara's. Meanwhile, Miles looks incredulous. *Kara Dunn go for months without email? Who is this imposter?*

Gene speaks up again, excitedly, "Mr. Williams, about reviving the franchise. We've got a great idea how to do it." He glances at Kara, "In fact, that's the whole reason we drove up here today."

She looks at him for a moment as though he's crazy, then it hits her. "Oh! Right!" She laughs nervously. "That's right, we had this idea for a competition. Invite all the *Rampant* players to one of a few centralized locations, have them compete for prizes and glory."

Gene grabs the verbal baton. "There's a strong online community of fans, a real cult following, and of course the competition would be open to new players as well. And the game's so unique, we think we could even sell it as a spectator event, for the people who don't actually play."

"But how would you pay for all this?" Miles asks dubiously.

"Sponsorships!" Kara and Gene say simultaneously. They glance at each other, and Kara continues, "It wouldn't require anything from DactiSoft—or Axmatik, I mean. And if it drummed up more attention for the game, it might get sales going again, helping to offset the company's loss on the game's development."

Gene opens his mouth to say more, but Williams beats him to the punch. "I like the idea," he says slowly, "and it wouldn't cost that much to make it happen. If we hold the competition at hotels and we draw enough participants, the management is likely to waive rental costs in however many conference rooms we require. And as far as the equipment goes… well, we just pick from among the cities in which Axmatik has a big presence, and we bring in our own equipment, using our own employees." He claps his hands together. "Excellent. Let's do it! And no other sponsors—I want Axmatik to get sole billing for the event."

"Oh," Gene looks slightly dejected. "I was hoping we could get the event televised, you know, as additional incentive for potential sponsors."

Williams smiles and seems to look at Gene for the first time. "Oh, I suppose we could do that too, whether or not we sell sponsorships. I've got friends in many places, you know."

[Chapter 18]

One Year Earlier

Friday evening
September 13, 2013

"Wow," Kara said, impressed despite herself. "This place is nice."

Paul Bandeburton just smiled, pleased at her reaction. It was the third time they'd been out together in the month since she moved back from Ashland. He was a post-grad student too, which meant a posh restaurant like this was normally outside his means... which in turn meant that he definitely had an interest in Kara. She wasn't sure what she thought of that yet.

"Ah, Mr. Bandeburton. Welcome!" effused a small Asian man in a tailored tuxedo, his accent faint. "And who is the lovely lady?"

"Alvin, allow me to introduce Kara. Kara, Alvin." Kara reached out a hand to shake, but the man bowed low.

"Your table is right over here, sir." He led them to a small, candlelit table in the corner. "Much quieter over here," he assured them, though the entire place was possessed of that hush usually characteristic of five-star establishments.

"Wow, Paul," she said again, as soon as Alvin was out of earshot. "You know the maître d'?" She wasn't actually that impressed, but she knew Paul would be hoping for such a comment.

His smile told her she knew him well. "Actually, he's the owner. Known him for years. Bit of a fussy sort, but all right."

Kara stifled a laugh; she might have used the same words to describe Paul himself. She considered asking after their host's real name—unless he was from Hong Kong, it most definitely wasn't Alvin—but decided not to put Paul on the spot. Instead, she asked, "So what's good here?"

"This place has the best sushi in all of Southern Cal," he announced proudly. "And I hope you like sushi, because that's *all* they serve here."

"Excellent," she smiled. "You'd probably better order for me, though. I really don't know the different types." That wasn't entirely true, but it would allow Paul to stick to whatever he'd budgeted for tonight. She had hoped to pay for tonight's date, set that precedent early on, but obviously Paul wanted tonight to be special. And she was okay with chivalry... to a point.

Raised voices at the front door attracted Kara's attention. "Franklin," said a powerfully-built, attractive man in a suit. He leaned over Alvin at the host's stand, obviously trying to stay quiet, but failing to keep his incongruously high-pitched voice from carrying.

Alvin's angry response also carried. "And I tell you, Mr. Franklin, we do not have you on our list."

"No, you don't understand me. *Ben* Franklin."

Kara lost interest as their voices quieted again, but she noticed a few minutes later when the man was seated two tables away. With him was another mountain of a man, also in a business suit.

"Well?"

"Sorry, Paul. What was that?"

"I asked what life was like in Ashland."

She laughed. "Very different." A waiter appeared with their drinks. "Very quiet, compared to here. But I liked it. There was more time there... you could get wherever you wanted in just a few minutes." He smiled. "I got at least a *little* more reading in."

Paul leaned forward interestedly. "So what do you like to read? Murder mysteries? Sappy romances?"

She barked a laugh; not a terribly lady-like sound, but he didn't seem to mind. "Journals mostly. And I like to hit all of the news websites most days—I'm a bit of a current events junkie. Though honestly..." She lowered her voice, as if imparting a secret. "I know I'm a professional geek, and this is probably heresy, but I prefer reading printed media. I already stare at a screen all day, and it gives me headaches sometimes."

Paul smiled approvingly, though at which part exactly, Kara wasn't sure.

"But the worst was the people," she continued.

"Really?" he asked in surprise. "Worse than here?"

"No, they were a lot nicer there. That's the problem—they're too nice. Smile at someone or make eye contact, and ten minutes later they're telling you about their grandkids. I mean, that's fine, it's just... I'm not that open with people I don't know. It was a little awkward sometimes."

Kara was really more of a listener than a talker—always had been. Usually she would grow uncomfortable under the kind of undivided attention Paul liked to give her, peppering her constantly with questions. But even on their first date a few weeks back, she'd found she didn't mind it so much. After all, Paul Bandeburton was a good-looking guy, and more importantly, an intelligent academic who could understand some of the struggles she was currently facing with her dissertation.

"So what was it like, leading your own project like that?"

"What, you mean the video game?" It had released over the summer, to much acclaim. So far sales weren't stellar, but Kara's team still had high hopes. The game had already been nominated for a few awards.

"Yeah, *Rampant*."

"It was really weird at first, having people report to me for direction. All that attention, and having to communicate abstract concepts clearly. Plus, it was uncomfortable letting other people do the work. I'm a perfectionist, you know? I tend to want to do things myself, make sure they're done right. But eventually I got used to the responsibility. Since I *couldn't* do the entire project myself, I had to learn to trust other people. Sometimes they failed, but most of the time they didn't. And I found out I'm pretty good at motivating people; it helped that they got excited about the same things I do." She smiled. "Now that it's all said and done, I think we did a pretty good job. It was a great experience."

"You never told me how you got plugged in with that company. Or even how you got started."

Kara felt a surge of gratitude for Paul's enthusiasm; coming from another academic, it meant a lot. "Believe it or not, my doctoral work centers around trying to develop a viable personal spacecraft: small, agile, robust, reusable, short-range." She ticked the attributes off on her fingers. "I know it's way ahead of its time, but that's the point. Looking forward to a day when there's a true economy operating in the vacuum of space. In the absence of gravity, of atmosphere, what would a personal vehicle look like? How would it work?

"I finished conceptualizing my model toward the end of 2010, and I'd done some coding on it—proof of concept stuff, really. It was time to secure funding, hopefully get on with NASA or any of the firms still performing zero G experimentation. Do some underwater testing, at the very least... Well, long story short, NASA wasn't interested. No one was. I kept hearing there's not as much money out there for aerospace right now. So I resorted to recruiting a small team of students—programmers—to help flesh out my concepts; it would've been part-time volunteer work for them, though, and we'd've been at the mercy of whoever schedules use of the supercomputer." She took a sip of her wine, eyes wandering around the room, before continuing. "Fortunately, that's when I got the call from Jamie Miles."

"He's the dude from DactiSoft, right?"

Dude. She smiled at the sobriquet. "Yeah. He'd heard about my project—something like a friend of a friend of my advisor. Jamie's a former prof in the state university system. Anyway, Dacti was looking to break into the mainstream entertainment market, but still maintain their commitment to solid educational products. It seemed like a good fit. Working with them, I actually had a budget and a bunch of fulltime programmers at my disposal, not to mention hundreds of beta testers eager to run my spacecraft through its paces in scores of scenarios. I'd never really considered a military application for my work, but the core project remained the same—and now I've got a lot more data to work with, to derive my findings from." She sighed, her enthusiasm ebbing suddenly, then smiled. "Assuming I ever finish my dissertation. *And* assuming my advisor doesn't cut me loose first."

"You know, you said something like that last week too." His tone was sincere. "What is it your advisor doesn't like?"

Kara laughed, suddenly bitter. "He doesn't like any of it." She sighed again. "No, that's unfair. I think he understood the situation I was in when I took my project to DactiSoft, that I wouldn't really be able to get the volume of data I wanted otherwise."

"So then..."

"It's the rest of the faculty. Definitely the chair—I know he doesn't approve."

"What, they've told you this?"

"Not in so many words, no. That's what's so *frustrating* about it. They won't address my project on its merits. They resort to making oblique references to it; you know, someone'll crack a joke about video games being such a rich vein for research. It's not original or funny, but it belittles my work without giving me an opening to defend myself. I'm not even there most of the time, but a few friends have repeated what they've heard." She sighed. "My advisor warned me it would happen, so I can't complain. But now that I'm back and actually pushing forward with my dissertation, he's catching a lot of flak."

Paul opened his mouth to say something, but at that moment a server appeared to take their order. Kara listened with only half an ear as her date picked items from the menu. This conversation was threatening her earlier good mood. At a nearby table, one of the two beefcakes appeared similarly put out, though she was too distracted to wonder why.

"That's a load of crap."

Kara looked up in surprise, but Paul wasn't talking to the waiter—he was talking to *her*, and he looked angry. "I'm sorry?" she asked.

"The way they're treating you. It's crap."

Kara felt a sudden warmth toward the man. "They're just embarrassed by how I collected my data," she said, wondering why she was bothering to defend them. "Imagine how that looks for the department."

"As if anyone would notice or care. Academics supposedly swear fealty to the pursuit of knowledge, but it seems to me all they care about is posturing and politicking." This time it was Paul who sighed. "Okay, not all of them. But some. They're just constantly comparing themselves to each other, and usually elevating themselves means tearing someone else down. Yeah, yeah," he shook his head, "it all happens beneath the veneer of civility. But it discourages anyone from rocking the boat." He took a big swig from his water glass. "Sometimes I wonder if things have really changed since the days of Galileo."

Kara laughed, feeling much better. "I don't know that it's *that* bad."

"What does it matter how you collected your data, as long as your methodologies were valid? They should be interested in what you learned. This stuff is *practical*... or will be, someday." He smiled.

Again, the sound of raised voices drew Kara's attention, and this time Paul twisted in his seat to look as well. It was the two men who'd been seated a few minutes after them. The hunks.

"I just want a hamburger, okay?"

Alvin did *not* look 'okay' with that. "We do not serve *hamburgers* here," he hissed.

"Well, I don't do raw fish."

"This is a sushi bar. What exactly were you expecting?"

"I don't— I just—" He broke off as his dining partner grabbed him by the wrist. The man glanced around, abruptly self-conscious of all the attention on him. His eyes locked briefly with Kara's before flitting away. His friend, meanwhile, was urgently stabbing at items on the menu and trying to placate Alvin.

"What a moron," Paul said, laughing.

Kara reached out and grabbed his hand, drawing his attention back to her. He flushed, obviously pleased with the physical contact. She decided she liked it too, and her own face turned crimson beneath the freckles.

All of a sudden, Kara felt like she was in high school again. Paul cleared his throat—twice—before finding something to say. "Listen, if you decide to change your focus," he offered, striving to be casual, "we'd love to have someone with your talents on our optics project." He cleared his throat again. "I mean, with your 3D modeling background, you could really take our brain function mapping to the next level."

Kara laughed, withdrawing her hand to tuck a strand of hair behind her ear. Paul looked disappointed, so she offered, "Hey, want to grab a movie after dinner?"

His eyes widened in triumph. "Sure!" He thought for a moment. "There's this great new action flick, *Return to Alcatraz*, about this special forces squad—" He stopped, suddenly unsure. "I mean, assuming you're into that sort of thing..."

"Sure," she enthused, "sounds great."

And so when Paul and Kara finished their meal, they walked five blocks to the nearest theatre and took in a movie. As it turned out, the movie was horrid, but they derived immense enjoyment from it anyway—poking fun at the absurdity of it all. And although there were very few people in that darkened theatre, the couple never realized that two of their fellow moviegoers had also come straight from the sushi bar... and those two men were laughing even more loudly at the movie's shortcomings than they were.

[Chapter 19]

Late October – Early November 2014

  The weeks that follow Kara and Gene's trip to DactiSoft are a flurry of activity. Gene spends far more time away from base than on, which is just as well since it makes for fewer awkward explanations in his meetings and communications with Williams' marketing people. Kara is mildly surprised to discover that Gene really is quite good at what he does; his slightly pretentious demeanor in their early discussions suggested a need to prove something, but as the Axmatik team grows comfortable working together, they increasingly seek his opinion, often deferring entirely to his suggestions.
  Meanwhile, Grant is ecstatic that Axmatik's sponsorship was purchased so easily. It seems his recent attempts to wrangle additional funding have fallen on deaf ears, though whose ears those may be is more than Kara is willing to guess. Despite now being privy to much more of the project, she has only heard one name in reference to their project's allocations; one day, when Grant was feeling especially depressed at the financial situation, she heard him speaking to himself: "I shouldn't have expected any differently. Novikov had it right."
  All in all, the subject of funding seems a tiresome one for Grant, so Kara avoids it, but it's clear that Grant doubts they'll be ready when the attack finally comes. The sentiment is understandable, considering that the first line of Destriers has yet to enter production. At least her design modifications have been completed, so the specs will be ready whenever approval finally comes through.
  In light of the fact that Kara will soon be reentering society—for the competition as well as, presumably, occasional meetings pertaining to her Axmatik consulting contract, which Grant approved—her need for personal security comes up almost immediately as a matter for reconsideration. During a long brainstorming session, she, Grant, and Stephens carefully craft a cover story that will not only help keep Kara's new association with Axmatik quiet, it will also help alleviate any of Jamie Miles'

lingering doubts regarding her uncharacteristic isolation from contact. As the story goes, starting in January, Kara began receiving disturbing anonymous messages on both email and voicemail. After finally calling the police about the matter, she was told she'd probably picked up a stalker, but that there was little investigators could do until the man either identified himself or committed a crime. Rather than wait around, Kara had abandoned much of her life in California and in February accepted the fictional research position she had described to Nate Williams. This cover story is brilliant in that it's simple, it's not terribly different from what actually happened, and—perhaps most importantly—it excuses the secrecy that's become part of Kara's life. It isn't all that hard to believe she can't reveal the name of her current employer or the nature of her research, what with the very real threat of corporate espionage these days. As for the stalker angle, it explains why Kara dropped out of contact, as well as the reticence she demonstrated in giving out her new email address.

When Kara nervously delivers the story to him via phone, Williams practically trips over himself assuring Kara of his understanding. As much as he wants to publicize their new collaboration, he agrees to reveal her involvement to just two project managers on the development team; these two will, in turn, be her only contacts vis-à-vis their contractual arrangement. Jamie Miles, though not directly involved in the ongoing project, is equally solicitous when Kara spins her story to him—so concerned is he, in fact, that Kara feels almost sick about the lies. She reminds herself, however, that she's lying only in the details, that there really *is* someone out there who wants her dead. Regardless, everyone agrees that her name will in no way be associated with the upcoming competition, and everyone understands—even if they consider it paranoia—why Kara refuses to attend except in disguise.

At the first opportunity, Kara pigeonholes Peterson and Stephens to ask if they've heard anything unusual about her old DactiSoft teammates, and the look they share is answer enough. It's no coincidence that these programmers were as inaccessible to Jamie Miles as Kara herself was—they have presumably been snatched up by "other interested parties," as Peterson puts it. "It should come as no surprise," he says, "considering they offer the same valuable insights you do." The two men assure her it's a developing situation that they're keeping tabs on.

Gene and his team throw together the competition in record time, scheduling it to begin less than a month after their discussion in Miles' office. Although Kara would expect surprise and resistance from Williams regarding the speed things are moving, he seems consistently pleased with every status report. The competition is to be a two-weekend affair, the first round held the second weekend of November at four sites across the country, the second and third rounds held the following weekend in Chicago at Axmatik's global headquarters. Gene's original plan called for that first round to be held in LA, Denver, Dallas, and New York City, but Nate Williams overrode Denver in favor of his main office. When Grant heard that Denver was being considered, he reacted with unexpected alarm, stating that Denver was out of the question, though he was unwilling to provide reasons. Between Grant's behavior and the news that begins coming out of the Mile High City as November commences, it's obvious he knows more than he's telling. And Kara begins to form a few suspicions as to the details.

Considering her renewed need for communication with the outside world, Kara is able to convince Grant to give her unfettered access to not just phone service but Internet and email access as well. Thus it is that she is able to follow the Denver situation with as much interest as the rest of the world. It starts with a drinking water scare, hundreds of children vomiting uncontrollably within an hour of taking sips from water fountains in school hallways. The cause of the reaction leaves the CDC people scratching their heads, even as things go from bad to worse; within three days, every bottle of water for sixty miles has been purchased. It seems that no bottled water has been shipped to Denver for over a week as a result of a logistics foul up—a foul up that somehow affected more than a dozen distributors simultaneously. What's more, these same companies seem to have trouble getting their systems to schedule future shipments. The whole thing results in a high tension situation that actually leads to isolated cases of looting; though the perpetrators are quickly arrested, it results in even more unrest among the law-abiding citizens. All the powder keg needs is a spark to set it off, but it gets a full-fledged firebrand in the form of a self-styled prophet named Vesuvius. When the media belatedly reports that this Vesuvius has been predicting the doom of the city for weeks, starting with the violation of their water, all hell breaks loose. Airlines and bus lines begin carrying the populace out in droves, and then the looting restarts in earnest. It's one of those situations that causes the rest of the country, watching the news safely from home in their bathrobes, to shake their heads in amazement that something like this could happen in the U.S. For those individuals, Kara among them, life goes on as usual.

On the bright side, Kara's access to a telephone allows her to actually speak with Viviane for the first time in almost nine months. She has harbored a small fear that Viviane and Gregoire would go forward with the wedding during her tenure with the military; Viviane can be spontaneous like that at times. As it turns out, however, Greg did indeed return to Versailles to care for his mother only a few months after Kara moved. Viviane is therefore just as much in need of Kara's encouragement as Kara is of Viviane's, even if Kara is unable to share the details of her current life. If anything, Kara feels as though their separation from one another has only strengthened their friendship.

One detail she most definitely *doesn't* share is that she may soon be deployed to outer space to defend against a vague military threat. Even she still has difficulty accepting that on most days. But Viviane's father, at least, proves to be someone Kara can confide in. High-ranking officer or not, there are times when he seems quite grandfatherly, and she mostly forgets some of the odd vibes she'd gotten from him in the early months of their association. With Grant, Kara is able to open up about some of her fears regarding actual combat. And for the most part, these interactions serve to reassure her, although one conversation in particular has the opposite effect.

Almost off-hand, Kara asks one day, "So who exactly is going to command these pilots in space?"

Grant is looking over her most recent report, and he shrugs, distracted. "The command chain is in place, my dear."

She freezes at this. "You don't mean that…"

Sensing her distress, he looks up, then squeezes his eyes shut in self-recrimination. "No, I'm sorry, Kara. I didn't mean to scare you." He returns to reading the report. "We would never place a person in such a position who was unprepared."

Placated, Kara lets the comment go... but on later reflection, she realizes Grant didn't outright say what she needed to hear—that Kara Dunn would *not* retain a command role in a combat environment. The realization feels like ice running through her veins, but she reassures herself: surely they would never expect her, a brand-new recruit, to actually lead troops in battle. Surely not.

Thursday and Friday
November 13-14, 2014

Kara surprises herself by thoroughly enjoying the first two days of the competition, which is scheduled across a long four-day weekend. Gene and the Axmatik team pushed the event so well that more than three thousand contestants signed up. The number of spectators who attend is nearly five times that, mostly families of contenders, but also some others who are attracted out of curiosity. Neither Kara nor her team of pilots participate themselves, content rather to wander the floor and watch, Kara adopting a different disguise each day.

Most of the Prometheus team is stationed in Chicago that first weekend, where Nate Williams has pulled out all the stops. The Axmatik campus is as well outfitted as any rich liberal arts college, and so it includes a massive convention hall of its own—nearly a quarter million square feet of open space that can be used for exhibits... or for piloting stations. The hundred stations at this, the largest of the competition sites, are equipped with the full contingent of eight screens. Since they take up a mere fraction of the convention hall's floor space, they have been spread out, interspersed with large displays where spectators can exercise some control over what is shown; in that fashion, family and friends can follow the fortune of loved ones in nearby carrels. Part of the remaining space is filled with food vendors, tables and chairs, and displays featuring Axmatik products and technology.

Even then, nearly half of the immense convention hall is still left unused, partitioned off by track-guided folding wall panels. In the center of the room, a large glass case encloses the two dozen high-end gaming computers that will be given as prizes to the pilots who make it to the final round the following weekend; their glossy black cases feature airbrushed representations of the various spacecraft from *Rampant*.

The first weekend of competition is highly forgiving, which allows for the minority of individuals who have never played the game to grow accustomed to it without being eliminated too quickly. Each pilot is assigned to a division with five other contenders, with game scenarios proceeding in a round-robin approach. At the end of each round—five missions played out over the course of four hours—the top three performers in each division advance and are reorganized into new divisions for the next round. In this fashion, each tournament location begins with upwards of 750 contestants on Thursday morning and will see that number whittled down to a single division of six contenders by Sunday evening, the end of the first weekend.

Mission scenarios fall into four categories—one-on-one dogfights, group furballs, convoy protection, and capital ship assaults—ensuring that each pilot has a chance to fly at least one of each type before being removed from play. Naturally the specifics and circumstances of each mission vary widely, generated at random from templates used by *Rampant*'s multiplayer functionality.

Unlike in traditional games or competitions, scoring is not based merely on the ratio of kills-to-deaths. Although there is definitely incentive to stay alive—namely, continuation in the competition—points are also awarded for tactics that promote mission completion, up to and including sacrificial maneuvers. Thus it is that some of the hot shot, hardcore gamers manage to maintain pristine kill-to-death ratios while nonetheless staying in the middle of the pack, much to their chagrin.

Of course, Kara and McLaughlin have carefully tweaked both the slow elimination and the scoring priority to reveal those pilots who have what it takes to fly for real. As Kara meanders among the carrels, ignoring the spectator displays in favor of watching the people operating the VR controls, she feels a nagging in the pit of her stomach that won't go away. To these men and women—some of them kids, really—this is just a game, with prizes for doing well. But the truth is that it's real, so very real, and for some of them the prize will be to die in quiet decompression in the dark of space; she tries not to dwell on this, however, as it strikes entirely too close to her own fears.

In a far corner of the convention hall, Kara comes across the twenty additional carrels set aside for the youth division. This offering for the teenagers, which in truth is an entirely separate competition, is the result of a compromise between Kara and Nate Williams. From the start, he wanted to test some new functionality that his developers had already thrown together, but Kara fought tooth and nail to keep the untested technology out of the competition; for one thing, it was unpredictable, but just as importantly it would skew pilot ranking if some missions incorporated the new options and others didn't. In the end, since the competition had until that point been for pilots 18 and older, they agreed to add the youth division to explore the modifications at the Chicago site alone. Now, as Kara watches the kids' performance, she is interested to see that the scenarios mostly pit pilots against identical craft, the storyline apparently one of civil war. This piques her interest, and she promises herself she'll find out more from Williams about the direction they're planning to go with the potential sequel.

Thursday passes quickly, as does Friday. Despite their efforts to slow things up, elimination nonetheless feels rapid, with half the contenders disappearing at the end of each morning and afternoon session. Gene gets his wish, as one of the major sports news networks sets up shop on Friday afternoon to provide commercial-free weekend coverage of the event... that is, if you can call the Axmatik convention hall, packed full of advertising, commercial-free. How much of the broadcast makes sense to television viewers is a question open to some debate, as the commentators tend to jump between matches quickly with little explanation, based solely upon what appears to be the most exciting. However, the interviews with the gamers are priceless. This is their moment in the sun, and they take the opportunity to enthusiastically describe intricate maneuvers and tactics, amid much hand waving, to the encouragement of their peers and the obvious confusion of the reporters.

Session 4 ends at 6 p.m. on Friday, and the carrels open up for free play by any interested party. At this point, seven out of eight pilots have been eliminated. With only a hundred contenders left at each location, Saturday's coverage will be much more focused on the true talent... as will the attention of Kara and her team.

Kara wanders about the exhibit hall, as she's done throughout much of the competition, observing the players taking advantage of Friday night free play. She stops to watch a young woman with bright purple hair display her considerable talent at the game; although everything about her is garish, from her hair to her clothes to her makeup, her movements are nevertheless graceful as she swoops around and blows two opponents out of the sky. Kara takes note of the carrel number and the time, intending to check into the girl, see if she would be a good candidate for targeted recruitment.

Stepping away, she rubs at her eye without thinking, and her finger comes away dark. Angry at herself, Kara draws a compact from her purse—an item she would never normally carry—and inspects herself in the tiny mirror. She barely recognizes the face looking back at her. Darker skin, heavily caked with makeup, the eyeliner and -shadow so thick and dark it changes the shape of her eyes entirely. Hazel contacts to cover her natural blue. Her hair has been uniformly darkened and braided into cornrows, which in turn changes the shape of her head by minimizing her hair's natural body. She smiles behind the uncharacteristically dark lipstick as she blots the smudge beneath her eye; she's pretty sure neither her father nor Viviane would recognize her even if they were expecting to see her.

Kara's stomach rumbles, reminding her it's about time for dinner. Looking around, she picks out a pizza vendor in a rolling cart against the back wall of the convention hall. It's not a solid wall, of course, formed instead of the louvered panels that can be moved to enlarge the main exhibit area; their competition simply hadn't needed the room. As Kara makes her way there, she doesn't bother checking for her shadows—the two men tasked with protecting her, plainclothes members of the Air Force Security Forces. On the off chance anyone were looking for her here, she would call far more attention to herself flanked by bodyguards than if they maintained their distance, as Grant reluctantly ordered them to do. Her best defense lies in the fact that she doesn't look like herself and is reportedly not in attendance.

She orders a bottle of water and a slice of sausage pizza, noting peripherally as a gap opens between the two wall panels behind the pizza cart. A uniformed workman emerges from the darkness and looks up at the ceiling, chatting quietly on a walkie-talkie as he tests how smoothly the panel rotates. Kara pays the vendor and turns to watch a nearby carrel while she waits.

A grimy hand suddenly clamps down over her mouth, and Kara is jerked backwards. "Hey, what—" she hears the vendor exclaim. "What are you—"

With a rattling crash, Kara's world is plunged into darkness. As if from a distance, she makes out muffled shouts and pounding, while closer at hand there are quick, furtive whispers. The hand disappears momentarily from her mouth as a flashlight suddenly blazes to life, directly into her eyes, but before she can more than breathe, something sticky is slapped down over her lips.

Kara's heart is pounding painfully against her chest and her head spins. The light dances off in another direction and she's dragged after it, the vice-like grip on each upper arm giving her little choice. Blinking back the disorientation, Kara sucks in air through her nose and yells at the top of her lungs; the soft chuckle that answers, right in her ear, is nearly as loud as her muffled shout. She tries throwing her legs out, kicking at the figures on either side, but that only leads to her being dropped. Moments later, she's being dragged again, this time with ankles taped as well.

Behind her, Kara can hear voices yelling—no longer muffled, but still distant. Sucking in deep breaths and pausing before letting them out, Kara slows her heart. The adrenaline is pumping and she's conscious of every extremity, but she realizes she's not scared... or at least, not scared stiff. She's easily as angry as she is frightened, and given the time to think, she seizes on that feeling.

Allowing her entire body to go limp, Kara makes it more difficult for her abductors to carry her by her arms. They have no trouble compensating, but while she takes the next several minutes to catch her breath, she begins to pick out some wheezing from her escorts. In all that time, they keep moving by the glare of the flashlight, sidling through gaps in the modular walls and, at one point, running down a long corridor with entrances to bathrooms. Finally they stop, throwing her roughly into a folding metal chair and taping her wrists to the metal bars of the chair back.

She looks around, trying in vain to identify her surroundings. Identical metal chairs stand folded and propped in rows as far as the eye can see—which isn't that far since the flashlight remains the only source of illumination. Distantly, some thought process concludes that they must have somehow sabotaged the fluorescents in this area of the convention hall, or by now her surely-frantic bodyguards would have brought everything online. She stops at that thought, listening hard, realizing she no longer hears shouting voices.

Abruptly, the tape is ripped from her mouth, and she lets out a momentary cry of pain before the hand slaps back over her mouth.

"Listen up," a gravelly voice barks in her ear. "Every wrong answer, you lose a finger. Same goes for screaming."

She coughs as the hand is removed. "So what? if you're just gonna kill me afterwards?" Kara bites out bravely.

The man grunts, and she can hear a chuckle from the other man, invisible behind the flashlight he holds. "Because," her interrogator rasps, "it'll be less painful that way."

"How did you find me?" she demands.

The blow to her face comes literally out of nowhere, followed by an explosion of white light in her retinas. She gasps, breathing in raggedly.

"I'm asking the questions," says the voice in her ear.

"Come on," she says, terrified, but playing for time as much as for info. "What does it matter if you tell? You're just gonna kill me."

She cringes in anticipation, and the blow comes again. She tastes blood as she coughs. So much for that.

"Question number one," the voice continues, and she stiffens at the touch of a cold blade to her left pinky. "What base are you operating out of?"

Kara swallows hard. "You already know the answer to that."

Another blow. "Last warning."

The blade presses into her skin, and without thinking she blurts, "Area 51!" She bites down on her own tongue then, angry, trying desperately to reassure herself that they probably already knew that, or else that the answer will seem ridiculous to them.

There's a long pause, but the knife doesn't press any further into her skin. "Good," says the thug approvingly. "I want access codes and passwords, starting with perimeter gate security, moving through the motor pool, all the way to your project bunker. *And*," he adds, as she gasps from a deeper press of the knife, "don't lie to me. I know the protocols better than you, so I'll know if you make something up. I also know you checked out a car and were passed through Gate 82 just last month, so you're familiar with the current code rotation."

Kara opens her mouth, but nothing comes out. She wracks her brain, but she's not sure she can provide the correct codes at this point, much less attempt to lie about them. "I—" She swallows. "I'm not sure if—" The knife digs deep, and Kara groans.

"Let me try," says a soft voice. The flashlight bobs closer, and Kara realizes it's the other man who has spoken. He hands off the light to the thug, who then steps back and trains it on her again. Her new interrogator kneels before her and grabs her wrists where they're taped to the chair's frame, then leans forward until his own face is visible. He locks his gaze on hers, and his eyes hold the sort of gleam she's always imagined characteristic of suicide bombers... or maybe it's just the glare of the flashlight. Finally he speaks, and his voice is still soft, modulated, even gentle. "Kara Dunn, I understand why you fight." He shakes his head. "But it's pointless. *K'lura* will take back what is theirs. We can either give it to them and live in peace... or we can die." Kara starts to speak, but he shushes her. "Don't be selfish. Consider all the lives you can save."

She doesn't answer. There's a long moment of silence before her interrogator leans back; the flashlight looms suddenly large before the thug's open hand lands once more. Spitting out blood now, Kara shakes her head to clear the stars, but they linger.

And as the soft-spoken one leans in again, a crazy idea occurs to her.

"You were correct earlier," the man continues mildly. "We cannot let you live. This is war, and you are a strategic enemy asset." His words, his enunciation, are very precise. "But before we kill you—humanely, of course—I hope you will make the right choice. We can neutralize the resistance at Groom Lake with a minimum of casualties, and that will be enough. No one else needs die after that, for there will be no hope of an American victory. The U.S. will simply retreat, as asked. Think of Viviane and Gregory and Sarah and Brady and Hannah, even Paul..." He smiles as he names many of her friends from California. "No matter your feelings for Paul, surely you wouldn't want to see him get hurt."

The silence lengthens once more, and with a sigh, the quiet man finally backs up again. And again, right on schedule, the flashlight lurches toward her. Except this time, Kara's ready—as the light comes within reach, she kicks out solidly, rising as far out of the chair as her taped hands will allow and pointing her bound feet right at that bright beacon. The thug's grip is strong, which is fortunate; as her feet connect, she hears a satisfying *crack!* and they are once more plunged into darkness.

And that's as far as her crazy plan went. From here on out, it's all improv, shored up by the confidence she's built in sparring sessions with Corporal Skewrs over the last several months.

Closing her eyes and focusing on her movements, Kara stands carefully and whirls, losing her balance again and going down as the attached chair connects with the flashlight-holder with a satisfying *clang!*. She manages to land in a sitting position once more. Pulling hard to separate her taped ankles, she experiences a surge of hope as her one of her thin leggings begins to split at the seams. Another hardy jerk, and her left leg is free of the fabric to which the tape remains stuck. She withdraws her now-bare foot, the low-heeled shoe lost early in her abduction, and jumps to her feet. A hand gropes at her calf, and she kicks where the associated face should be, earning a grunt of pain in response.

Chair still glued, in essence, to her rear end, Kara leaps in the direction she saw the other chairs folded and propped in rows. She collides almost immediately with them. Balancing on her right foot, she thrusts her left blindly into the collection, between chairs, pulling at them desperately. In the darkness, the sound of a few chairs clattering to the ground rings out, but it's not enough. She can also hear the grunting of two angry men picking themselves up off the ground. Near panic, clenching her teeth on the emotion that wants to burst free, Kara kicks again and again and then, finally, she feels the subtle shifting she's been hoping for, the start of a domino effect. Suddenly, the sound of falling chairs is cacophonous, growing louder and faster and, most importantly, *moving away*.

At that moment, Kara does the most difficult thing she can imagine doing in that situation. She very quietly lowers herself once more into a sitting position on the chair.

One of the men lets out a savage curse, and his voice is so loud she can almost feel his proximity through the darkness... but then the angry voices begin moving away, chasing her phantom form as it wildly knocks down chairs in a desperate bid to escape.

Pulling hard now, Kara begins working at the bonds holding her hands, gritting her teeth as the tape pulls her skin. Adopting an up-down motion, she senses that the tape on her left wrist has begun rolling. Just a little bit more, and she should be able to rip free.

And then the unthinkable happens—the ceiling lights finally come to life.

Looking up through dazed eyes, Kara sees the two men clearly for the first time, and they're not nearly as far away as she'd hoped. Whipping their heads around, they quickly locate her, and the fanatical visage they share sends a chill straight up her spine.

The big man, the thug, is just feet away when she finally jerks her left hand free. Standing and whirling a full $360°$, Kara swings the metal chair—still attached to her other wrist—right into his face. The man drops like a rock, letting out an extended scream that tells her she inflicted serious pain. She jumps back out of his reach, swinging the chair again, now at the smaller man. She misses, but with a tearing sound and a great deal of pain, the chair finally rips free.

She cocks back with her right fist as if to throw a monumental punch, but as the little man counters by leaning in, her left foot comes up in a limber kick to connect with his chin. There's barely enough power in it to stun him, but it's all she needs as she then replants that foot and pivots for a solidly-delivered right sidekick to the gut, relying thoughtlessly now on her training. The crunching sound that accompanies her foot's landing suggests she broke at least one rib. Angry now, she kicks him wildly in the face one more time as he drops.

Spinning on her heel, she locates the nearest gap in a wall and flees in that direction. *Clack!* The loud metallic sound comes from behind her, and she feels something whip past her face, even as a big hole magically appears in the louvered wall before her. Changing direction instinctively, she makes for another opening between walls, running for all she's worth. *Clack!* the sound rings out again, another hole appearing in yet another wall nearby. It's only then that Kara realizes someone must be firing a *gun* at her.

As she dives through the gap, there are two more shots, one exploding all the way through the flimsy wall material behind her and into the new room she's entered, knocking over a nearby chair. Rising up again, Kara takes in the most unexpected and joyous sight imaginable: a petite, sandy-haired young woman standing frozen not fifteen feet away—with a drawn pistol in her hand. Anna Haynes. With a sudden surge of hope and a grin as fierce as the anger on Anna's face, Kara throws herself further in the other direction with a deliberately loud groan. She rolls over in time to see her interrogator, the big guy with the gravelly voice, tear through the opening far closer on her heels than she'd guessed. His head jerks left at the unexpected sight of another person, but Anna doesn't give him any more time than that.

Boom! Boom! There's nothing quiet about the bullets that tear into the large man's chest. He stares at Anna in shock for a long moment before he totters and falls. Kara leaps up and toes the man's gun carefully out of his limp hand before bending over and retrieving it; Anna, meanwhile, is at the opening, easing an eye into the next room.

"See him?" Kara asks, breathing hard.

"Nope. Just one more?"

Kara nods.

Anna turns and runs a critical eye over her, and Kara realizes how bad she must look, battered and bruised. "Stay here," the other woman suggests. Then, without waiting, she moves through the door.

Within half a minute, Kara hears Anna's yell of "Freeze!" followed immediately by two more booming shots.

"Kara?"

She turns in surprise to see John McLaughlin approaching her, handgun at the ready. "C'mon," she tells him, and together they pass through the next room into the one where Kara had been taped to the chair. Anna is standing over the supine form of the soft-spoken man.

She turns at their appearance, fury still etched on her plain features. "I tried to take him alive," she complains, nudging the body. "Took him in the shoulder." Turning, she punches the wall in frustration. "I didn't know anyone actually *made* suicide pills. I thought that was movie crap."

With surprise, Kara looks down on the face of the man, still foaming at the mouth and rapidly turning blue. She looks up at McLaughlin, then again at Anna, at a total loss for words. Then, utterly exhausted, she gingerly hands McLaughlin the gun and drops heavily back into her interrogation chair.

Returning to the main exhibit hall, Kara marvels at the fact that barely forty-five minutes have passed since she purchased her uneaten pizza. More amazingly, no one outside of her team ever became aware of the deadly game playing out practically under their noses. By the time Kara's detail had gotten through the locked wall panels, she and her abductors were so far gone into the warren of unlit rooms and corridors that her people weren't sure which way to go. Grant had called in the rest of the team and put them under McLaughlin's command for a coordinated search, while Grant himself harried the facilities supervisor about bringing up the lights in the unused areas of the building.

"She's my favorite granddaughter, and she's just wandering around all by herself," he had whined repeatedly, maintaining the man's sense of urgency. It was twenty minutes before the supervisor finally found the disconnect that had prevented him from raising the lights. Twenty minutes during which Kara had been interrogated, escaped, and fought her captors, and during which her team had stumbled carefully in the pitch black, listening in vain for out-of-place sounds in an area over a hundred thousand square feet divided into scores of rooms. Anna had been the one to hear the clattering of Kara's chair dominoes.

Locating Grant, Kara moves in his direction, flanked much more closely now by the bodyguards—both of whom remain shame-faced. McLaughlin, Anna Haynes, and the others remained behind with the bodies, and Stephens was coordinating with them by phone when she left; with any luck, the facilities management people would never find anything more inexplicable than two large stains in the garishly patterned carpet. Grant stands now on the fringes of a group surrounding Gene Jenkins, among them a dozen or more reporters with microphones. Grant, dressed incongruously in street clothes, has his cell phone plastered to one ear as he turns in her direction. His face, rigid with stress, loses only some of its tension as he catches sight of her. He merely nods, turning away again.

It's not at all the welcome Kara expected from him, but she shakes it off as she watches Gene begin fielding questions. Absently, she clasps and unclasps her hands, intertwining fingers, happy to still have ten of them. Looking at Gene, it's clear he remains completely oblivious of how she spent the last half hour. He catches her eye and smiles, and she's glad she took the time to clean up and cake another pound of make-up over the bruises before reappearing. It would be refreshing to take in something as mundane as a press interview.

Unfortunately, it becomes immediately clear that for all of Gene's talent, his confidence, even his pluck when speaking with the rich and powerful, the man has zero aptitude in front of the camera. And yet, paradoxically, he just as clearly thrives on the attention.

"Mr. Jenkins, a question for you!"

"Y-yes, of course!" Gene is sweaty and rosy-cheeked, which on a man of his complexion is quite an accomplishment.

"Can you please tell us a bit more about how this competition came about? Where did you get the idea?"

Gene beams for the cameras. "Oh, well, Kara and I—that's Kara Dunn, the gal who designed the game—she and I met each other at a hotel in Vegas. That's where we—" Suddenly his face goes slack and his color drains as he realizes how that may sound. "No! What I mean," he laughs suddenly, "is that me and her, er, she and I met there with a group. Gamers. *Rampant* gamers. A bunch of people who played a lot together but never met each other in person. But," he adds, belatedly remembering Kara's incognito status, "I'd like to stress that Kara had no involvement in the planning after that. And she's *definitely* not here today." He looks directly at her as he says this, and Kara just closes her eyes tiredly. "As for the rest of the folks, *don't*"—Gene holds up a hand suddenly—"ask me their names, because then I'd have to kill you." He chuckles nervously, then adds for clarification, "I'm happily married, you know." And he glares at the half dozen reporters, as if daring them to contradict him.

For a moment, they seem as nervous with the interview as Gene does, which ironically seems to calm Gene. Judging by the self-satisfied smile he adopts, one which Kara has come to know well, she suspects he's pleased with his perceived success at fending off probing questions.

"Um, Mr. Jenkins, about the competition," one reporter finally hazards. "In short, *why?* I mean, clearly it's a success," he waves his hand about the hall, "though based on game sales, I wouldn't have thought it likely."

Gene is beaming once more. He taps his head self-importantly as he says, "To be successful at event promotion, you must understand a bit about human psychology; I was a psych minor in college, you know." He attempts to smile in a sophisticated manner, to dubious effect, considering the twitch that has seized his right eye. A few of the reporters begin glancing around, clearly hoping to find someone better to interview. Sensing his audience escaping, Gene says hurriedly, "As to your other question, we thought it important to identify the next generation of pilots, the men and women who will defend our American way of life when we're attacked by the invaders from outer space." He smiles nervously and actually winks at Kara, "All in the game, of course."

Kara groans audibly, and she feels a hand grip her upper arm; she glances over to see Grant, now off his phone. "We need to cut this short," he growls. "Grab that idiot and let's get out of here."

"But what about—" she begins to protest.

"Your cover doesn't matter anymore—it's happened."

She frowns. "*What*'s happened?"

He waves dismissively and begins dialing another number. Kara turns to look him full in the face, and she's struck anew at his appearance. The man is white as a sheet and uncharacteristically grim. "It's happened"—those were his words... and she realizes that whatever happened, it was really, really bad.

"Okay," she responds, turning back towards Gene. He's now telling the cameras how the new game will explain the origins of Area 51. From the surprise exhibited by Nate Williams, who has been drawn to the cameras like a mosquito to fresh blood, it's clear that this particular plot point is news to him.

It's anyone's guess what Gene might have said next, but even as Kara grabs his arm to pull him away from the cameras, everyone's attention is diverted by the sudden, almost-simultaneous ringing of half a dozen cell phones. The sound grows in the moments that follow as more phones join the symphony.

Slapping shut his own phone once more, Grant turns and begins steering Kara and Gene away from the crowd. "We're leaving," he hisses.

"What?" Gene demands, confused. "Why?"

Quietly, Kara asks, "What's happened?" as she tries to catch Grant's eye.

Grant heaves a sigh. "The attack has come." Grant's gait stalls momentarily, and he turns to look at her. The rigid set of his face cracks, and for an instant she sees a play of emotion: grief, anger, guilt. His eyes are bright as he says, "They hit Denver."

[Chapter 20]

The 35-foot-long unmarked matte-black projectile, fired from orbit, enters Earth's atmosphere for the first time at 8:35 p.m. MST and within two minutes reaches maximum velocity, over 2,000 miles per hour. Its movement is detected almost immediately by radar defense systems, and yet just three minutes after launch, it has already dropped to an altitude of 900 meters above the Mile High City—where it detonates.

The air surrounding the device is almost immediately superheated to millions of degrees by the release of thermal radiation. This fireball expands rapidly, and where it encounters the tops of the first skyscrapers, they are quite literally vaporized.

The force of this outward expansion forms a shockwave within the fireball, but after just a fraction of a second, this wave has burst beyond; the momentary obscuring of the fireball by the expanding pressure front causes the characteristic double pulse of light so long associated with a nuclear detonation. Even miles away, humans looking the *other* direction are temporarily blinded by this release; those looking directly at it are blinded for life.

The well-tended greens of the Denver Country Club cease to exist as the shockwave reaches the ground directly beneath the explosion's hypocenter. The awesome force of this wave expands into the surrounding downtown area, and even the quakeproof foundations of the newer buildings are utterly destroyed.

In just eighteen seconds, this pressure front has flattened every non-reinforced building for two miles in every direction. The majestic edifice of the Cathedral Basilica, which has stood for more than a century, simply collapses. Cars are hurled off Valley Highway.

The bodies of humans who somehow survive the danger of falling buildings and flying objects are no less affected. Any person close-in to the hypocenter is simply incinerated by the fireball, which grows to a mile and a half across. Outside of that, the shockwave rips muscle from bone as it passes through human tissue, also causing immediate hemorrhaging of the lungs and stomach. At the outer edge of the still expanding perimeter, eardrums burst. And even after all this, most will experience third-degree burns and take in enough radiation to kill them within 24 hours.

At twenty-eight seconds past detonation, the shockwave has definitely slowed, now moving only 300 miles per hour rather than 13,000, as it had in that first half-second. This is still enough pressure to pulverize every window it meets, and every shard becomes a killing tool. The three-story glass façade of the Colorado Convention Center blows back and flays the hundreds of people flocking to the lobby to stare down 14th Street, where the rising mushroom cloud is visible over the city.

Exactly two minutes after detonation, to the second, the shockwave reaches I-70 to the north. By now, many motorists have pulled to the shoulder to stare in shock, but others have sped up, attempting to get away. The hurricane-force wind that blows into them—still traveling 100 miles an hour—causes countless accidents. Those drivers able to regain control in the wake of the blast nevertheless lose power steering, just moments later, as their vehicles' electronics are fried by electromagnetic radiation. This burst of radiation is produced by gamma rays from the explosion itself, and as it follows behind the shockwave, it destroys every circuit board it encounters and causes voltage surges in power lines.

It is five whole minutes before blast winds drop to mere gale force, with impact from flying debris now resulting in serious injuries rather than death. The continuing effects of thermal radiation cause combustible materials to burst into flames, and exposed humans sustain first- and second-degree burns, but the temperature of the wave front is also beginning to fall. The electromagnetic burst, however, continues. Eight miles, nine miles, ten miles from the hypocenter before it tapers off. From the origin to that 10-mile mark, every light winks out and every moving vehicle careens out of control as the electromagnetic pulse expands.

Even still, the deaths continue.

Twenty-eight miles distant, Denver International Airport is safe from the immediate effects of the blast, as are the aircraft on its tarmac. Not so for the dozens of airliners in the process of taking-off, landing, or simply holding in air. Fifteen of these are caught in the electromagnetic burst, and they tumble from the sky, instantly killing all passengers and leaving deep furrows of destruction across areas of Denver otherwise unaffected.

And even *then*, the weapon is not done killing. Even after all other movement has ceased, after the shockwave has dissipated, the dust has yet to settle. The radioactive particles forming a cloud above the city have already begun drifting northwest on a gentle breeze. As that cloud moves eight miles over the next six hours, fallout will result in vomiting and eventual hair loss, destruction of bone marrow, or death for those downwind. The men, women, and children who survive will face a long-term risk of cancer. But only half of the radiocontaminants will land in the local area over the next 24 hours. The cloud will persist even as it is blown far and wide, fallout occurring on a much less noticeable level even hundreds of miles away over the month that follows, causing more damage to the ecosystem than can ever truly be determined.

This is not a blockbuster disaster flick. This is not entertainment for the masses. This is the reality of nuclear detonation over a major population center: 40,037 dead only ten minutes after the missile is first detected; another 10,705 dead within the next week; countless more who will live with disfigurement or cancer in the years that follow.

And yet when compared to the vast array of nuclear weapons humans have constructed in the last century, for the express purpose of killing one another, the four-foot wide, 250-kiloton warhead that caused all of this ranks as only *moderately* destructive.

The End of Book One

Day 143 of Incarceration

Interrogation Room #3, Bosman-Alpha Facility
30°06'27" N, 95°10'19" W – Elev. sea level
  (49 feet below ground)

The room is dirty, nasty. Row upon row of 6-inch lime green tiles cover each wall, stretching from floor to ceiling, the grout between tiles black with mildew. Many of the squares are cracked or missing entirely. The floor... it's best not to look closely at the floor. Water drips steadily somewhere nearby, and an analog clock tick-tocks a steady cadence detectable by keen ears.

The prisoner has keen ears. Of the five senses, hearing remains the strongest; smell and tactile touch were damaged irreparably in the fire.

The fire at the crash site.

A faint squeak sounds from a corner of the room—a rodent? The prisoner shifts forward to relieve one of many aches and pains, the movement causing a soft rattle in the chains binding hands and feet to chair.

A throat clears, and the prisoner's blue eyes snap open. These eyes are sharp, intelligent, pained... set deep in a mottled face crisscrossed by scars and bandages.

"And why should we trust you?" *Across a small table from the prisoner sit three men; the speaker, red-faced and perpetually angry, is between the other two. All are pale-skinned, middle-aged, in uniform, but the speaker has the biggest splash of color across his chest.*

The prisoner winces at the question, forehead wrinkling. On top, where hair should be, there is only rough, brown stubble sprouting in patches. "Why should you... distrust... me?" *The questions and answers always return to this point.*

The man in the middle scowls. "What were you doing here? I don't suppose you crash landed your spaceship on purpose, just so you could bring us this warning."

"No..." *The prisoner winces again. Cerebral trauma was severe, and thinking, remembering, remains both difficult and painful.* "My ship was damaged, in the battle. I told you."

"Right, by... what did you call them? Kay-loo-ran spaceships?"

"*K'luran.* Yes." *The voice was melodic once, but now it is rough, gravelly—vocal cords damaged, like the rest of the prisoner's body.*

"And why were they shooting at you?"

An angry gleam appears in the shackled creature's eyes. "As I've told you, I was stationed in orbit, defending this planet."

"You and your faction of the military."

"We are hardly a *faction*—"

"Whatever. So they just shot you down last month, but they're going to hold off on actually attacking the planet."

"I know it's hard to believe, but none of this will happen for another thirty years, including—"

"Let's back up and talk about you again. You claim to be a friend."

The prisoner jerks forward against the chains, almost furious. "Look at me. Listen to what I'm telling you. How can you doubt me?"

"Oh, well, I don't know." *The man examines his fingernails.* "You *did* shoot your nifty gun at my soldiers. Around here, we call that an attack—not the sort of thing friends do." *He shakes his head.* "I don't know where you learned English, but you're obviously confused on some of the finer points."

"I am *not* your enemy. I made a mistake… I thought your men were—"

The man just talks louder. "Okay, fine, we'll assume you're my new best friend. You were protecting Earth from invaders. So why *do* your Kay-loo-rans want to invade?"

"*K'lurans.*" *The prisoner breathes deeply, causing a new, wracking chest pain.* "How many times will you ask the same questions?"

"Until I'm satisfied with the answers. *Why?*"

Angry, the gaunt figure tries to shift in the chair, grunting in pain. "This planet belonged to the *K'lurans*… first. Before there were humans."

"Of course. And now the Kay-loo-whatever want it back?"

"Just North America."

"Well that's right generous of them. Doesn't do *me* a whole lotta good."

The prisoner's head jerks back and forth, frustrated. "That's why you need to prepare! I can help. And... and the technology in my ship. You have time, before the first Zenith."

"Right, your Zeniths. Let's talk about that. Tell me again when the first is supposed to happen?"

The prisoner sighs, a very human sound. "November... 2014, I think."

The interrogator scoffs, again, as he's done every time he gets this answer. "Sure. Just thirty years from now. Can't you give us an exact date while you're at it?"

Dates... details. The prisoner finds them hardest to remember, harder than anything. For a long moment, the poor figure cuffed to the chair is distracted by the surrounding stimuli: the ticking clock, the dripping water, the offensive colors. Then—

"Hello?" *The interrogator waves a hand.* "Do you read me?"

"I'm trying to picture the timeline in my head... I'm sorry. I can't remember the exact date."

The man grunts, exasperated. "You're missing my point. How—"

One of the other men, usually silent, interrupts. "Sir, this isn't unreasonable." *He gestures at the prisoner.* "Loss of memory regarding specifics—like dates—is a commonly documented side effect of head trauma in humans."

The man in the middle grows even angrier. "You're not here to talk, Captain. Shut your flap."

"Yes, sir."

The interrogator turns back to the prisoner, but the willowy figure—eyes clenched in concentration—speaks first. "I'm trying, believe me. I have to work backwards... The final offensive will come in May 2016. I know that for sure. And—"

"That's when this fleet of yours arrives."

"Yes... although smaller elements will begin arriving in the months leading up to that. Some of them will carry nuclear warheads, and they'll target cities within the *K'luran* tract."

"*Which* cities?"

The grimace deepens. "I never found out. As long as you intercept them before—"

"Helpful as always," *the caustic reply cuts in.*

"These smaller elements are your little black ships? The triangular airframes?" *the other man, the nicer man, asks in genuine interest.* "The... Nymphs you've told us about?"

"Yes—" the prisoner begins.

"Captain, kindly *shut up*."

"Yessir."

The prisoner is speaking again. "But working backward... I know the second Zenith attack happens the previous August. Their plan is to target Chicago, but—"

"Yes, yes, August 2015. And before that?"

"The previous November. The first Zenith."

"Which would be November 2014. Denver." *The heavy silence stretches long.* "And you're telling me they'll attack without warning? Without provocation?"

"Yes. They will send a message to the world at the second Zenith, claiming that warnings were given. But it's propaganda—intended to undermine resistance, erode public trust in the government."

"You seem awfully sure of all this."

"Trust me, that's how it will happen." The bound figure leans forward, the scarred face earnest. "I've seen it—I can tell you—"

"I think that's enough for now." *A long silence follows, broken only by tick-tocking and dripping.* "I just don't buy it. You spin this story about an invasion, but you can't give me any details—"

"*What?*"

"And thirty years away?" the man forges on. "As a career military man, I can tell you, planning in detail that far in advance is asinine. Hard to believe anyone would do it. Hell, I'm not sure who my enemies'll even *be* in thirty years. *Back* thirty or forty years, it was us and the Russians fighting the Nazis; now the Germans are our allies against the Russkies."

"This goes *far* beyond planning. This is established. This is *fact*, I just—"

Again, the objections are completely ignored. "I don't doubt you're who you say you are. How can I? Your level of technology is beyond what we've seen anywhere. But this timeline of yours? This supposed future war, set in stone—"

"I didn't say that! Let me help you prepare!"

"No." *The word is firm, final, absolute.* "I don't believe you."

"But why would I lie?"

"Make yourself seem useful? Valuable? To get better treatment? If *any* part of what you say is true, you're stuck here—you can never go back." *He leans forward, his face nothing short of malevolent.* "What matters is, I don't trust you." *He leans back.* "I think it's time we tried more effective forms of questioning."

"Sir!" *The other man speaks out again.* "You can't—"

"What did I tell you—"

"No. The general would never approve, and I'll make sure he knows."

"You listen to me, you upstart. Just because of your success in Suffolk—"

The prisoner's eyes squeeze closed. Keen hearing and raised voices only multiply the never-ending headache, and the argument grows heated, stretching on, and on, and on.... "Stop! Just… stop. Please." *The figure looks so small in that moment, cuffed to the chair, looking up beseechingly. The eyes focus on the man challenging the interrogator, and something flickers there… Recognition?* "From now on…"—*breathe*—" I talk to no one…"—*breathe*—"but *him*." *The eyes, so clear and bright, refocus on the man in the middle.* "Not you, never again."

The man laughs. "Sorry, but you're not in a position to negotiate. Now, Johnson, have Samuels prepare for—"

A new voice sounds from above: "Harrell, all of you. A word in the hall."

The interrogator's red face grows pale, and the three exit. The prisoner relaxes, if only slightly, and the clock ticks and tocks at length before one man finally returns. The nicer man—the… familiar man.

"Apparently you *do* have some negotiating power." *He smiles, just a little.* "Here, let me get those cuffs off you… On behalf of the U.S. Government, I am sincerely sorry for the treatment you have received up 'til now. The questions, the repetition, it was all necessary… but your story has remained consistent. Not that it makes any difference to Colonel Harrell…" *The man chuckles.* "I'm sorry, I'm Captain Carl Grant. I'm now your primary liaison." *He affects a light air, but his face is concerned as he finishes with the restraints and sits back on his heels; he inspects the various wounds on his new charge's battered face.*

As the chains fall free, a three-fingered hand comes forward tentatively... then rests lightly on the man's cheek. The man chuckles nervously. "Um, let's go get you cleaned up."

BOOK TWO
PROMOTION

Energiya launch system employs four RD-170 strap-on rocket boosters around a massive fuel core; a premise similar to that used by NASA's STS, but on a much larger scale

Canards offer pilot greater maneuverability and finesse on reentry

Energiya's expendable launch system and booster originally developed by the Soviet Space Program, resulting in only a single successful launch

Embarkation via gantry access through two hatches

Debarkation (both scheduled and emergency) via any of the four hatches

Wings and Fuselage constructed primarily from a proprietary Aluminum Alloy

cabin windows scratched from final ODC order due to cost overruns

Conventional aircraft flap design provides control for atmospheric reentry and landing

Cockpit Crew of 6:
Commander
Pilot
Co-pilot
Navigator
Relief Pilot
Mission Specialist

Maximum Passenger Capacity: 204

swept-back cropped delta-wing design

Propulsion Systems follow same principles used in shuttle program's SSMEs

Engine structure composed of Titanium Alloy

Energiya system conceptualized 1976, developed by Soviet Union 1976-1987

Longship orbiter conceptualized 1997, developed in secret by American company "Out of this World Tours" 1999-2014 under code name "Galera Vickeengov"

Energiya Launch System with
LONGSHIP
Reusable Orbiter

*If you know the enemy and know yourself,
    you need not fear the result of a hundred battles.
If you know yourself but not the enemy,
    for every victory gained you will also suffer a defeat.
If you know neither the enemy nor yourself,
    you will succumb in every battle.*

~ Sun Tzu, *The Art of War*

I recently learned something quite interesting about video games. Many young people have developed incredible hand, eye, and brain coordination in playing these games. The Air Force believes these kids will be outstanding pilots should they fly our jets.

~ Ronald Reagan
Orlando, Florida
March 8, 1983

[Chapter 21]

**Friday evening
November 14, 2014**

The sleek aircraft is already taxiing by the time Grant leads Kara to facing seats in the midsection of the craft, which has seating for about twenty. Gene has been instructed to remain in the back row with McLaughlin, who, to add insult to injury, takes the aisle seat. The rest of the Prometheus personnel remain in Chicago. Satisfied that they have all the privacy they'll get, Grant indicates that Kara can finally ask the question that's been burning ever since his announcement about Denver.

Except by now, it's no longer a question. "You *knew!*" she hisses, furious.

His eyes widen slightly at the anger writ large on her features.

"You knew the place, you knew the time! You didn't want us running the competition in Denver this weekend! How could you—"

"No," he cuts in quietly. "I knew the place, but I didn't know the time. Not exactly." Grant pauses for another accusation, but Kara's willing to listen. Ready for answers. He sighs. "Kara, we've known for thirty years this attack would come. We knew it would hit Denver this November. As for the specific date, our... source of intel... was never sure."

She's speechless. Thirty *years?* Before she can say anything, the copilot steps out of the cockpit and hands Grant a slim folder covered with numerous dire warnings about the consequences of unauthorized reading.

"Thank you," he says, and the uniformed woman returns to the front. He skims the report, eyes narrowing, then sighs.

"What?"

"It's not as bad as we feared," he responds.

"It's not?"

He catches her hopeful expression. "Oh, it's still very bad."

"How many... died?"

"It's too early to know," he says, shaking his head. "But satellite photography reveals the destruction is much more contained than I'd expected." He sighs again. "But it was a nuclear weapon… The city has been devastated."

"Who launched it? It was an ICBM, right?"

"The warhead was delivered by missile, yes," Grant confirms while evading her real question. He pulls off his glasses and rubs the bridge of his nose, eyes closed. "Launched from orbit, as we knew it would be."

"So who was it? Who attacked us?"

Grant sighs again. "It wasn't a foreign nation, Kara."

"Terrorists? But which—"

"Aliens, Kara." He says the word slowly, enunciating each syllable.

She stares at him for a long moment, frozen, because that word is incongruous. It doesn't belong in a serious discussion of war and death unless denoting something other than 'extraterrestrial'—and it takes that long moment for Kara's suddenly sluggish mind to confirm that Grant doesn't mean the word in any other sense. Nor is there any trace of a smile on his face. "*Aliens*," she repeats dumbly, only beginning to accept that he's dead serious. For Kara the skeptic, the concept of extraterrestrials has always been a lighthearted one belonging to fantasy and entertainment; to lay the deaths of countless people at the feet of *aliens* is therefore… irreverent. It sounds like a bad cliché, not an authentic headline. The idea of this happening in the real world, innumerable *real* lives being snuffed out in an instant by creatures of myth… it cheapens those deaths. It makes her angry.

But Carl Grant's steady eyes confirm his absolute belief that space-faring *aliens* committed this atrocity. At length, he asks, "Have you ever heard of Rendlesham Forest?" She shakes her head, and he sighs. "About thirty years ago—no, almost thirty-four years now—a spacecraft crash-landed in a forest in Suffolk, England. An honest-to-goodness unidentified flying object. Between the heightening tensions of the Cold War and the growing number of UFO claims worldwide, the Air Force had dedicated immense resources to investigating any reports of airborne phenomena. I was team leader for one of several commando units that would respond to these reports—and it was my team that was assigned this one." Pause. "You look confused."

Kara finds her voice. "Even thirty years ago… you can't have been young. But you were leading commandos?"

Grant can't help but chuckle. "That's one of the things I love about you, Kara. I tell you about a UFO crash landing, but you seize on a far subtler detail. Bravo." He sighs again as his smile fades. "I was forty-five at the time. Not old, though certainly the oldest on the team. But we were specialists… and I was looking for answers. Twice I had refused promotion, because it would have taken me out of the field—and I wanted to be there when we finally made that big discovery. I wanted to see it in person.

"Well, that time, I did." He settles his aging frame back into the seat, eyes flicking out the window and off into the distance. "It was the night of Christmas, 1980, and I was alone as usual. Quarter way through a bottle of scotch when the call came. There'd been a sighting in southern England just a few hours before, around nine or ten local time. Hundreds—maybe thousands—had seen what looked like a meteor streaking out of the western sky, trailing flame." He steeples his fingers. "We had two Air Force bases there at the time, rented from the Brits, and our people had seen something too, had seen what looked like a fire in the forest just outside one of the bases. A patrolman had gone out to investigate… and he reported he'd found something. Sleek, black, swept-back wings. He even touched it before it lifted off, silent as a ghost, disappearing into the night. Oddly enough, said it felt almost like fabric.

"The facts didn't fit, but it didn't matter. Six hours later, my team was on a plane, and ten hours after that, we'd arrived on the scene—unbeknownst to our people there. We began our search just before dusk… and that was the night we met KLINE."

"Kline?" Kara asks.

Grant nods, still staring out the window. "Our codename, for the pilot of the downed craft. And what a sight, too. Badly injured in the crash: suffering from head trauma, severe facial burns, numerous broken bones." He shakes his head, eyes distant. "I'll never forget that nightmarish face, never get it out of my mind. But those eyes… those large, shockingly blue eyes…"

He seems to slip into a reverie for a few moments, and when he returns, it is with obvious difficulty. He speaks almost casually, but it seems forced. "The poor soul was terrified. Fought like a cornered animal, firing repeatedly and injuring three of my men. But my troops had strict orders: non-lethal force only. I was not going to lose this prize. Finally, after an hour-long chase through the woods in the dark, we connected with a tranq round.

"We found where KLINE's ship, badly damaged, had finally come to rest, and by the end of the next day we had removed every trace of it. That was the 27th. Barely twenty-four hours had passed since our arrival, and we were winging our way back across the Atlantic with our first recovered UFO and its pilot, safely sedated." He smiles wanly. "Our boys stationed at the British air bases never even knew we'd been there. There was an investigation, of course; they knew *something* had happened in the woods that night, and we had a few close calls with one of their search parties while we were sanitizing the area. They even found the crash site later—we couldn't hide the burn marks or the damage to the trees. But when they eventually told the world their story, especially the part about chasing after lights in the forest, it was hard to take them seriously. After all, there was a lighthouse just a few miles away on the coast, and it was only too easy to believe *it* responsible for what they thought they saw."

Grant is now in full story-telling mode. Angry though she is, and scared too, Kara drinks in every word. She knows she hasn't been cleared for any of this, and she's not about to interrupt.

"Of course, it almost fell apart two days later, back in the States. The... 29th. We were transporting our cargo—first by air, then by rail—to a classified installation not far from Houston. The last leg of the journey, under cover of night, the container was airlifted by a half-dozen big choppers to the base, fifteen miles from the closest bend in the railroad.

"Unfortunately, we were seen, by several groups of people. By itself, that wasn't an issue, but... Well, because of concerns about alien bacteria, my people and KLINE were in quarantine; the cargo container holding the wreckage was also being continually sprayed down with a chemical neutralizer. Heavy-duty weed killer, in essence. No one really knows for sure, but we think three of those witnesses were misted as we flew directly over them.

They all complained of a burning sensation, experienced health problems for the rest of their lives. Problem is, they went public about it. Sued the government for millions. They lost, but it drew unwanted attention to the area where we were conducting research, eventually necessitating relocation to Groom Lake."

He pauses again, even longer this time. "Nevertheless, we weathered that storm. KLINE was kept in an induced coma for more than a month while our people treated the burns and trauma... and tried to decide what to do."

Kara clears her throat. "Your first introduction to alien anatomy, and you just waded right in. Sounds like the military."

Grant shakes his head. "KLINE was in bad shape, and there was extensive head trauma. Our doctors did the best patch-up job they could. Besides," he offers a wry smile, "you'd be surprised at the similarities to human anatomy.

"In any case, after awakening, KLINE had several long talks with us. That was how we learned about today's attack, about a whole campaign that would be waged against our world, and especially against the people living in North America."

"What, he just told you?" Despite the gravity of the situation—or perhaps because of it—Kara entertains the image of a little gray man flashing a rude hand gesture and saying in a nasally voice, *Your doom is upon you. And by the way, we'll start by attacking Denver in November of 2014. Just so you know.*

Grant snorts. "I use the word 'talk' euphemistically. 'Interrogation' would be more accurate. It never got violent, but it wasn't very nice either. After several months, though, two things happened. First, the officer in charge of the operation decided to take KLINE at face value, tentatively at least, accepting our guest's warnings about the attack that would come someday." He sighs forlornly. "The attack that came *today*. And second, KLINE refused to speak with anyone except me ever again." Grant smiles sadly, wistfully. "It was my ticket up the promotion ladder, the ticket I'd been avoiding until then. We eventually became great friends, remaining close right up until... well, until KLINE's death a couple years later."

For a moment, at least, Kara's anger is dulled in the face of this man's pain, evident even after all these years. "That must have been about the same time you lost your wife."

Grant's face falls at the mention of his wife. "Yes, Callie... KLINE... it was a rough couple of years." Then he brightens slightly. "But in the end, I got the answers I was searching for.

"And that's how Project Prometheus came about. You like that? Prometheus? I confess I misled you, Kara—that codename, at least, *does* mean something. Prometheus stole fire from the gods and gave it to men. In the same way, KLINE brought us knowledge of the aliens' timetable, their technology, their intentions." He sags in his seat. "I thought that knowledge would give us a chance, but..."

It's way too much to take in all at once. Kara objects, "But how did you know the date wouldn't change? It was *thirty years ago*."

Grant's face clouds. "That nitwit who's running this country said the same thing. Thanks to him and the guy before him, we *weren't* ready. We spent most of the time since '80 planning, only to get our funding cut at the end, when we needed it most."

"But— But what about Star Wars?"

"The missile defense system?" He nods. "See, *that* President was a real leader. I showed him the proof, and he recognized the threat; KLINE was part of the impetus behind the system. The President told the world it was about defeating Soviet ICBMs—intercontinental missiles—which were designed to escape the atmosphere and travel halfway around the globe before reentry and detonation over their target, so an orbital defense network made sense. But in the original specs, the system was also tasked with defeating extra-orbital attacks." Grant rubs his eyes again. "None of it was ever actually implemented, though. The Presidents who followed never took the threat quite as seriously."

The general turns away, looking out the window for a time. Compared to the destruction of Denver and Grant's revelations, Kara's short-lived kidnapping just hours before seems distant and inconsequential. And yet it raises questions, questions Grant may for once be disposed to answer.

She wracks her brain, searching for the name she heard just that once while taped to the chair. "Kalura?" she asks tentatively.

Grant gives a start, turning back to regard her with incredulity.

"They mentioned it earlier—the men who grabbed me." She shakes her head. "I thought it was the name of an organization, a terrorist group, or maybe mercenaries, but... it's not, is it?"

Shaking his head, Grant settles back into his seat, looking away again. "No."

"But... what then? That's the aliens?" She leans forward, angling for his attention, but apparently Q&A time is over. "Grant?"

He doesn't answer, and they lapse into silence. Grant's mind is clearly a thousand miles away again... or perhaps just thirty years away. Kara eyes him for a long time. Without the conversation, however, without Grant's story to distract her, she can no longer hold back the crushing weight of emotion she's held at bay until now. She doesn't know how many people lived in Denver, can't really think of the attack in those terms. The grief that floods over her now is an ache, a wrenching pain, as if from losing an unimaginable number of loved ones suddenly and unexpectedly. She doesn't consciously notice her senseless adoption of these victims as loved ones; as the despair wells up, unrestrained, her analytical mind finally shuts down. The tragedy is so devastating, so impossible to comprehend, that it attacks her on a personal level.

Her shoulders begin heaving silent sobs, tears streaming down her face, making a mess of the caked makeup. She digs tissues out of a nearby bin and begins urgently, almost desperately, wiping at the offensive grime all over her face. Grant senses her distress and finally turns from the window. He settles a comforting hand on her knee, but she jumps to her feet to avoid him—or tries to jump, instead jerking painfully at the seatbelt. Fumbling at the latch with shaking hands, she finally gets it undone.

Slowly, Kara looks up to meet Grant's eyes. There are tear tracks running from his eyes as well, and his vitality seems finally to have fled him; for the first time, the man really looks his age. And yet even now, his emotion is contained, controlled. That simple fact, in light of what has happened—in light of what Carl Grant failed to prevent—disgusts her.

Anger mixes once more with grief. Anger over how this man plays fast and free with the truth, living above the law, shirking his duty to the people he has a responsibility to look after. Anger over countless preventable deaths in Denver—this man not only knew, he *believed* in the threat, yet didn't raise the warning when he realized they'd run out of time. All of this merges with the anger and hurt she's vicariously absorbed from Viviane over the years. Even anger at the perpetrators of this atrocity—this too, Kara directs at the man beside her in lieu of the distant, faceless beings she cannot imagine. Words form in her mind, accusations, and in her mind she rails against him as outwardly her sobs continue. With a stuttering breath, she stands and moves to sit across the aisle, averting her gaze, no longer able to look at him.

Looking at the back of her head, Grant knows the time has come. He will never again share a conversation with this delightful, inspiring woman. Never again see her smile, never again see those eyes flash, or that face blush in unnecessary embarrassment. Never again will he argue with her over matters important or not. The sense of this loss is not distinct from his pain over Denver; it is all a terrible emptiness he feels physically, in the pit of his stomach. He failed. He doesn't need to see the accusation and disgust in Kara Dunn's eyes to tell him that.

In that moment, Carl Grant feels what Kara has already seen—the loss of the energy that has driven him for the past three and a half decades. For the first time in his life, he truly feels *old*.

And yet he is not bereft of hope. He knows that his own role in this story is now complete, but he also knows that others, Kara among them, will take up the cause and ultimately—he hopes—succeed where he failed. "You're the one, Kara," he says softly, but loud enough that her head turns. "*You* will lead our pilots in battle." Yes, Carl Grant knows she is the one who will, in so many ways, take up his burden. And it's encouraging. But ultimately, his hope is based on so much more than that—he believes firmly that a loving, almighty God is completely in control, scripting events from on high and allowing pain and suffering precisely because it draws wandering hearts back to the one source of true peace they will ever know.

Into these hands, General Carl Grant of the United States Air Force commends his life's work, feeling sudden peace. It is no longer his responsibility. It never really was.

Their wheels touch down, the flight over far too fast. They bump unevenly over Groom Lake's salt pan runway, but Grant stopped noticing the discomfort decades ago. Instead, despite the peace he felt just moments ago, he experiences a sudden twinge of fear. Though he knows the way this must end, he doesn't know exactly how the next scene will play out.

As soon as the jet stops moving, he hears the hatch opening and the stairway descending. Several sets of heavy feet come clomping up the steps, and Gen. Peterson enters the small cabin, flanked by an Air Force cop and another of the generals. Grant is standing at attention by the time they arrive, comporting himself with all the dignity of his station, despite being out of uniform.

Peterson stops three feet away, face impassive. "Brigadier General Carl J. Grant, I am placing you under arrest on charges of treason and domestic terrorism." He turns to the cop. "Take him into custody."

[Chapter 22]

Late November 2014

 With Grant's arrest and Peterson's subsequent promotion to commander of Prometheus, Kara herself is catapulted to the second-in-command position... for the moment, at least. The rapidity with which these events transpire again leaves her head spinning, and the confirmation of her worst fear—that Grant expected her to not just train but *lead* the pilots stationed in orbit—compounds the sensation. She can only hope that he was alone in that expectation, which he quietly revealed to her that last time she saw him. After all, Peterson is in charge now, and surely Kara would not be *his* top choice... although at this point, Kara is rapidly losing her faith that logic plays any role in military decision making.

 Despite her horror at the semi-promotion she's received, Kara would welcome access to additional information—and yet, to her consternation, the shift does not result in an upgrade of her security clearance. If anything, Jerome Peterson becomes even more tight-lipped than before, and that's saying something.

 Kara is left to gather information the same as every other American, from the news networks. Within a day, details are leaked to the media regarding the warhead's method of delivery, and the information evokes powerful emotions in a scared populace. For the first time in over two decades, American citizens remember the fear of nuclear holocaust with which they lived during the Cold War. Except that now, no one seems to know which of America's enemies is behind the attack.

 An investigation is immediately launched, of course. Forensic examination of downtown Denver provides little useful intelligence; given the manner in which a nuclear weapon creates such force, and the massive area over which the radioactive debris falls out, determining the provenance of active materials is impossible. A far more promising avenue is to backtrack the missile's entry into Earth's atmosphere. Although there was no reason to give it any special attention before 8:35 p.m. MST on November 14th, that missile—or rather, the body that launched it from orbit—had been tracked for days, one of the thousands of unidentified bodies orbiting the planet at any given time, all monitored by elements of the U.S. military. Nevertheless, investigators ultimately report uncertainty as to where the craft originated.

The talking heads explode into conjecture: Who would dare call down American wrath? And why? Who even has the capability? What's the next target? These questions and more are punctuated with frequent recriminations about the Denver attack, in which the death toll has not been established and perhaps never will be. Although the city had boasted a population of more than six hundred thousand as recently as the previous month, optimistic estimates suggest that only 80% of those people remained in the city following the doomsday panic in the weeks prior to the attack. Others point out that detonation occurred above the downtown area, which was not only more densely populated, it was home to those less economically capable of relocating on short notice.

The official report, when it arrives, estimates the current death toll at 45,000.

As for the doomsday panic that had seized Denver before the attack, no longer are the rest of the nation's inhabitants watching their news stations interestedly in their bathrobes, shaking their heads at how crazy the world is. Now they too are close to panic, for the threat has possibly come to their doorstep as well. Now some of them are staying home in their bathrobes all day, while others are packing up to get away from population centers.

Predictably, racial tensions begin to flare, and the media makes sure each incident is well publicized. Within the first week, a dozen men of apparent Middle Eastern descent are murdered by angry mobs in unrelated incidents. Never mind that five of them were born in the States, or that one of them is actually Indian. In fear, the mob is looking no more than skin deep. It needs to lash out at something, someone, to void its collective feeling of helplessness, much as Kara wanted to lash out at Grant just before his arrest.

She regrets that now, for she now finds herself in Grant's shoes. She knows the truth, that it's not humans—and certainly not Arabs—who are responsible for the attack. And yet she does nothing, says nothing, even as more innocent men die for reasons no more significant than their dusky complexion. But who would believe her even if she did come forward? What *reasonable* person would believe her? She suddenly has a much better understanding of the burden Carl Grant has shouldered for the past three decades.

And yet she still doesn't know what to think of the man. No explanation has been made for his arrest. Interpreted one way, the charges could imply that Grant himself had something to do with the Denver attack. But Kara doesn't believe it. Whatever the man may be, he would never be party to mass murder. Whatever decisions he made were ultimately motivated by compassion; she knows him that well, at least. That doesn't mean he always made the right decisions. As Kara's mind churns through her many questions over and over, her frustration with the clandestine nature of the military grows. How can any organization succeed in a culture of such oppressive secrecy?

As a week passes, then two, Kara's bruises slowly fade. Regarding her kidnapping in Chicago, at least, she manages to get some information out of Peterson; he himself insists upon walking her through a recitation of her interrogation more than a dozen times, taking careful note of every implication and innuendo buried in her attackers' questions. He is naturally angry when he learns that Grant informed her of the alien angle, but her exposure to the truth simplifies matters. Peterson shares the results of background checks on her abductors, namely that both are former U.S. military, dishonorably discharged. He admits that this has been true of many of the men already killed or captured in Kara's previous kidnapping and assassination attempts. In addition, both of her Chicago attackers were known UFO quacks; one of the men had even been based at Area 51 for several years before he was discovered leaking mildly sensitive information to fringe websites.

Although neither of the two survived to be questioned, interrogations of her previous mercenary attackers revealed how they were generally recruited. It was always ex-special forces operatives the aliens went after, ones known to be conspiracy theorists... and sadly, these aren't that uncommon. Such a mercenary would be approached by individuals purporting themselves to be agents of the *K'luran* aliens—agents who would then play upon the mercs' awe to convince them of America's impotence in the face of the *K'luran* war machine, then play upon their patriotism to convince them of the moral need for short-circuiting any human resistance. In this way, some of the ex-soldiers apparently proved easy to manipulate, with the remainder won over the old-fashioned way—with cold hard cash. The entire discussion leaves Kara with raised goosebumps, because it isn't just fanatics who have been coming after her... Peterson quietly confirms that a number of the mercs seemed to be reasonable people operating with noble intentions. She can only imagine what sort of presentation the recruiters are making that's so convincing.

Also disturbing is the question of how, despite all of her preventative measures, the attackers were so confident Kara would be in attendance at the competition, and in Chicago specifically. By now, the enemy surely knows it was the government that snatched her up, and thus—even given Kara's association with *Rampant*—she wouldn't have attended something as meaningless as a video game competition unless with an ulterior motive related to the war effort. Therefore, they shouldn't have been looking for her there unless they knew the Air Force was behind it... *or* unless they had some other reason for thinking Kara was personally involved. And the only five non-military personnel aware of her collaboration were Gene Jenkins, Jamie Miles, Nate Williams, and the two Axmatik PMs working on the *Rampant* reboot. Despite Gene's disastrous press interview, there's no reason to disbelieve his assurances that her name was never mentioned *before* the competition took place. Unfortunately, it's all too easy to believe that one of the Axmatik folks might have revealed her involvement, even innocently. There's little they can do about it now, but that doesn't stop Peterson from launching yet another investigation, this one looking into Axmatik's top leadership.

On the national scale, violence and unrest continue to escalate during the two weeks following Denver. Yet during this time, the President remains strangely silent, offering token broadcasts of encouragement but little explanation. Just as his lack of visibility begins to spark speculation that he was actually in Denver when it went up—notwithstanding the appearances he *has* made—Air Force One lands at Groom Lake and Kara finds herself called into a rather intimate meeting with the great man himself.

**Thursday afternoon
November 27, 2014**

They sit around the now-familiar conference room table—the President, his chief of staff, Peterson, Kara, Gene, McLaughlin, and the chairman of the Joint Chiefs of Staff, the body that comprises the leadership of all branches of the military. Kara can't help but think it's the oddest Thanksgiving get-together she's ever attended... though she has to admit, had she not caught a few minutes of the Thanksgiving Day parade earlier while flipping news channels, she wouldn't even have realized what today is.

The first order of business had been to establish firmly in everyone's minds that the enemy here was aliens, actual extraterrestrials, not terrorists or some other foreign power. Although Kara had spent the last couple weeks adjusting to this revelation, it took McLaughlin and Gene by complete surprise. The Air Force pilot raised numerous objections, many of them quite creative, until the President revealed the actual findings of the Denver investigation—which are far more conclusive than the press was led to believe. Rather than tracing the craft that fired the weapon back to a launch point somewhere on Earth, and rather than failing to trace it at all—as had been reported—investigators discovered that the craft had quietly slipped into Earth's thermosphere days earlier from outer space... where it returned immediately after its devastating attack. Though still not entirely convinced, McLaughlin ultimately gives up arguing, and the meeting proceeds.

The question on the table now is whether announcing the existence of aliens, not to mention their malevolent intent, is likely to increase public hysteria or not. The President is hesitant about making full disclosure, and Peterson, predictably, is also strongly opposed; Kara and Gene, the closest thing the meeting has to civilians, are just as strongly supportive of the idea.

"The important thing," Jim Maccabee, the President's chief of staff breaks in, "isn't so much *what* you tell the people. Sir, what's important is what you tell them you're *doing* about it. As such, I would have to side with Dunn and Jenkins. If we handle it right, telling the truth would short-circuit the ethnic violence, probably even lead to unity in the face of a common threat."

"Assuming the public actually believes it," the chairman of the Joint Chiefs retorts. "It's a bit much to take without proof, you have to admit."

Maccabee snorts. "The American people can't believe we'd lie about something like this." He stops short, then everyone at the table bursts into laughter at the same time, Peterson included. "Okay," Maccabee admits, "maybe they could." The laughter has just the slightest tinge of hysteria to it, but it's still a good release.

"Regardless," Peterson says, "we need to get moving on manufacture of our defensive craft, not to mention the orbital barracks."

"Well, we can solve that problem if we just tell the public the truth," Gene blurts out. He has remained mostly silent thus far, probably out of shame for his performance in front of the cameras in Chicago, which he later admitted was foolish. He forges on, "Think about World War II. Everyone got behind the war effort, and productivity shot through the roof! I say we forget about all the secrets. Well, *some* of them, at least. It takes too much work to keep them anyway. Tell the people about the threat, and allow anyone who wants to get involved to do so. Even if, say, a quarter of the steel fab plants in this country committed a small percentage of their manufacturing capacity to national defense, we could have our Destrier chasses ready in only a couple months."

"It would help if we had a better idea when the next attack will come," the President says thoughtfully. "General, is there any indication on timing in the KLINE Document?"

Peterson gasps. "Sir! No one here— These people are not cleared for that information. Not even the name!"

The President cocks an eyebrow at Peterson, then almost lazily shifts his gaze to Gene. "Come to think of it, Gene, I'm beginning to like your idea of throwing out all the secrecy." He turns back to the new commander of Prometheus. "The KLINE Document, General. I'd like to see it please. While you're at it, why don't you bring in any other paperwork that's been retained since Prometheus was established in the 80s. Every scrap." He adds under his breath, "The way you people take notes, there'll be precious little of it."

Silence reigns during Peterson's absence, and when he returns he's wheeling a stubby two-drawer file cabinet before him. Kara recognizes it as having belonged in Grant's office. Peterson's office now.

Peterson removes a key from about his neck and twists it into the keyhole in the top drawer, meanwhile punching a twelve digit combination into the digital keypad. That accomplished, Kara catches several soft *snick*s and the hiss of decompression before the drawer pops open a half inch. The President pulls it out further, and Peterson guides him to a particular folder. "I must beg you, sir. Unless you feel it is absolutely necessary, please do not reveal this information even to the people in this room."

The President is flipping through the folder he selected. "That son of a gun," he whispers softly. "Grant finally showed me this last month, but even then, it was just an excerpt. This transcript..." he hefts the folder, "they had more than one interview with KLINE."

"Sir, please."

The leader of the free world drills Peterson with his piercing green eyes. "General, is there any mention in this document about timing? Dates?"

Peterson sighs. "B-12," he responds, and the President flips to the proper page.

"Ah." After reading silently for a minute, he begins to do so out loud:

PANDORA: SO JUST TO SUMMARIZE, THE DENVER ATTACK WILL BE NOVEMBER OF 2014. AFTER THAT--

KLINE: THEIR INTENTION IS TO HIT CHICAGO, THE FOLLOWING AUGUST... WE HAVE DISCUSSED HOW YOU CAN HANDLE THAT. AFTER THAT, EVERYTHING WILL HAPPEN QUICKLY.

PANDORA: RIGHT. ABOUT THE--

> KLINE: WAIT. THAT'S JUST DIRECT OFFENSIVES. YOU MUST KNOW, THEY WILL ALSO HIRE MERCENARIES TO UNDERMINE EFFORTS TO PREPARE, TO FIGHT BACK. SABOTAGE. ASSASSINATION.

"What's this?" The President interrupts his own reading. "Right after that, it says 'REDACTED', and a whole block of the transcript has been blacked out."

Peterson clears his throat. "Um, sir, that information—whatever it was—was probably deemed too sensitive to commit to paper. Or they decided that later, and had it removed."

"Who did?"

"Probably General Grant."

"And you don't know what it says?"

"Um, no sir. Probably just General Grant."

"Son of a—" He brings his irritation under control. A few moments later, he flips a page and resumes reading:

> KLINE: ORBITAL DEFENSES, YOU <u>MUST</u> DEVELOP THEM AS SOON AS POSSIBLE. SHIPS, PILOTS, STATIONS. BUILD ON THE TECHNOLOGY FROM MY SHIP. IT'S YOUR ONLY HOPE AGAINST THE K'LURAN FLEET.
>
> PANDORA: TELL ME MORE ABOUT THIS FLEET.
>
> KLINE: THERE WILL BE FIGHTER CRAFT FIRST--VERY QUICK, AGILE. WE CALL THEM NYMPHS. THEY CAN BE EQUIPPED WITH NUCLEAR MISSILES, LIKE THE ONES THEY WILL LAUNCH AT DENVER AND CHICAGO. THAT IS WHY YOU NEED YOUR OWN FIGHTERS IN ORBIT, TO INTERDICT THEM. THEY WILL BEGIN AMASSING NO LATER THAN SEPTEMBER THAT YEAR, IN PREPARATION FOR THE FINAL ASSAULT THE FOLLOWING MAY.
>
> PANDORA: WHAT DO THESE NYMPHS LOOK LIKE?
>
> KLINE: BLACK, WINGED. TRIANGULAR. AND SMALL--MAY BE COMPUTER-OPERATED, OR ELSE A SINGLE PILOT. <u>VERY</u> HARD TO KILL.

PANDORA: WHAT ELSE?

KLINE: WHEN THE MAIN FLEET ARRIVES IN MAY...

PANDORA: YES?

KLINE: IT'S THE END. THE LAST BATTLE I KNOW OF. HONESTLY... I DON'T KNOW HOW YOU CAN PREPARE. THEY WILL BE THROWING EVERYTHING AT YOU. THE DREADNOUGHTS ARE MASSIVE, HARDENED AGAINST NUCLEAR STRIKES.

PANDORA: DOZENS OF DREADNOUGHTS? HUNDREDS? MORE?

KLINE: A DOZEN, MAYBE MORE. STILL ENOUGH TO LAND TEN MILLION TROOPS.

[LONG SILENCE]

PANDORA: AND THEY WANT OUR LAND?

KLINE: THEY SAY THIS CONTINENT IS THE ANCESTRAL HOME OF THE K'LURANS. THAT THE K'LURANS WERE HERE FIRST.

PANDORA: YOU DON'T BELIEVE IT?

KLINE: I DON'T KNOW. THERE'S NO WAY TO KNOW FOR SURE. BUT THE K'LURAN AMBASSADOR WILL MAKE THAT CLAIM. THEY WILL RELY HEAVILY ON MISINFORMATION TO UNDERMINE YOU.

PANDORA: TELL ME ABOUT THE AMBASSADOR.

KLINE: HE WILL CONTACT HUMANKIND WHEN THE SECOND ATTACK OCCURS. WHAT HE HAS TO SAY--

A pause in the President's narration. Then—"Looks like another redaction, right in the middle of that sentence. Also something about KLINE's recurring headaches interfering with the interview and... how taking Aspirin would cause him to go into seizures."

Kara chuckles.

"You have something to add, Colonel?" the President asks coldly.

Her face reddens, and she searches desperately for something to say—certainly not the humorous thought that just ran through her head. "Um, no sir. Just—I know KLINE suffered significant head trauma in his crash."

"*What?*" Peterson demands, his face the epitome of barely controlled fury.

The President's gaze is more calculating, but no more friendly. "How did you come by that information?"

Kara stammers. "General Grant... He told me about KLINE... right after the Denver attack."

"As if we needed one more example of his treason," mutters the chairman of the Joint Chiefs.

The President holds her gaze several moments longer, then glances at the chairman. "Anything new from Grant? I understand he spent more time with KLINE than anyone."

"No, sir. He's still not cooperating."

The President sighs.

"I'm sorry," Kara breaks in, "but sir...?" She trails off, suddenly unsure what to say, feeling the heat crawl up her cheeks. "What exactly is the deal with Grant? What did he do?"

"You're not—" Peterson begins.

"—cleared for that information," Kara finishes for him, surprising even herself and definitely flushing now. "Yes, I know," she says, continuing anyway. "How am I supposed to help you lead this effort if I get left out of the loop on major details?"

The President waves a hand dismissively. "Not going to happen. Can we move on?"

"I just—" Kara sighs, unwilling to let this go now that she's finally had the courage to bring it up. "Okay, what about Grant's daughter, Viviane? Does she even know what's happened with her father?"

"Would she even care?" Peterson asks pointedly.

"Do we have to discuss this now?" the President demands, actually rolling his eyes. He points at Kara. "You have my permission to inform Grant's daughter that he'll probably never see the outside of a jail cell again. Give her whatever reason you want. Happy?"

Hearing this definitely does *not* make Kara happy, but she senses the finality in the President's tone. Peterson doesn't appear happy either, but then, he never does. He just as wisely stays silent.

The President blows out his breath in noisy frustration. "So... what do we actually know? They'll be gunning for Chicago come August?"

"Assuming nothing has changed in the last thirty years," the chairman says.

"Which is a big assumption," Peterson agrees. "Still... that intel was spot-on regarding Denver."

An awkward silence follows the comment, and this time it's the President who looks distinctly uncomfortable. "It would be nice if we knew more about these *K'lurans*," he muses finally. "Their society, their culture, what makes them tick, whether they can be reasoned with. I assume there must be factions—this KLINE is obviously not towing the official line. But how strong are these detractors, assuming KLINE wasn't the only one, and are they in any position to help us further?" He poses the questions almost rhetorically, but when no one says anything, he gets a little testy. "Well, Peterson? Any further info about any of this in here?" He indicates the rolling cabinet.

Peterson shakes his head. "You're welcome to read it all, sir, but it's mostly just restatement of the same, along with logs of the milestones reached since that time. There *are* a number of"—He pauses, then speaks more carefully—"*unusual* bits of information. But nothing pertinent to this discussion."

"What about the bottom drawer?"

Peterson opens his mouth to speak, but pauses. "Umm," he clears his throat. "I'm afraid I can't give you access to that drawer."

For the first time, the President truly looks like he's going to blow a gasket. Before he can speak, however, Peterson hastens to explain.

"I mean, I don't have access to it myself. No key, no code."

"So bust it open."

"No sir, we can't. To do so would activate the cabinet's failsafes. I don't know the details, but improper entry would probably cause a few chemicals to mix, destroying the contents."

The President turns to the Chairman. "So we lean on Grant some more—"

"*Sir*," Peterson interrupts. "Grant doesn't know either. These documents...from what he told me, they were his predecessor's. From back in the beginning of Prometheus. The man never passed on the codes before his heart attack."

"A classic case of knowledge loss," Gene interjects sagely in the sudden silence. "Not an uncommon problem in poorly managed organizations." Peterson shoots the dark-skinned man a murderous look, but everyone else ignores him.

The President eyes Peterson for another long moment, chewing on the inside of his cheek. The only sound in the room is the soft drumming of his fingers on the tabletop. "Fine. Peterson, make copies of whatever you need out of that top drawer, because we're taking the whole thing with us. Jim, you'll interface with CIA, FBI, NSA—I don't care who, but get someone working on cracking this thing."

"Sir!" Peterson blurts, horrified.

"It's not doing anyone any good right now, so I don't see the risk in trying. If there's anything in there that can help..." The President shuts the KLINE folder and returns it to Peterson. "So. We'll need to have our own defensive force in place before next August, in preparation—initially at least—for repulsing one-man spacecraft, these... Nymphs. That gives us a timeframe and something specific to defend against. I'm not sure if it's a *feasible* timeframe, but it's a start. I'll also get the ball rolling with FEMA... when it comes right down to it, we may need to evacuate."

No one actually moves in response to this statement, but to Kara, it feels like a collective shudder runs through the group. The idea of retaining any sort of control while attempting to evacuate the third largest U.S. city... "Sir," she says tentatively. "Just one more thing to consider while you're discussing evacuation. The aliens have agents here—we know that. If you try to evacuate the city, it'll be all over the news within hours... That means these *K'lurans* will know about it, and then they'll just revise their plan of attack, switch targets, and what'll we do then? I'm not saying we don't try, but..."

The thought sobers them all, as if they needed a reminder of how serious this situation is. Jim Maccabee shakes his head. "It's a no-win situation. Damned if we do, damned if we don't."

The President sighs. "Enough about Chicago for now," he says, gently but firmly. "Let's be working on some ideas there, but for now, we need to keep moving."

"Okay," Maccabee responds obediently, "say we go public about the Martians. Or Kalorans. Whatever they are. What exactly *are* we doing about it, and how much do we make public? I'm talking about our orbital defenses here."

"I say we go all out," Gene offers, surprising no one. "We tell them about the aliens, but we also tell them about Prometheus, though maybe not in so many words. In fact..." His eyes grow distant. "Yeah, we go *all* out. A whole new branch of the military, the Space Defense Force or something like that. That would do it." His eagerness fades somewhat as he notices the skeptical expressions around him.

"Gene..." Kara begins.

"No, listen. Let me tell you something." He furrows his brow, and it takes Kara a moment to realize that he's angry, *very* angry. "You know how I became part of this project? This goon and his friends" —he thrusts a finger towards Peterson—"show up at my door, tell me that my skills are needed for purposes of national security, but they can't tell me anything more. They give me twenty minutes to pack, during which time they don't let me out of their sight. I'm not allowed to leave a note for my wife and kids, who are out buying new winter coats. I have to trust these men to give my wife some explanation that won't cause her to worry to death. I didn't get to speak with her myself for a week! You know what? That's kidnapping under any reasonable definition of the word. And why? Why was that necessary? Because of all these secrets you have to keep.

"Well, I'll say it again. Throw out the secrets and tell everyone the truth—not about Chicago, I mean, but about the true nature of this threat. Let the manufacturing base *volunteer* their extra capacity, rather than being conscripted. And as for pilots, we've got hundreds to pick from; thanks to our competition, we can work up evaluations on all of the men and women who competed, even though we never got to the second weekend. I say we recruit a few more pilots," he nods to McLaughlin, reminding everyone of the Air Force pilots already on board, "and we use them to promote the poo out of this thing. This new branch of service, it's highly selective; it has to be, starting out with fewer than—what is it, two hundred pilots? We push the honor, the duty, the glory—heck, we show off the new uniform, because a sharp uniform will get anyone's heart pumping.

"And then, only then, when we've gotten the collective heart of the nation beating in excitement about this whole thing, *then* we approach our top picks… but we *ask* them to serve—we don't force them. Because if you expect them to fight and even die for their country, maybe for their world, you can't force them into it. It has to be their own choice."

There's a moment of silence, during which Maccabee's small smile gradually widens into a broad grin. "I think he's onto something, sir. We create a new generation of heroes for the people to rally behind."

The President smiles too, in pointed contrast to Peterson's scowl, though it's not clear whether Peterson dislikes the proposal or is chafing at being labeled a goon. *Probably both*, Kara decides.

"General?" The President asks. "Your thoughts?" It takes Kara a moment to realize he's not talking to Peterson but rather to the chairman of the Joint Chiefs.

He takes his time in responding. "It would be different, I'll give you that. The only new branch of service this nation has seen since its founding is the Air Force, and it was operated by the Army for forty years until Truman reorganized the armed forces after World War II. Still, even if we call it a distinct branch from the outset, we can integrate it into the existing command structure. It would have representation on the Joint Chiefs through the Air Force, much as the Coast Guard does through the Navy in wartime." He shrugs. "Operationally, it might as well be staffed by Air Force personnel; it really doesn't matter how you, um, *market* it to the general public. In fact, I'm not sure it really makes much practical difference once you get past recruitment."

"Excellent!" Gene enthuses. "I'm envisioning a goodwill tour of sorts…" He frowns thoughtfully. "Who's actually in charge of all this anyway? That will be the most critical role for reassuring the public."

"General Peterson is—" the President begins, but Gene cuts him off without thinking, much to everyone's horror.

"No, no. The man has no charisma. He'd never inspire the people's trust."

"What I was trying to say," the President continues testily, "is that Peterson would be the point at which this new branch merges with the existing Air Force command structure, for all intents and purposes leading the new organization." He looks to the chairman of the Joint Chiefs, who nods. "In terms of putting a public face on it, well... I suppose the so-called 'commandant' of this new service could be the top-ranked pilot deployed into orbit. But that individual would still report to Peterson, who would report to me and the Chiefs."

Kara feels a jolt of fear. An irrational jolt, she assures herself.

"If I may, sir," McLaughlin speaks up, "Kara Dunn is perfect for such a role."

"*What?*" she hisses.

"And she already fills a similar niche in the command structure," he persists.

Gene looks delighted. "The public will love it, sir."

"No!" she exclaims, louder now.

The chairman nods confidently, Maccabee smiles encouragingly, and even Peterson fails to object or even, for that matter, look up. The President glances around, then pronounces, "Kara Dunn is indeed the obvious choice. Congratulations, Colonel."

Kara's sense of panic blossoms, and she fights hard to avoid hyperventilating. Were she more observant in that moment, she might have noticed just how... scripted that whole exchange seemed. The President making historic military policy decisions just like that, without previously consulting the Joint Chiefs? The chairman accepting the nomination of a brand-new recruit—one he'd presumably never heard of before today—to lead, in essence, a new branch of service, without even requesting additional information? And Peterson... not objecting? It should all seem highly suspicious, and indeed, John McLaughlin is quite surprised at how quickly his nomination is acted upon. But Kara Dunn... Kara is simply trying to control her breathing.

The President glances around the table, seeking out any further comments, and Peterson obliges. "Mr. President, I'd like to state for the record that I think going public with all this is absurd. Maintaining operational security through secrecy is proven. What you're considering could have unpredictable consequences."

"Okay," the President nods, "you're entitled to your opinion." He smiles grimly. "But let me make this perfectly clear: while everyone here gets a vote, mine's the only one that counts. And I say we play things Gene's way."

"John!" Kara hisses, as soon as she's got the man by himself. "What were you *thinking*?"

McLaughlin wears a look of deep concern as he eyes the closed door to the conference room; Peterson remains inside with the players from Washington, and Gene is already halfway down the hall, muttering excitedly about possibilities. "That was very odd."

"Tell me about it! What makes you think *I'm* a good choice for this role?"

He blinks. "Oh, that? Kara, you're a natural leader. You're smart, you think quickly on your feet, and—most importantly—you care about the people you're responsible for. You're the kind of person I want to serve under."

The endorsement leaves her speechless for a moment. "But John, you— Then what do you mean, 'that's odd'?"

"It's just the way that played out," he responds slowly, glancing back at the door. "Nothing happens that quickly in the military. Or that unanimously, not among the big decision makers at least. I wonder…" He pauses. "You know the brass who used to oversee Prometheus?"

Kara nods.

"They were in there with the President before us. Not Peterson, but the rest of the ones we used to report to. I got here early, as they were leaving, and they looked furious." He shakes his head. "With the whole Grant thing—"

"Do *you* know what that's about?" she interrupts.

"No. But considering that, I bet the whole committee got canned. I just wonder if..."

"What?" Kara insists.

"Just... the only thing I can think is that those officers put forth your name even before I did. And they must have made a compelling case, considering how fast the President and the chairman rolled over." He pauses. "But even then..."

Kara grabs her head in both hands and knocks it gently against the cinderblock wall: once, twice, again. "No..." she moans softly. "I can't do this. I'm not the right person. John..."

"Kara, it's okay—"

"No, John. There have to be hundreds of pilots better suited to this, more experienced," she says, so low it's almost a whisper. "Just look in our unit. Skylar? Or you—you would be perfect." She looks up hopefully.

"No." He snorts softly. "I'm a good pilot, and I can certainly lead others in combat. But this role requires more than just leadership skills." He pauses, searching for the words. "It calls for someone... visionary. You've shown your vision, your creativity, your... unorthodox thought process in so many ways. If it weren't for you, we wouldn't even have the Destrier, much less a tactical framework within which to operate it. You may not be experienced in the military, but you have a better grasp on our tech than anyone else ever will. And charisma?" He shakes his head. "You have a way of inspiring confidence... I don't just mean people are able to trust you, but you have a way of building people's confidence in themselves." He pauses again, this time for emphasis. "Gene is right, Kara. This may well be a fight for the survival of our species. We need more than a leader, we need a figurehead. A single face to reassure the public, to draw out the people we want to recruit, and to truly inspire the pilots who go into battle on this nation's behalf. A person we believe is actually capable of winning this fight." He smiles, taking in a breath. "If that person isn't you, Kara, then I'm not sure where to start looking."

Hand clasped over her mouth, Kara squeezes her watering eyes shut. "I'm sorry," she whispers. "I have to find the bathroom."

[Chapter 23]

Thanksgiving weekend 2014

And so it seems that the more responsibility Kara inadvertently amasses, the less control she seems to have over her own life. It's ironic—as she awakens the next day, she needs to seize upon a clinical observation like this in order to avoid the crushing feeling of inadequacy that threatens to pull her under. The feeling that not only is *she* being swept along by events outside her control, but that faceless masses of people will somehow be jumping in after her in the mistaken belief that she knows what she's doing. It's almost debilitating, knowing that people will be looking to her, and worse, her not even knowing how she ended up in this position. Her stomach twists into a knot that simply will not unwind, and she spends an unseemly portion of the weekend perched over a toilet, retching in agony.

Yet she forges on. Never a fatalist before, Kara is beginning to see life through a slightly different lens; whether she was ever truly in control of her own destiny, she's clearly not now. Maybe the feeling of control was always an illusion. Regardless, all she can do now is accept her lot and make the best of it… and when it comes right down to it, there are many worse situations she could have been plopped into. Her position right here, right now, actually enables her to touch the lives of millions of people—just as Grant promised her all those months ago, when he first recruited her.

More than anything, however, it's the continued demands placed upon her that keep Kara getting up each morning, putting one foot in front of the other, day after day. Before that fateful Thanksgiving meeting adjourned, the President penciled in the evening of December 15th for his broadcast regarding this all-new branch of the military. Which means that Kara and her team have just over two weeks to bring said organization into being before it is introduced to the world. Two weeks to establish an identity, traditions, a unique look—not to mention a name. And then there's that matter of preliminary recruitment, which Gene had made an issue of.

"What we need are some poster boys," he'd said. "And... um, you know, girls too." And he was right. When the President makes his announcement, that would be the moment to introduce the very first pilots in this new defense force. The faces who would serve as media darlings—thankfully, Kara needn't be completely alone in this—simultaneously encouraging a scared populace and inspiring those talented pilots who would later be recruited.

There was some discussion as to just how many pilots are needed for this role, but in the end, those who had an opinion agreed upon twelve. For one thing, twelve is the number of pilots per squadron in *Rampant*. More importantly, twelve pilots means they could include all six of their existing Air Force transfers—including J.T. Faulk and Kevin Smith—and add six new recruits. This half-and-half constitution would make a strong statement about their priority in recruiting the best, be they current service personnel or not.

With Kara and Gene already onboard, this means they need only four more pilots to round out their dozen "poster kids." That said, it will take far more time than they have to run down the history on the pilots identified through the competition... which means they're back to square one, recruiting from among the pilots whom Kara has already identified, whose dossiers have already been prepared.

"Remember," Gene says repeatedly, "we need men and women who look good in uniform, who will do well with media attention." Kara's eyes shift to McLaughlin's the first time Gene says this, and they can't help but smile. It's clear they're both remembering how well Gene handled the media attention in the moments before the Denver attack.

In Kara's mind, appearances are a poor thing to base the defense of a planet on, but it means they're able to quickly agree upon Roger Harris, Shaniqua Watson, and Jose Morales for three of the four slots. Gene is pleased that Shaniqua's and Jose's inclusion will project an air of a multicultural response to the alien threat; as far as Kara's concerned, they're just good flyers who have proven themselves as team players.

Filling that last slot proves far more difficult. Gene rules out most of their prospects outright, citing various reasons why they would have a negative impact on the program's image. They're left with two files laid out side by side: Philip Brinkman and Donald DeMaria.

"Brinkman will bring respectability," Gene argues. "Just look at the man. Conservative haircut, pleasant smile, thin-rimmed glasses. When you add in what he does for a living, it's clear—he's our man."

Despite the general feeling of malaise that seems to permeate her life right now, Kara has enough tact to feel uncomfortable as she objects. "It's... well, it's what he does for a living that bothers me. I mean," she hastens to add, "from an appearances standpoint. He's the pastor of a megachurch, described here as 'extreme right-leaning' and 'hyper-fundamental.'"

"First of all," Gene responds equitably, "Five hundred members is hardly a megachurch; it's merely above average."

"Okay," she says slowly, still pensive. "I'm just surprised you'd want someone with that kind of image added to the mix. Extremists tend to worry people, especially when you hand them multi-million dollar weapons."

Gene is dumbfounded. "How do you get off calling him an extremist?"

"You read the file. His political positions are far outside the mainstream, and his rhetoric is..." She clears her throat. "Well, hateful."

"How's that different from our current President? Some of his positions are just as extreme, only in the opposite direction; that didn't stop the vast majority of Americans from voting for him." He shakes his head. "So maybe Brinkman's words sound hateful when you boil them down and summarize them, but that doesn't mean his beliefs are motivated by hate. My beliefs aren't significantly different. Does that make me hateful?"

Kara is silent a moment. "I don't know, but it does explain why you're so high on the guy."

Gene's breath rushes out in an audible display of frustration. "I don't understand why you suddenly care about the squadron's image anyway. I thought your only concern was our performance in orbit, and it's clear that Brinkman's is top-notch."

"You're the one who thinks I make a great charismatic figurehead," she retorts. "You don't think I'm concerned with image too?" She exhales noisily. "Okay," she admits finally, "I'm concerned with the effect he would have on the rest of the team. Having this guy preaching at us day in and day out probably won't be very good for morale. He probably thinks this alien attack is judgment from God, something we deserve." She shakes her head. "Besides, would he even *want* to join? 'Pastor' doesn't seem like the kind of job you can just quit on a whim."

Gene can do nothing but shake his head in turn. "So you'd rather take DeMaria? The guy's thirty-nine and single and he still lives with his parents, for crying out loud!"

"If I may make an observation," McLaughlin breaks in calmly. "No matter who you choose, chances are we will fly with both of these men before this is all over. As far as it's possible, try to keep your comments from becoming personal. These things have a way of getting back to people, and it can make things really uncomfortable."

Gene scowls at Kara, as if pained that she would violate confidence and share with Donald his scorn for the man. Kara just rolls her eyes. Then she remembers something the President said in that meeting, and her lip quirks at one corner. "Gentlemen, I appreciate your input. Gene, I'm afraid I'll have to pull rank on this one. Sorry."

There's no real sense of victory as she delivers this line, however. There's only a momentary peace as she tosses back the last swallow from a bottle of antacid.

Monday morning
December 1, 2014

Kara and McLaughlin depart well before dawn the next morning, rocketing east in an F-15 Strike Eagle with McLaughlin—call sign "Joker," predictably—at the controls. Gene is left to his own devices, a division of duties that suits everyone. "I've got a lot to do," he insisted the night before. "Develop imagery, insignia, slogans, not to mention uniforms." Whether or not the work would be enough to keep Kara busy for a day, it's obvious Gene feels hard pressed to complete it before the deadline.

The flight is like nothing Kara has ever experienced, which is both good and bad. Her generally positive outlook on life had reemerged that very morning, for the first time since Thanksgiving Day; as she walked out on the tarmac, she even felt a thrill of anticipation for what the day would bring. And so throughout the first leg of their flight, she remains flushed in exhilaration… but she never quite escapes the specter of regurgitation. The fighter's operable range has been stretched to over 3,000 miles without need for refueling, what with the substitution of extra fuel tanks in place of ordinance. Along the way, they are escorted by two groups of other fighter craft—the responsibility for Kara's safety being handed off from one flight group to the other when they reach the Mississippi—and these escort craft most definitely have *not* had ordinance removed. Without the need to refuel, McLaughlin completes their landing in Atlanta at 9:30 Eastern, having traversed nearly 2,000 miles in just over two hours.

Climbing into the glossy black government sedan moments later feels like hopping onto a kiddie ride after exiting a rollercoaster—it's simultaneously restorative and devastatingly boring.

Gazing out her window, Kara shakes her head in wonder at the half-dozen apparently civilian vehicles that pace the sedan through downtown traffic. When it came to recruiting these four new pilots to round out their goodwill tour lineup, she and Gene had leaned heavily on Peterson to let Kara make the pitch personally. Grudgingly, he had acknowledged the need to bring people on board in a less vindictive frame of mind than Peterson himself had caused when "recruiting" Gene—and Kara is someone these people already know, at least virtually. This morning, though, reminded again of the expensive and disruptive security measures that now accompany her wherever she goes, Kara wonders if there wasn't another option they should have considered. At least she doesn't have to worry about an attack today—unlike Chicago, where Kara's presence made sense, there's no way anyone could predict her appearance at any of today's stops.

Their first "appointment" of the day is with Roger Harris at 10 o'clock, and, unlike the rest of their interviews, this one actually *has* been scheduled in advance. Under false pretenses, of course. When they'd called Roger's investment banking firm on Friday, they simply implied to the receptionist that they had a notable sum they were interested in plowing into a few high-risk stocks. A half-hour window magically appeared in Roger's tight schedule.

Roger is a harried-looking man with a growing forehead and deep crow's feet about his eyes, despite his forty-three years. He rolls his sleeves up to the elbows as he shows them into his office, where Kara and McLaughlin seat themselves on a rich leather sofa. Through the floor-to-ceiling glass of the office's interior wall, Kara recognizes a few of her escorts milling busily amongst the cubicles beyond, and she wonders how they're able to do that without attracting attention as strangers. Turning back to their host, she watches as Roger folds his frame into a desk chair and throws one leg over the other, fingers interlaced around one knee.

"Amanda tells me you're interested in some high-performance investments," he says, getting straight to the point.

The others exchange a look. "Actually, Mr. Harris, that's not entirely true," Kara admits.

His eyes narrow uncertainly.

"We needed to see you on short notice, and this was the easiest way to do so without drawing attention. We're... I guess you'd say we're from the government."

In an instant, the tension in the room seems to ratchet up at least two notches, and with the office door closed, Roger looks to the clear office wall for comfort—as if reassuring himself that Kara and McLaughlin can't do anything too horrible to him in open view of the office staff.

McLaughlin hastens to say, "We need your help with something. You're not in any kind of trouble."

The other man relaxes slightly, responding slowly. "Okay... what can I help you with?"

Kara smiles brightly, trying to put him at ease. "Our records show that you spend a great deal of time playing video games online. Your favorite is *Rampant*, which you are quite good at. You go by HarryChest71, right?"

Roger blinks, and his eyes again slide nervously to the interior wall, this time finding reassurance in the fact that the door is closed.

"Um, yeah. What's that got to do with the government?"

"You know what happened to Denver?" It's not so much a question as a segue, but Roger nods anyway. "Our military response will involve space combat, and we've identified you as one of our top prospective recruits. The military hasn't exactly been preparing for space battle, you know, so we need to find as many qualified pilots as we can, as quickly as possible. I was actually on the development team for *Rampant*, which is how I got involved."

To say that Roger's face registers skepticism is something of an understatement. "You expect me to believe that? I don't even know you people."

"Um, well, you actually *do* know me... sort of," Kara offers hesitantly. "We've flown together. I'm CareerStud."

"Oh," he says, momentarily stymied, adding stupidly, "I thought you were a guy."

"Yeah," Kara says, coloring slightly. "It was supposed to be CareerStudent, but it got truncated to ten characters when I signed up for my first gaming account, and I never changed it. I didn't expect to ever meet any of you people in person."

Her vulnerability finally puts him at ease, if only momentarily, and he barks a laugh.

"Look, Mr. Harris," Kara says, "call the White House and ask for the President."

He just stares at her for a long moment. "Seriously? The President?"

"Seriously. Here, the number is 202-456—"

He waves her off, reaching for his computer mouse and focusing on the screen. "Not that I don't trust you... actually I don't. What I mean is, no offense, but you could give me any ole number." He taps a few keys on his keyboard, presumably bringing up a directory, or perhaps the White House website.

He lifts his office phone and begins punching in a number... pausing to assess Kara's reaction. When she doesn't back down, a cautious smile plays about Roger's lips and he finishes dialing. After a moment, he reconsiders and switches over to speakerphone.

"Thank you for calling the White House," a pleasant but efficient female voice answers. "How may I direct your call?"

"Uh," Roger flounders, "may I speak with the President?"

"May I ask who is calling, sir?"

"This is Roger. I mean, Roger Harris."

"Ah," she says with evident recognition. "How are you, Mr. Harris?"

"Oh. Great. Um, how are you?"

"Very well, sir. Please hold for the President."

A silly grin spreads across Roger's face. To the President's credit, they only have to wait through two minutes of elevator music before he picks up.

"Roger!" He sounds genuinely pleased to receive this call.

"Um, hi, Mr. President."

There follows an awkward silence. The exercise has accomplished its purpose, but it leaves Roger on the line with the President of the United States—and no idea what to say. Finally, the President says, "Roger, I hope you'll agree to work with Kara and John. They can't give you much detail just yet, but let me underscore the fact that your involvement could save millions of lives."

"Thank you, sir. That's— just, wow."

"Maybe we can meet in person some time."

"Yes, sir."

"Good bye, Roger."

"Yes, sir. Thank you, sir." The line disconnects, and Roger stares off into the distance for a while. "Is this for real?" he asks softly.

"Yeah," Kara says. "We really can't tell you much more right now, but I *can* say it will involve a lot of publicity. You'll become an American hero, a well-known face. There'll be danger, of course—"

Roger waves this away. "When do I start?"

She glances at McLaughlin. "Actually, today," he says. "In the next few hours, you'll be picked up here by some people from military intelligence. They'll follow you home so you can pack your bags."

"Wow," Roger says again. "That's... quick. What should I tell my wife? My kids?"

"Just tell them you'll be doing some consulting work for the federal government. No need to worry them yet."

"Worry them? Ha!" he laughs. "When will they find out the truth?"

McLaughlin blinks, surprised at the other man's reaction. "Oh, well, within a week or two, I guess."

"*Ex*cellent," Roger intones, grabbing a framed photo of his family from the desk top. "How ya like me now, you little snots?"

Kara turns to find that John McLaughlin is as taken aback by this as she is. "Right," she says, all business. "Mr. Harris—Roger—we have more appointments to get to, but we'll see you again very soon. I, um, look forward to working with you."

Monday noon
December 1, 2014

Fortunately, all four of their stops are on the East coast, so they were able to plan each leg based upon the most viable time to approach the next recruit, rather than be limited by travel constraints. When you're flying a supersonic jet with top speeds around 1,600 miles per hour, a flight from Atlanta to Raleigh really is just a hop, skip, and a jump. In fact, as it turns out, taxiing and awaiting clearance for take-off and landing consumes far more of the day than the nineteen minutes spent in transit.

They find another unmarked black sedan waiting in the hangar in Raleigh, and twenty minutes after climbing inside, they pull up in front of the DeMaria residence. The time is 12:17 as Kara walks up the pathway to the door, amazed at the sudden increase in neighborhood joggers and dog-walkers in the minute since they pulled onto the street.

An older woman in a house apron answers the door with a pleasant smile. "Hi," Kara says. "Is Mr. DeMaria at home?"

"I'm sorry, honey, he's at work right now."

"At work... actually, we're looking for *Donald* DeMaria."

"Oh!" she seems surprised at this, but she recovers quickly. "Please, come in, come in. Donald's office is this way." They follow her up the stairs to a closed door, upon which she knocks. "Donald, honey, you have visitors."

After a moment, she opens the door and waves them in. Donald is seated at a large desk, the innards of a tall computer tower lying exposed before him, a can of compressed air in one hand. Kara and McLaughlin stand awkwardly near the door for a long minute as the man painstakingly sprays dust out of every nook and cranny of his machine—though if there's much to be removed, Kara certainly can't see it from where she's standing. She lets her eyes rove about the room. Other than the desk, the only other furniture is two large bookshelves, a sofa, and an office chair. The shelves are packed full of books, mostly textbooks, though Kara notices a number of works by both renowned physicists and fantasy novelists, all mixed together.

Finally, Donald sets down the can with a tolerant sigh, and turns to acknowledge them. "Do you have an appointment?" He is a thin man, wearing sharply creased khakis and a heavily starched white shirt, short-sleeved, buttoned all the way to the throat. The presence of browline glasses completes Kara's first impression of this man as a nerd who just escaped the 50s.

"No, I'm afraid we don't," she says.

The man sighs again. "Very well," he says, then settles back in his seat expectantly.

Kara waits a very long moment, thinking the man will at least offer them a seat on his couch, but she decides to move on before the silence can grow too awkward. "Mr. DeMaria," she says finally, reaching out her hand, "I'm Kara Dunn. I was part of the team that developed the game *Rampant*."

"No, you led the team," he corrects as he grasps her hand and shakes it in a precise down-up-down motion. Rather than complimentary, his correction comes across as arrogant. "I authored the wiki article on the game, you know." He absentmindedly produces a bottle of hand sanitizer and rubs a generous dollop between his hands.

"Oh. Right." She smiles slightly. "Did you know I'm also CareerStud?"

"You..." The revelation has the intended effect of throwing him slightly off kilter. "No, I did not. Funny, I always though CareerStud was a—"

"A man?"

He looks at her like she's crazy. "No, a horse breeder."

McLaughlin stifles a laugh behind her. "Well," Kara says defensively, "how do you know I'm not?"

"Because I authored the wiki article on you as well."

"Oh. Wow," she says. McLaughlin is now openly laughing, and Kara smiles too, though Donald clearly doesn't understand their levity. She introduces the men, then gets to the point. "Mr. DeMaria, I'm currently working with the U.S. military in preparing a response to the Denver attack. If you know so much about me, I'm sure you can connect the dots and figure out what sort of combat that will entail. We're here to recruit you as part of the effort."

Donald nods contemplatively. "This is not unexpected."

"It's not?"

He looks up. "Oh, I hardly expected you to come to my door and ask me to join. But a military response to the Denver attack is a given. To say the timing of last month's *Rampant* competition was coincidental strains credibility, and even before it was announced, my bots notified me of an inexplicable surge of interest in backtracking known *Rampant* pilots. You do the math." He pauses, sipping daintily at a bottle of brand-name spring water. Kara can't do the math because she's not even sure what he just said, but she lets it pass. "Incidentally," Donald continues, "I saw a news piece on that competition—you really should hire a PR professional, because your man Jenkins is an informational sieve."

Kara can only shake her head. "So, about joining up. Will you?"

"It certainly sounds fun." He delivers this line deadpan.

"So you're in?"

"Affirmative."

"Okay, then," McLaughlin says. "I suggest you go ahead and pack a few bags, as the military intelligence people will be here later this afternoon. Please don't share any details with your mother—in fact, it would be better if you let the intelligence people explain. This will all become public knowledge very soon anyway, so your parents won't have to wonder about you for long."

Donald takes this in stride, his nod as precise as his handshake.

"Any questions?"

A precise left-right-left shake. "Negative."

"Right."

As soon as Kara and McLaughlin are safely back in the car, they both start talking at once. He defers to her, and she says, "Did you notice he didn't smile even once? Even people with no sense of humor smile. It's a bit spooky."

"Hey, you picked him," he reminds her. "But look on the bright side: he'll probably keep his uniform looking pretty sharp."

**Monday afternoon
December 1, 2014**

Shaniqua Watson proves to be the easiest interview of the day. She greets them as soon as they walk through the door of her coffee shop in Connecticut late that afternoon. Her smile for them is brilliant, just as it is for each of the three customers she serves before they reach the counter.

"What a day, huh? Winter already! What can I getcha to warm you up?"

Kara smiles back. The other woman's enthusiasm is infectious. "A large latte, please. John?"

"Just bottled water, thanks."

As they wait, their barista is maintaining an energetic, nonstop monologue about the beauty of the fall and winter months, all while whipping up Kara's drink.

"Shaniqua," Kara breaks in when she sees a polite opening. It doesn't even occur to her to say 'Ms. Watson.' "My name is Kara Dunn. I'm actually here to meet you in person. You know me as CareerStud."

The other woman's jaw drops momentarily, and she shouts, "No way!" even as she comes around the counter to envelop Kara in a hug. This draws some looks, but Kara notices they're amused looks; no doubt most of the regulars are already familiar with Shaniqua's antics. "Listen, Kara," she says as she hands over her latte, "I can take my break in about ten, if you don't mind waiting."

Kara smiles. "Not at all," she says, turning to discover a line of six people stretched out behind her. She makes a move toward a quiet corner table, but McLaughlin steers her toward the door instead. Outside, he claims one of the many empty tables standing so forlorn in the early winter cold—of course, out in the cold there will be no one to overhear their conversation... except maybe the two large men in bulky coats seated at the only other occupied table. Kara catches one man's eye and smiles, and he nods formally in return.

She and McLaughlin enjoy the lull in what has otherwise been a nonstop day, savoring their drinks and huddling against the cold. When Shaniqua joins them fifteen minutes later, she is full of questions, and their conversation assumes the tone of long-time friends catching up after only a short period apart. McLaughlin eventually clears his throat and taps his watch, and Kara turns reluctantly to business.

"Listen," Kara says, "there's something important we need to discuss with you." She glances around and leans in closer. Shaniqua nods eagerly for her to continue. "John here is with the Air Force. We're working with a team to prepare a military response to what happened in Denver." The other woman's face adopts a look of immense sorrow, but she nods just as determinedly. "We expect there to be some space combat," Kara says, "and we want you on the team. I've flown with you, and I think you'd be a great addition."

Shaniqua smiles in gracious acceptance of the praise. "Space combat, huh? *Real* space combat?" She's silent for a bit. "Wow." Then "You know, I didn't get into that game for myself. I bought it to play with my brother—he's got a lot of problems, addictions really, and it was a good diversion that we could work our way through together. I guess what I'm saying is that the flying itself is fine, but I could take it or leave it." She holds Kara's gaze with her large, liquid brown eyes. "Do you really think I could help people by doing this?"

Kara marvels at how trusting the other woman is, not just taking their pitch at face value, but apparently valuing their opinions.

"Shaniqua," McLaughlin pipes in, "you're in a unique position to save millions of lives. And I think you would add far more to the team than just your talent in the cockpit. Your enthusiasm and... your *vibrancy*... would do so much for morale."

Kara nods her agreement. "We want you." She meets McLaughlin's eyes. *More than anyone else we've interviewed today*, she adds silently.

Shaniqua breaks into a wide smile. "Okay then. So what's the next step?"

**Monday evening
December 1, 2014**

In contrast with their previous stop, nothing goes quite right from the time Kara and McLaughlin hop out of their fighter in Miami. They're here to see Jose Morales, who works as a sanitation engineer for the city of Coral Gables. It's clear from the dossier that the title is simply a euphemism for garbage collector, which is why they left this interview until last—there would have been no convenient opportunity to talk to Jose, much less find him, while he was out on his rounds.

Kara had hoped to be waiting for him when he got off work at five, but a few minor delays earlier in the day joined forces to bring them to their last stop over an hour and a half late. Now they discover that, despite their tardiness, their car isn't ready. By the time they finally pull up at Jose's apartment building, they're pushing 7:30.

The interior hallway they take to find Jose's door is old but clean; the walls and especially the doors could use a coat of paint, and the carpet has gone from thin to threadbare in places. Twenty feet down the hall, a couple is making out, but there's enough light for Kara to see that the man's eyes are open; the woman, her back to them, is presumably keeping watch in the other direction. *What a life*, Kara thinks, shaking her head. McLaughlin finds the right door and gives it a good rap. They wait a minute, then he gives it another try. Nothing.

"I guess that's what we get for not calling ahead," Kara says with a wry smile. "Other than this, we've been pretty lucky. Harris could have called in sick, or Shaniqua might have scheduled a day off—either way, we'd have been out of luck."

"Maybe," McLaughlin says noncommittally. "What's his file say? How does he usually spend his evenings?"

"He usually stays home; that's why we came here first. But let me see..." She pulls out the slim folder. "Okay, looks like he frequents a club called the Purple Flamingo, or used to—not so much since his girlfriend dumped him. Since then he's spent more time at the movies, usually by himself. Two nights a week he's in class, but tonight's not one of them... oh wait, sometimes there are study sessions." Her shoulders slump. "Trying to find him would be hard, impossible if he's in some dark movie theatre."

"Why don't you give General Peterson a call."

"Peterson? Why?"

He shrugs. "I'm just saying."

Eyes narrowed, Kara pulls out her cheap phone and speed dials the man.

"*Speak.*"

"General, it's Kara. We're outside Morales' apartment, but he's not here. We got delayed."

"*Okay, hold on.*" The line clicks, and she knows the receiver has been turned off on the other end. She looks suspiciously at McLaughlin, still at a loss as to how Peterson can be of assistance. After about a minute of silence, the man comes back on. "*He's down at a nearby night club. The Purple Flamingo. Back corner booth.*"

"How do you know that?" Kara demands. She's already striding briskly down the hall toward the outside door.

"*Ask Joker.*" The line clicks off.

"John. How does Peterson know where he is? I mean, not just the address, but which seat his butt is currently occupying." She doesn't give him a chance to answer. "He's got someone tailing him, doesn't he?" She grabs McLaughlin's arm to stop him on the top step as they exit the building into the darkened night. Peripherally, she notes no fewer than three loiterers; this neighborhood, she realizes, represents the easiest assignment any of her security details has encountered today.

McLaughlin grimaces. "Yeah. All of them do."

"All of them? Everyone we talked to today?"

"Everyone on your original list, all the people you had files prepared on." He gives an embarrassed laugh, perhaps at her naivete. "I mean, Kara... how else do you think our people found out so much about them?"

That certainly makes her stop. She really hadn't given it much thought before now. "But is that really necessary?" she asks finally. "Seems like overkill."

"As soon as you wrote up that list, these people were identified as a vital national resource. Ever since then, each one has been monitored every minute." Angry, she turns back toward the car, but he grasps her shoulder. "You know, when something is valuable, you want to know where it is at all times. So you can protect it. So that no one can steal it."

"Steal it? Who's gonna steal a garbage collector?"

"Actually..." He suddenly looks far more uncomfortable. "When it comes to video gamers, the U.S. is filthy rich. Outside the U.S.... not so much. What if some other country wants a space defense force of their own? Where will they get the pilots?"

"You've gotta be kidding me!"

He shrugs. "I'm just saying it *could* happen."

"So even the people that we've ruled out, the ones that will never be part of this thing—they're being watched?"

"Yeah. But they'll never know it. Most people aren't that observant."

Their path to the Flamingo skirts the city, and they run into traffic; Kara begins calculating just how late they'll be when they get back to base, just how little sleep she'll get before the next morning's debriefing.

It's after nine when they enter the smoky, laser-lit warehouse known as the Purple Flamingo. There's no telling if their man is still sitting in the corner, but it's as good a place as any to start, so Kara leads the way across the dance floor. With all the visual pollution, not to mention oscillating human bodies, visibility falls somewhere shy of twenty feet. She wonders what her detail makes of this—on the one hand, it's easier to blend in; on the other, the press of bodies is so tight it would probably give Peterson a conniption to see Kara's exposure as she pushes through. Eventually the back wall of the place emerges from the swirl, and a moment later Kara has located their quarry.

"Jose Morales?" She has to shout to be heard.

The diminutive Hispanic man, looking painfully young, inclines his head to acknowledge her. He's leaning back in the circular booth seat, each arm draped around a less-than-modestly dressed woman. One of them glances up at Kara, then goes back to a giggly conversation with the other.

"I'm Kara, this is John. Mind if we talk?"

Jose waves his hand as if to say "whatever," and Kara makes a move to climb into the booth. The girls stand abruptly, the simultaneous movement reminding Kara of a flock of birds unexpectedly changing direction together. "Hey!" Jose says plaintively. "You coming back?"

"I don't know," one of them says thoughtfully, with a coquettish bat of her lashes. "You still buying?"

"Yeah, sure."

"Okay then!" she says brightly, and the two disappear into the crowd.

Jose's eyes follow their departing forms longingly as Kara and McLaughlin crawl into flanking positions in the booth.

"You're not an easy person to find," Kara says to break the ice. When the small man just stares at her in confusion, she forges on. "You're Slickster, right? Your gaming handle? I'm CareerStud."

Pause. "In *Rampant*?" It takes him a moment to switch mental gears, but his eyes widen when he does. "CareerStud? *Dude*, I thought you were a— like, a dude," he finishes lamely. After a moment, he brightens considerably. "But hey, you're not. Cool."

Kara feels herself flush, and she knows John McLaughlin well enough by now to guess that he's probably stifling laughter; she keeps her eyes on Jose, willing herself not to look up.

Jose turns to McLaughlin, "How 'bout you? Do I know you too?"

"No," Kara answers. "John's a player, and a hot one too, but he never played online until recently."

"Cool. So how'd you find me?" He waves at a passing server, indicating his need of a refill; the other two decline to order.

"Um, well, we're actually working with the government," she says embarrassedly. She'd rather not just come out and say, 'Gee, Jose, we've had a spy watching your every move for the last two months.'

"What?" Jose says sharply.

"It's— The situation is that they need our help. What went down in Denver, they think we can be part of the solution."

"You mean... what do you mean?"

"I mean there's going to be space combat, and we're the best at that."

"So you're trying to recruit me? You want me to join the Air Force or something?"

"Not exactly. We've got something different in the works, but you're close."

"Forget it."

Kara blinks, surprised at how quickly the Latino reaches his decision, without even hearing them out. She glances at McLaughlin, who speaks up.

"Jose, listen man. This is the opportunity of a lifetime. The chance to be part of something brand new, a whole new branch of the military. For one thing, you'll be famous. But you'll also be saving lives. Because of your experience with this game, you're more qualified than just about anyone else we could recruit."

As McLaughlin's voice grows more insistent, Jose's head-shaking becomes more pronounced. "No way, man."

Kara's at a loss. "But why? Why not?"

Jose buries his head in his hands. After a moment, his voice emerges. "Let me tell you somethin'. The army told two of my buddies the same thing. Told 'em they could be part of something special, told 'em they would wear a uniform and people would respect 'em. Told 'em they could save lives." He leans back and drops his arms into his lap. "And ya know what? They wanted that. We love our country, man. You probably think I'm from Cuba or something, just 'cuz I talk different, but I'm not. I'm an American. I was born here. But most white people, they treat me like a foreigner, like some immigrant right off the boat.

"My boys, they had something to prove. They never got as much opportunity as I bet you did, but they wanted to show they took their responsibility serious. So they joined up." He rubs his face again, silent for a long moment. "They got killed in Iraq, man.

"And you know what they got for it all? A medal. So much for the glory and respect. Their moms got a folded flag and a medal from some guy in uniform who couldn't wait to get out the door, probably to give a flag to some other mom. So yeah," he concludes, "you can forget it."

Kara meets McLaughlin's eye, feeling deflated. There's not much to say. She reaches over and squeezes Jose's arm, and his eyes shine overbright as he looks up. "I'm sorry, Jose." She sighs. "We'll let you get back to your drink."

He nods and they exit.

Kara's ears are ringing when they get back to the car. She fishes out her phone and dials Stephens. "No go on Morales. Looks like we'll be making the pitch to Brinkman tomorrow after all."

"*I see... I'll go ahead and arrange for a detail to meet you in Houston. Say... 9 o'clock?*"

"No, I can't get away tomorrow—too busy. It'll probably be John, since we need everyone on base by Wednesday for our first meeting."

"*Okay. As far as your other new recruits go, pickup went smoothly. They should be settled in by tomorrow night, all the forms signed.*"

"How are they feeling, do you think?"

Stephens chuckles. "*Nervous, maybe scared. But they're definitely eager to know more. If I had a nickel for every probing question I got from DeMaria...*"

She smiles tiredly. "Great. Thanks." She flips the phone closed and looks at McLaughlin. "I guess we go home now."

He smiles back. "You sure there's nothing you want to do in sunny South Florida while we're here?"

She snorts at the word 'sunny' as she looks out at the darkened sky, then turns back to him. "Hmmm… Can we find a drive-thru somewhere? I haven't had a real burger since Grant recruited me nine months ago."

[Chapter 24]

**Monday night
December 1, 2014**

  Gazing out the cockpit window from the F-15E's WSO seat—the station designed for a weapon systems officer—Kara finds herself enjoying the return leg of their flight far better than that first sprint from Nevada to Georgia. As McLaughlin put it, she's earned her 'air legs,' having now logged several hours in the cockpit. She knows that at least part of her newfound aplomb is due to the fact that there's no longer anything to be seen out the window. Whereas that first flight was a ground-hugger, with plenty of banking and swooping and scenery to watch zipping past, McLaughlin is minimizing fuel consumption on their longer return from Miami by grabbing more altitude. Since it's almost midnight, details are harder to make out in any case. Whatever the reason, Kara finds the trip peaceful, something she really needs right now.
  Of course, there's nothing like a solid fast food combo meal to bring contentment after almost ten months of bland 'healthy' food.
  Kara heaves a sigh and tries to pick out individual constellations to her left and right. In the tight cockpit, darkened but for the dim glow of numerous instrument panels, she can almost believe she's on a road trip. Though in this case, the driver is sitting directly in front of her rather than to her left.
  "Everything okay back there?" McLaughlin's voice crackles over her helmet's speaker.
  "Yep," she responds, speaking into the oxygen mask-cum-microphone strapped over her nose and mouth. "Just doing a little stargazing."
  "Enjoy it while you can. I hear these new spaceships you're cramming us into have no windows."
  She laughs but feels an odd pang. The reasoning behind that decision was more than valid, but it does seem an awful waste—to be out there, actually floating in space, but visually locked away where the stark beauty of the heavens can't be appreciated. She

sighs again. "John, off to our left, that funny triangular constellation right on the horizon... what is it?"

His voice sounds a little worried as he responds: "Yeah... the one that seems to be keeping pace with us?"

Kara's heartbeat quickens as she realizes he's right. "Right, that one."

His answering laughter is full and reassuring, not the least bit mocking as he says, "That would be one of our escorts."

"Oh," she says, feeling stupid.

"No worries. Hey, you never told me how you handled the thing with Grant's daughter."

Kara grimaces. "I didn't really. It's not like I wanted to tell Viviane her dad was in jail; it just seemed like something she should know. But actually getting her on the line yesterday... I didn't see how it did anyone any good. It's not like she'll find out from anyone else. And by not telling her, I save myself at least one reason for Peterson to be angry with me. So we just talked... As seldom as that happens, I'm glad I didn't ruin it with bad news. Viviane can be emotional at times."

"I didn't realize you two actually knew each other."

Kara smiles. "For years now. We're like sisters." They lapse into silence for a time, then: "How do you deal with all the secrecy, John? It puts such a strain on relationships."

"That's a good question," he replies. "Let me know when you find the answer." He chuckles. "But seriously... it's just a matter of how strong the relationship is. The people you keep up with... your interactions have to be based on something deeper than sharing the details of your day, obviously. But I enjoy having intellectual discussions with my ladies, you know, talking over the occasional profound thought or philosophical question that comes to me. We often share from our quiet time, too." He laughs. "Nothing classified about that, fortunately."

Kara frowns. "Quiet time?"

McLaughlin chuckles quietly. "Sorry. I mean when we read our Bible. Pray. That sort of thing." He pauses, maybe a bit uncomfortably. "I know you're not religious. But we like to share what we're learning with each other."

Kara's lip quirks into a lopsided smile, a little surprised at the realization that his mention of faith doesn't bother her. For whatever reason, the occasional times that McLaughlin's brought up the subject, it hasn't bothered her the way it does coming from some people—like Gene, who seems to think everyone believes the same way he does. It helps that McLaughlin doesn't wear religion on his sleeve... but probably more so, it's the fact that he obviously accepts her exactly as she is, despite all the valid reasons he has to resent her. John McLaughlin is just genuine.

What makes her smile now is his apparent admission to being a ladies' man. "So," she asks playfully, "you have lots of women waiting for you back home?"

There's a momentary pause, and when the man speaks, he sounds confused. "Um, I guess. I just mean my mom and my wife. Evelyn moved in with Mom when I was first stationed at Groom Lake. My dad died a while back."

Now Kara feels incredibly stupid. "Oh. I didn't... I mean, you're married?"

"Definitely." McLaughlin sounds more uncomfortable now than confused. "I didn't give you a different impression, did I? That I was available? Or..." She can almost hear him swallow with embarrassment. "Or... looking?"

Kara erupts into laughter, unable to contain it. "No, John, not at all. I've never felt like you were coming onto me. Far from it. You're the very image of propriety."

"Okay, good. Because that would be bad on multiple levels."

Still laughing, Kara says, "I agree. Sorry, I just... I haven't tried getting to know you and Anna and the others on a personal level. And I feel bad about that."

"Well, we do get pretty good at secrecy, even about stuff that doesn't need to be secret."

"I'll make a better effort of drawing it out of you," Kara assures him. "So tell me about your wife. Evelyn, you said?"

"That's right." His voice is subtly different as he describes her, and Kara can easily believe she's the center of his world. "I met her while I was at the Academy. She was a few years older, already teaching second grade. Compared to some of the huge egos in my class, she was a breath of fresh air. She's quiet, but just a naturally encouraging and supportive person. From the very beginning, whenever we'd go out together, I always had this feeling like, as far as she was concerned, there was no one else in the room but me."

He talks more about their courtship, their wedding, and the early deployments of his Air Force career post-academy. Kara is struck by the fact that, for all the wonderful things he has to say about his wife, he never once mentions any physical characteristic: not the color of her hair or eyes, not her height or whether he finds her smile infectious, nothing. Perversely, Kara wonders if she should read meaning into that omission.

"It was hard when we finally discovered that Evelyn—" He stops. "Sorry, I, uh… we don't usually share this with people. But…" He pauses again, speaking hesitantly. "Well, we both love children, and we discovered last year that we can't. Have kids, I mean." He falls silent for a moment, then laughs a little. "You're a good listener back there, drawing stuff like *that* out of me."

She smiles a little. "I'm sorry to hear that."

"It's not a major loss. We always knew we would adopt a few kids. This just means we get to adopt all of them. I guess that's an answer to your question too…" He trails off.

"Which question?"

"About how we deal with the secrecy. We deal by making plans for the future. By looking forward to the big family we'll have when I'm out of the service—when I don't have to worry about secrecy anymore. When I can have a real life."

"Oh. I assumed you were a career officer."

"Well… that's usually a good impression to project. Actually telling your CO that you're not planning on re-upping is generally considered a bad idea." He laughs. "And that's exactly what I just did."

"Why is it bad? Sounds like more of this secrecy crap to me."

"It can be bad for morale if people think an officer has his mind on anything other than the service."

"If you say so. How much longer are you in for?"

"Three more years on this commitment. I guess it all depends on how this alien thing plays out, though, doesn't it?" There's more gravity in his voice as he says this.

"Yeah, I guess it does."

They continue to talk, the mood lightening again as they chat back and forth about their childhoods. McLaughlin is in the midst of a hilarious tale about a particularly elaborate prank he pulled as a kid, when suddenly he stops mid-sentence. "Hold on."

Silence stretches over the headset. As if from a distance, Kara can hear the muffled sound of McLaughlin's voice directly, from within the cockpit, but barely audible over the noise of rushing air and roaring engines.

"That was the controller," he finally tells her, transmitting once more over the cockpit radio channel. Kara can feel the jet executing a sharp bank. "They just detected a UFO in close proximity to us."

"*What?*" Kara blurts.

Despite the obvious tension in his voice, McLaughlin can't help but laugh. "UFO just means we don't know what it is: unidentified flying object."

"Oh," she replies, again feeling foolish. "So what? Something just took off nearby?"

"Well... no." The humor is gone. "This object entered atmosphere from orbit. It's probably just a meteor, but its point of entry is awfully coincidental, so we're diverting to be—"

In that instant, McLaughlin's voice again cuts out, simultaneous with the winking out of every display and instrument in the cockpit. Kara gasps. Reminding herself there's nothing she personally can do—though she'd much rather there were—she focuses on breathing and sits back to wait it out.

She catches the sound of a muffled voice, and it takes her another minute to realize it's John speaking from outside her helmet. She unsnaps the mask and lifts her helmet—remarkably difficult with the canopy window directly above her head. "What was that?" she belts out.

"I said I've lost all control! We'll give it another twenty seconds, but then we'll have to punch out!" Even though he's shouting, he sounds calm.

"What?" she yells back.

"I mean eject! Make sure your helmet and mask are strapped on! Do it now, and sit tight! I'll take care of everything!"

Another short eternity passes, during which Kara directs her attention at the constellations, looking to them for comfort. And then suddenly, rapidly, the stars begin disappearing. Simply reacting to the perception of an object looming straight toward her, Kara ducks instinctively, right before the jet bucks with a resounding *clang*. Ahead of her, McLaughlin is yelling, but she can't make out the words. She can't make out anything—it's as if a blanket has been dropped over the cockpit window, shutting out even the minimal illumination of the starry night.

McLaughlin yells something along the lines of "Here we go!" and in the next moment, the canopy glass implodes into thousands of tiny pieces.

They both howl in pain as shards of superheated glass rebound unexpectedly, reentering the cockpit instead of blowing out and away. Suddenly the decibel level is unbearable, and Kara feels the passage of cold air on the exposed parts of her face and neck. But the actual ejection doesn't happen.

A light suddenly appears, resolving itself into a beam and jumping around erratically within the cockpit. It takes her a moment, but Kara realizes McLaughlin is using a flashlight. By its diffuse glow, she sees that the window above her no longer exists, having been shattered intentionally as part of the manual ejection sequence; however, something dark and menacing is holding station directly above their craft, almost within arm's reach, making successful ejection a lethal proposition.

Staring hard, she begins to make out weird, complex geometric designs as her eyes adjust to the light. *Boom! Boom-Boom!* McLaughlin, with no other course of action left to him, is firing his sidearm point blank at the thing above them. *Boom! Boom!* She registers that the air is growing rapidly cooler, almost frigid now, and realizes that they're gaining altitude rapidly. And since their craft is without power, that must mean—

McLaughlin fires again, and after that, events speed by too quickly for her to comprehend. There's a sudden *whoosh*, and she's being torn every which way, head whipped back and forth painfully. She clamps down on the bile rising up her throat—greasy hamburger, half-digested—still buffeted back and forth until finally, finally, she feels her passage stabilizing. From the rush of frigid air against her neck, she knows she's been successfully ejected, but otherwise it feels as if she's floating. Although these facts should reassure her, there's nothing calming about the prospect of freefall thousands of feet above Earth's surface. Opening her eyes tells her little more, except that the stars are back, as they should be.

A sudden radiance flares above her, and for just an instant, she makes out what appears to be a triangular white body—not illuminated by some external light source, but actually *glowing* brilliantly. The next moment, that shape disappears into a billowing white cloud that nevertheless continues to shine diffusely. And then the whole thing explodes.

The shockwave hits her like a physical thing, a maelstrom of superheated air, blasting her, blasting past her, and throwing her acceleration seat off on a bucking, twisting, tumbling tangent to put her initial ejection to shame. Screaming uncontrollably, Kara can't stop the vomit that erupts into her mask, and in another instant she's choking, gagging, suffocating, unable to get any oxygen. Fighting the forces pushing and pulling at her tumbling body, Kara manages slowly, ever so slowly, to reach up, fumble at the catch, unsnap the mask strapped to her face. She expels the vitriol filling her mouth in a violent cough, then sucks in a huge breath of too-thin air...

And blacks out.

Kara comes to slowly, the pounding in her head intense. She takes three deep, sating breaths before realizing the significance of that and gasping, which sends her into a fit of coughing.

"Colonel, it's okay."

She blinks open her eyes and struggles to focus. She's in a small room, with someone leaning over her. No, it's the back of an ambulance, and that someone is John McLaughlin. "John?"

"Yes, ma'am." His uncharacteristic deference confuses her, but she becomes aware of others crammed into the space as well.

"Um..." She struggles to sit up, but they push her back down. "Where are we?"

"We're..." John pauses. "Actually, I don't know."

"Welcome to the middle of nowhere, Nebraska," a cheerful voice sounds, "where you're lucky to have fields of corn to break your fall."

"What happened?" She finally manages to focus on McLaughlin's face. "That UFO, was that—"

His eyes flash a warning, and Kara realizes that, of course, they're surrounded by civilians. And she herself is no longer a civilian, no longer free to speak freely.

"I still think we should take her to a hospital, check her out more fully," the friendly voice continues. "She's got a fractured ankle, and there's no telling how long she suffered oxygen deprivation."

"You have no idea how much we appreciate your quick response," McLaughlin says placatingly, "but we've got to get going. Our transport will be here soon." To Kara, he adds, "Congrats, by the way. You just earned yourself a Purple Heart, not to mention a nifty lapel pin for surviving an aircraft ejection. Ma'am."

Kara rolls her eyes and groans. "I didn't even do anything. I was just a passenger."

"Don't complain," he says, laughing, though she can see sadness in his eyes. He leans in and lowers his voice. "Gene will be pleased you've got something to fill up all that empty space on your brand-new uniform. Appearances, you know."

She smiles and tries to speak, but he just lifts another finger to his lips. Distantly, she makes out the sound of chopper rotors. Giving in, she flops back on the stretcher as they pull her from the ambulance and begin wheeling her across a parking lot.

"I'll tell you more on the ride home," McLaughlin promises as the chopper heaves into view.

[Chapter 25]

Tuesday morning
December 2, 2014

John McLaughlin proves true to his word, sharing with Kara what they know as they chopper back to base under heavy escort, this time flying so close to the ground—below radar coverage—that she's glad to be stretched out flat on a gurney where she can't see. McLaughlin admits that the object plummeting from orbit was, after all, a UFO in the popular sense: an actual spacecraft operated by their enemies. As soon as it was within range, it had fired some variant of EMP, an electromagnetic pulse generating enough radiation to overwhelm nearby electronics. It was this pulse that caused their fighter and those of their escorts to suddenly go dark. At the speed they were moving, there was only limited time in which to reboot their systems, and none of the pilots managed to do so.

As for the craft that practically landed on McLaughlin and Kara's F-15, radar evidence confirms it was the original bogey. After their two blips merged on the scope, the UFO had indeed begun dragging them into high-altitude at orbital escape velocities, probably employing a magnetic grapple of similar design to the Destrier's. Although no one would ever vocalize it, now or later, Kara imagines the words that will be running through everyone's head: alien abduction. It would probably never be clear the exact effect McLaughlin's small arms fire had, but presumably it damaged the alien craft in some way, because within a minute of their successful ejection—before they even reached the proper altitude for their chutes to deploy automatically—the UFO had undergone a devastating chain reaction so intense it left no meaningful wreckage for the forensics people to analyze. Judging by tiny spatter burns on their clothing and ejection seats, the strange craft's destruct sequence had involved some sort of highly-destructive phosphorous agent.

It is with infinite sadness that McLaughlin shares of the death of two of their escort pilots. The first, Lt. Zachary Burke, never managed to eject. The second, Lt. Abby Williamson, became tangled in her parachute lines in the wake of the enemy craft's explosion, and the twisted chutes were unable to properly slow her before she hit the ground. Like Kara, both will be awarded Purple Hearts for their sacrifice, though posthumously, and Kara cannot help but feel even worse about receiving the medal herself—simply because she broke an ankle upon touching down; she wasn't even conscious at the time. Needless to say, the senseless deaths of these brave pilots add just a little bit more to that persistent weight which pulls her down.

Following their return to base, Kara is admitted to the infirmary in their bunker, where a kindly, elderly doctor by the name of Jacobs is very thorough in checking her out. As he fits her with a walking cast—the ankle break is clean, likely to heal quickly—they talk through her medical history. He shows particular concern when she mentions her asthma, presumably in light of the oxygen deprivation she suffered, but his dismay only grows as he returns to her records and studies them with renewed intensity. In the end, he discharges her with assurances that all is well and she'll make a full recovery… but he's no longer smiling.

Fortunately, the time zones work in Kara's favor. Even with their late departure from the East Coast and the incident that followed, it's still shy of 2 a.m. on base, and she hurries quickly to bed. Before turning in, she's happy to discover a message from Peterson releasing her from their scheduled 7 a.m. debriefing. She never gives the doctor's strange behavior another thought—not until years later, at least, when she'll wish she had.

With her debriefing temporarily postponed, the first item on Kara's agenda the next morning is a 9 a.m. bureaucratic rendezvous involving the Joint Chiefs and representatives of the Air Force Space Command, or AFSPC, headquartered at nearby Peterson AFB in Colorado. The purpose of this second meeting is to establish chains of command and spheres of responsibility. Technically, defense against extraterrestrial threats would fall under the purview of the AFSPC, but in truth, the AFSPC's charter was written with a more Earth-centric mission in mind: namely, surveillance of enemy nations and defense against ground-launched ballistic weaponry. As such, it is ultimately decided that Kara's new, as-yet-unnamed branch of the military will be completely independent of the AFSPC, whose charter will be rewritten to reflect a narrower focus. Both will answer to U.S. Strategic Command—USSTRATCOM—a multi-service unified combat command which has maintained ultimate responsibility for all military space operations since 2002, when Donald Rumsfeld reorganized the Defense Department.

The meeting would normally prove tedious for Kara, who is hopelessly lost amidst the red tape, but after the events of the previous evening, she welcomes a little boredom. Nevertheless, what she cannot get over is just how long it takes to establish *officially* who is responsible for what and how they will all communicate with one another, considering that all parties appear to be in complete agreement on these points even from the beginning of the meeting. Fortunately, she has no need to understand any of it, as her chain of command will continue to run straight through Peterson. She is on hand simply as insurance against the occasional arcane question.

The discussions wax straight through lunch, which is catered, and Kara is finally dismissed at almost 2 p.m. She and Peterson return to his office—Grant's office, as she cannot help but still think of it—for the delayed debriefing, which lasts a further hour. Although the original intent of the meeting was to review Kara's recruiting efforts from the day before, fully forty minutes is spent instead analyzing the implications of last night's attack. Although nothing about the clash is certain, what they find most disturbing is that the enemy knew exactly when and where to strike—even which craft Kara herself occupied. This could be due to a leak in Peterson's organization or *K'luran* technology so advanced as to cut through Air Force security measures, but neither option is encouraging; at least in this case, they can rule out the possibility of Axmatik's people being involved. In addition to the penetration of their secrecy, Peterson and Kara also have to consider the fact that the enemy is now targeting Kara directly rather than working through human intermediaries. Just one more thing to worry about.

At 3 o'clock, Kara is available to welcome her new recruits as they begin arriving on base, and after the morning she's had, it proves a welcome responsibility. They're being given the same treatment she was, namely sequestration while dozens of pages of forms are read and signed. Kara, concerned that too much time alone with such paperwork will scare the average person out of his wits, makes sure to poke her head in every hour or so to encourage them.

The surprise of the day comes just after dinner, as Kara is stumping down the hall towards her quarters. Looking up, she comes face to face with Jose Morales flanked by two members of the Security Forces. Her shock prevents her from uttering anything intelligible, but he favors her with a murderous look anyway before continuing on his way.

**Tuesday evening
December 2, 2014**

Kara taps lightly on the door; it's almost ten, and she doesn't want to disturb the room's occupant if he's already asleep. There's no sound from within, but after a moment, the door is pulled open about a foot. When no face appears, Kara pushes into the room and closes the door behind her.

Jose is already crawling back onto the bed. His room is laid out with the bed in a corner, and he wedges his back into that corner without meeting her eyes. She considers asking his permission to sit, but thinks better of it. Settling into the desk chair, she says, "General Peterson just told me what... what they did to you."

No response.

"I'm sorry, Jose. I didn't even know. Seeing you here... it was a complete surprise, honestly." As was finding out that Peterson had simply canceled McLaughlin's trip to recruit Phil Brinkman this afternoon.

Motionless but for his eyes, Jose glances at her, glances briefly at her leg cast as if mildly surprised, then quickly looks away again. Kara struggles mightily with her emotions. This crap about forced recruitment in the name of national security just isn't right. It happened with Gene and now with Jose, and who knows how many others? Kara is almost biting her tongue to keep that frustration from spilling out. She hates that Jose obviously thinks she's in on it, or at least condones it. But to undercut her boss would be bad even in a civilian organization; she's beginning to realize that doing so in the military can have consequences that are actually dangerous. She grinds her teeth. She can hold her tongue, but she can't stop anger coursing through her at the injustice of the situation.

"Look, when we meet tomorrow for the first time—as a group, I mean—you'll meet Gene Jenkins. You know, Jinx. They did the same thing to him, and I worked with him for over a month before I even found out about it." She sighs, trying to find a way to be encouraging without being insubordinate. "This is not the way I want to operate this unit. If we're going to expect people to fight and maybe even die"—Jose winces at this—"we can't force them into service. But we're not there yet. What we're building right now is just a small group of pilots to create a public face and reassure the public. After that, we should have enough volunteers with the right skill set that we don't have to force anyone.

"Unfortunately, we're in a time crunch. The President wants to go public with all this on the 15th, and there were only a few people we felt comfortable bringing in on such short notice. You were one of them."

She waits, but still nothing. With a sigh, she gives up on tact. "Look, I know how you're feeling, okay? You have no idea just how closely I identify. I hate what they did to you—you didn't even get to pack a bag. That's wrong. But Jose, neither of us can do anything about it. And whether it's right or wrong, the motivation behind it is commendable... because you have a talent that could save millions of lives." She heaves a sigh. "When we meet tomorrow, will you try to put a good face on it? The others won't know what happened, and I don't want them to. Talk about a morale killer..." she chuckles tentatively, but she's alone in this.

"Kara," he says weakly, then clears his throat. "You need me for a bunch of photos and interviews and stuff. When that's over, you'll have the pilots you need. Will they... Do you think I can get out then?"

He looks at her with such hope, his face almost childlike, that Kara feels she would do anything to ease his torment. "I don't know, Jose, but I'll do everything I can to get you released."

He nods, swallowing hard. "I *do* love my country. But I don't want to die for it."

She nods back, blinking away sudden tears.

A minute later, as she limps down the hall to her own quarters, she reflects that Jose's situation really *isn't* terribly different from hers. Both of them are being swept along by events outside their control, not being given much of a say in the matter. The realization doesn't make her feel any better, but it does challenge her to accept the very encouragement she offered him—to remember that she's in a unique position to defend people who can't defend themselves. Inadequate or unprepared as she may be, Fate or random chance or *something* has put her in this position… and if she can do something to help, then she's obligated to give it her all.

[Chapter 26]

December 2, 2014
Tuesday evening

    Anna Haynes sips her drink, watching disinterestedly as the man enters. It's obvious he doesn't belong, and Anna's not the only one to glance his way. Other than the ball cap, which the man should have removed, there's nothing unusual about his clothing; he's dressed as casually as everyone else. But the way he carries himself, the way he stands there gaping at the unusual sights... she's a little surprised he doesn't have a camera slung around his neck.
    "So who ya think it was?"
    "Huh?" She turns away from the outsider; the guy's probably just a tourist who wandered too far from Vegas. "What are you talking about?"
    Barrett gives her a look like she's crazy. "What do you *think* I'm talking about?"
    "Oh." She grimaces. "You know we shouldn't be discussing that."
    Barrett scoffs. "It's not like we know more than anyone else." He waves a lazy hand to encompass the pub. Behind the bar, the TV is tuned to a 24-hour news channel, and even without audio, it's obvious what the current story's about. It's been several weeks, but most national news segments are still focused on the attack and its aftermath.
    "True," she admits. Of course, the people they work with probably *do* know the full story, including who it was that perpetrated the first nuclear bombing on U.S. soil. But whatever they may know, they've not seen fit to tell Anna squat.
    "So..." Barrett prompts. "Who do ya think it was?"
    "Well, there aren't that many possibilities," she says, leaning back in her chair and looking around the bar. It's a slow night, of course, being a weekday, but there's still a fair representation of pilots: Herc drivers, Viper drivers, Eagle drivers... Among their ilk, Nellis is known as "the Barndoor," because operators of all types are constantly passing through on their way somewhere else.

Which is exactly why she and Barrett had driven up for the day, so they could run down a few potential recruits for their new unit.

"North Korea," Barrett offers, "Pakistan or India. *Israel...*"

"China and Russia," Anna adds, finishing out the list. "That's it."

Across the way, she notices the tourist snapping photos after all, using his cell phone camera, clearly in seventh heaven as he takes in all the trappings typical of a pilot bar. She watches idly as he photographs the personalized beer steins stacked behind the barkeeper, the squadron paraphernalia adorning the walls, the parachutes hanging from the ceiling.

"Terrorists?"

She shifts her attention back to Barrett again. "No way, man." She pauses, drops her voice. "This wasn't some suitcase nuke, Twix. Someone launched against us, and they hid their point of origin." She rubs finger against thumb. "That kind of tech *costs*. 'Sides, Grant already confirmed this was a foreign power."

"*Did* he?" Barrett asks with a knowing smile.

She frowns, thinking it over as she watches the tourist making a fool of himself in the corner of the room, posing with an old ejection seat while a longsuffering pilot dutifully captures the ridiculous image. She tries hard to remember Grant's exact wording... but she can't. She *does* remember quite clearly when the old man first spoke to their team—introducing them to this brand-new theatre of warfare they were to be trained for—but he gave very little detail about *who* they would be fighting. Her limited exposure to Grant in the four years since that time only reinforced her first impression of the man, that he played his cards *very* close to the vest.

"Well?" Barrett interrupts her thoughts, feigning impatience. "Who do you think?"

Anna sighs. "I think we can rule out Israel. And too pricey for Pakistan or Korea."

"What about France and England?"

She just rolls her eyes.

"Which leaves Russia and China, like you said."

Anna nods slowly. "My money's on China."

Barrett perks up. "How much?"

She barks a laugh. "Not again, man. You're always taking my money." Still, she hesitates, sorely tempted. "'Course… depends who *you*'re betting on, Twix."

"Aw, Sweeps, that's easy," he says, using her callsign the way she's been using his. An establishment like this has many unspoken rules, and 'callsigns only' is one of the most basic. He clears his throat, grinning impishly as he leans forward. "It was E.T."

Anna frowns. "E.T.?"

"C'mon, man, you know—*aliens*."

Anna bursts into laughter. "Make it a buck then." She takes a pull on her beer and looks around curiously for that tourist, wondering what he's gotten into now. She finds him at the crud table, carefully reading the mounted sign which outlines all the house rules, clearly very confused about this obscure version of billiards which requires only the cue and eight balls.

"A hundred? I'm not *that* sure," Barrett admits.

"Huh?"

"About the aliens." His face twists. "Make it a ten spot?"

Anna shakes her head in wonder. "You're serious? You really think aliens just nuked us?" Her friend begins to object, but she waves him off impatiently. "I mean, you think that's a serious possibility?"

Barrett shrugs, uncharacteristically serious and uncomfortable. "Nothin' else fits," he says slowly. "Grant knew the attack was coming a *long* time before. Seems like he even knew *where*."

Leaning back, Anna tries to follow his logic. "So you're saying… if Grant knew when and where, it stands to reason he knew *who*. But if he knew *who*…" She trails off.

"If he knew *who*," Barrett completes the thought, "we woulda gone preemptive on 'em. Exactly."

"But we couldn't prevent the attack through traditional military means, because the attack *originated* in outer space?" She scowls "I dunno, man… that's a huge leap. You've dreamed up a whole new species of sentient beings solely based on what you *think* Grant might or might not've known ahead of time."

Barrett shrugs, overly casual, his momentary disquiet long gone. "Maybe," he allows. "So… ten?"

Anna bites her lip, fighting a smile, and feeling horrible about it. It's such an appalling thing to be discussing so nonchalantly. For that matter, if she's honest, it feels wrong that life has continued on as usual these last few weeks, wrong that she and Barrett are sitting here shooting the breeze like this, in light of the unprecedented loss of life that just occurred.

And yet, normality is what she desperately *needs* right now. The bombing was bad enough. But she'd been forced to kill two men that same day—her, personally, shoot and kill a pair of enemy agents. Right now, her bond with Barrett is the only thing keeping her sane, and if their joking is a bit insensitive, what of it?

"Fine," she says, "I'm in."

But Barrett's no longer paying attention to her. His eyes are focused over her shoulder, no hint of a smile on his face. "Look out," he says softly, "Nosejob on your seven."

Reflexively, she begins to turn left, then checks the movement. Her caution is wasted, however, because the man has apparently already seen her. Or, more likely, he's seen Barrett.

"Well, well, well..." Captain Andy Craft launches his opening salvo like a line out of a bad movie. "If it isn't Lieutenant Hayseed." His expression is gleeful, but she can see the hatred burning in his eyes, stronger than ever. He's accompanied by two men who assume flanking positions, acting for all the world like henchmen. Sneering, Craft says, "I been lookin' forward to the day I see you again."

Anna tries and fails to keep from flushing; she'd always hated that awful callsign Craft assigned her when she first joined his unit. Of course, as a wet-behind-the-ears rookie named Haynes, hailing from rural Oklahoma, the appellation was probably unavoidable, but most squadrons generally give their newest members *some* say in the choice of callsigns. Not Andy Craft, though. Oh well, she'd had her revenge...

Casual as can be, she says to Barrett, "Well lookie, Twix, it's ole Andy Nosejob." She deliberately shifts her gaze to stare at her antagonist's flattened nose, smiling in satisfaction. She herself was directly responsible for the new callsign Craft inevitably picked up following their last run-in.

Craft is no longer smiling. "That's *sir* to you, Lieutenant," he says quietly, menacingly. His stooges crowd a bit closer on either side, one of them going so far as to flex his well-developed muscles, in response to which Anna barks a laugh. Her former CO's eyes narrow in confusion, and she can tell he's suddenly unsure of his standing. He glances around, then tries again to get a rise out of her. "I don't see your fairy godfather here to protect you this time."

Anna resists the urge to stand up; she's so short she'd only come half-high on him. Instead, she stretches out, putting her feet up in an empty chair, forcing nonchalance. "I don't need Grant's protection. Those trumped up charges of yours are long gone."

It was the right thing to say if she wanted to make him even angrier. Craft glances at Barrett for the first time, then back at Anna. Exasperation mixes with anger as he says, "Who *is* this Grant anyway, that he can steal away two of my pilots and interfere with an Article 15?"

"Someone with an eye for talent, apparently," Anna quips before she can stop herself, a frequent problem for her.

Craft steps closer, fists tightening until the knuckles are white. Looking up at him, Anna wonders if the man would stoop so low as to throw a punch at a seated woman, but she'd rather like to see him try. It's been a while since she had a decent bar fight, and no matter how good a showing she made of it, the aftermath would be satisfying for sure.

Whatever might have happened next, their confrontation is interrupted by a loud electronic clamor from the bar. A civilian might take it for the sound of a slots machine hitting the jackpot, but the pilots know better. Already, a dozen operators have converged on the feckless tourist, slapping him good naturedly on the back as he smiles uncertainly, obviously confused about his sudden popularity. The man is still—even now—gripping the joystick mounted on the bar... the one non-pilots can never help but touch whenever they enter a bar like this. Finally the man lets go, jerking away from the bar with a look of horror as the pilots explain the situation: he's now on the hook to buy drinks for everyone present.

Nosejob Craft is trying to regain steam when Anna turns back to face him, but he's lost all control of the situation. "Well, I don't care who this Grant is, but I do expect proper respect from my subordinates." He glares at her, waiting.

Slowly, Anna rises to her full height of five-foot-two and fixes Craft with a look of her own. "As do I," she replies dangerously.

Craft is clearly bewildered and trying not to show it; meanwhile, Barrett stands to join Anna, stretching casually. His timing and delivery are perfect as he says, "I think it's time we head back to base, Major."

Her former CO blanches. "No way," he whispers finally, sounding half choked. "They promoted *you*?" he stammers out, disbelieving. It's an officer's worst nightmare, running into an old subordinate you used to pick on, only to discover they've now been promoted above you. And considering Anna Haynes' documented history of insubordination, it must be especially surprising in this case.

"It's amazing, really," Barrett says conversationally, "how some officers flourish if you just put them under good leaders." He shrugs and smiles at Craft's goons, who abruptly seem very interested in the free round of drinks going around at the bar.

Anna has eyes only for Craft himself, who stands directly between her and the exit. She could easily go around, of course, but… "Out of the way, Nose."

The man desperately wants to swing on her, she can see it in his eyes, but he hasn't yet built up the necessary liquor courage. "Fine," he eventually bites out, stepping aside.

"What was that?" Anna asks softly, not moving a muscle.

It takes Craft a long moment, during which he grinds his teeth almost audibly. "Yes, *ma'am*."

She deliberately bumps him on her way out the door.

Once outside, she and Barrett break into huge grins almost immediately. "That was great!" he enthuses.

"Better than I ever imagined," she agrees.

Her friend checks his watch. "It's 8 o'clock… We can knock around here another hour and still be back by midnight."

Anna snorts. "Way you drive, we got another *two*."

Barrett glances up and down the street. "So you wanna find another place?"

"Nah." She sighs. "Might as well get back. Big briefing in the morning, remember. Maybe they'll finally tell us something.

He chuckles. "Dreamland it is, then…"

[Chapter 27]

Sixteen Years Earlier

**Monday morning
August 17, 1998**

"Hey, Kara!"

Kara smiled. "Hey, Robin. Good to see you."

"You too. Good summer?" With a little wave of her hand, the other student dismissed the question unanswered. "More importantly, how was that hot date this weekend?" Eyebrows waggling suggestively, she added, "Luke Harrington, yeah?"

Kara can't help but laugh. "You heard about that?" She shrugged. "Not so hot, I guess. He took me out for fast food, then some action movie."

"Ooooh," her friend said, cringing. "A real romantic. I thought better of him."

"I don't know. It wasn't a bad movie. Just suspension of disbelief, you know? As if, with this big threat from outer space, the best solution the federal government can dream up is training a bunch of unruly civilians to be astronauts?"

Robin smiled. "Oh, I know the movie you're talking about. Yeah, kind of an overused plot device."

"Yeah. Anyway."

"So what brings you in today?" The other student straightened, then added mock-officiously, "What can the Registrar's Office assist you with?"

Digging through her bag, Kara retrieved her schedule of classes for the fall semester. "Just need to drop a class." She handed the paper over, tapping the circled entry on the page.

"You signed up for *tae kwon do*?" Robin asked, looking surprised.

Kara barked a laugh. "That's just it—I *didn't*."

"Oh. Well, let's see." The other student pounded an entry into her keyboard, adding absently. "Didn't this happen to you once before?"

"Yeah," Kara nodded. "Last fall. Comp Sci 101. Guess you've got some bugs in your system."

Robin shrugged. "If so, they only affect some students. It's not like this is a common occurrence." She frowned suddenly. "Huh. It's not letting me remove the class."

Kara groaned. "Seriously? *Again?*"

"Yeah. It says the drop/add period is over."

"Robin, the semester hasn't even started yet."

"Hey!" the other woman objected, hands raised defensively. "Tell it to the computer."

"This is exactly what happened last year!" Kara growled. "There's nothing you can do? I mean, your boss can fix it, right?"

Robin looked suddenly embarrassed. "Yeah… can we not take this to him? He already thinks I'm computer illiterate."

Now Kara looked suddenly embarrassed—she couldn't prevent the thought running through her head, that if Robin couldn't handle something as basic as a drop/add, maybe she *was* a little underqualified for the job. But that was stupid. She'd been working in the registrar's office since sophomore year.

"How about this," her friend said brightly. "How about you just take the class."

"Robin—"

"No seriously. It's just one credit, and it's not like they'll be giving you homework. Besides, it's probably great exercise, and you learn some cool self-defense moves…"

"Sounds like maybe *you* should sign up."

Robin shrugged. "I've thought about it off and on. I mean, c'mon, it's paid for in tuition, and you get credit for exercising. What's not to like?"

"Um, the exercising? The sweating? Being in a room with a bunch of testosterone-fueled post-adolescents swinging punches?"

The other woman laughed. "Sounds like fun to me. Seriously, I'll do it with you." She dropped her voice. "Just please, don't make me admit to my boss that I still can't figure out this system half the time."

Kara sighed. "I don't know…"

"I do. You're going to do this with me, Kara, and you're gonna realize you love it. Just like last time—you hemmed and hawed that you didn't want to take Comp Sci, but in the end, what happened?"

Kara didn't answer immediately. "I loved it," she mumbled finally.

"And?" her friend asked leadingly.

"And..." she sighed. "And I ended up adding it as a second major."

"See?" Robin said in conclusion, the matter clearly settled for her. "It's almost like Fate is helping you pick your classes. Don't fight Fate, Kara."

[Chapter 28]

**Wednesday morning
December 3, 2014**

Jose doesn't exactly have a bounce in his step when he enters the conference room the following morning, but at least he's not openly scowling. He chooses a seat at the far end of the large table, though not actually on the end itself; a prime position for remaining aloof from proceedings.

Kara glances at the clock above the marker board, sees they're still ten minutes early. The last two members of the group enter a moment later, and she decides to begin. She's feeling understandably jittery about today's meeting, but there's nothing more she can do to prepare; best just to start. "Morning, everyone," she says with a warm smile, only slightly forced. "We're still early, but we're all here, so let's get going. I guess you must be eager to find out what exactly this is all about."

There's a low muttering of general assent from the room, including the Air Force pilots Kara has already been training with; she reminds herself again that even they don't know the full truth, despite the fact that some have been stationed here far longer than she. Only Kara, Gene, and John McLaughlin have been made aware of the alien angle prior to this briefing.

"Each one of you comes to this meeting today with some of the facts, but few of you know the whole story, so I'll start from the beginning." She looks around the room, meeting each of the other eleven pairs of eyes, all of them intent on what she has to say. She's glad she insisted on leaving Peterson out of the meeting; she needs to start building trust, right from the get-go, and Gen. Jerome Peterson is not exactly a trust-inspiring individual. "Some time ago, the Air Force received intelligence to the effect that a nuclear ballistic weapon would be launched against a major U.S. city in November of this year. The source of this info indicated that the weapon would actually be launched from space, making defensibility difficult because it would cut out most of the travel time that a traditional ICBM would require, arriving on target within just a few minutes. Our source further implied that this attack would be only the first in a series of space-based assaults against major U.S. population centers.

"An initiative known as Project Prometheus was put in motion for the express purpose of preparing an orbitally-based combat force capable of intercepting and defeating these attacks." As she speaks, Kara feels a little of her tension fade. "R&D began on several theorized models of space superiority fighter craft, but these were ultimately abandoned in favor of the Destrier—the primary player craft from the space combat game *Rampant*, which is what led to my recruitment into Prometheus, since I led the *Rampant* team. Extensive design modifications were necessary, of course, but by leaping past the conceptualization stage and straight into development, we were able to save considerable time and expense.

"Unfortunately, certain details of the predicted attack seemed a bit... farfetched, so the threat was not taken as seriously as it should have been. In short, we didn't get the funding needed to prepare in time. When the attack came, we only had one operational Destrier, and it was hanging useless in space where we left it after its first test flight; of course, as a prototype, this craft doesn't have the most recent design improvements. Regardless, even if we *had* possessed the equipment, we were still short on qualified personnel to operate it—and that's where you come in."

"Ma'am, who was behind the attack?" asks Kevin Smith, one of the two new Air Force transfers. Kara's not spent much time with him yet, just enough to characterize him as a quiet, morose sort. Stephens found information on the man's background to be sparse, so Kara knows little about him beyond what McLaughlin was able to share.

"I'll get to that in just a moment," Kara says, in answer to his question. "Everything I'm sharing with you is top secret, but much of it will become public knowledge on the 15th, as the President will be making some pretty big disclosures. This is part of the reason for the hasty recruitment of our newest members. We wanted the inaugural unit of this space combat force to be on hand for the President's announcement for two main reasons.

"First, it shows the public that the government has a strategy in place for dealing with the threat. You've seen what's happened since Denver; we're just this side of mass hysteria, and the existence of a group of capable, confident-looking pilots—no matter how few—will go a long way towards defusing tensions."

Jose clears his throat. "Why twelve?"

"Why twelve pilots?" Kara can't quite determine whether it's petulance or genuine curiosity motivating the question... then it clicks: if ten's as good as twelve, Jose's involvement wouldn't be necessary. "Several reasons," she says firmly, "the most important of which involves tactics. As you know, allied tactics used in the game were based upon squadrons of twelve, generally broken into four flights of three. In the real world, it turns out that's a bit simplistic; however those maneuvers will still form a basis for our operational playbook. One of our many duties in the upcoming months—those of us sitting here, I mean—is to begin working together within the game, identifying what tricks and tactics we can bring with us into the real world. Hence, twelve."

"But we won't actually be flying in squadrons of twelve?" Roger Harris asks in evident confusion.

McLaughlin speaks up. "We will likely fly in groups of twelve, subdivided into flights of three, yes. But the game uses the word 'squadron' to refer to a unit of twelve pilots, each of whom had their own ship. It won't work like that here—when we're up to full fighting strength, each squadron will consist of several dozen pilots who share the same twelve to fifteen Destriers. Think of it as shift work, so that your ship is almost always in use, even when you're not."

A laugh comes from the other end of the table. "It ain't like ownin' a car," Barrett Williams, another of the AF boys, pipes in. "These puppies cost millions—you gotta share!"

"Which brings me to the second reason we'll be on stage when the President makes his announcement," Kara breaks in, bringing the discussion back on track. As silly as it is, she feels a surge of confidence just from running this meeting; management is something she's good at. "We need about two hundred more pilots to volunteer in the coming months, and our faces will serve as their inspiration.

"In truth, very little of what you do these next few weeks and months will be military in nature—the tactical sessions will probably be the sole exception. The day will soon come when we desperately need each one of you in fighting trim"—she avoids looking in Jose's direction at this—"but in the meantime you will each be a poster child for one of the most hastily thrown-together marketing campaigns of the last century." She smiles wanly as she delivers this last, and it draws a few chuckles.

Roger raises a hand. "I'm sorry, I just don't understand. Why do we need all this? Why spend all this money on new technology—if we know who attacked us, can't we go after them with more traditional weapons?"

There are nods around the table. Kara clears her throat, "Well…"

"We *do* know, don't we?"

She trades a long look with McLaughlin. "Yeah, we know. But… well, this is one of those farfetched details." She forces herself to meet eyes around the table. "We weren't attacked by humans. The attack was alien—extraterrestrial."

Kara watches the play of shock across each face, completely understanding the emotional confusion that each man and woman is experiencing, anticipating the types of questions that will come. She was, after all, in their shoes just days ago.

The first response to make the transition into the verbal realm is not, however, quite what she expected. "Man, I *told* you!" Barrett all but shouts. The comment appears directed at his longtime friend Anna Haynes, whose jaw is still hovering somewhere between ajar and agape. "Cough up!"

Most of the room's occupants seem to transfer the focus of their amazement onto this interplay between the two pilots. Noticing this, Barrett explains, "We had some money riding on this. She thought it was China. I said, 'No way, man, it's totally E.T.!'"

Somehow the absurdity of it breaks the tension, and peals of laughter break across the room. Even Donald cracks what appears to be a small smile.

"How much?" Roger can't help but ask.

"Ten spot. Guess I shoulda made it more."

"The odds were against you," Roger protests. "You should've gone 5-to-1."

"Man, I'll lay my wager with you next time."

"Not me," Anna breaks in. "I'm done rolling the dice with you, Twix," she says to Barrett. "Uncle Sam don't pay me enough." She shares an exasperated smile with Kara, who'd found herself warming to Anna ever since the other woman saved her life last month.

The room's laughter continues for a moment, then dies away, leaving a certain warm quality in the air that was previously lacking. "I suppose you would have delivered the punch line by now, if there was one," Donald says. Kara can only smile in response. "You realize," he continues, "just how statistically improbable it is that we would ever run into a life form from outside our planet, much less an intelligent one? Not that they do not exist," he hastens to add, "but this universe is immeasurably large."

Kara nods, returning soberly to the briefing. "I know. I never would have dreamed it either, but it's true."

"How can we be sure?" Shaniqua Watson asks, obviously a little unsettled at the idea of alien life.

"Because it was one of the aliens who told us about all this," Gene inserts nonchalantly. "He crash-landed here several years ago " He breaks off suddenly, wilting as he falls under glares from Kara and McLaughlin.

Donald sits up so quickly that his chair makes a smacking sound. "We actually have an alien? In custody? What—what is it like?"

Kara again trades glances with McLaughlin and sighs. "Actually, we don't have him anymore. He was injured in the crash and... well, he didn't last very long after that." In truth, Kara knows he lived at least a few more years, but she holds that datum back. Up until Gene's unfortunate interruption, she'd been fairly pleased with her ability to pick and choose what to divulge. In the Jerome Peterson School of Sharing Information, only the details that really matter are worth revealing, even if the listener has been cleared for the info; she's willing to play by that rule sometimes if it means less of the man's constant disapproval.

Donald isn't letting go so easily, though. "But what do these creatures look like? How big are they? How many appendages... or do they even have appendages? Are they methane-breathers?"

Kara opens her mouth to respond, then realizes she doesn't know. "I honestly can't tell you," she says, perversely pleased at her growing fluency in double-speak. "What's important is that, because of him, we have some idea what to expect."

"And let us be clear," McLaughlin breaks in, uncomfortable, "all of this will probably stay top secret long after we're dead, so keep a lid on it, even from your future squadmates."

"Right. Thanks, John."

He nods, giving Gene another long, measuring look.

"So, according to this source," Kara continues, "additional attacks are on the way, but we probably have a... a lull, maybe eight or nine months, during which we stand a chance of preparing a defense." Again, no need to reveal just how precise KLINE's predictions were.

"Assuming nothing's changed since the little guy landed here," adds J.T. Faulk, a dark-skinned ex-linebacker with a basso voice. Several of the pilots in the room chuckle at hearing J.T. refer to the alien as 'little guy,' since most of them could also be called 'little' next to J.T.

"Of course," Kara agrees. "But we can only prepare as fast as we can prepare, and that's exactly what we're gonna do. Like I said, our first duty is getting out there and being seen. In essence, we're responsible for bringing in the personnel, though we've already got a number of qualified prospects identified—some of you may not realize, but Axmatik Limited ran a *Rampant* competition last month, and even though it never finished, we got all the player data and statistics. Military intelligence is currently running background checks on all of these people, so pretty soon we'll know who we want. Our job is to make these people *want* to join up. This has got to be a 100% volunteer outfit; since we won't be able to accommodate more than two or three hundred pilots anyway, depending on ship production capacity, it shouldn't be that hard to recruit the right people.

"Once we've got our people and we've reassured the public, it'll be time to hunker down into some serious training. That's when we'll pass along what we've developed during our tactical sessions, drilling our pilots on both the standard battery of team formation maneuvers and on anything new and creative we've come up with. Ultimately, those of us here will be split up into different units once they're established."

"Will all this be in simulators?" Shaniqua asks. Kara belatedly realizes just how quiet the woman has been; apparently she's not as comfortable in large groups of new people.

"We'll go as long as we can with the simulator rigs. Obviously it's not logistically feasible to ferry us back and forth from here to orbit, so once we're launched, we'll be there for the duration. Before we get to that point, several things have to happen, including construction of the ships and the stations we'll be using for orbital barracks. Of course, there's also the physical training that each of us will undergo to prepare for prolonged space habitation," she says.

"May I ask," Kevin interjects, ever polite. "How *are* we going to get into orbit? To my knowledge, there's nothing out there capable of launching more than ten or fifteen people into space at a time. And if you're talking hundreds of pilots..." he shrugs. "That translates into maybe a thousand people total, if you count support staff."

His question draws more than a few odd looks. "You been livin' under a rock, man?" Barrett asks.

Kevin blinks. "I... well, yeah, I guess so. I haven't been back in the country long."

McLaughlin leans forward. "One of those space tourism companies went public a few months back. They have a 200-seat spaceliner prototype—the Longship—and it's already been through a successful test flight."

A somewhat excited look crosses Kevin's dour face. "Really?"

McLaughlin nods. "Yeah, so the technology is out there."

Kevin glances around the table. "But how? I thought spaceplanes that size were still decades away. I can't believe they managed something like this without word leaking before now."

"Word *did* leak," Donald says. "It was simply dismissed as unlikely."

This is news to McLaughlin. "Really?"

Donald nods gravely. "If you dig far enough back into OWT's history—" He glances at Kevin. "I refer to Out of this World Tours, the company that built the Longship—you will find that much of their R&D work was performed at a remote site in Siberia. And even ignoring that fact, the technological whitepapers regarding the Longship's rocket launch system make it obvious."

He falls silent, waiting patiently for someone to ask. Gene obliges. "What's obvious?"

Donald smiles. "The Longship was born from the ashes of the Soviets' Buran orbiter—their version of the Space Shuttle. And there have been rumors ever since the 1990s that the Russians were trying to resurrect the project; it simply seemed unlikely given the political realities." His smile grows. "But it was *not* the Russian government; they sold or leased the leftovers of the space program to OWT, an American company with considerable upfront capital. A win for both parties. The Russians earn money back on a program they can do nothing with themselves, and OWT acquires technology, facilities, cheap labor, and—because they are operating in Siberia—it becomes much easier to maintain secrecy about the project." He trails off at the dubious looks of the men and women around him.

"You know all this?" McLaughlin asks skeptically.

"Well, no, but it *is* obvious." Suddenly frustrated, Donald hastens to add, "Consider the Longship's launch system—similar to what our Shuttle used, but on a larger scale, four solid rocket boosters instead of two. That is *exactly* the Energiya system developed by the Soviet space program to put Buran in orbit."

Kara clears her throat. "Regardless, as John said, the technology exists to put us in space sometime next summer. In fact, this will be public knowledge soon, so I'll go ahead and tell you—the President is moving to nationalize Out of this World Tours. Soon enough, the existing Longship orbiter will belong to the U.S. government, along with two more that are currently under construction.

"Getting back on track," she continues—running right over another attempt by Donald to seize control of the conversation—"Shaniqua's question about simulator training brings up another important point. You'll be briefed on all the modifications to the Destrier, but the most important one you'll have to familiarize yourself with is the overhauled display system. We've done away with the 360-degree monitors and are going completely virtual. Doing so will mean less equipment that might be damaged either in launch or during combat, but I believe it'll also mean a far more intuitive visual interface. Any display matrix that relies on physical methods of representation will require some distortion in order to represent every line of sight leading away from your craft; it's unavoidable. But the VR goggles can display the appropriate line of sight precisely, no matter what direction you're looking. It will, in essence, be like floating alone in space, looking straight through the invisible walls of your craft."

"Yeah, but what about—" Roger cuts himself off, nodding suddenly.

"If you're asking about the light pollution, you're right. Such a detailed overlapping VR representation would be hard to make out against the surroundings while playing *Rampant* in your living room; even with lights out, there's usually *some* ambient light." She smiles. "But that's not a problem when you're packed inside a hermetically-sealed sphere in outer space."

Kara opens the floor up to questions, and she and John McLaughlin spend the next hour addressing concerns about tactics and craft responsiveness, among others. The pilots are getting ahead of themselves with most of their queries, but Kara chooses not to put them off; they've already exercised enough patience for a lifetime, and besides, their eagerness is almost tangible. Side conversations begin to form, and she notices that while Shaniqua's bubbly personality is reasserting itself, Jose isn't participating overmuch, though he is listening as Barrett and Anna discuss a new maneuver they've been working on. Kara realizes suddenly that she never had the members of the squad introduce themselves to each other. She corrects this mistake, insisting that the pilots share call signs—or screen names, in the case of the new recruits—while they're at it.

After that, it's time for a bathroom break, which Kara limits to fifteen minutes. She pulls Gene out of the line shuffling its way out the door. "Are you ready to share your stuff when we get back?"

He reveals an anticipatory smile, having reestablished his equilibrium. "As ready as I'll ever be."

As the men and women filter back in from the bathroom, Kara is pleased to see that they are more intermixed than before. She'd been fairly confident that the Air Force pilots, the four she'd known a while at least, would prove welcoming of newcomers, and it's good to see that she was right.

"Okay, team, listen up. There's something pretty major I didn't tell you before, because I wanted to hold it 'til after the break."

"Guess she was afraid we'd whiz our pants," Barrett stage-whispers to Shaniqua, next to whom he's now seated himself. Shaniqua, being Shaniqua, smiles.

"That major thing," Kara continues, albeit smiling at Barrett also, "is that our unit is not actually an Air Force unit." She derives some pleasure from Barrett's wide eyes; indeed, this announcement surprises all of the soon-to-be former Air Force pilots. "We'll be breaking away to form a new branch of service, one dedicated solely to defense against threats from the direction of outer space. Practically speaking, very little will be different; we will initially retain the rank structure of the Air Force, as well as pay grades and commendations. As..." She takes a steadying breath. "As the highest-ranking officer in this new service, I will nevertheless report to General Peterson, who will retain his Air Force commission. We will therefore have representation on the Joint Chiefs of Staff through the Air Force. All this will probably change in time, as our numbers grow and career officers climb the ranks, but for the time being that's how it will be."

"So..." Roger speaks up tentatively. "We'll have ranks? What are we, enlisted?"

"You mind answering that John?" Kara prompts. "And..." she starts to say, then chuckles. "And just so you know, John is my XO—that's executive officer, basically the second in command for you newbies."

"And Kara's our CO—commanding officer," McLaughlin adds, at which Roger and Shaniqua trade delighted smiles, clearly enjoying the military jargon. "To answer your question," the tall pilot continues, "yes, you'll have ranks, but you'll all be officers. The Air Force—and now our unit, too—is kind of backward compared to the traditional military hierarchy, in which the enlisted men and women are the most forward deployed while the officers stand back and direct operations from afar. With us, the officers are the flyers who engage in combat, while the enlisted folks stay behind and provide support, mostly as mechanics and air traffic controllers.

"As for rank, our Air Force transfers here will retain their current ranks. The rest of you will be commissioned as second lieutenants."

Donald furrows his brows. "So we should be addressing you and Kara as... what?"

"Kara and I are both full colonels, though she enjoys the seniority of overall command. As far as how we talk to each other," he smiles, "it's just the way we're talking right now—relatively casual. It's long been the tradition of special forces, no matter what their branch, to maintain informal relations within combat units. Situations are often fluid and unpredictable, and when team members feel comfortable with each other, they're able to offer ideas and suggestions—which is what we want. At the end of the day, everyone knows their place, so it's not usually necessary to enforce a rigid pecking order. Again, you won't find that everywhere in the Air Force, but for our purposes at the moment, it's really the only practical way to operate." He waits a moment for any questions, then nods to Kara.

"For you transfers, I know this may seem sudden," she says. "You take pride in the Air Force, and you have your traditions. I welcome you to bring all of that with you. This new space combat service is, in many ways, ours to shape as we see fit. We don't even have an established name yet, much less a uniform or any of the necessary iconography. The President has afforded us a once-in-a-lifetime opportunity—really, an opportunity that will probably never come again in the future of this country—a chance to make our own initial proposal on all of this."

"Our own proposal on... what, exactly?" Skylar McClinic asks with a frown. Unlike McLaughlin, with whom Kara is very comfortable, Skylar never fails to intimidate; not only is the other woman gorgeous, she's brilliant, having earned a master's degree in classical studies of all things.

"Our own proposal on *everything*," Gene replies, and all eyes turn to him. "The name of the new branch, its slogan, its imagery—including logos, patches, roundels, and so on. And uniforms, obviously."

"Gene has already been working on this," Kara tells the group, "so I'd like him to lead us through this discussion. Just keep in mind, there's no guarantee that the President or the other decision makers will accept our recommendations, so keep it reasonable." She nods back at Gene.

"For each of the other branches," Gene says, "these things are defined by hundreds of years of history. Decades in the case of the Air Force. What we want to do is simulate that same kind of history, generate our own traditions, develop a culture of our own that people will look at and respect. Take the uniform, for example. It needs to be sharp, similar in fashion to the dress uniforms of the existing branches, but also distinctive enough to really stand out. When the average man, woman, or child sees one of our pilots out and about, we want there to be recognition that this serviceman or -woman is not just a defender of our country; he or she is a member of that most elite branch of the service, the…" He trails off. "Well, fill in the blank.

"As Kara said, I've been working on all this, and I've got some concepts I'd like to share with you. None of this is set in stone, so anyone who has a suggestion or counter-proposal is welcome to share it.

"Therefore," he says, standing and unzipping a large portfolio case with an air of drama, "I give you… the Space Defense Force!" With a flourish, he pulls out a three-foot tall black foam board upon which have been mounted several images.

Everyone crowds around, the people at the ends of the table standing and leaning in on elbows or coming around the back to get closer. Nobody speaks for a long moment, and there are a number of smiles, a number of nods, but they're mixed in with a few unreadable faces.

"What's with the logo?" Kevin Smith wants to know.

Gene grins. "You like that?"

Kevin shrugs noncommittally.

Roger speaks up. "This emblem here in the middle… can you even use that? I would assume it's trademarked."

"Yeah, it is, but so what?" Gene counters, a sudden edge to his voice. "The government can take whatever it wants, right?

And in this case, they already *have*—Air Force Space Command uses it in *their* logo, so I just borrowed from them." His smile returns. "Besides, it's *perfect*. People grew up with that TV show, and now, what we're doing, it's like it's starting to come true!"

"Well *I* find it offensive," Donald offers. This causes everyone to step back a bit and focus on the man.

"Offensive?" Kevin questions.

"It is *offensive*," Donald insists. "You are talking about entertainment for the masses. To say it is based on pseudoscience would be an undeserved compliment. I find almost every aspect of the show to be absurd in the highest degree." He sniffs. "Why we would want to encourage any association between that *fiction* and what we are doing in the real world is beyond me."

Several pairs of eyes meet others across the table, uncertain what to say in the wake of the pronouncement.

McLaughlin clears his throat. "Since we won't be actively involved with the AFSPC," he says, "I think we'd be better off avoiding the similarity anyway."

"Oh?" Gene responds. "I assumed we would fall under their jurisdiction, or report to them or something." He reddens. "Did I say that right? I don't really have the lingo down yet."

McLaughlin smiles. "It was an understandable mistake. But no, our branch and the AFSPC won't have much to do with each other. They're more... inward-facing, helping us defend against other countries."

"They better change their name then," Barrett says with a glint in his eye. "We gonna be the space commanders now." The man seems incapable of anything but levity.

"To get back to my presentation..." Gene says with a bit of huff in his voice. "Besides the logo, which I will rework, what do you think? What about the uniform?"

Everyone leans in again to trace the images with their eyes.

"I guess it's okay," Anna Haynes says.

"Okay?" Gene repeats.

"Oh, Gene, it's really good," Shaniqua offers encouragingly.

"Sure," Roger shrugs. "It's good."

Gene sniffs. "Is that all? I was going more for... awe-inspiring."

"Well, it's definitely not that," J.T. says firmly. "No offense."

"Shaniqua's right," McLaughlin soothes, "it *is* good. But it's fairly traditional. The dress uniform you've drawn up has a very similar cut to the current Air Force uniform. And it's, what, a deep blue?" He gets a nod in response. "You said you wanted 'distinctive,' but I bet most people would see this and think Air Force."

"But what about the sash? The epaulets? The filigree on the cuffs?

"I like the sash," Shaniqua enthuses.

"Woman, that sash is *wrong*!" Barrett exclaims. "It's…" He makes a face. "It's *purple*."

"Nobody else has a sash," Gene offers helpfully, trying desperately to put a positive spin on it.

J.T. laughs, and Kara can feel the vibrations through the table. "The *Boy Scouts* wear sashes."

Gene stares at him aghast. "Okay," he mumbles, "no sash."

"Look, Gene, you were right on," a voice chimes in. "We want unique. We want distinctive. We want something that screams 'elite!' It's just not this." Kara cranes her neck to try to see who's speaking, and she's surprised to discover it's Jose. "What we need is something dramatic…" He thinks for a moment. "All the other services, they wear a tie, right?"

"With their dress uniforms, yeah," McLaughlin answers. "The men, at least."

"What if we go more stylish?" Jose asks. "How about… a cravat?"

"A what?" several people ask.

"A cravat. It's a sort of forerunner of the modern necktie."

"I know what you're talking about," Kevin says, smiling slightly. "Sure, that would be dramatic."

Jose chews absently on his lower lip. "I'm thinking we go with black for the jacket, button it up higher than a traditional suit jacket. Wide lapels—continue the dramatic, nineteenth century look with a Grafton collar to set off a Regency knot on the cravat. But we get edgy with the colors. What do you think of a deep blue, fine silk dress tunic with the same color for the tie? The accoutrements—you know, the buttons, epaulets, rank insignia, and medals—we do all of those in silver with a strong blue cast, the same hue as the shirt and tie. We keep all the patches duotone—predominantly shades of blue and white. I think the overall effect would be one of understated elegance, subtle but stunning."

He drifts off into further thought, while everyone else stares in shock. Kara realizes that at some point, Jose's barrio accent, his slangy delivery, morphed into something more professional. And the passion with which he spoke...

"What?" Jose stammers, surprised to find everyone staring at him still.

"Dawg, you lost me when you started talking about Grafton knots and collar styles and stuff," Barrett says. "I thought you said you were an engineer."

Jose snorts. "Sanitation engineer—I pick up your garbage on Thursday mornings. But I'm studying..." He clears his throat, flushing suddenly. "I'm taking classes, working on a degree in fashion design, specifically designer clothing." His eyes dart around the room, as if expecting someone to mock him.

Surprisingly, it's Gene that speaks up. "I think I have a general idea what you're describing, and I like it."

"You do?"

"Yeah... what do you think about adding the cuff filigree back in?"

"Man," Barrett intones, "just don't call it filigree!"

"Might as well give us back the sash," booms J.T. in agreement.

"What about headgear?" McLaughlin asks.

"I like the beret," Kevin offers.

Jose nods. "That or a caubeen. It's sorta like a beret with a band tied around it."

"Great," Gene breaks in with a note of finality, "moving along, we—"

"Hold up now, Lieutenant," Kara says playfully. She trades glances with Anna. "Are you gentlemen forgetting something?"

Jose smiles. "I've got some ideas. Just give us some time to put it all on paper."

"Okay then." She nods at Gene, giving him the go-ahead.

"Next: symbolism," he announces, with a certain amount of grandeur.

Wednesday afternoon
December 3, 2014

To describe in detail the exchange that follows would be a challenge. While exciting for those involved, it becomes lengthy. Gene opens with a discourse on the importance of the bald eagle in American iconography, not to mention that of the Air Force. It is his opinion that the eagle should be prominent in whatever imagery is developed, given its connotation of freedom and power.

This proposal is met with numerous counter-suggestions; following Jose's impressive ad hoc presentation, everyone feels a bit more comfortable with challenging Gene's proposals. Gene does an admirable job of taking this in stride. A strong argument is offered against using eagle symbolism specifically because of its association with the Air Force.

Such is the mood that a number of rather ridiculous alternatives are mentioned, most of them winged creatures, including dragons or bats. Kevin raises the possibility of a chimera, which leads to an explosion of overlapping comments, most of them along the lines of "A *what?*" or, in Donald's case, "A lion with a snake for a tail and a goat sticking out of its back? Oh yes, very inspiring." All of this necessitates a clarification from Skylar that the term can refer to any mythical creature that incorporates parts from more than one animal. At this, someone raises the broader question of what exactly this new service branch *does* stand for, suggesting that the symbolism should follow the meaning rather than the other way around. The conversation devolves completely when part of the group becomes hopelessly embroiled in the question of what to name the new branch… a question that poor Gene had thought already settled, having heard no disagreement following the announcement of his own suggestion more than an hour before. Kara calls another bathroom break, and McLaughlin makes arrangements for a late lunch to be brought in.

Upon resuming, Shaniqua Watson calls attention to the fact that Skylar never left the room. Blushing, the blonde pilot hesitantly hands over the notebook she's been doodling in.

"It's a griffin," she explains. "Kevin got me thinking when he mentioned chimeras. The upper body of an eagle, the lower body of a lion. They were traditionally thought of as divine creatures, since they combined the bodies of the king of birds and the king of beasts." She shrugs. "And in the myths, they often defend treasure. It just struck me as rich imagery, the kind of thing we're looking for."

"What's this here?" Kara asks, indicating the sketch.

"It's holding the globe, with wings wrapped protectively around it, shielding it."

"That's *awesome*," Barrett says with a grin.

"There's... something else, too," Skylar says with an apologetic smile. She gets nods, so she continues. "Griffins are supposed to be monogamous."

"They have lots of sex?" Barrett says, surprised.

"That's 'promiscuous,' you dork," Anna retorts, swatting him.

"They only ever take one mate," Skylar clarifies. "And they stay faithful to that mate even if it dies. I just thought... it's an all-or-nothing sort of commitment. And that's where we are. We may be the only thing standing between humanity and extinction. If we fail and the attackers get past us, even if we survive, there'll be nothing left to go home to. And so we'll fight with utter abandon, never letting go until our world is safe... or we're dead. All or nothing, no in-between."

Kara speaks solemnly into the silence that follows. "I like it." There's muttered agreement around the table, all of it solemn. Jose studies the wood grain in the table before him. "This is a good start," Kara continues. "We can work more on all the little stuff later today and tomorrow, but I've got a conference call with the President in less than an hour. Let's go ahead and revisit the question of what to call our newest branch of military service."

Suggestions are offered that incorporate the word "interstellar," but it's pointed out that this implies travel between star systems, whereas their unit will remain relatively stationary in orbit above earth. This leads to the comment that their team really isn't a space defense force so much as an orbital defense force. From there, Roger suggests the use of the word 'corps,' because "It just sounds cool, you know? Elite." And just like that, the newest branch of the U.S. military is born for real.

"The Orbital Defense Corps," Kara intones. "Humanity's first line of defense." She shrugs. "Actually, humanity's last line of defense, too."

"Shouldn't we have a squad name too?" Kevin asks.

"That's right, baby," Barrett speaks up, unable to restrain his oversized sense of humor any longer. "E.T.'s Worst Nightmare." He grins maliciously and looks at Skylar. "I can just envision the squad's *un*official emblem, can't you?"

"I'll get right on it," she says.

[Chapter 29]

**Monday evening
December 15, 2014**

"On November 14, 2014, our great nation was the victim of a devastating attack. Tens of thousands of Denver's citizens were killed in one of the most disastrous events to take place on U.S. soil in our two-and-a-half century history."

Skylar listens with half an ear to the President's voice coming from the press briefing room next door. She's never understood why politicians feel the need to state the obvious. As if there's anyone in that room who doesn't know what happened on 11/14. Her eyes take in the room around her, and she's overwhelmed anew at the circumstances she finds herself in. The White House. It would be a fascinating study for a psychologist, her emotions at the moment. She's just discovered the existence of alien life, *malevolent* alien life, and she knows she'll be personally responsible for operating brand-new (and probably inadequately tested) equipment to fight them off. And yet what scares her right now is the prospect of entering that room in a few minutes and being presented to the world as its salvation.

Not all of her fellow pilots are as apprehensive as she is, or at least they don't show it; in truth, she too is successfully maintaining a calm façade. Several of the pilots are talking quietly, though they all keep an ear out for their cue to be ready. Roger is the most animated, still flushed after encountering the President personally; he has repeated several times now his story of their short phone conversation two weeks back. Barrett has been a non-stop source of jokes about aliens ever since Kara's initial briefing, and he's found a willing audience in Shaniqua, who always appears genuinely interested in what anyone has to say about anything.

Pilots, she muses, eyeing the newest recruits. It's hard not to be skeptical of them, or even of Col. Dunn, even now. But Skylar's time in the Air Force—now abruptly ended—gave her plenty of practice at keeping her opinion to herself. And in this case, at least, she's not entirely sure of her opinion.

Donald catches her eye and strides over, his posture as stiff as any career military man she's known. She sighs; his attentions are becoming uncomfortable.

"Did you know the press room used to be an indoor swimming pool?" he asks.

She raises her eyebrows, feigning interest.

"Indeed. Installed during FDR's time. Nixon was the one who had the room converted."

Skylar nods and lets her eyes rove, trying to find that tricky balance between showing enough interest to be polite but not so much as to encourage further conversation. She apparently errs too far on the polite side; but then, Donald is not your average human being.

"The room is named in honor of James Brady... you know who that is?"

She shakes her head, trying desperately to catch John McLaughlin's eye. The man has saved her rear many times, but he's badly neglecting his wingman duties at this particular moment.

"Wow, you are young, aren't you?"

She blinks at this and focuses on Donald.

"James Brady," he says. "He was shot in 1981 during an assassination attempt on Reagan. He was the press secretary."

She looks him up and down. "And exactly how old were *you* when that happened?"

The man colors slightly. "Six."

"Congratulations. That's two years you've got on me." She tugs nervously at her collar.

"You look great in your uniform," he says, then almost visibly cringes.

She decides not to punish him any further for the comment. "Um, thanks. I need to get used to this tie."

"Cravat."

"Right." Even considering all the other impossible things happening lately, Skylar still finds it amazing that some tailor somewhere had churned out these outfits to Jose's exact specifications on such short notice. In the end, Jose had done little to distinguish the women's uniform from the men's. The jacket was cut just a tad differently, and he chose a different tie knot. As with the other services, the ODC women were given the option of pants or skirt. For today, the four of them agreed to opt for the skirt; it would more clearly highlight the unit's gender representation.

Donald is opening his mouth to say more when an outburst of echoed human voices travels down the hall. The pilots cease conversing as they recognize their cue to be ready—the President has just announced the existence of hostile extraterrestrial life. Almost immediately, the din from the other room quiets. Skylar knows that the President is not planning to take questions at this point, and the press undoubtedly wants to hear what he says next.

"Although defending against such attacks doesn't fall under the purview of any of our existing armed services," the President continues, "this government was not caught entirely unawares. For several months now, we have been preparing to wage a defensive battle in space above our great land. The attack came sooner than we were prepared for, but I am now able to reveal to you the United States' response to this alien threat. May I present the inaugural unit of this nation's newest branch of military service, the Orbital Defense Corps."

Kara glances quickly around, then leads the pilots into the press room. The colonel is trying hard, but Skylar can still detect a slight limp; Kara had insisted her walking cast be removed for today's event, and Gene had backed her up vociferously. As they enter the room and line up in front of the small stage, the President leads the press in a round of applause. Given that half of the room is operating recording devices, and many of those that remain are madly shouting questions, the clapping sounds a bit weak. Skylar and the others come to a stop in their assigned spots, and she thanks the heavens that she was never cursed with claustrophobia; the small, crowded room has just become far more so.

While the President outlines the organizational structure of the USODC, Skylar keeps a pleasant but sober smile on her face and stares towards the back of the room, avoiding eyes. Beside her, Gene seems a bit jumpy, which surprises her; it was he who coached them on how to behave in front of the cameras. He recommended against expressionless faces, because that could imply arrogance or disconnectedness, but he similarly warned against showing too much excitement, which might give them the appearance of being overeager. Skylar imagines Donald trying desperately to force a smile while Barrett, next to him, tries desperately to keep his in check. Those mental images are enough to upset her own facial balance.

"So as you can see, this is just the beginning," the President continues. Skylar can almost feel the man's imposing presence behind her on the dais. "Recruitment for this new branch of service will be a priority in the coming weeks. In addition, I will be calling upon our civilian manufacturing facilities to contribute unused capacity to the war effort, so that the necessary ships and equipment will be in service by the time the next attack comes. All of the details, including recruitment information and answers to many of the questions I know you have, can be found on the ODC's new website—OrbitalDefense.com—which," he waves at an aide standing in the press room doorway, "will come online in about twenty seconds. And now, I will be happy to take any questions."

Skylar almost falls backward at the force with which the entire room's occupants jump to their feet shouting.

"Yes, Frank?" the President acknowledges one reporter.

"Mr. President, could you please tell us a little bit more about these aliens?"

"No." Skylar glances over her shoulder to see him smiling apologetically.

"But sir," Frank overrides the din. "Anything—"

"I'm sorry, Frank. That kind of information is highly classified at this time. Julie?"

"Sir, what has been the reaction of other heads of state to this threat? Will they also be preparing? Will we be cooperating with them?"

"Good question, Julie. At this time, the focus of the alien threat seems to be centered on North America, though it certainly makes sense for every capable nation to prepare. And yes, as in the past, we will be sharing our technology with allies. Unfortunately, very few of our friends around the globe have already developed the infrastructure for manned space flight—and that includes our neighbors to the north and south. The United States will therefore be shouldering the entire burden of this defense. George?"

"But if other nations *are* attacked—outside of North America, I mean—will we respond?"

"I imagine that will depend upon the situation. However, I'm not sure how responsive we could be if a call for help comes from halfway around the world. Anthony?"

"How do you intend to fund all this?"

"I intend to go before Congress to seek an emergency military subsidy."

"Follow-up, please. How will you respond to accusations that this subsidy is a violation of campaign promises to *cut* military spending?"

The room holds its collective breath for a moment. "I'm not going to dignify such an absurd question with a response," the President responds evenly. "Carlene?"

"In light of today's disclosure, can you confirm or deny whether the mid-air explosion over Nebraska on December 2nd, which resulted in the loss of five Air Force jet planes, was in fact the work of these alien invaders?" The woman sucks in a huge breath after getting the question out, and everyone pauses for a long moment. An hour ago, a reporter would have been laughed from the room for asking such a question.

The President recovers quickly. "I can confirm that the Air Force encountered and destroyed a scout ship on December 2nd, resulting in the unfortunate loss of two pilots—a man and a woman who died heroes." He pauses only barely. "This encounter only underscores the importance of the Orbital Defense Corps, who will be better positioned to intercept such threats before they can get that close in the future." He takes a sip from his water glass as numerous voices begin shouting once more. "Bob?"

"Mr. President, what's the makeup of these officers?" The man indicates Skylar's squadron. "I know you said the Orbital Defense, um, Corps would operate under the umbrella of the Air Force... are these all former Air Force pilots?"

"Some of them are, Bob. As for the others, well, let me start by telling you a story..."

Late December 2014 – February 2015

To say that the media gives the Orbital Defense Corps a less than ringing endorsement in its first week of existence would be something of an understatement. The only topic that engenders more broadcast discussion is the President's revelation about the existence of hostile aliens, and that coverage is no more positive. Most pundits express skepticism in light of the government's unwillingness to provide proof. And unsurprisingly, at least a few bold talk-radio moguls go so far as to suggest that the whole thing is a front, that the proposed Congressional subsidy will be funneled toward some darker purpose.

Congress itself is no less explosive in its reaction than the media, but it falls into line after endorsement by certain key members of the House and Senate armed services committees— officials who have been cleared for some of the sensitive information from Prometheus. The President's proposed subsidy passes with a healthy margin; however, the armed services committees settle in for a longer discussion on some of the finer points of the establishment of this new branch of service, such as recruitment practices.

What both the media and Congress are having trouble swallowing is the idea of putting video gamers at the forefront of a fight for the nation's survival. This sort of contentious reaction is not inconsistent with the press's established *modus operandi*, but the struggle of Senators and Congressmen has an understandable root cause—at an average age of above 50, few of these men and women grew up in a generation for which video games were a valid pastime. They can't help harboring a stereotypical image of a maladjusted young man who never quite escaped adolescence, still living in his parents' house and unable to hold a meaningful job. In fact, many *gamers* hold this view, believing themselves to be exceptions to the rule; this was the very reason Gene disapproved of Donald DeMaria's participation in the goodwill tour, though fortunately, none of the press seems to pick up on Donald's former "occupation" as an opportunity for embarrassing the ODC.

Fortunately, there is data to at least partially refute these preconceptions. What few people seem to realize is what an

American institution video games have become. Two in three American households play video games, and the average age of the most dedicated players is around thirty-five. Most surprising is that 30% of all gamers are adult women, contributing far more to the game-playing population than adolescent males. Statistics also make clear that three-quarters of game units sold are rated appropriate for teenage audiences or younger; considering the excessive violence and mature content in many recent high-profile games, it's become easy for the average American to forget that such games are not the majority.

Nevertheless, preconceptions die hard. In the end, it's Col. Kara Dunn who captures the confidence, if not the hearts, of a nation—despite her self-doubt, she proves perfectly suited for this role. Female, in her mid-thirties, and holder of graduate degrees in multiple disciplines, Kara was not a gamer herself until recent years, when it was a love of *science* that brought her to gaming—and not just to playing them, but to developing them as well. Entirely against her will, Kara even speaks before a special joint session of Congress, immediately prior to their vote on the ODC legislation. Whatever their thoughts on her presentation, Congress ultimately allows creation of the new branch to go forward as planned, without forcing itself into the details of recruiting practices.

In the week that follows, Kara and team embark on a goodwill tour planned out by Gene with assistance from a few Air Force public relations types. The first month is murder. No matter what certain members of the media say on-air, the general public is indeed feeling reassured by the policy the President has chosen for their defense. They are desperate for hope, so local leaders of all stripes—business, church, civic—all log requests for appearances from the ODC's First Defense Squadron.

As they travel from city to city, the unit's members grow accustomed to the guidelines under which they live. They understand that all interviews are to be handled by Kara, that it is their job to smile, nod, wave, and occasionally hug or play with children. Not that they are to rebuff anyone asking innocuous questions, but—for the sake of simplicity as much as consistency—they are to defer most questions to Kara. On a few occasions, special dispensation is given for unusual situations in which a team member other than Kara is either requested or more appropriate. One such situation is Jose's invitation to speak to Pittsburgh's inner-city school children. Kara's gut twists at the prospect that his lack of commitment will be exposed, but that evening's news coverage paints the event as a positive experience. Returning to the hotel later that night, however, Jose seems to brood more than usual.

In the first several weeks after the President's announcement, the ODC's popularity results in an unexpected turn of events. What with the Corps' prominent use of Skylar's stylized griffin in its publications and the rich imagery it entails—not to mention the fact that "the United States Orbital Defense Corps" doesn't exactly roll off the tongue—Kara's troupe finds itself increasingly referred to simply as "the Griffins." Never one to miss an opportunity for branding, Gene soon begins incorporating the name into the advertisements and press releases he now designs on an almost daily basis. It's not long before one of the other pilots takes notice.

Donald holds up a full-page newspaper ad one evening just before the squadron's tactical session is to begin. "Can someone offer an explanation for this?"

McLaughlin's brow furrows. "Looks like an announcement about Saturday's meet-and-greet." Like many of the advertisements they've seen in other media over the last few months, this one includes color pictures of each of them, something which had taken a bit of getting used to. "Why?"

Wordlessly, Donald taps one line of bold text: *Come meet the Gryphens in person!*

"Yeah, you like that?" Gene asks, beaming. "I only regret I wasn't able to secure the website domain name. Some hack author already registered Gryphens.com—cashing in on our fame, I bet."

Kara experiences a sinking sense of *déjà vu*, and not because they missed out on registering a domain name. It's Barrett who finally verbalizes what Donald is really pointing out. "But dude, Gene—you *spelled* it wrong."

Dropping the ad onto the tabletop, Donald produces a pen and rather ostentatiously makes the editorial correction.

Gene's mouth drops open. "But—" he splutters. "I could swear I saw it spelled that way…" He whips out his laptop and pounds away for a few minutes before burying his face in his hands. "Oh man, oh man."

"It'll be fine," Kara assures him. "Just use the correct spelling in the future."

"You don't understand," Gene wails. "I've already got a month's worth of approved publications in the pipeline. It's too late!"

There follows an awkward silence, which Skylar unexpectedly breaks. "Actually, Gene's using a valid spelling—uncommon, maybe, but not wrong. The word's not originally English, you know." She pauses, then smiles. "I think we're fine to use that spelling. It'll be unique to us."

"I agree wholeheartedly," Donald adds, his sudden reversal prompting much laughter and eye rolling.

"In that case," Gene says tentatively, "I was kinda wondering anyway... You think maybe we could lean on this author, make him give up Gryphens.com? You know, nationalize it or something, the way the President did with OWT?"

Kara sighs. "I don't know, Gene... that seems a little silly."

"You *know* Peterson would go for it," Jose offers darkly. At a level look from Skylar, he clears his throat and adds, "Um, General Peterson, I mean."

Kara resists the urge to roll her eyes. "We already have a website, Gene."

"Yeah, but OrbitalDefense.com is our *official* site. With Gryphens.com, we could do something fun and different, something—"

"Gene. Seriously, enough." She shakes her head, bringing the evening session more fully to order. "Moving on... Tonight, I'd like to talk through some flight formations that may prove helpful on escort duty. You know I'm not generally a fan of formation flying, but..."

Most of the unit's free evenings are spent thus, in general discussion as well as development of tactics. Kara finds herself particularly fond of role-playing—calling out a pilot and quickly describing a scenario, asking how that individual would react—and she crafts these situations largely based on the limited information she's been allowed to read from the KLINE Document. The team also spends time huddled around whiteboards and, often, playing the game on a closed network connection. Such evenings are typically grueling, but the tie that binds these men and women grows exponentially as each gets an increasingly clear idea of how the others think, of what drives them.

In these times, Kara strengthens her rapport with all eleven of her squadmates, but in addition to McLaughlin, she grows especially close to Shaniqua and—surprisingly—Anna. As Kara had already gathered, Anna Haynes is a woman who judges others entirely on their merits, and so she exhibits none of the fawning or even deference that Kara now sees from almost everyone; for Anna, Kara is just another person, and so Anna is someone with whom Kara can let her hair down. The many frank discussions the women have regarding policy, ethics, even politics—often late into the night after the others have turned in—result in a strong sense of mutual respect and appreciation. Kara comes to rely upon Anna as someone who will give it to her straight, and for her part, Anna has never had any compunction about speaking her concerns unbidden.

On the far end of the personality spectrum, Shaniqua Watson is nothing less than a delight to be around, anytime, all the time. Though embarrassed to even remember it, Kara had wondered early on if the woman's bubbly demeanor evidenced a lack of substance. That proves far from true, however, as Kara finds that Shaniqua is game for any debate, though she has little tolerance for cynicism. It's the other woman's penchant—and really talent—for encouraging others that ultimately draws Kara to her; whereas interaction with Anna keeps Kara from losing track of the person she's always been, it's Shaniqua's constant optimistic support that helps Kara grow more confident in her new position of authority.

But when those times come, inevitably, that Kara must vent her frustrations or else face meltdown, there remains only one person with whom she can share: Viviane Grant. And although there are very few details Kara can actually disclose in their phone conversations, Viviane is a reliable shoulder to lean on emotionally.

Meanwhile, Peterson is spending his newly acquired funds with a rapidity that would make any billionaire catch his breath. His staff starts by working their way through established GSAs— government service agencies, contractors that have worked directly for the government before and maintain the appropriate clearances.

Several hundred more prospects have already been identified by intelligence colleagues of Stephens, and over the coming months their checks and paperwork will be completed to give them GSA status as well. Security is still a concern, for although the secret of the alien attack force is out, the technology and tactics that have been developed to rebuff future attacks will remain a closely guarded secret.

In fact, in a very real sense, the confidentiality of the ODC's equipment specifications is better protected in this new environment of openness than if the President had never made his announcement. The reason is simple and it involves, ironically, compartmentalization. By farming out the production work to hundreds of contractors rather than keeping it closer to the vest, the military ensures that no one or even ten of these companies see enough of the picture to be capable of reproducing any significant module, whether intentionally or under duress. Given the aliens' documented use of mercenary organizations, traditional security measures are as applicable as if the U.S. were facing a terrestrial foe. As work orders are completed, the components are shipped on a randomly-established schedule to Area 51, where Air Force personnel take possession at the gate. Final assembly—as much of it as will be completed on Earth—is performed by contract workers who have been voluntarily sequestered on the base for the duration of the conflict.

Thus the first two months of the New Year pass quickly for those involved in the defense of the planet, and recruitment and manufacturing capacity goals are both realized. Kara's team's last day "on the outside" before splitting up for training assignments is spent in New York City, where they are given leave to spend it however they wish.

Saturday afternoon
February 28, 2015

Kara spends the morning catching up on correspondence and signing photos for children. It's after noon by the time she leaves her suite and wades through the heavy hallway rugs to the suite shared by J.T. and Barrett. Although New York's preeminent hotel offered each of the pilots a complimentary 900-square foot luxury suite of his or her own, Kara made the executive decision that accepting would be just a little *too* over the top. So they shared, two to a room. Nevertheless, the antique furniture in any of the apartments—for that's really what they are—is more than enough to seat the entire group.

She knocks, even though her key card has been programmed to open all of their doors. After a moment, Barrett pulls the door open, his back to her as he keeps eyes glued to the big screen TV. Cheers erupt and he goes bounding back into the room without even a word to Kara.

The door closes automatically behind her, and Kara takes in the scene. J.T., Barrett, Anna, Kevin, and Roger lounge around the screen, a basketball game and some chips and salsa their only concern. Donald is hunched over the dining room table working intently on something, and across from him, Jose flips disinterestedly through a magazine.

"What's wrong with you people?" Only Jose looks up; the rest are too focused. "Hasn't anyone left the hotel at all?" she asks him.

"Donald and Barrett went out earlier. That big toy store, right?"

Donald nods distractedly.

"Wait—you and Barrett went to a *toy store* together?" It's an odd pairing, not to mention an odd destination.

"Yeah, check it out!" It's commercial time, and Barrett is once again interacting with the world this side of the television. He climbs over the couch, a maneuver that would surely cause the hotel manager to gulp, and bounds across to the mini bar. A recently delivered six-foot sandwich runs the length of the bar, and standing in a row right behind it—

"What are those?" Kara asks a bit sharply. "Are those *action figures*?"

"Awesome, isn't it?" He hands her one, a four-inch plastic model of a person—Kara herself, in full uniform. "Hold on, you gotta see the package." He fishes it out of the trash and hands it over.

'Wing Commander Kara Dunn' it says prominently beneath her press packet photo; in smaller text below is the caption *'in dress uniform'*. On the back is a rundown of her life along with vital statistics. There's also a picture of the entire squadron, their figurines at least. Kara's not sure how she feels about being a doll, though Barrett is clearly enthused about it. "Barrett, it says to visit the website for info on future releases. Are there more? More than these twelve, I mean?"

"Oh, yeah. These just came out today. They're also planning a line of figures in flight suits, and after that, I think there's supposed to be a set that shows us pre-ODC. You know, you dressed up as a student, Roger in a suit. Us old Air Force kids'll be in our old uniforms." She glances up to see what everyone else thinks of this and catches Jose scowling. She understands; it's one thing to find you've become a doll, but it's another thing entirely to be a doll dressed up as a garbage man. "But they're doing the Destrier too," Barrett continues, "and our space base. Eventually, they're supposed to do a line with the aliens and their ships too, but I guess that'll come after we've actually seen them." He shrugs.

"So you bought everything they had so far?" she asks, somewhat incredulous. "The whole line?"

"Yep. They're gonna be collector's pieces. Only $12.99 a pop."

She shakes her head. "Not that I'm into collecting, but... well, you unwrapped them."

"Oh, no—these are just to play with. I bought a whole 'nother set. I already packed and shipped that one home to my mom's place."

Kara turns on Donald, about to ask if he too had bought a whole line of action figures. But now she sees what he's working on. It's a model of the Destrier—not a toy, but a kit including a hundred or more small pieces in need of assembly. Donald is applying a thin line of glue with a toothpick, now pressing two pieces together. He appears to have already painted the individual pieces, which are set out to dry on paper towels. She sees a completed cockpit assembly sitting to the side, remarkably detailed.

"Um, Donald? Why bother with the innards? The Destrier doesn't have any windows, so how would anyone know once you glue it all together?"

"The outer hull has a break away section—see these two pieces?" He holds them together to form a complete sphere. "This top piece is hinged so you can pop it open to look inside. But the instructions make it very clear this is not a hatch. Just something that has been added for the reason you mentioned."

Another cheer goes up from the people on the couches; the game has clearly resumed.

"Why didn't you wait until we get back to put it together? Won't it get crushed in your luggage?"

He shrugs. "Perhaps. This model is simply to occupy my time today. The kit is only a level 2; ultimately I expect them to release a more detailed version."

He squints through his glasses and leans back over his work, and Kara decides to leave him be. In fact, with the exception of Jose, it doesn't look as though anyone in the room is looking for something to do. She tosses her head in Jose's direction. "Hey, wanna take a walk? Grab some lunch?"

"Do I have to get into uniform?"

She doesn't bother answering this; standing orders are not to be seen in public in anything less than full dress uniform. "Come on, it'll be good for you."

Jose returns to his own suite to dress, during which time Kara consults with the head of her security detail, stationed in the hall. There's the usual argument regarding placing herself in an unpredictable environment, but after two-plus months of interviews and events and unpredictable mingling with the masses, his argument is weak. Never in all that time, despite opportunities, has there been another attempt on Kara's life. The man ultimately backs down and approves Kara and Jose to leave the hotel on foot, under the loose supervision of an SF squad.

Jose emerges shortly thereafter, resplendent in his dress blacks. She tells him as much, her words a compliment not only of how the uniform looks on him but also of how the uniform looks on everybody. It's sharp and totally unique, and they have Jose to thank for it. They ride the elevator down twenty-seven floors and exit onto the street, pulling on their uniform gloves and great coats and picking up their escort.

It is a beautiful winter day, chilly with a deep blue sky showing between the tops of buildings. They get polite stares from passerby, but most faces smile when they realize they've been caught. Occasionally, people stop them to ask for autographs or a photo with them. A few such instances seem to draw Jose out of his funk; to his credit, he never stays down for long, but Kara knows that this emotional struggle nonetheless plagues him everyday. They don't talk much as she guides him the ten blocks from the hotel to Central Park, stopping briefly to snag pirozhkis and soda from a street vendor.

Kara finally calls a halt next to a pond she found on a previous visit, years before. They settle onto park benches as their guards form a wide perimeter, allowing them a degree of privacy. The stuffed sandwiches are perfect on such a cold day, and she savors the warm ground beef and onions, appreciating the scenery; though most of the trees have lost their leaves, the stone bridge spanning the water is crawling with ivy. Kara smiles in satisfaction.

They sit for a long time, neither talking, both thinking their way through the inevitable conversation. Jose speaks first. "How're the numbers looking?"

She takes her time in responding, not because she has to think hard, rather because it's that kind of leisurely conversation. "Good. We've got 212 volunteers who made it through both the pilot proving exercises and a newer, more rigorous background check. About half of those were ones we identified through the competition."

He nods, his eyes following a stray duck who missed the memo. "What was the point of the competition, anyway? You never told me."

"Originally?" She smiles wryly. "Originally, it was a way to identify the people we would later recruit. And to a degree, that's how things worked out—those that performed well eventually got personal visits from recruiters, though many of them had already shown up at Air Force recruiting offices. Before Denver, though, the plan was to have all the background checks completed first, then send one of our team—at the time, me, Gene, and the old AF pilots—to invite them personally."

Jose raises his eyebrows at this. "Invite them?" he asks, placing just the slightest emphasis on the word *invite*.

She shrugs. "That was my understanding." *Peterson, on the other hand...* She can't help but wonder about that now.

The conversation lapses as Jose undoubtedly looks for a way to broach the matter of his own involvement. Kara genuinely feels for him, but she waits on him to speak. She knows now that most of the fresh recruits on the goodwill tour have shared this struggle to some extent in recent months; Kara and Jose are not the only ones to have questioned their own adequacy or even desire to fulfill their allotted responsibilities. At length, Jose asks, "So do you think we've got enough?"

She notes the 'we,' responding, "Initially, yes. Assuming a 25% washout in training, we're left with 159, which is forty pilots per squadron. That's enough pilots for 24-hour coverage on 8-hour shifts, plus subs, and we don't have capacity on those bases for many more in any event." She crosses her legs and turns to fix him with her gaze, neither challenging nor encouraging.

"So, if—" He cuts himself off. "If I were to—" he starts again, with no more success. He meets her eyes with a miserable look, then turns away.

She knows exactly what Jose's feeling. He knows what he wants, but he feels guilty about it, feels ashamed; he hopes she will take the initiative to release him, even to reassure him that leaving is okay. "I spoke with General Peterson. In light of our successful recruitment, your participation from here on out is voluntary or not at all."

Jose lets out his breath, but it doesn't quite sound like a sigh of relief.

Kara continues. "Jose, the choice is entirely yours. But you've been with us now for a few months. You know what could be at stake. You're one of a rare class of people in a position to do something about it. What's more, I see a leader in you. You have the raw talent for command eventually, and you've also been part of all our tactical planning, so you would be a huge help to your new squadmates in training." She knows these arguments well, for they're similar to the ones she uses even still to bolster her own confidence. She pauses now, knowing that her next statement will hit Jose like a ton of bricks. "*You* have to decide whether it's your responsibility, your duty, to stay on. *You* have to sleep with that decision."

She leaves it at that. His eyes are shining, but the tears don't flow like they did that first night on base. After a moment, he expels his breath again—this time with a note of decisiveness. "I can hardly leave now, anyway. Not when they've made an action figure out of me." His wry smile can't hold out against the broad grin that stretches across Kara's face.

"So you'll stay, then." She gets an answering nod to this. "I'm glad, Jose. And I say that not just as a commander who needs good pilots, but... as a person. You add something to this team; I think everyone would have been hurt to see you go." She reaches over and grasps his shoulder. "And I promise you, I will do my utmost to make sure you walk out of this alive, which is no more or less than I will do for any of my people. I know everyone else will do the same."

He nods again and swipes at his eyes a few times.

"Moving on to more important things," Kara says brightly, "will you be joining us for Chinese tonight? I think most of us are going to be there."

He shakes his head. "Not to be the black sheep... I'm only here one night. I wanna do something I can only do here... I just don't know what yet."

She thinks for a moment. "You could join up with Shaniqua and J.T.," she says tentatively, adding quickly, "if you're up for company, that is."

He pulls a face. "Go shopping?"

Kara laughs. "If *that* were the plan, I think Shaniqua would have already lost J.T. too. No, they're hoping to catch a Broadway show, though I think they'll both be happier if it's not just the two of them alone. Anyway, they're meeting back at the hotel first."

"Won't it be too late? I mean, those things sell out."

"Ah, but Jose, you're forgetting—you're famous now. If you want to go, you shouldn't have any more trouble getting a last minute ticket than they did."

**Saturday evening
February 28, 2015**

Jose ends up joining Shaniqua and J.T. for a quick bite before taking in that Broadway show, and the remaining three quarters of the squadron head out for a long supper at an upscale Asian eatery. They are joined by McLaughlin's wife and Gene's family, resulting in a party of thirteen. Upon arriving, they're shown to a private room in back. Away from curious eyes, the group is able to let down its collective hair. Everyone joins in the merrymaking, though at least a modicum of respectability is maintained. The pilots all realize what Monday will bring: a much more serious phase of their involvement in the ODC.

Barrett and Anna, who have been flying together for years, share a number of probably-embellished stories about saving each other's life; instead of sobering the group to the dangers they will face, the pair's tales have the effect of underscoring the team's feelings of camaraderie. Gene's children, John and Jen, drink this in, casting frequent admiring glances their father's way; it's so unusual to see teenagers engaged in hero worship of their own parents that Kara can't help but smile. For her part, John McLaughlin's quiet but pretty wife Evelyn appears no less proud of her man; they share numerous asides throughout the meal, and it confirms Kara's previous impression that they are devoted to one another.

Kara gets another lesson in obscure military tradition following one of Barrett's more outlandish stories. While the Jenkins kids lean forward in rapt attention—and, truthfully, Gene does as well—McLaughlin raises an eyebrow. "Ten percent?" he asks simply.

"Absolutely," Anna confirms instantly.

"Fifteen at the very least," Barrett adds before resuming his narrative, and McLaughlin subsides with a small smile.

Leaning across Donald, Kara asks Skylar, "What's this about ten percent?"

Skylar grins. "Standard rule of aviation. When you tell a story, it has to contain at least ten percent truth."

McLaughlin is the first to offer a toast, and in keeping with his personality, it is serious but optimistic. Barrett follows with a toast to the diversity of their team, after which he proceeds to list the idiosyncrasies of each pilot, finishing with an admirable impersonation of Donald obsessively wiping down the table surface and squirting sanitizer into his hands. Donald feigns offense, but it's clear he's grown accustomed to the good-natured ribbing.

After the plates have been cleared, fortune cookies are passed around, and the group derives great enjoyment from listening as each member reads his or her fortune aloud.

"'Keep in mind your most cherished dreams of the future,'" McLaughlin reads, then turns to smile at Evelyn, who beams. There is appreciative muttering around the table.

On McLaughlin's other side, Skylar cracks her cookie open and crunches on a piece before reading aloud: "'Everything that we see is a shadow cast by that which we do not see.'" She pauses. "Interesting."

Donald is next, his placement at Skylar's side the result of great persistence despite her attempts to subtly escape to another empty seat. He daintily cracks open his cookie and quickly brushes off his fingers, as if the feel of the crumbs is abhorrent to him. "'You will not find success in romance,'" he intones seriously, then scoffs. "What kind of fortune is that?" The ubiquitous mini-bottle of sanitizer is back in hand as he turns to Kara. "I hope yours is better."

Kara smiles and unfolds her paper, having already munched on the cookie itself. Its words stop her cold: 'Your death is inevitable.'

"Well, what does it say?" Barrett prompts impatiently from down the table.

Closing her fist suddenly, Kara crumbles the paper. "Nothing. It's stupid." There's a moment of uncertainty around the table, but Kevin Smith—seated at Kara's right—intuits her shift in mood and draws the group's attention to himself by cracking open and reading from his own cookie. The amusement continues as recitation proceeds around the table, but Kara's heart is no longer in it.

[Chapter 30]

March – April 2015

Kara's thoughts return to that fortune cookie prediction frequently over the next several days. Her analytical mind can't help but scoff, because on the one hand, the statement is obviously true. Of course she'll die, because everyone does. Still, it's more than a little unsettling.

Fortunately, there's plenty to distract her over the next two months, and eventually the fortune cookie's dire warning fades from the forefront of her attention. It's during this period that the members of Kara's goodwill team go their separate ways to begin training in earnest. For the former civilians—Gene, Roger, Donald, Shaniqua, and Jose—that means an abbreviated form of Basic Officer Training at Maxwell AFB in Montgomery, Alabama. For Kara and the rest of the team, it means something a little bit different.

In point of fact, Kara's commissioning to the advanced rank of colonel was not as unusual as one might think. It is common enough, in fact, that the Air Force has an established and specialized training regimen specifically for non-military professionals who are recruited as Kara was. Although Kara never went through this training, known simply as Commissioned Officer Training, the month of March holds something similar for her. And she's not alone in this.

All told, there are 126 new ODC senior officers that assemble in one of the innumerable subterranean facilities at Groom Lake on Monday, March 2nd. The vast majority of these are individuals accepting a parallel transfer from one of the other branches of service, but there are a handful who, like Kara, have no previous military experience. Two of these are medical professionals with multiple specialties, while the others are former NASA employees with very specific knowledge regarding the operation and maintenance of spaceborne facilities, of which the ODC will be operating and maintaining four.

The various backgrounds of the military transfers are far more diverse. Despite the ODC's strong ties to the Air Force, it's actually former Navy personnel who demonstrate the strongest representation. The simple fact of the matter is that life onboard an orbital defense installation is far more akin to that aboard a seagoing vessel than anything an Air Force officer is likely to have encountered. Thus it is that the highest-ranking ODC base personnel are all former submarine or aircraft carrier staff. The submariners bring an experienced understanding of how to provide leadership for hundreds of people cramped together in a tiny, enclosed space without fresh air or sunlight for months at a time. The carrier officers, meanwhile, comprehend the delicate balance that must be maintained in order to run a mobile, isolated military facility while simultaneously supporting an aviation component.

Of course, some of the officers involved in logistics, utilities, spacecraft maintenance, and installation defense at each of the four orbital defense bases, or ODBs, come from the other services too—Army, Marines, and Coast Guard. It seems that, even in outer space, there will always be a need for cooks, janitors, handymen, and security, and it will be the responsibility of many of the ODC's officer transfers to oversee exactly this sort of work. Although it is Kara's pilots who face the dangerous combat mission, that mission wouldn't be possible if someone else were not available to handle the more mundane tasks. Of the pilot transfers, there are forty-one—forty-one men and women who will form the backbone of the Orbital Defense Corps' fighting force.

Organizationally, the entire deployment of some 800 personnel is structured as a single wing with Col. Kara Dunn in command, reporting to Gen. Peterson on the ground. It will be Peterson's prerogative to issue orders of strategic import, but it will be Kara's responsibility to determine how best to execute those orders in space. Ultimately, that means she will be the one held accountable for everything that occurs outside of Earth's atmosphere. As wing commander—or "wing king," in flyer parlance—Kara will have eight direct subordinates: the squadron commanders of the four fighter units and the four base commanders. It's something of a hybrid arrangement, since the base commanders must maintain final authority aboard their facilities; however, they and their counterparts in the pilot cadre will, for the most part, enjoy a peer relationship.

Of the four squadron commanders, three posts are filled from Kara's original crew—John McLaughlin, Skylar McClinic, and Kevin Smith—necessitating a promotion from lieutenant colonel to full bird colonel for the latter two. The fourth post is given to a Col. Joe Midgett; it is with Midgett's squadron that Kara herself will fly when she takes her turn at the helm of a Destrier.

For the most part, the sessions attended by the ODC's leadership during the month of March are specific to their areas of responsibility, and so class sizes are small. Kara, naturally, spends a bit of time in each of the various areas, familiarizing herself with the responsibilities of the people under her command. Of course, she and the other newly commissioned officers have training of their own to endure—an abbreviated form of what she would have found in the Air Force's Commissioned Officer Training. Topics run the gamut from military customs and proper uniform care to administration of first aid and the history of warfare. Just like any history course, there's homework, and Kara is amazed at the age of some of the texts on her reading list. As her instructors reassure her, however, the principles of warfare are often applicable regardless of the form a battlefield takes. A perfect example is the fact that even modern businessmen find it beneficial to read the 3,000-year-old *Art of War* by ancient Chinese strategist Sun Tzu. That text in particular proves fascinating, but for Kara, the secret highlight of her training is the instruction she receives in small arms marksmanship.

Once upon a time, she would have questioned why a pilot needed training with handguns, but her two most recent near-death experiences preempted that; it's obvious that she wouldn't be alive today if not by the pistols carried by John McLaughlin and Anna Haynes whenever they're on duty. Although Kara has trouble with the idea of pointing a gun at another human being, she nevertheless takes to this segment of her training with alacrity. Indeed, even her instructor comments that she has an intuitive touch and unerring accuracy, something that in many cases cannot be taught. Thus it is that, with little trouble, she earns her certification on both the M-9 pistol and the M-16 rifle.

Much of Kara's time is spent with her eight direct subordinates, as will remain true once they arrive in orbit. Teambuilding exercises seem the order of the day, which she finds amusing, as it's the sort of thing she would associate more with corporate culture than military. But it makes sense. The thirteen of them will have direct responsibility for 800 ODC officers and enlisted, and by extension, for the lives of countless millions of Americans. It is imperative that they be capable of working closely together. They don't have to like one another—and indeed, Kara quickly realizes that a few of her newer associates do resent her shortcut career path—but they must learn to respect and trust each other. One of Kara's detractors is a former naval captain by the name of Junior Randolph, which is unfortunate since it is on Randolph's base that she herself will be stationed once they reach orbit. And yet she cannot fault the man. Though he's rather crotchety, he never treats Kara in less than a professional or respectful manner. It's just in his eyes... she can see his disapproval there. There are others, however, who seem much less reserved about working with her. In particular, a submariner by the name of Franklin Bauman proves to be quite the encourager. He is a positive individual who greets his coworkers with enthusiasm every morning, somehow managing to remain dignified despite his obvious zest for life. The friendship that leaps up between Kara and this man doesn't have to be forced.

It is with her fellow pilots that Kara spends the most time, of course, and thus she gets more individualized interaction with Skylar McClinic and Kevin Smith than had been possible even during the goodwill tour. Kara will never cease to be intimidated by Skylar, and they will probably never grow to become close friends—their interests and passions are simply too dissimilar—but the women's mutual respect only grows as they spend more time together. Kevin Smith, on the other hand, fascinates Kara more and more as she gets to know him. So much of his past remains shadowed, for even though Stephens finally got the man's official record released for his and Kara's perusal, there's precious little detail in it thanks to Kevin's involvement with special operations. The little intel the document *does* provide implies that he's done a lot of ops in war-torn regions, including relief work and refugee evacuation. And yet, secret as his past may be, the man himself doesn't strike her as guarded. What Kara initially thought was a gloomy disposition proves nothing of the sort; Kevin Smith simply has a very serious outlook on life. He has obviously seen much pain in his lifetime, but rather than make him more cynical, this seems to have made him more compassionate. He's the sort of person who has no use for pointless convention, and despite being a career military officer, he doesn't allow himself to be trapped by others' expectations of him. Kara is impressed to learn that he's mentored several troubled teens during his Stateside postings. Kevin Smith is a complex individual, but his selflessness and heart for others impresses Kara more and more. She even recognizes the stirrings of real affection building within her... If it weren't for their superior-subordinate relationship and the fact that they'll soon be fighting a war together, she wonders whether something might have come about between them.

Flight training is a necessarily significant part of what occurs among the pilot transfers during that month. Kara, McLaughlin, Skylar, and Kevin lead these sessions for the most part, working through the tactical playbook they took from *Rampant* and then modified heavily over the two-plus months of their goodwill tour. Very soon, the pilots they train will turn around and share those same drills and exercises with their own subordinates, who are currently working through basic training at Maxwell AFB. It is mostly during these sessions that Kara has the opportunity to see the remaining members of her original crew—J.T., Barrett, and Anna—and it does her heart good to chat a few minutes each time with Anna in particular. And yet, the realities of military life are such that, more and more, Kara feels the need to establish a degree of separation from those further down the command chain from her. Although her rapport with Anna Haynes is and will remain strong, Kara fears that their days of frank discussions late into the night are past.

And of course, every day at Groom Lake ends with a group session for all 126 members of the ODC leadership. During this time, they cover the material that is truly brand new to each and every one of them: the culture of this new organization known as the Orbital Defense Corps, including procedure, standards, and nomenclature.

Throughout all of this, the ODC's 200-plus brand-new pilot recruits—including Gene, Roger, Donald, Shaniqua, and Jose—are having quite a different experience in Alabama. Like Kara, they receive instruction in military history, customs, leadership, and the use of small arms. Unlike Kara, they face a significant focus on physical training as well. Kara and her squadron commanders take several opportunities to visit Maxwell AFB during this two-month period, and she's struck by just how similar the proceedings are to what she's always seen portrayed in Hollywood movies. Drill instructors screaming into recruits' faces, dragging them out of bed at ungodly hours, pushing them far past the limits of physical endurance. She understands the logic behind it all; besides preparing personnel for the physical rigors of combat, training of this kind enables the recruit to set aside his individuality for the good of the unit. In a very real sense, the process transforms free-thinking human beings into highly functioning automata who respond quickly, though at times creatively, to orders. While Kara's once-civilian mindset rebels at this, she also recognizes how necessary this responsiveness will be in combat.

She is nevertheless pleased to see how Shaniqua Watson flourishes in this environment, using her gift of encouragement on those around her. The woman always seems to intuit when someone is most in need of a smile, a joke, or an encouraging word, and her efforts quickly make her a favorite among the new recruits. Shaniqua uses this acceptance in turn to facilitate the interaction of others within the group, thereby helping to weave a tighter fabric of solidarity overall. It's a team-building effort of an entirely different kind, and when Kara hears of it, she can't help but wonder whether this is nothing more than Shaniqua's gift at work... or if the grueling physical drills are designed in part to bring about this result.

Regardless, as this all takes place, it helps that Shaniqua is already in prime physical condition. Others, unfortunately, struggle far more. Roger, already in his forties, is crippled at times by joint pain, as are some of the other older recruits. A schoolteacher named Krista Givens bursts into tears whenever the insults are screamed in her direction. Chip Conroy, an auto mechanic by trade, breaks frequently into fits of dry heaving. Shaniqua is always ready to uplift, and most of the recruits stick it out; Conroy in particular, who hails originally from Denver, exhibits a level of commitment that challenges them all.

Some recruits are not so admirable in their efforts, and it is from these that their first washouts emerge. Most notably is a beast of a man by the name of Gage Dixon, a body builder from the West Coast. His breathtaking musculature notwithstanding, the man rebels against the unending aerobic exertion as much as he does against being ordered around. He is the first to quit, and a spate of others follow in quick succession, their pride no doubt appeased by having outlasted such a magnificent specimen as Dixon.

    The biggest surprise, both literally and figuratively, is a man by the name of Willie Cobb. At just over 300 pounds, little of it muscle, he is a specimen of a whole different kind. He was one of the pilots on Kara's initial list of suggestions, perhaps the most gifted pilot Kara has played the game with. Notwithstanding their mutual history, the first surprise is that Willie would volunteer knowing the physical condition he would need to achieve. By far the greater surprise is that he survives the experience without quitting. He proves surprisingly resilient despite his girth, not exactly light on his feet, but not too far from graceful. Predictably, his shape is an instant source of sarcastic amusement, not just for the drill instructors but for the other recruits as well. Despite discouragement from Shaniqua, the jibes don't cease until Willie himself shocks them all into silence. They're on a ten-mile run in full gear when the recruit in front of Willie goes down, tripping up Willie and a half-dozen others. Though several of them stay down, nursing bruises, Willie leaps to his feet and goes another two miles—missing one shoe. He doesn't quite complete the run, ultimately passing out from exhaustion with his foot bleeding freely, but the instructor personally helps carry him back to the barracks. The mockery mostly ceases after that, though the recruits who failed to get back up from the fall are unceremoniously sent packing. There is more to Willie Cobb than meets the eye, as Kara knows from having read his file.

    Several of Kara's other initial picks—the ones who made it through screening, at least—are part of her training group, and she finally gets to meet them in the flesh. Jeremiah Blankenship, better known as Brewtus, is a friendly but extremely reserved man; having lived years on the streets as a panhandler, his body is more hardened than the others, but he endures the added burden of giving up his booze cold turkey. Shannon Dembry is a slight young woman with close-cropped purple hair who cops an attitude at every opportunity; Kara recognizes her as one of the contestants she observed in Chicago, that fateful November 14th night. She's surprised to also recognize a man named Ben Bechtel, whom she always knew as Fa8z—pronounced "faze," the '8' silent. He turns out to be the very same stringy-haired conspiracy theorist who ran their car off the road last autumn, though he wasn't permitted to keep his long hair when he began training. Fa8z is perhaps the most vocal of the recruits, always willing to share an opinion about what the government is not yet telling them regarding the aliens. Pastor Phil Brinkman, the man Kara rejected from their goodwill team, did indeed give up his ministerial role to join the ODC, and he proves to be a very reserved individual… at least in the face of the drill instructors' many barbs. Ultimately, Phil and a few other specific recruits will take on some of the responsibilities typically associated with service chaplains, but space aboard the ODBs is simply too limited to accommodate a dedicated chaplaincy.

Marksmanship training proves to be one of the most popular components of instruction the new recruits receive, just as it was with Kara. She has no idea what the dynamic is like with a randomly selected group of recruits, but it's clear just how eager hardcore video gamers are at the idea of firing real guns… though she's not sure whether to be worried by this or not.

As that first month goes by, the rate of dropouts slows and the sense of unity among those who remain grows even stronger. During one of their forced marches, one of the drill instructors even christens his trainees with a name that one of the squadrons will eventually choose for themselves; what was intended as an epithet proves surprisingly apropos, and the First Defense Squadron of the ODC soon becomes known as the Vacuum Suckers.

Saturday morning
April 25, 2015

    For Willie Cobb, the second month of basic training is like night and day difference from the first. While physical drills continue, it is now the classroom instruction that takes the lion's share of each day. Dress uniforms are worn when not on the parade field or out on a run, and attired thus, the pilots cannot help but feel more respect both for themselves and for their fellows. They indeed begin to feel part of something elite… but with an element of humility that comes from only recently having done hundreds of pushups in the mud while serving as the target for grave insults.

    It seems almost a surprise, therefore, when training comes to completion. A ceremony is held to commemorate the occasion, and as Willie files in with the rest of the officer candidates, he's pleased to see there's no media present. Off to the side, seated among the other families and waving with absolutely no care for how foolish she may look, Willie's wife Sam beams with so much pride it's obvious even dozens of yards away. His face splits wide into an answering grin, desperate as he's been to see her again after so long. Sneaking peeks at his fellow recruits, he finds that smiles are apparently the order of the day, and so he worries less about comporting himself with the appropriate dignity for this occasion.

    The proceedings unfold much as he remembers his own high school graduation. In one sense, the speeches offered by many of the instructors are so dry as to induce catatonia, yet the import of the ceremony—the transition it represents for each of the new officers—is such that not one eye droops; each individual sits ramrod straight, feeling both relief and expectation, not to mention pride. Following their general remarks, the instructors take a few minutes to recognize those recruits they feel excelled in training. Those graduating at the top of the class are called to stage to receive special ribbons for their uniforms, and Willie is surprised to hear his name announced along with Shaniqua Watson and several other highly deserving individuals. Similar recognition is afforded to those who earned expert certification with small arms marksmanship. Each of the newly established ODC ribbons is the same dark blue, inscribed with white, gray, and light blue stripes in various configurations. As each commendation is awarded, the issuing officer performs the duty of reaching inside the recruit's uniform jacket and affixing the ribbon in its appropriate place.

Finally they reach the point in the ceremony when the commissioning itself occurs. Willie watches as several of his fellow candidates are called up by name, and then it's his turn. Following the taking of oaths, each recruit has a gold second lieutenant's bar pinned above the left breast by one officer while two others slip looped rank insignia over the epaulets. This completed, each newly-minted officer salutes first and maintains the salute as a sign of respect while the higher-ranking officers on stage salute back.

Eventually, Col. Kara Dunn is introduced, and Willie sits up with some expectation. Although he'd never met her in person until just a few weeks ago, he had flown with Kara often in online *Rampant* matches. Among the thousands of people who frequented the game servers, there were some folks whose gamer handles he came to recognize over time. CareerStud was one of these, and by flying with her often enough, it was amazing how much Willie learned of her personality and character. He didn't even know she was female, and yet he came to respect her as a team player, one who often put the team's fictional mission ahead of her personal player statistics; moreso, she was always one to welcome newbies with respect and enthusiasm, even though she herself remained one of the highest-ranked pilots and could have chosen to fly exclusively with those equally experienced.

It wasn't until the middle of basic training that Willie learned Kara the media personality was the same gifted individual as CareerStud the online gamer. It took him some time to adjust to the idea. Perhaps the biggest difference was that she didn't seem as open or welcoming as he would have expected; the first time she arrived to observe their training, she seemed rather aloof. She certainly made an effort to meet everyone in Willie's unit, and her familiarity with their names and backgrounds was impressive, but she often seemed preoccupied—not that anyone could blame her, given the burden of responsibility that had been placed upon her. There'd been some talk among the other recruits, disappointment really, that Kara wasn't as inspiring in person as they'd anticipated. Willie was willing to give her a chance, however;

certainly those new recruits that had already worked with her—like Shaniqua—were immensely loyal. And truthfully, no one could find any fault with Kara; the woman obviously took her responsibility seriously and had made a commitment to knowing those officers under her command. In the final analysis, Willie thought these facts said a great deal about her.

The colonel's keynote address is passionate but short, for which Willie is grateful. He knows all of the new recruits are eager for some time with their families after being separated for so long. Following her closing remarks, Kara Dunn steps back from the podium. In one motion, the 133 brand-new ODC lieutenants, along with their 41 commanding officers—who had traveled from Groom Lake for today—rise to their feet to salute their commandant. The tassels of her unique commandant's epaulets glittering in the spotlights, Kara snaps off a sharp salute in response, and the room erupts into cheers.

As the auditorium's seven hundred occupants lose all semblance of dignity, Willie Cobb pauses long enough to drink it all in. He is a terminally optimistic sort, much like Shaniqua Watson—with whom he'd struck up an instant friendship—and so he can't help but feel positive about the ODC and their mission. And yet it adds to his joy to see that his squadron mates—no, his friends by now—are also exhilarated. Families crowd in for photos, fathers and mothers and spouses and siblings, and a fair number of sons and daughters too. Seated near the middle of his row, Willie waits his turn to get out; despite now being in the best shape of his life, he is still a very large man, and maneuvering in cowds is difficult.

Then Sam is there, appearing just a few feet away, her small frame hidden so easily by the crowd. Her radiant smile continues unabated. More than two months now he's gone without her, without even communication, as is normal in basic training. He wraps his arms around her, takes a deep breath, and lets it out contentedly. "I've missed you so much."

Her muffled response, spoken into Willie's chest, is unintelligible. Laughing, he pulls away slightly to look into her bright eyes. Cupping one side of that still-smiling face in his hand, Willie says, "Your face must be getting tired by now."

"I can't help it."

"I know, impressive, aren't I?" He takes two steps back, grabbing the hem of his uniform jacket and snapping it with a flourish. "Lieutenant William Cobb, United States Orbital Defense Corps, at your service."

Sam gives him a sly smile. "Oh, that? That's pretty cool too…" She trails off.

Eyes narrowed in good-natured suspicion, Willie awaits the punchline.

Her joking manner falling away, Sam steps close once more and rises up on tiptoes. Whispering into his ear, voice thick with emotion, she says, "Honey, it finally happened… We're pregnant."

[Chapter 31]

**Sunday evening
April 26, 2015**

"*Hello?*"

"Viviane?"

"*Kara!*" The younger woman's voice is abruptly more animated. "*I've missed you... I guess you're out of training now?*"

"Yeah..." Kara sighs. "I just really need you right now, Viviane."

"*Of course! What's up?*"

The silence stretches long. She tries to speak, but before she knows it, she's crying instead. Quiet though she is, the sound apparently carries across the line.

"*Kara! What's wrong?*"

"I— I just..." She trails off.

"*It's okay. I'm here. Take your time.*"

She does just that, releasing all the pent-up emotion in a rush. Eventually, finally, she settles somewhat. "Sorry, Viviane, I just..." She sighs.

"*I know, it's okay.*"

"I just feel so much pressure, you know? This just— It goes so far beyond being a good manager. People are looking to me to lead them in a war zone. Hundreds of people, expecting me to keep them safe. No—more than that, this whole country really. I—" She chokes up again, throat thick. "I'm not up to that, Viviane."

The other end remains silent as Viviane listens.

"I'm sorry," Kara sniffles, breathing deeply to calm herself down. "I know I always dump this on you. I just don't have anybody else I can talk to, not about this." The tears continue to stream, even as her breathing steadies. "I've made some good friends, and they're all great people. But I can't show them how terrified I am. *I* have to be reassuring *them*."

A pause, then: "*Kara, I thought you were feeling better about all this. Is there something in particular that brought it all back up?*"

She sighs. "No… I guess… it all just seemed far away until now. There was so much else to do, and that was scary enough. But now that I've actually been through some real military training… it's just—it's official now. I'm really in charge of an entire branch of the United States military… and in barely two months I'll be living in space, fighting a war." Her throat thickens again on that last word, cutting it off slightly.

"*I can't imagine what this is like for you. The stress alone.*"

Kara feels just a bit of that relief that comes from knowing someone else understands her pain.

"*But Kara, you're the best person for this job.*"

She sighs, seeing the comment as just another pleasant but empty reassurance. "Viviane…"

"*Obviously all the old farts in uniform think so, and that counts for something. I guess it proves you qualify for the job.*" She pauses. "*But Kara, this conversation we're having, right now, it proves to me that among the qualified candidates, you're the* best *person for this job.*"

"Why?"

"*Because you* are *worried,*" she insists passionately. "*Because you* do *feel the weight of all those lives hanging on your decisions, and you'll be more careful not to make stupid decisions as a result. And you're courageous. Despite your fears, all along, you've stuck with this even when you probably could've gotten out. Me… I would've just panicked, gone bonkers, and they would've been forced to fire me.*" A moment passes. "*You know that scary guy you're always talking about? Peter something?*"

"General Peterson?"

"*Yeah, him. You think he loses sleep over lost lives?*"

Kara's not sure how to answer.

"*There's a reason your people trust you, Kara. You're a trustworthy person. Don't try to ignore that pressure, just don't let it overwhelm you.*"

Kara laughs, still emotional, but suddenly feeling a little better. "That was a pretty inspirational speech. Maybe *you*'d like my job?"

"*Not a chance. Bonkers, remember? Besides, I'm too* selfish.*"

Kara smiles, formulating an objection to that characterization, then cutting herself off—"Oh shoot, I have to run. I'm being paged." Swiping at her eyes, she adds, "But Viviane—thanks. For helping me keep it in perspective."

"*Of course.*" Viviane pauses, and Kara senses there's something more she wants to say. "*Kara...*" she begins hesitantly.

"Yeah?"

"*You talked to my dad lately?*"

Kara feels a slight jolt at the question, a sudden surge of guilt. "No... why?" she asks, feigning casualness.

"*Oh, nothing. I've just been thinking about him lately... actually thinking it would be kinda nice to catch up a little.*"

Kara cringes. "Sorry. We're... working out of different bases these days."

"*No big deal, just thought I'd check.*"

"Of course."

As the conversation wraps up, Kara can't escape the feeling of guilt over not being open with Viviane about her father's incarceration. And despite the other woman's encouragement, Kara can't help but think that this proves she's not really all that courageous.

[Chapter 32]

Late April – Mid-May 2015

    As April leads to May, Kara receives the encouraging news that production of the space habitats the ODC will use as bases has been completed, and orbital assembly is set to begin mid-May. That accomplished, every square foot of the nation's spare manufacturing capacity has turned to fabrication of the components that will make up the ODC's V-2 Destrier spacefighters. The timeline calls for the fighters to launch into orbit in June, with the ODC personnel to follow a few weeks later on July 4. When it came right down to it, an Independence Day launch was the obvious choice, at least for the politicians and PR people. For Kara, it makes little difference as long as they have a few weeks to settle into their habitats and run drills in preparation for resumption of hostilities, which could come as early as August.
    Once placed in orbit, the dozens of new habs will be linked to form four separate space stations, one for each of the ODC combat squadrons. Following a petition sent up the chain of command, the Gryphens are given permission to name the stations in honor of their favorite science fiction writers of the past century; thus the first four orbital defense bases are christened Asimov ODB, Clarke ODB, Verne ODB, and Zahn ODB.
    The fifteen modules, or habitats, that form each station are of the XA 420 design, developed by Xavier Aerospace for a government-sponsored project they ultimately lost the bid on. The modules provide 420 cubic meters of livable space—roughly 13,000 cubic feet—and are made of a strong fabric-like material which is resistant to micrometeorite collision, but also collapsible for easier transport into space. Twelve of these habitat modules form the main complex of each ODB: six dedicated to living quarters, with five more for HQ/communications, kitchen/dining, exercise, flight training, and life support, the twelfth module to serve as a machine shop for the techs' use in maintaining both the station and the fighter craft. The modules are arrayed along a corridor that sports a recyclable airlock at each end as well as one in the middle. The Destriers dock along a 120-foot-long girder

which meets a station airlock at one end and, at the other, the module used for storage of ordnance. The two remaining modules are defensive gun emplacements located at the end of similar girders emerging from opposite sides of the main corridor, placed near the airlock halfway down the corridor's length. Neither the ordnance module nor the defensive modules are pressurized, due to the presence of explosive munitions; were they to be included as part of the main complex, any explosion in one of the three—no matter how small—could take out the entire base. Since the cockpits in the Destriers themselves are also unpressurized, there is no need for a "covered" passage to the ships. In total, each base measures 250 feet long and 100 feet across in the main complex, not counting the outlying gun emplacements. It's not terribly pretty to look at, sporting none of the sweeping curves characteristic of so many fictional space stations, but it's functional and as safe as the engineers know to make it; compartmentalization is key, as each module will remain closed off from others in combat situations, preventing destruction of the entire base in the event that any of the habitats are compromised.

The May 9th launch of four medium-lift rockets, each bearing four collapsed hab modules to low Earth orbit, is the start of a media circus that will last a week. Kara stations herself at Cape Canaveral, one of the four launch sites, to field interviews; rather than take rooms at a local hotel, she and her security detachment are billeted on the base itself, well within Canaveral's own security cordon. Over the next four days, the remainder of the habitats are catapulted into space aboard ten more rockets, and the first three of six shuttle missions are launched to ferry the engineers in charge of assembly. Brought out of retirement especially for this purpose, *Discovery*, *Atlantis*, and *Endeavor*'s reappearance proves quite popular; the shuttle program had, of course, been terminated in 2011.

The estimated cost of the entire ODC venture finally begins to firm up at just shy of $500 billion—well above the emergency defense subsidy secured by the President. Neither Congress nor the press makes much of an issue of this.

May – June 2015

Immediately following commissioning of its newest recruits, the entire ODC officer corps is relocated to Johnson Space Center outside Houston, where they join their enlisted support personnel. The enlisted folks are all transfers from the other branches, and they've spent the last couple months going through a streamlined training regimen similar to what Kara and her command staff experienced. Johnson Space Center, or JSC, is home to the neutral buoyancy lab which has been used in astronaut weightlessness training for decades. The lab's primary feature is the world's largest swimming pool, some 200 by 100 feet and more than forty feet deep. Over the previous three months, its full-sized mockup of the International Space Station has been replaced by a mostly complete ODB—a fifth copy purchased from Xavier. For the next two months, the pool will be used almost non-stop in preparing the ODC's 800-plus deployable personnel for long-term space habitation. Unfortunately, the protocol is by necessity accelerated from the normal twenty-month methodology undergone by NASA astronauts.

When not in "the tank," the pilots spend every spare moment drilling tactics and maneuvers using a now highly-modified version of the *Rampant* game. The display functionality has been adapted to use only one monitor for textual output, the entirety of the graphical representation being handled by the VR goggles. Fortunately, the buildings leased to the ODC by the center include enough subterranean square footage that the pilots can train without significant ambient light. In fact, with the final display modifications, the game can now be run fully-functional on a limited system costing less than $300 to assemble; it's ironic, given the price tag of the rest of the training program.

Just as the First Defensive Squadron—with Midgett in command—established its own identity as the Vacuum Suckers, so too did McLaughlin's Second, Skylar's Third, and Kevin's Fourth Defense Squadrons as, respectively, the Alienators, the Space Cowboys, and E.T.'s Worst Nightmare. As each unit's sense of identity solidifies, so too does rivalry between the fighter squadrons. The struggle for supremacy in training exercises leads to the creation of many new tactics not previously considered.

Nevertheless, tension continues to grow among all involved as Independence Day nears. In recognition of this, Kara and Peterson agree to allow ODC personnel six discretionary hours each Sunday evening. It's almost a joke, offering so little free time, especially after two solid months of training, but they have no choice; it's all a balancing act, a matter of finding equilibrium between vital training and the moments of leisure that will prevent the pilots from losing their minds entirely.

Members of the Corps use the time in various ways. For many, it is a prime opportunity to catch up on lost sleep, though others feel such usage is a waste. Reading is popular with Donald and others who might be described as lifelong students. Some personnel take the opportunity to drive into Houston for a movie or a show, though Peterson's standing orders require guard details and full dress uniforms. An even dozen, not counting guards, take the opportunity to attend Sunday evening church services; these include Shaniqua, Willie, and, predictably, "Preacher" Phil, who has no chance of escaping such a moniker despite his new profession.

Love is also in the air. Place enough stress on a group of people for long enough, and relationships will sprout up out of desperation if nothing else. Ultimately, human beings are incapable of going through life's challenges alone, and another person—even religion, Kara admits—can provide much-needed support. Many ODC families relocate temporarily to the Houston area to spend even a few hours a week with their loved ones, Willie's and McLaughlin's wives and Gene's family among them. Kara hears tell that Shaniqua has begun a romance with a local man, and though she wouldn't have believed it possible, the other woman's smile indeed seems brighter than usual. Several relationships emerge from within the Corps itself, including between Jose and a young woman named Shannon Dembry who had been on Kara's initial recruitment list. Regulations prohibit such liaisons between officers and enlisted, as well as within the command chain, but beyond this Kara cannot conscience interfering; after all, the line between a good friendship and a romantic relationship is often a blurred one... and besides, doesn't the ODC encourage friendships among its personnel?

What Kara refuses to admit until much later is that she herself may be developing feelings for one of her colleagues.

Thursday night
June 18, 2015

"Burning the midnight oil again?"

Kara glances up to see Kevin Smith poking his head through the doorway of her temporary office. She smiles, her work abruptly forgotten. "Always. What's up?"

"Do you have some time to talk? It's important."

Kara belatedly notices just how worn her friend appears, how emotional, as if he's barely holding it together. She starts to invite him in, then realizes the time. "Oh, Kevin, I'm sorry—I have a meeting starting in just a couple minutes. Maybe afterward?"

Kevin glances to the side at that moment, and it's like he's flipped a mental switch; gone is the simmering emotion, replaced immediately by detached professionalism.

"Colonel," Peterson says by way of acknowledgment, nodding as he sidles past Kevin through the doorway.

"Later is fine, ma'am." Kevin turns to leave.

"Just a sec!" Kara calls. Dropping her voice, she asks Peterson, "What do you think of Kevin joining us? He's cleared, and he already knows most of the story. Given his experience with rescue and evacuation scenarios..."

Peterson considers it for a long moment, then grunts. "Fine."

"Kevin," Kara calls, "I'd like you to join us for this meeting."

The other pilot looks a little surprised, but he dutifully files in and finds a seat. Within a few minutes, they're joined by John McLaughlin, but the four of them remain mostly silent until Gene Jenkins finally arrives; there's nothing like the mere presence of Jerome Peterson in a room to kill all possibility of small talk.

"I'm sorry we had to schedule this so late," Kara begins after closing her office door. "But we wanted to stay under the radar;

besides, our various schedules are fairly incompatible at this point." Her subordinates all nod, though of course none know why they were called in. "General?" she invites.

"We're here to continue a discussion we began last November. Colonel Smith wasn't with us at that time, but we believe he brings a unique perspective." Peterson focuses on Kevin. "You know we have a source of intel, one of the aliens who crashed here years ago?" Kevin nods. "Well, he says the aliens' next target is Chicago. The attack should come in August." As is his fashion, Peterson delivers these lines in a gruff, matter-of-fact tone.

By contrast, Kevin Smith's jaw drops open in astonishment—a rather over-the-top reaction, but then, this isn't your typical conversation. He recovers quickly. "I thought this alien was supposedly dead? Are you saying he's still..."

"Oh, he's dead all right."

"Have we actually heard from them yet?" Gene breaks in. "The aliens, I mean." Ever since the end of the goodwill tour and the start of training, Gene has chafed at being just one of many ODC pilots—and a junior officer at that—rather than someone with a say in policy decisions. He is clearly eager to be part of this discussion. "KLINE's information is thirty years old. What if it *is* out of date?"

Thirty years? Kevin mouths in further surprise.

"Nothing yet from the *K'lurans*," Kara confirms, looking questioningly at Peterson as she says it, never certain even now whether she herself is being told everything. "But I'm sure it's as KLINE said. They're softening us up before making any demands."

"*Do* we have any idea what they want?" Kevin asks.

"Do we ever!" Gene enthuses. "According to KLINE, they want us to cede half the country to them."

Kara sighs.

"That's... that's what they want?" Kevin asks in evident confusion, and Kara feels sorry for him. He hadn't asked to be dumped into the middle of this discussion, and she'd forgotten how bewildering some of the details would seem at first.

"Yes, that's what they want," Peterson cuts off Gene's response, clearly grumpy at having his meeting hijacked by all of these questions and answers. "In any case," he continues, "we don't believe the attack will occur until several weeks after the ODC is on station in orbit. But just in case, the President wants to continue exploring evacuation scenarios."

"*Evacuation* scenarios?" Kevin asks in amazement. "Do you have any idea what you're saying?" No one responds immediately. "There are *millions* of people living in Chicago!"

"Roughly ten million in the area, yes," Peterson confirms, not the least bit affected by the number.

"It's actually worse than that," Kara adds gently, almost apologetically. "If we evacuate, we have to do it quietly or else the K'*lurans*' spies will get wind of it. And then they'll just switch targets, leaving us worse off than we are now."

Kevin slowly sags back into his chair as the full weight of the problem becomes clear to him.

Peterson seizes on the silence to continue. "The President asked us before to be thinking about 'creative solutions' to this. So that's why we're here."

"All due respect, sir," McLaughlin says, "but we're pilots. Most of us aren't qualified to offer an opinion on something like this." He glances briefly at Kevin Smith as he says this, obviously aware that Kevin's background is a little different.

"It's simply a matter of keeping this intel contained," Peterson responds. "With the exception of Smith here, the rest of us already knew about this. As long as possible, POTUS wants to avoid informing anyone else." By POTUS he means, of course, the President of the United States, though Gene looks slightly confused at the term.

Or maybe Gene is confused for an unrelated reason: "Are you saying that ten million people would die if Chicago got nuked?" he asks. "I thought it was only like 50,000 when Denver was hit."

Kara cringes inwardly. She knows Gene isn't being flippant, but his casual-sounding question nevertheless makes it seem that way. She sees her disquiet mirrored in Kevin's eyes.

Peterson addresses Gene's concern. "It's unlikely they can or would destroy the whole city. Predicting the effects of a nuclear blast is hard, but to take out the whole metropolitan area would probably require a 10 megaton bomb. If the aliens have something like that…" He sighs. "Then God help us."

"So what exactly *are* we expecting?" McLaughlin asks.

"The Denver device..." Kara begins slowly. "That was 300 kilotons, wasn't it?"

"Between 200 and 300, we believe," Peterson confirms. "Though again, it's hard to know for sure. Assuming they used a similar device on Chicago, they—the President's scientists—think the death toll would hit 160,000 by the end of the week."

Kara sucks in her breath. "So many..." she whispers. "Why?" She speaks up louder. "Why so many more than Denver?"

"Chicago is a much more densely populated city—three times as dense, I think," Peterson shrugs. "That compounds the problem. For one thing, Chicago O'Hare is a busier airport. In fact..." He checks his notes. "The death toll could go up as much as 20,000, depending how close the hypocenter is to the airport."

"Yeah, but that's still less than 200,000—a drop in the bucket compared to ten million!" Gene insists, again causing Kara to cringe.

"Except that we don't know exactly where the strike will occur," Kevin says quietly, then pauses. "Or do we?"

"No," Peterson assures him.

Kevin exhales, a tortured sound. "I'm sorry, I just don't see how it's possible, even under the best of circumstances, even if we *did* know exactly where and exactly when it would happen. If you level with people, they'll panic and transportation will bottleneck city-wide—then no one will get out. But if you try moving them under false pretenses, many people will simply refuse to leave."

"And either way, there's still the issue of the spies," Kara reminds him, and Kevin nods sadly. She shares a look with Peterson, then says quietly, "I think we've all accepted that no matter what we do, if it comes down to an attack in August, there will be massive loss of life. This meeting..." She takes a deep breath. "This meeting is about finding creative ways, anything we can think of, to save as many lives as we can while fully expecting—and hoping—that the measures we come up with won't be necessary."

"And what if the attack comes earlier than August?" Kevin questions.

"We're confident," Peterson assures him, and certainly Peterson does seem confident. Kevin doesn't look nearly as sure, but he lets it go.

"Well," Kara says slowly, "just to get us started... I'm sure the President's people have already considered this, but"—Peterson waves irritably, impatient with the qualifications—"I think we *could* actually issue a warning... we'd just have to make it general." She pauses to let that sink in. "We encourage anyone living in *any* large city to consider moving in with friends or family in rural areas."

"You don't think an announcement like that would undermine all the confidence we've been trying to build these last few months?" asks McLaughlin, not skeptically, simply raising a concern.

"It certainly could," Kara agrees, nodding. "But it doesn't have to, if they handle it right. The government could present it almost like a PSA, one of several things families can do to feel more sure of their safety." She shrugs. "From the news right now, it sounds like a lot of people are already moving out to the country."

"It's a good idea," Gene decides. "And they could take it a step further, actually develop a whole line of PSAs, you know, 'Tip #17 for Keeping your Family Safe from Alien Invaders.'" He chuckles.

McLaughlin nods. "Sometimes people stick their heads in the sand. A series of announcements like this would be a good way to keep them constantly reminded of the threat without accidentally inciting a panic."

"And it's helpful regardless of where the aliens strike," Gene adds. "So even if they do switch targets..."

Peterson grunts, scribbling notes on his pad. After a few moments, he looks up. "What else?"

There's another long pause as everyone thinks hard. "I wonder..." McLaughlin begins. "Would there be any way to *entice* people away from Chicago, rather than trying to scare them away?"

"Like what?" Gene asks. "You mean a sporting event or something?"

"Maybe," McLaughlin agrees. "Something like that would be less likely to make those spies suspicious."

Kevin shakes his head, frustrated. "It wouldn't work. For one thing, it would have to be a huge event to make a dent in the death toll. Regardless, you can't schedule it at the same time as the strike, because—again—you don't know when the strike will occur."

"You could just schedule it early, then kidnap everyone once they get to the event—prevent them from going home," Gene suggests. "What?" he demands as Kara rolls her eyes. "I'm being serious! It would be a lot easier than trying to kidnap people from within Chicago."

"Gene..."

"You just have to make up a good reason why they can't go home!"

Kara sighs. She glances at Peterson and is surprised to see him gamely recording Gene's suggestion. But then, something like that *would* appeal to him, wouldn't it? "What about something that lasts longer?" she asks. "Like a music festival?"

Kevin seems determined to defeat every idea. "You do understand the difference in scale, don't you?" He shakes his head. "How many people could you possibly draw? Ten thousand? Twenty? And only some of those would be from Chicago, since the venue would obviously have to be somewhere else. So how many Chicagoans would you actually be saving?" He sags once more. "There's just not a way to save enough people."

"Actually..." Peterson says, narrowing his eyes and staring off into the distance, "you'd be surprised. I saw Rod Steward in concert at Copacabana, back in... '94?" He shakes his head. "There was something like three and a half million people there—" He breaks off as he notices the shocked expressions turned his way. "What?"

"Oh, um..." Kara equivocates. "I guess I'm just as surprised as Kevin that an event could draw that many." Which is of course a bold-faced lie. The pilots are all struggling with the mental image of Jerome Peterson at a rock concert.

"What about that big summer music festival?" McLaughlin asks.

"Which one?" Gene responds, confused.

"I don't know what it's called, but I know it draws something like a million people..." He trails off, smiling expectantly at Gene.

Gene slaps the arm of his chair in sudden excitement. "I know the one! And it's just outside Indianapolis—just a couple hours from Chicago!"

Kara frowns thoughtfully. "I think I know the one you're talking about. The real patriotic one, right? I read they ended up canceling this year, because it coincided with our launch date."

"Don't you see?" Gene asks elatedly. "We could have them reschedule for August, get them to stretch it longer than usual—maybe a whole month instead of a few weeks. Then we push it hard, and I mean hard, make it even more patriotic than usual. Maybe have a portion of proceeds go to the survivors of Denver." His eyes literally glaze over as he considers the details.

"You realize you wouldn't have anything to do with this personally," McLaughlin asks with a slight smile. "Right? We're just brainstorming here."

"It's a good idea," Kara concludes, watching as Peterson scribbles it down. "As long as they avoid any hint of federal involvement, because again, that would clue in the K'luran agents. Together with the PSAs, something like this could save a significant number of lives," she says positively.

"Really?" Kevin retorts, unusually caustic. "Run the numbers here. Even if we're wildly optimistic, no more than 10% of people would actually move away from home because of a PSA—Joker's right, people stick their heads in the sand instead. And this music festival. Assume you actually get two *million* people—fine. Assume even half of them come from Chicago—fine. Even assume those million Chicagoans remain at this festival for the entire month—ridiculous, but fine. That's one million out of ten. Assuming that this million is drawn evenly from across the Chicago area, that's *at best* another 10% removed from the area where the strike ultimately occurs." He rubs his temples fervently. "So best case scenario, your estimate of deaths drops by 20%... That's even less than the amount of variation already existing in the estimate—that doesn't sound to me like we've made any significant difference."

Kara scowls, feeling a little hurt. "Kevin! Every life saved is significant—and we're talking about saving as many as thirty or forty thousand here."

"No, you're talking about giving up on *a hundred and twenty thousand*."

Any excitement that had been generated by the musical festival brainstorm has now been leached from the room. Kara is quiet as she responds, "As we've already established, if it gets to this point, loss of life is inevitable."

Kevin shakes his head. "How firm is the President on his alien agenda?" he asks Peterson.

The general frowns. "What do you mean?"

"Any chance he would give in to this demand? Assuming the aliens actually communicated it to him?"

There are several sharp intakes of breath.

"You mean *give up*?" Peterson demands. "Half our country!?"

"Kevin, what are you saying?" Kara asks, dismayed.

"No chance in hell," Peterson concludes.

Kevin just shakes his head more urgently. "No chance? Even if it meant saving countless lives? After they destroy Chicago, what's next? How many more cities will be destroyed? What other option do we have in the face of such overwhelming force?" His voice cracks. "A few strikes like this, and that's a million dead. A few more, another million. How many millions of lives is our pride worth?"

Everyone is silent for a long moment. "But Kevin," Kara finally says, quietly, "we *do* have a workable response to this threat. The ODC—it's why we exist. And we *will* be in position before August to block this attack." She nods firmly. "This is all just... contingency planning."

The assembled officers lapse into another long silence, and it eventually becomes clear that Kevin Smith's outburst has sucked a bit of energy out of everyone, no matter what reassurances Kara may make. At length, Peterson adjourns them, promising to share their ideas with the President, and even complimenting Gene on his participation.

Kevin is moving the slowest as the rest rise to leave, and therefore he's the last to go. Kara calls to him as he reaches the door: "What was it you needed to talk to me about?"

"Oh, it was nothing," he assures her.

Kara inspects the man as she walks across the room to join him. All of that tension and uncertainty, the tamped-down emotion she saw in him earlier, is back—in fact, much of it had reemerged during the meeting. Kevin Smith is clearly a very empathetic person, and she can only imagine how much worse tonight's discussion made him feel than when he first walked in. "You seemed pretty upset earlier," she probes gently.

"Okay," he admits, "it wasn't *nothing*." He breaks eye contact to study the floor. "But... compared to what the people in Chicago are facing... It's just family stuff, and I needed someone to talk to. But... I guess this Chicago thing helped me put everything in perspective." He looks up sadly, his face belying his next words: "I'm fine now, really."

"All right then," she responds, not the least convinced. She wants to say more, wants him to know she really cares about what's going on in his life, even if whatever it is seems small next to the big picture.

Kevin turns to leave.

She reaches up quickly to grab his hand, and they both freeze; even Kara is surprised. She has to swallow once to find her voice. "I hope everything's okay... with your family, I mean." Squeezing his hand briefly, she releases it.

His face screws up with emotion, but he acknowledges the sentiment with a nod. And then he's gone.

Kara spends a solid five minutes chastising herself for her juvenile behavior, then an even longer time mulling over the Chicago situation. The launch of the ODC personnel into orbit really is the crux of the matter. If for whatever reason that failed to happen, then Kevin is right—the death of a hundred thousand or more people in Chicago would be unavoidable. But then, the Chicago situation is just a microcosm of the greater challenge they face. Without a defensive force in orbit to defend against attacks, their enemy could rain down fire from heaven all day long. The fact that they haven't done so yet causes her to stop and wonder, and not for the first time. Is it possible that the aliens really *have* attempted negotiations with the President already, only to be rebuffed? Would it even matter if they had?

She shakes herself to dispel the questions. They're honestly not worth her time, because—brainstorming sessions aside—she has more immediate things to worry about. The matter of delivering her people safely to their orbital bases... yes, that's something she can affect. As crucial as it is to the survival of Chicago, not to mention the entire nation, cost should be no object in regard to their security measures the day of the launch. She makes a note to address the matter with Peterson. There can be no possibility of security lapse for the July 4th launches.

[Chapter 33]

Late June 2015

July speeds ever closer. Final assembly of each V-2 Destrier takes place at Canaveral—under tight security and under cover, so as to avoid any spying eyes from the sky—after which each craft is fitted into a shipping brace that will protect it during launch. By the third week of June, the last of the subcontracted work on the fighters is complete and, while the final runs are being assembled, the initial batches are catapulted into orbit atop the same brand of two-stage, medium-lift rockets used for the habitats, three Destiers per rocket.

Those habitats, meanwhile, are coming together nicely. Zero G engineers, mostly on loan from NASA, have worked around the clock for five weeks to inflate and connect the modules, forming the 15-bulb design chosen for the U.S.'s first four orbital defense bases, or ODBs. During this period of construction and assembly, everything is kept in a centralized staging area in very low orbit; it is only after completion and full staffing that the bases will be towed out to their final, far-flung geostationary positions. The decision to stage centrally was arrived at for several reasons; spaceborne people resources are naturally limited, and it also makes sense to work directly from the point at which the collapsed habs and other materials enter orbit. But just as important is the challenge of providing at least *some* protection during the ODBs' period of greatest vulnerability.

This planned two-month-long exposure was the crux of several heated arguments among Peterson, Kara's staff, and the ODC's NASA liaisons. Some were in favor of sending some of the experienced ODC pilots—Air Force transfers—along for the ride when the habs were launched, along with several Destriers, so as to provide a limited border patrol during construction. Others argued that the weightlessness training at Johnson had already been abbreviated more than was safe, and further accelerating the launch of any personnel would only leave them less prepared for the realities of long-term life in space. Kara saw both sides as well as the need to make sure the ODBs survived long enough to be used; for her, the need to maintain a consistent training regimen overrode the other risks. In typical fashion, Peterson made his own decision to uphold the training regimen, ignoring all opposition. Although, naturally, he did not share his reasoning with everyone, he simply felt secure in KLINE's timetable, which said the next strike wouldn't come until August.

Thus it was decided that the ODB modules would be accompanied by the first two Destriers hot off the line, and the crews of construction workers—most of them trained astronauts anyway—would include an additional six shuttle-rated astronaut pilots. While these men and women would not be trained in ODC tactics, they were without exception former Air Force fighter jocks; given the benefit of an abridged Destrier training program, they were deemed capable of a reasonable showing should there in fact be an attack on the staging area. It was hardly an ideal situation, but then nothing about these circumstances was ideal, and at least some protection was being afforded—and perhaps more importantly, the *appearance* of protection was being projected.

As Kara begins preparations for her own July 4th launch from Cape Canaveral, she is breathing easier in the knowledge that nothing ever came of their concerns. As of June 29th, the last of the kinks are worked out at Asimov, and each ODB is prepared to receive its new tenants. That means she can now focus all of her worries on strapping *herself* to a highly combustible launch vehicle for rapid transport into space.

Saturday morning
July 4, 2015

Independence Day 2015 dawns bright and clear as the sun crests the Atlantic: a perfect day for a launch or two. Long before that first glow appears on the horizon, though, preparations for both of the day's two launches were already well underway.

"Kara must be going out of her mind right about now," Jack Dunn says softly, a smile tugging at his lip.

Viviane laughs. There's a pause, and then Gregoire says, "Why?"

She flashes him a smile of her own. "Because Kara *hates* sitting around with nothing to do—and they boarded those Longships, like, three hours ago. Everyone's just sitting in there, on their *backs*, with nothing to do but pick their noses. Except they can't, 'cause they're in full spacesuits." Her eyes return to the spacecraft several miles distant, parked on the tarmac with its nose to the sky. Impatient, she bounces absently on the balls of her feet, even as her fiancé squeezes her hand reassuringly.

"But they can listen to music, no?" Greg asks. "I heard they built MP3 devices into the spacesuits. Since many of these people, they will be in those suits all the time..." He trails off at a look from Viviane.

"Trust me," she says. "Kara's bored stupid, music or not."

"Still... she's dreamed of this all her life, you know," Mr. Dunn puts in, a faraway look in his eyes. "She watched every televised Shuttle launch as a kid—did you know that? She'd get down on her knees, right in front of the TV, just staring in wonder..." He sighs.

With a huff, Viviane seats herself, Greg joining her. She's been alternating between standing and sitting for hours now. They'd arrived around 4 o'clock to claim good seats, and even though it was still dark then, she'd enjoyed the carnival-like atmosphere—after all, everyone loves funnel cake, right? But as the hours dragged on, her enthusiasm waned in favor of the anxiety she'd felt since first learning Kara would be deployed to orbit. At this point, there's still half an hour remaining until the first launch, and it can't come soon enough.

In truth, she's probably casting a lot of her own impatience onto Kara; but seriously, if Viviane's this bored on the outside, with food and amusement and bathrooms and the chance to stretch her legs, it's *got* to be bad for Kara on the inside.

In front of the grandstands, NASA has setup a small stage, which has now hosted a number of different experts, each providing information or entertainment—sometimes both—as a way of passing the time. Right now, some public relations guy is describing the equipment the Gryphens will be using to reach orbit.

"No doubt, you've noticed the similarities between what you see on the tarmac today and what you've seen on television over the last twenty-four years. Much like the more famous STS system used in conjunction with the Space Shuttle, the OWT system—developed by Out of this World Tours—employs a large expendable liquid hydrogen-oxygen fuel tank, along with reusable solid rocket boosters or 'SRBs'. The fuel tank is what you see in orange, while the SRBs are in white, the same color scheme used on most Shuttle missions.

"The first difference you'll note is one of scale. Proportionately, the OWT system is almost twice the size of the STS, with the OWT fuel tank standing more than 300 feet above the jetty. The more observant among you have probably also noticed that we're using *four* solid rocket boosters today, rather than two." The man pauses. "But I suspect most of you have eyes only for the Longship, which is the spaceplane of choice today, in place of the Space Shuttle.

"The Longship—which we refer to as the orbiter—was conceptualized by Out of this World Tours in 1997, then developed at an undisclosed location between 1999 and 2013. It features a swept-back cropped delta-wing body design—see the way both wings are triangular in shape, like the Greek letter *delta*? This is a design you often see in fighter jets, but not as often in commercial liners. You'll also notice the existence of two much smaller wings near the nose of the craft, just back from the cockpit. These are known as canards, another feature more traditionally associated with fighter jets. And yet the size of this orbiter is much more consistent with that of a jetliner.

"That has led some of my colleagues to describe the Longship as the lovechild of the Space Shuttle and a Boeing 747." He pauses a moment for laughter. "Functionally, the Longship certainly inherits from both traditions—boasting both the space-worthiness of the Shuttle and the passenger cabin of a large commercial aircraft. And while its capacity for 204 passengers might be considered only midsized among airliners, the Longship ranks as far and away the largest spaceplane developed to date.

"This particular Longship, launching here from Complex 39A, is known as the *Herald*. The *Harbinger* is the Longship launching from 17B three hours from now. Once they deliver their passengers to their respective orbital defense bases, the two Longships will reenter atmosphere and land here at Kennedy five days from now. At that point, preparations will begin anew for launching the second half of the ODC personnel into orbit two weeks from now.

"In addition to *Herald* and *Harbinger*, there's a third Longship known as *Hermes*, which will sit out today's launch. You've probably heard that the…"

Viviane turns to Kara's father in confusion. "Did he just say this is the *Herald*? I thought we were going to see Kara launch, and she's on the—"

Mr. Dunn makes a shushing motion, even as Greg squeezes her hand warningly. "It's supposed to be secret who's on which orbiter," Dunn says quietly.

"Oh," Viviane colors. "But—"

"After this launch, we'll have plenty of time to make it to 17-B." He smiles. "Don't worry, we'll get to see *both* launches."

"Okay," Viviane subsides.

"… were christened in honor of Mercury, the messenger god from Roman mythology," the speaker is now saying, "also known as Hermes to the Greeks. I can't tell you for sure why these names were chosen—those sorts of decisions are above my pay grade"—more laughter—"but there are theories floating around. For one thing, it's been said that the personnel of the Orbital Defense Corps will be delivering a message to the aliens for us." The laughter is more forced this time, but it's there. "It's also been noted that the Longship's canards are reminiscent of the wings sprouting from Mercury's head in most depictions—"

At that moment, a loud wailing sounds, coming from the direction of the launch pad.

"Oh," the speaker says, sounding a little confused. "I guess they're moving the gantry back from…" he trails off. The alarm sound continues, but the gantry, designed to roll away from the launch pad before launch, remains stationary.

"What's going on?" Viviane hisses, heart in her throat.

"I don't know," Mr. Dunn says slowly. "Probably just part of the launch," he adds, but his tone is concerned.

The PR guy is now explaining that this is an unusual departure from normal pre-launch procedures, but that there's nothing to be concerned about. He's drowned out by a sudden swell of voices. "Look," someone yells from nearby.

Miles distant, a swarm of ants appears to be forming at the foot of the gantry. But Viviane knows they're not ants, they're people in spacesuits—and they're moving as fast as possible away from the launch pad. The tension in the crowd grows as the minutes pass, even as a new speaker mounts the stage to explain that there's nothing to be concerned about.

And then the *Herald* disappears in an intense flash of light as a thunderclap rattles the grandstands.

[Chapter 34]

Saturday afternoon
July 4, 2015

"We had a tech up on the gantry, checking on an error code we were getting. It really was long past the time everyone should've been gone, but there was still plenty of margin."

"And he saw something?" Kara asks.

"No," responds Dr. Andrew Potteiger, the flight director on loan from NASA. "He actually *heard* something. A dripping sound... so faint, he wasn't even sure he actually heard it, but that's the kind of thing that makes our blood run cold here."

Kara nods.

"Anyway, he started a walkaround and eventually discovered a small pool forming below the external tank—a leak, apparently. He called it in, and that's all we needed to abort the launch and initiate evacuation."

"And that's when..." Kara's voice trails off.

There's a long pause before Peterson speaks up soberly. "Actually, we managed to get everyone off the *Herald* before the explosion happened... we just didn't get them to a safe distance in time. But a few of the folks who *did* make it safely, they said..." He stops, uncharacteristically shaken, and glances at Potteiger. "Said they heard... howling, almost a low moaning... right before the whole thing went up."

There's another awkward pause. "And we don't know what caused it?"

Peterson scowls. He clearly has an opinion, but Potteiger replies, "We've launched an investigation." He glances at Peterson. "And a search of the immediate premises. But you should also know that..." He pauses. "Well see, that error code? If I didn't know better, I'd say the system had been tampered with."

"Which further suggests sabotage," Peterson grunts.

"No, you misunderstand," the flight director objects. "The subroutine generating that alarm was non-critical—it couldn't have had anything to do with the explosion. But the thing is, I don't see how the system could have gotten into that state by itself. It's as if…" Potteiger shakes his head. "If we're indeed looking at sabotage here, well, it's as if someone else—someone else entirely—manipulated the system to be sure we'd have a man on the gantry at the last minute. If that hadn't been the case…" He sighs, silent for a moment. Then: "Colonel… I know you lost some good people. Not to mention the *Herald*. But it could have been much worse. If that tech hadn't started poking around… Well, when the engines ignited, we would have lost everyone." He opens his mouth to say more, then just stops.

Kara gazes out the window at the charred, gutted hull of the distant Longship, lying upside-down amidst the debris of its fuel tank and rocket boosters, and at the blackened streaks leading away from it in all directions for hundreds of feet. Dozens injured and twenty-two confirmed deaths, including Chip Conroy… and Anna Haynes.

Struggling to speak through the lump in her throat, she turns to Potteiger and says, "Please express to your technician just how much I appreciate what he—how many lives he saved." And then, with a weak attempt at an appreciative smile, she flees the room.

She makes it as far as the first unoccupied corridor she can find, then sinks to a crouch. Back to the wall, head in her hands, Kara gives in to her grief.

July 2015

Two searches of the surrounding area reveal nothing, but on the second day after the incident, a sharp-eyed chopper pilot notices something unusual a quarter mile to the east: a series of geometric shapes cut into the long-bladed grass that grows wild on the Canaveral headland. It's the sort of discovery that sends a jolt through even the most reasonable of individuals. First an accident of this magnitude, and then the discovery of crop circles, one of the quintessential indicators of alien visitation. In truth, the whole scenario is just a little *too* perfect; nevertheless, for a time, it seems to keep the inhabitants of Cape Canaveral on tenterhooks, peeking over their shoulders whenever they find themselves outside.

Meanwhile, the investigation into the disaster itself turns up precisely nothing; deriving meaningful information from the burnt wreckage is nearly impossible. Even identifying the locus of the original leak amidst the debris would be like finding a needle in a haystack; to attempt to then backtrack its original cause would be an exercise in futility. And thus the official ruling is that the explosion was an accident... even though said accident was both theoretically and statistically impossible. Suffice it to say that no one really believes the official ruling—it's just that there's no real evidence of sabotage.

In light of the situation, the authorities make the decision to block all egress from the promontory's secure areas, while also limiting the arrival of new personnel. Unfortunately for most ODC servicemen and -women, this puts them on opposite sides of the fence from their families, as the spectator grandstands were outside the security perimeter. For those news people trapped inside, the measure proves quite easy to swallow; after all, they're at the center of the biggest developing story of the moment, and no additional media is being allowed in. What's not so popular is the gag order handed down twenty-four hours later: no information will leave Canaveral in any form. In the name of national security, a total media blackout has gone into effect.

By Wednesday the 8th, at least, one unexplained phenomenon is, in fact, explained. Review of the past week's logs by a maintenance supervisor reveals unauthorized use of lawn mowing equipment by one Jodie Chin, a groundskeeper. In the face of mounting hysteria amongst the people trapped at Canaveral, Kara can't help but shake her head at this most obvious of causes. Nevertheless, investigators initially hold off on confronting the man, in hopes of determining his intentions and ferreting out any compatriots. This delay leads to nothing, and the eventual interrogation reveals a very scared man who thought that crop circles would be a fun prank for the morning of the Gryphens' launch. In the wake of the disaster and faced with a team of angry interrogators, he quickly changes his mind on that score. In the end, however, investigators conclude that he is indeed a harmless prankster... which isn't to say that he won't face criminal charges.

Outside the blackout zone, the media continues to run rampant. Even as candlelit vigils continue across the nation, experts and pseudo-experts from various fields take up residence on talk shows as they discuss theories regarding who was behind the attack—not that very many of them doubt the aliens were ultimately responsible; the question is whether they actually perpetrated the act themselves. Despite the official ruling that the catastrophe was an accident, the talking heads take sabotage as a given. Is it possible that the aliens have, in fact, secured a foothold in this country and are capable of moving about undetected—either because they're of similar physiognomy to humans, or because their technology allows them to masquerade as such? Or are they working in concert with some human faction, perhaps terrorists? Even this late in the game, it seems the media is not aware—as Peterson's people obviously are—of the alien aggressors' cooperation with human mercenary groups. In the absence of any news from on the ground at Canaveral, the theories proposed grow only more outlandish as the weeks slip by. Perhaps the perpetrators were fringe radicals—humans—operating independently of any organization, just one or two half-crazed fanatics who believed the world was rightfully coming to an end and humanity should accept its fate rather than fighting back. Or maybe it was an agent of some foreign government happy to see the U.S. exposed to attack. For that matter, a few pundits still hold to the opinion that the entire alien attack is a farce staged by a foreign power.

Through all of this, launches from Canaveral remain on hold indefinitely. Kara's staff chafes under this—they quite appreciate the danger to themselves, and yet they also feel that August deadline looming; and besides, they've spent the past several months preparing themselves mentally for facing danger. Instead, they find themselves billeted in old barracks-style housing on base and placed under heavy guard until the investigation is completed. As the delay stretches on, Kara and Peterson devolve into a number of bitter arguments, but as he repeatedly points out—and validly so—they can no longer take confidence in the security measures there at Kennedy. And though the ODC personnel are willing to risk their lives for the greater good, it won't do anyone, including the people of Chicago, any good if they never make it to orbit. Peterson implies that drastic steps may need to be taken to address their security situation before he's willing to risk another launch; but as is too often the case, he refuses to share the details with Kara.

Then in the wee hours of the 17th, drama leaps to a new high. Returning from a nocturnal trip to the restroom, Donald DeMaria stumbles upon what appears to be a bomb in his barracks. Reacting to the perceived threat, he immediately pulls a fire alarm. Within half an hour, a bomb disposal team has arrived onsite... only to discover that what Donald thought was a digital countdown timer is actually a standard alarm clock. Humiliated, feeling a hundred pairs of eyes upon him, Donald stammers an apology, admitting that he was half asleep when he leapt to his conclusion. Nevertheless, the relief of the evacuated personnel is a palpable thing... right up until the moment the alarm clock goes off, at 4 o'clock sharp. The subsequent explosion is deafening, even to those still outside the metal building. Within the building, the four members of the bomb squad are thrown more than ten feet. Miraculously, no one is killed; the device was a small one, and the response team was already on its way back outside, having concluded it was a false alarm.

This second sudden reversal, right on the heels of the first, leaves the assembled personnel in shock. Someone had indeed planted a bomb in the midst of their sleeping forms—a bomb that undoubtedly would have killed dozens—and they had wrapped it in the innocuous form of a common alarm clock, the sort of thing one sees all the time and thus never really notices. And yet Donald DeMaria, possessed of an overly active imagination and still half dreaming, stumbles across the thing and leaps to the right conclusion for all the wrong reasons... saving lives in the process. It leads to a dubious notoriety. Donald is openly hailed as a hero, and yet he knows his compatriots are privately shaking their heads, fully appreciating the irony that no one died precisely because he *is* an idiot.

If possible, security is tightened even more. Unfortunately, investigation into the barracks bomb also leads nowhere, as the explosion has left nothing for the forensics people to dig their forceps into. And though no one was killed, the incident still serves to ratchet up the tension for the thousands of people trapped at Cape Canaveral.

For Kara, the weeks following the disaster mark a return to the feelings of inadequacy she's never quite banished. The ODC wasn't even able to make it into orbit without losing people, and the loss of Anna in particular... On several occasions, Kara must take extended trips to the bathroom simply to grieve properly, away from curious eyes. Anna was there for her when Kara desperately needed it, and yet Kara—ultimately responsible for the safety of her people—couldn't protect her in turn. Never mind that there's nothing more she could have done; never mind that, by all accounts, Anna was one of the last out of the Longship specifically because she stayed behind to make sure everyone got out. Logic has no place in Kara's self-recrimination. For all of her rough edges, Anna Haynes was a fiercely loyal friend, and she could always be trusted to crack a tension-releasing joke when things got too stressful. It goes without saying that the woman leaves a gaping hole with her passing.

And Kara could use some Haynes-style levity right now. She can't help but feel even more stress over the fact that Peterson has closed her out of both the investigation and his plans for moving forward from here. Having grown unexpectedly accustomed to leadership over the previous year, she now finds herself without any particular responsibilities until Peterson decides what's next; all she can do is try to reassure her people, precisely when she's feeling as uncertain as ever. With too much time on her hands, she again finds herself almost overwhelmed by thoughts of death. During all the months of training, with not a single attempt on her life, Kara had almost managed to forget the danger she was in. Yet now, when she's not reliving the moments of terror before Anna's timely rescue, she's left thinking about her many other close calls in the months leading up to that, not to mention the abduction attempt just weeks later. If anything, the knowledge is more sobering now than it was at the time, maybe because she feels far more *mortal* now than ever before. In the words of that stupid Chinese fortune cookie, 'Your death is inevitable.'

It's enough to drive her stir-crazy, just like all the other ODC personnel locked up at Canaveral for the last month. And just like them, she begins yearning for an opportunity—any opportunity—to escape this crazy place.

Then she gets one.

Sunday evening
July 26, 2015

Kara slumps into the seat beside McLaughlin. "Hey, guys."

Across the table, Skylar clears her throat uncomfortably, and Kara straightens her posture with a start. This temporary building may have been setup as an officers' mess, a place for eating and letting down, but that doesn't mean Kara shouldn't always appear confident and professional in front of her people. Especially considering how demoralizing the last month has been for everyone.

"Sorry," she says.

Skylar gives her a convincingly oblivious look. "For what?"

"You heard the news?" Kara asks them, letting it drop.

"About General Grant?" McLaughlin clarifies. "Yeah, we were just discussing." He takes a breath, lets out a frustrated sigh.

Skylar shakes her head. "I barely knew him, barely saw him after he recruited me. I guess I'm saying I don't have any particular loyalty to him, but still… that's a rough way to go. Serve your country half a century, then spend your last eight months locked up, branded a traitor." Even as she's speaking—softly—she keeps an eye on the people around them, ensuring no one is close enough to overhear. "Did they ever actually *charge* him with anything?"

"Not that I heard," McLaughlin says, and Kara shakes her head in agreement.

"Peterson says you're attending the funeral?" Skylar asks.

This time, Kara nods. "More in a personal capacity—Grant's daughter Viviane is one of my best friends."

Skylar blinks. "Really? I didn't know that… That's a crazy coincidence."

Kara gives her a wry smile. "I know, right?"

"Good to hear *someone* has permission to leave Canaveral," McLaughlin gripes, but there's more humor to it than sarcasm. "Make sure you find a drive-thru and enjoy a real burger while you're away."

Kara smiles at the inside joke. "I'll probably be with Peterson and a full security detail the whole time." She pauses. "Can't you just picture us all stuffed into a booth together at a fast food joint?"

"Peterson included?" Skylar asks, then laughs outright.

The levity doesn't last, unfortunately. In the silence that follows, Kara catches sight of Barrett Williams slumped at a nearby table, not the least bit confident or professional in his bearing. She nods in his direction, and Skylar sighs.

"I don't know what to do with him," the other woman says frankly. Barrett is, after all, one of Skylar's direct subordinates. "After that first week, I made sure no one would serve him alcohol, but..." She trails off with a suddenly guilty look.

"Why?" Kara asks.

"Well, he sorta... went on a bender."

"*What?*" Kara demands. Dropping her voice, she adds, "You didn't tell me that."

McLaughlin leans into the conversation. "There are times for discipline, and there are times for understanding. You know how close he and Haynes were—as close as you and Viviane Grant."

That takes Kara aback somewhat. "I wasn't saying—I'm just surprised this is the first I heard of it."

"Well," Skylar says, "better that you and Peterson didn't have to address the issue. It's on my head." She sighs. "Thing is, ever since that first week, Barrett's performed his duties fine, anything I've asked of him. But his downtime..." She gestures at him. "All of it, just like this."

"And the grief counselors we brought in?" Kara asks.

"I ordered him to attend a few sessions. Don't know if it helped." Skylar pauses. "On the upside, he *did* crack a joke earlier today. I think that's the first one I've heard from him since the Fourth."

Kara nods, wishing she had a solution. But the fact is, Barrett is only an extreme example of how poorly *all* of her people are coping right now, not the exception to the rule. "I think Kevin is really struggling too," she says slowly. "Though he hides it well."

Skylar smiles sadly. "Better than Barrett, at least."

"Any idea why it would affect him so badly?" Kara asks, then hastens to add, "I mean, obviously it's affecting all of us badly. But... I didn't think Kevin was close to anyone we lost."

"He wasn't," McLaughlin puts in, "not that I know of. But some of them were his people, and he's protective of his people." He chews his lip. "Plus, he saw something rough at his last posting. I don't know the details, but..." He shrugs. "I know *that* affected him deeply too. And that kind of thing starts adding up after a while. Regardless, everyone handles loss differently. You know that."

"Yeah..." Kara says. "I just wish he wouldn't shut me out like this."

"I know what you mean," McLaughlin agrees. "We just need to give them time—Barrett, Kevin, all the rest. Time, counseling... and we need to get them off this base and into orbit."

"Hear, hear!" Skylar raises her paper cup wryly, as if joining in a toast. "This place isn't doing anyone's mood any good."

They fall into companionable silence for a few minutes, then McLaughlin stirs. "Well, I'd better get going," he says, his expression brightening considerably. "Date with the wife." At Kara's confused expression, he adds, "She's arriving tonight."

"Really?" Kara smiles genuinely. "That's great." With the ODC trapped here on the promontory indefinitely, and with the flow of communication with family outside all but blocked, Peterson had made the concession that spouses could apply to join their loved ones in enforced isolation. More than a few had done exactly that, but it was a difficult commitment to make, not knowing when they would be released again.

"Tell Evelyn I said hey," Skylar puts in as the three pilots rise from their table.

"Ditto from me," Kara adds. "I think I'll go force my company on Barrett."

After all, Kara thinks as McLaughlin and Skylar leave the mess together, she has no real desire to return to her quarters any earlier than necessary. And while she may not have been as tight with Anna as Barrett, they were still close. Maybe reminiscing together will help Barrett. It'll certainly help Kara.

**Tuesday morning
July 28, 2015**

As it turns out, there's no real funeral service for Gen. Grant, just a few words spoken at the graveside; although Grant was of the Christian faith, his duties chained him to his office and apartment at Groom Lake, and he seldom had the opportunity to attend services off-base. The eulogy is delivered by an unnamed Air Force chaplain.

Kara and Viviane share a hug following the burial, but words are long in coming. What with the media blackout, they haven't spoken in a month.

"You've been good?" Viviane finally asks.

Kara just nods, unable to find the right words to comfort her friend.

"I can't believe it..." Viviane begins, starting to tremble. "All those years just trying to be rid of him, and now I actually miss him. Already."

Kara quickly pulls her friend back into an embrace.

Voice muffled against Kara's neck, Viviane continues: "I hated him sometimes, but he was my dad—I didn't want to lose him. And now I know at least that he was working on something important all those years. I just wish... I wish I could've seen him more... at the end. But it's like he dropped off the face of the planet."

Kara feels the inevitable rush of guilt, but she swallows the temptation to finally tell Viviane the truth of the last eight months. It might help the other woman to know that her father didn't contact her because he *couldn't*, but the knowledge that he was being jailed for treason... No, that knowledge would only hurt her friend. "He..." Kara begins tentatively. "He told me one time that he always thought of you while he was working, that it was you he was working to protect. He—" She searches for the words. "He wasn't clueless; he knew he didn't give you the time you deserved. But he loved you." She pulls back and forces Viviane to look her in the eye. "He loved you," she repeats, nodding, "even if that was hard for you to believe sometimes."

Viviane's expression sours again. "You had all that time with him. *You.* I wish I could've had that."

Kara sighs and nods. "There were a lot of ways that he failed. But you can take comfort in *knowing* he loved you, and in knowing that his love for you will save millions of lives." The words taste bitter in her mouth, reminding her of all the lives lost in Denver, lives Grant had the foreknowledge to save. She experiences a rekindling of the anger and confusion that had slowly faded since the previous November—along with more guilt simply for feeling angry, since part of her nevertheless wonders if she would have handled the situation any differently from Grant—but she forges on regardless. "You can be *proud* of him, Viviane. And when you're tempted to feel sorry for yourself, you can remember that your sacrifice—the fact that you didn't have the dad you should have had—was part of what will save all those lives." She tries a tentative smile. "Hey, it ain't ideal, but it's something."

Viviane wipes her nose and smiles bravely, pulling out the triangularly-folded American flag for a closer look. "You're right. You're always right. I guess Dad's a bit of a hero, isn't he?"

"He sure is." Looking past Viviane's shoulder, Kara catches sight of Gen. Peterson standing under a nearby tree, watching them closely. Gregoire stands awkwardly beside him. Kara thanks the God she doesn't believe in that Peterson—gruff, insensitive Peterson—also had the tact to maintain the illusion about Grant.

As they walk back to the cars, talk turns to Viviane's upcoming wedding. "I've decided on May."

"Oh yeah?" Kara responds, happy for a more positive topic.

"Yeah. Outside Paris—Gregoire has an uncle with a farm... from the photos, it's perfect. Anyway, not a big affair, just close friends. And you *will* be maid of honor—" She stops moving and turns to eye Kara. "Right?"

Kara sighs, stopping also. "We've discussed this. I want to, but... there's no telling what the next several months will bring." She smiles. "I can't just hop a shuttle down, you know."

Viviane nods sadly. "I know. If we have to, we'll hold the wedding until—"

"No you won't! You schedule that wedding, and if I can be there, I will. I don't want to miss it. But even if I do, we've still got the rest of our lives—that wedding is just the official start of your life together with Greg, and I'll be a part of that life. You guys will make lots of beautiful children, and I'll be that spinster aunt that visits from time to time that you can never get rid of. In the grand scheme of things, it doesn't really matter if I miss the kickoff party, right?"

"Okay then." Viviane smiles warmly. "Take care of yourself. I'm sorry about July 4th... I know you lost some friends."

Kara just nods.

"Colonel Dunn?" They both jerk slightly at the realization that Peterson has crept up on them. "We really should be going. I hope you don't mind riding back with me. There's a matter I'd like to discuss with you." He smiles awkwardly at Viviane and waves his hand dismissively. "You know, just a logistical... thing."

Kara pulls Viviane into a last tight hug. "I love you, my friend, and I'll miss you too."

"You'd better come back. Those kids will need their spinster aunt."

[Chapter 35]

Nine Years Earlier

Saturday afternoon
March 11, 2006

Kara stood staring at the casket, lost in thought and reflection. Off to the side, her father quietly accepted the encouragement and consolation offered by a long line of individuals. Kara's mother had been well-loved in the community.

As was so often the case, Kara stood aloof. She knew that people would simply assume she was wrapped up in her own grief, and that she needed the time to herself. She let them think it. And certainly, she was grieving... but her mother's cancer had taken a long time to kill her; there was no shock to her passing. Mostly, Kara just felt uncomfortable with the hugs and sympathy. These weren't people she knew, not really. They were friends of Mom's, other socialites and volunteers and committee chairs from the community; as much as Kara loved her mother, they'd never really understood each other—not the way Kara and her father did—and the prospect of accepting banal platitudes from the people Mom *was* close to just wasn't appealing. The only hometown friend of Kara's that had actually shown up at the funeral was Allie McCullough, and after more than seven years out of touch, that had been nearly as awkward. Allie had waited through the funeral, offered Kara her condolences, then beat a hasty retreat.

Kara sighed, just wishing the day was finally over, and immediately regretting the thought. Her dad was the real victim here, and she couldn't help but respect his strength in the face of this onslaught of well-meaning acquaintances. It made her feel selfish, the fact that for a few minutes, at least, she had so completely forgotten how difficult life was for Dad right now.

Someone came alongside, brushing Kara's shoulder. Kara squeezed her eyes shut, willing herself not to be annoyed; fixing a smile on her face, she turned to greet the person. But it wasn't someone she was expecting.

"Viviane?"

"Hi, Kara," the girl responded, if anything, more awkward than Allie had been.

Kara stared at her new roommate in appreciative surprise. They had just moved in together in January, and although they'd had some great late-night discussions, they still barely knew each other. Kara certainly wouldn't have expected the younger woman to fly coast-to-coast on such short notice for the funeral of a woman she'd never met. "I didn't even know you were here."

Viviane shrugged. "I tried waving earlier, but I guess you're a little distracted. There's a lot of people here! Your mom must have been really well liked."

Kara nodded, turning back to stare at the coffin once more. "She was," she said simply. There wasn't much more to be said, and they lapsed into silence. Comfortable silence, Kara realized after a moment. They might not have known each other long, but somehow she felt comfortable with this person—so different from herself in so many ways—to a degree she'd experienced with few besides her father. It was a welcome realization in that moment.

At length, Viviane stirred, looking embarrassed. "Um, I know this isn't the best time, but... I don't think I can make rent this month. Maybe next month, but..." She met Kara's eyes briefly, then looked away, flushing.

Kara regarded the girl with genuine amusement. Just entering their third month together, and she was already having trouble with rent for the second time. Considering the amount of money the college junior apparently spent on clothes and at the clubs, not to mention crazy whims—such as this last-minute plane ticket to Maine—it was no wonder she was always short. But she was helpless in so many practical respects; Kara could hardly feel any rancor toward her, though it would certainly make the next month difficult financially. She needed to sit the younger woman down at some point soon and begin working through a few of these failings in her upbringing.

Kara sighed. "We'll get through it... though I think that puts you on kitchen duty for a while."

"Kitchen— You mean, like, cooking food...?"

"Yep." She didn't add that it would help Viviane's financial woes if she didn't eat out so often; she'd see for herself. Kara laughed lightly, pleased to have escaped the emotional weight of the funeral, if only briefly.

Viviane was eyeing her still. "It's really okay?"

Kara smiled and shrugged. "What other option do you have? It's not like I'm going to kick you out." And she realized it was true; she felt an unusual amount of protectiveness for this new friend of hers, vulnerable and unprepared for adulthood as she was.

The young woman broke into one of those brilliant smiles of hers. "You really are great, Kara, just like Dad said."

Kara's forehead crinkled in confusion. She hadn't yet met Viviane's father, and thus far, the girl had steadfastly refused to talk of her family.

Misunderstanding the look on her friend's face, Viviane hastened to speak. "I know, I know, I could ask Dad for money, but... don't you see, Kara, I can't, I *can't*." Just like that, she began losing control of her emotions. "I only finally moved out on my own. If I admit I can't make it on my own, it would be... it'd just be bad," she finished, tears welling in her eyes.

"Shh, it's okay," Kara comforted her, giving her a tentative hug. "We'll work it out." Smiling slightly, Kara laughed to herself at the role reversal here, as she comforted this flighty creature over something so minor while standing beside her own mother's coffin.

Viviane's smile was back as they came out of the embrace. "You really are great, Kara. One of the most giving people I know."

Kara pondered that for a moment, having never thought of herself as generous. Then her attention was called away. "Kara," Mr. Dunn called. "I'd like you to meet Mrs. Klugman-Anderson. She and your mother were..."

With that, Kara's self-imposed sequestration was defeated; she could no longer avoid standing alongside her father as the remainder of the line streamed past, offering their sweet comments about her mother. But her spirits were lifted knowing she had a friend of her own who cared enough to fly 3,000 miles to be there.

And although Viviane spent the night with the Dunns before flying home, and although Kara and Viviane filled many hours with conversation over the months that followed, Kara never once thought to follow up on that odd comment Viviane made about her father.

[Chapter 36]

Tuesday noon
July 28, 2015

Kara settles back into the plush leather seat of the sedan as Peterson enters behind her and pulls the door shut.

"Corporal?" Peterson makes a circular motion with his hand when the driver looks back, and a moment later a privacy screen rises between the officers and the front of the car.

Reaching into the inside pocket of his dress uniform jacket, Peterson removes a slim hinged case—almost like a flattened jewelry box, but in leather instead of felt—and tosses it casually into Kara's lap. Tentatively, Kara raises the lid, which creaks as it opens. Glittering inside is a pair of silver stars.

Her eyes go instinctively to Peterson's shoulders, and she's surprised to see that his rank insignia now consists of two stars on each shoulder rather than one. No longer a mere brigadier general, he's apparently now a major general. "But—" she begins, confused.

"I already got mine. Those are for you," he grunts matter-of-factly. "Long overdue in both cases."

Kara sucks in a breath. *Her*, a general officer? Brigadier General Kara Dunn?

"They gave me a seat on the Joint Chiefs." He barks a laugh. "I'd usually need a few more stars for that, but tradition hardly matters much in wartime. Anyway," he continues, "we needed more depth throughout the entire organization. And it's absurd to think of conducting a war without a single general officer in theatre. So there you go." And apparently that's all he intends to say on the subject.

"General," she begins, and she remarks to herself that she's not even *more* shocked—and terrified—by this unexpected turn of events. Apparently she's experienced this sort of thing often enough in recent months that it just doesn't phase her the way it once did. Still… "General, one year ago, I was a civilian. It doesn't seem absurd to you that I'm now a one-star *general*?"

The man's face cracks into one of those rare, seemingly-genuine smiles. "Like I said, unusual things happen in wartime. I don't really care who you were a year ago. It's who you are today that matters"—Kara tries momentarily to parse this seemingly back-handed compliment before giving up—"and by now you've proven yourself the most talented Destrier pilot in this organization." He shrugs. "And a talented leader." No, for Peterson, it's just a statement of fact as he sees it, not a compliment.

"I just don't see how I'm supposed to inspire confidence and respect when I'm wearing a rank I didn't earn."

"I thought we'd settled this," he retorts angrily. "You earned this responsibility, you just didn't join the military until late. So what? You're the expert and every Gryphen knows it. Case closed." He starts to turn back to his window before swiveling abruptly and jabbing a finger at her, almost as a parting shot. "And don't let your people hear you talking like this," he bites out. "It's my prerogative to put you forward for promotion, and the President and Joint Chiefs approved it. No one inside the ODC will question that, and hell if I care what anyone outside this organization thinks of it." With a final grunt, he settles back in his seat and shifts his attention to the passing trees.

"So," Kara asks after a moment, unable to resist the urge. "Was this the 'logistical matter' you wanted to discuss?"

"Hardly," he responds, but he doesn't elaborate, and they lapse into silence. Content with the quiet, Kara ruminates awhile on what this promotion means, but her mind soon wanders. For the first time in years, she finds herself thinking about her mother's funeral—not surprising, given the funeral they just left—and about Viviane's surprise appearance there.

"General..." she says at length. Her forehead is crinkled in confusion when Peterson turns distractedly to look at her.

"Yes?"

"I've known Viviane Grant for..." she pauses to consider. "Almost ten years. Since before I ever came up with the concept for *Rampant*."

There's something in the man's eyes as she turns to meet them. "And?" he asks evenly.

"And... with everything that's happened, doesn't that strike you as an incredible coincidence? It just seems too perfect... Usually I'm able to convince myself that Grant knew of my work *because* of my connection to his daughter. I think he even said as much. But... I was just remembering something *she* said, way back when we first knew each other. Something about her dad's opinion of me."

Peterson grunts and turns to gaze back through the car window. A light drizzle has begun, appropriate after the funeral.

"Well?"

"Kara, Grant's been keeping tabs on you your entire life," he says matter-of-factly.

She experiences a weird feeling in her belly at this revelation. "What do you mean? And how do you know?"

"His files are mine now, remember?" He sighs. "I don't know *much*, because he didn't document much. But he's got files on you going back as far as 1984."

"'84? But I was *six* at the time."

Peterson nods, still gazing out the window. "And he wasn't just watching. In addition to copies of all your transcripts and applications and so on, there's evidence he had a hand in all the scholarships and grants you received over the years."

The odd sensation feels more like a gut punch now. Peterson might as well say that all of her hard work was a sham, that she hadn't actually earned any of her accomplishments over the years. "But..." She struggles to process this. "That doesn't make any sense. I mean, *why* would he have an interest in me?"

"There's a lot in his files that doesn't make sense," Peterson agrees.

"Was there anything in there about me and Viviane living together?"

The man shakes his head.

"I always thought we'd been connected randomly through a roommate matching service."

"All things considered, I doubt it was that random."

Kara sits back, frowning. Every mild sensation of creepiness she ever felt around Carl Grant is back in force. Her face twists, and she turns to find Peterson watching her.

"It wasn't just you," he assures her. "The man spent the last few decades stalking half of the ODC's top leadership."

Somehow Kara still has a reservoir of shock to draw from in response to this statement. "Who?"

"Joker, for one. Grant made sure the boy's application got pushed through at the Academy, even though there were a few flags. For one thing, he's technically too tall to be a fighter jock. But even after graduation, Grant kept an eye on him, made sure his COs always noticed him, saw his potential. He got a number of peach assignments thanks to Grant's interference.

"Haynes too," he continues. Kara feels the customary jolt at the reminder of her dead friend. "She was up on a charge a few years back, insubordination. Her captain was a bad apple, but she went about things the wrong way. Grant waved his hands and it all went away, and a year later she and Williams were quietly transferred to my unit at the Lake.

"Heck, just the fact that they've stayed together as long as they have, same as McLaughlin and Skylar McClinic… it's unusual. Not unheard of, but definitely unusual that they've gotten so many postings together. As if he wanted to make sure they'd built a strong trust in one another."

"But," Kara objects, "that could just be Grant showing an interest in promising careers. Right?" Even as she asks the question, she doesn't really believe it.

Peterson barks a laugh. "Oh, there are other examples. Ever wonder why Morales has such a guilt issue?"

"You mean because of his friends?"

"It's not just that his friends died, Dunn. He was supposed to be in Iraq with them."

"What?"

"I'm sure they wouldn't actually have been stationed together. But they all joined up the same day, the three of 'em. The boy's paperwork was all approved, and then one day he gets a call from the recruiter—'sorry for the confusion, but you've been deemed physically unfit.'"

Kara shakes her head in amazement.

"Watson too."

"Shaniqua?"

"Yeah, though I can't see that he actually interfered with her life. He just watched." Peterson scratches his chin. "There's other stuff in that cabinet too. Dossiers of pilots and other personnel Grant had blackballed along the way—like what he did with Joker, but the opposite, making sure certain careers tanked early. Some very odd coincidences among those folks..." He drifts off a moment, as if something has just occurred to him. Then he shakes his head slightly. "And mixed in with all of it, there are weird personal effects, plus letters to his dead wife." He sighs. "Anyway, I think you get the picture."

"You didn't know anything about this? His... interference, I mean?"

"Me? I'm in the same boat. I didn't know how deep his manipulations went until I got access to his files. But I was in there too, along with the rest of you. He'd been watching me just as long. Funny, I always thought he hated me as much as I hated him... didn't realize it was him who requested me specifically."

"But how could he have known we would be part of the ODC so long ago? I mean, knowing about the attacks from KLINE is one thing, but this...?"

"Ah." Peterson leans forward, an odd twinkle in his eye. "How do you know it's not the other way around? Maybe you're all Gryphens now because Grant first identified your potential years ago."

"But that can't be true! Not for Shaniqua and Jose, at least— we recruited them because they'd flown with me online."

"Yes, but how did they get involved with the game in the first place? From what I understand, it's the only video game Watson's ever played."

Kara just sits in stunned silence, trying and failing to trace through all the causes and effects. Trying and failing to remember exactly what first sparked her own interest in zero G transportation, without which the Destrier, the game, the *ODC* never would have happened.

"Grant was a strong proponent of childhood testing to spot potential future leaders," Peterson speaks into her thoughts.

"And you think that's how he identified all of us?"

The man simply shrugs. "Who's to say? I just know that Grant played a deep game."

Kara pauses. "You sound almost like you respect him."

The man flashes another rare smile. "Yeah, I guess I do... even if he was a sanctimonious, self-righteous little... Anyway."

"But what about... Just what was it he *did*? Why did he spend the last year of his life locked up?"

Peterson is silent for a long while. Finally: "He committed treason."

"*Seriously?*"

He sighs. "Yes, seriously. He led a rogue CIA team to engage in domestic terrorism."

"The more I learn about the man, the less I understand."

Peterson grills her with that look, the practiced military stare that some officers nevertheless seem born with. Peterson is a natural at it. "You were angry with him, weren't you? That he knew about Denver but he never warned them?"

She shifts uncomfortably. "Well, yes."

"That's just it," he grunts, grudgingly. "He *did* warn them, the best way he knew how. It's not terribly different from what we're trying to do in Chicago, coming up with creative ways of getting people out of harm's way." His eyes continue to bore into hers. "Except that he went behind the President's back, violating his oaths of secrecy—that's the treason part—to save as many residents of Denver as he could. And the methods he chose weren't very nice. That's where the terrorism part comes in: he abused his authority and clearances to co-opt a CIA black ops team, which he used to run operations on U.S. soil, for the express purpose of scaring those people out of their minds. Two of his pet spies poisoned Denver's municipal water supply, while another hacked into shipping manifests and ensured all the bottled water dried up." He snorts as he realizes his unintended pun. "And of course there was that street preacher—Vesuvius, he called himself—screaming doom and gloom; he was a CIA agent too. Grant caused all of that. Terrorism by any definition... and yet because of it, there's no doubt in my mind that he saved lives."

Kara finds her eyes misting. She's immediately furious with herself at displaying such weakness in front of Peterson, but she can't help it. The emotion of the funeral; the pain she felt vicariously for Viviane, not to mention the guilt; the sudden shame over her anger towards Grant, and the confusion from today's revelations—all of it is a bit overwhelming.

"I was livid when I found out," the general continues, "we all were. Bad enough the man endangered national security—risking the lives of *many* more people just so he could soothe his conscience over those few in Denver—but he did it in such a sneaky way. At the time, I was disgusted; the man was too weak to do what needed to be done, too weak even to openly defy the President. He undermined our security and then hoped to get away with it."

He takes a deep breath, lets it out slowly, and continues. "Now, though, I'm not so sure. That holier-than-thou crap I always put up with... a man like that doesn't expose himself; he takes the moral high ground and finds a way to cover his rear if he ends up being wrong. Grant didn't do that. He had his protection—the President himself ignored his warnings repeatedly. But Grant chose to do what he felt was right... and I realize now he didn't wimp out in the way he chose to do it. I've played it all back and forth a hundred times since then. He found the best way to save the most people without actually revealing *anything* about the true threat. Shoot, even if Uncle Sam *had* forced an evacuation, it's questionable we could have gotten more people out—especially if we'd told them it was an imminent alien attack." He shakes his head ruefully. "It really *isn't* any different from the problem we're facing with Chicago right now." He grunts. "The hell of it is, treason and terrorism are only part of it. They didn't even catch him on the embezzlement."

"*What?*"

"It's true," Peterson confirms. "In the early days of Prometheus, Grant was given a huge budget—an *obscene* budget. But only some of it was spent directly on Prometheus. He plowed a significant percentage into other, more speculative projects at Groom Lake, which he thought might have application for us today. But even still... there's a lot of money unaccounted for. As in hundreds of millions of dollars over the last twenty years."

"No," Kara shakes her head. "I can't believe it. Even if he *did* line his own pockets, someone would have noticed that kind of money in a private individual's hands. Especially a military man."

"I agree," Peterson nods. "But just think. *Someone* had to pay for OWT's development of the Longship."

"Wait—the tourism company? But they were private until last year. They were never funded by the government."

Peterson nods again. "Yes, but how does an unknown private company afford a fifteen-year development cycle on something like the Longship?"

"Lots of private investors?"

"With no publicity and never a penny's return on investment?" Peterson shakes his head. "No, not lots of investors; they were too secretive for that. Just a *few* investors. Here's the thing... when they went public, an audit of their records caused one early donor to stand out—to the tune of hundreds of millions of dollars over the years. A board member by the name of Carl Janus, who apparently lives in the Caribbean... but does not actually exist."

Kara just stares at him.

"I say all of that to say this..." Peterson pauses for thought. "What you said to Grant's daughter, about him being a hero—it's true. Not just in the future, if the ODC fights off this threat. He's a hero now. He's already saved lives. And without him, I don't think we'd have any way of reaching orbit."

Peterson sits in silence for a long moment after that, as if reviewing everything he just communicated, then settles back into his seat. Apparently, he's said all he wants to say.

Kara wipes her eyes, then asks, "I guess that means the charges have been dropped?"

Peterson looks at her sharply. "Hardly. He's guilty—textbook example. But at least now you know the mitigating details." His face softens slightly. "My guess is they'll drop it all eventually—with him dead, there's no benefit to anyone to air all of this." He turns away to look out the window. "And if the President's a big man, he may even see his own mistake in handling the situation and recognize Grant's contribution posthumously."

Kara nods thoughtfully and turns to look out her own window. With everything else going on today, she'd managed to keep from obsessing over Chicago for a few hours... but that was becoming more difficult with each passing day. After this discussion, of course, she can't help but sit and agonize over what might happen if the Gryphens cut things too close. If only—

Peterson breaks the silence: "I wasn't lying to that girl; I actually *do* have a logistical matter to discuss with you, regarding your new launch schedule." He smirks wickedly. "You'll never believe how drastic our next step will be. It seems another of Grant's projects will come in handy after all."

Friday night
July 31, 2015

The night life at Cape Canaveral leaves much to be desired as the trapped personnel and media end another week in limbo, yet many still put forth an effort at forgetting their woes for a few hours. One small band of revelers moves loudly down the street, talking and laughing, making their way from one modest party to another. The many warehouses and hangars they pass stand still and silent in the night.

A pair of shadowy figures rendezvous in the shadows between two such buildings, and they freeze momentarily as the partygoers pass by just feet away.

"You have it?" the nervous one asks, after the boisterous pilots are finally beyond earshot again.

"Yes," the other replies, handing over a slim silvery object which glints momentarily in the moonlight. "The sabotage gave us the extra time we needed to put it together. All you need to do is—"

"I remember," the first replies quickly, eager to be away from this suspicious meeting. "And..." A pause. "You took care of the other thing?"

"I did. You're covered, no matter what happens."

The nervous one calms slightly. "Okay. Good then." Pause. "They're moving us, tomorrow."

The reply is sharp. "Where?"

"I don't know yet."

"Very well." A much longer pause follows this time. Finally: "You've made the right decision. Don't doubt that."

The first conspirator doesn't look so sure.

[Chapter 37]

**Sunday afternoon
August 9, 2015**

Kara sits patiently—or at least, patiently on the outside—as the makeup artist covers over a supposed imperfection. When she first started the promotional junket several months back, this was one of the hardest parts for her; she's never been one for wearing much makeup, and to let others cake it on until she met *their* ideal image of her was galling. Of course, she realized quickly it was far worse for John McLaughlin and the other strong military men, so she held her peace. By now, of course, it's old hat.

No, it's not the injustice of having someone else apply her makeup that makes Kara want to fidget; it's the fact that they're now well into August. As each new day dawns, with Chicago still standing, she feels a glimmer of relief and yet an added burden of stress as well— it's only a matter of time before the attack comes. It actually won't be long until the first ODC elements are catapulted into space. But even after the ODC personnel reach orbit, it will take time to settle in at their ODBs, then to tow those bases into the proper position in orbit to form an effective picket. Will their defensive screen be in place before the Chicago strike comes?

"Five minutes," the director calls to her. She nods, though in truth, a minute here or there hardly matters—despite their change of venue, they're still under a media blackout, and this interview is simply being taped for broadcast later.

"General Dunn, so nice to meet you," comes a recognizable voice, and Kara turns to see journalist Hayden Vaughn approaching with hand outstretched. To look at him, he really *does* seem pleased to meet her, despite all the hardship her cronies have put him and his people through this past month-plus. Not to mention this last week, which has been craziest of all. Then again, he's about to get an exclusive interview with Gen. Kara Dunn… and after that, though he doesn't yet know it, some even *more* exclusive footage.

She shakes the proffered hand, smiling. "It's just Kara, really. Off camera, at least." Her eyes flick to the beautician. "On camera, I suppose I have an image to uphold."

"I understand that," he says, eyeing her shoulder hungrily. It takes Kara a moment to realize the man is staring at her shiny new general's star, which will undoubtedly bring more value to this interview than if she'd still been wearing her full-bird colonel's insignia. The beautician closes up her kit, and Vaughn meets Kara's eye again. "About the interview, you've not given us a lot of time, so I think we should jump right into the questions—you know, instead of talking through it all before the taping."

"That's fine with me," she says.

"I'd like to start with your personal history; most of the reel I've seen on you doesn't get into those details, and I'm curious as to how your background shaped you for this position of leadership. After that," he glances at his notes, "we can move into current affairs. In particular, I want to get your take on preparations being made by other countries to combat this threat. Ultimately, of course, we'll have an opportunity to discuss the military's revised schedule for putting our people in orbit, is that right?" She sees the gleam in his eyes—this is the exclusive portion of their talk—and confirms with another nod. "Great," he enthuses, though respectably. "Of course, if I see us running out of time, I might skip ahead to that point."

Kara represses a smile. Most of the journalists she's met prefer complete control of an interview, and it's obvious Hayden Vaughn is no different; one would never suspect there was anything unusual about this particular taping. In point of fact, however, Vaughn and his crew are little more than prisoners at the present moment. He had been awakened abruptly by a PR officer a week ago at Canaveral, offered this unique opportunity—with plenty of strings attached—and given just five minutes to make his choice. Naturally he leapt at the opportunity, and ten minutes later he and his crew were being hustled quietly away from Florida under cover of night... along with the entirety of the USODC. *Exciting*, they had agreed at the time.

She can only wonder if they still feel the same way. They probably hadn't thought it possible, but the ODC managed to sequester them even more completely than they'd been at

Canaveral, with not a clue as to where in the world they currently are. But this interview—and the opportunity to follow—should make it all worth it.

"Great, great," Vaughn repeats, running a hand through his trademark wavy, red hair.

"We're ready, Hayd!" calls the director from behind the camera #1 operator.

Vaughn smiles professionally towards one of the three cameras, a momentary flash of straight, white teeth. "Good evening, this is Hayden Vaughn broadcasting from an undisclosed location somewhere in the Northern Hemisphere..." He pauses dramatically. "And that really is all I know of my current location. It is my privilege tonight to interview Brigadier General Kara Dunn of the Orbital Defense Corps."

"Glad to be here, Hayden."

"General, there's been a great deal of talk in recent months about the ODC and its mission, but I'm curious to know more about the woman who will be leading our troops into battle." He turns to her as an aside and says, "Kara, we'll just take this chronologically for now, but edit it later as necessary."

She nods.

"Tell me about your childhood."

And so she does, sharing about her family, her upbringing, and her interests, throwing in the occasional anecdote. Vaughn walks her through her high school years after that, drawing out her opinions on various fads of the time, how she related to her parents growing up, her experiences with dating. Although they had not, in fact, talked over each question before filming began, there had been a great deal of communication back and forth between their "offices" in the past week as they determined jointly which topics would be addressed. And the interview itself is without doubt a team effort, very much a choreographed dance through which she and Hayden Vaughn move in concert; they are working together to form an image of her that the general public can identify with as a real human being. Whereas previous interviews focused on her ability to command or even attacked her inexperience, this tape will depict her as a leader to be trusted not because she's anything special but because she's *normal*—confident, in control, fit to lead, but very much an average, accessible American. Which is ironic considering her ongoing struggle with having that confidence in herself.

They've talked for nearly thirty minutes when the parade of questions finally halts. Vaughn casts a frown at the clock. "It looks like half our time is already gone." He scans over his notepad. When he looks up again, his demeanor is much more business-like. "Recent reports from overseas indicate that a number of other countries have begun building and training their own 'space navies,' as I believe they've been dubbed. What are your thoughts?"

"I think it's an excellent idea. After all, that is exactly the response our own military is taking to this threat."

"Of course, many people point out that the U.S. government has not been very forthcoming as to the details of this threat. When it comes right down to it, how much does the American public really know? Denver was destroyed in a nuclear blast on 11/14 of last year. There have been no attacks of that magnitude in the nine months since"—he throws up his hands to ward off her objection—"for which I am very grateful. But that means there's been no further evidence of this supposed extraterrestrial threat. Surely you can imagine how that looks. Some critics are claiming there really is no threat, that this is all an elaborate deception, though frankly I don't see the point. Far more people are questioning why our President hasn't shared the missing details and evidence—at the very least, with the governments of allied nations."

So much for dancing on the same team. "Well, I can hardly speak for the President, Hayden. All I can say is that I'm sure the State Department is sharing what information it can with its counterparts around the world." And that quite literally *is* all Kara can say; she herself doesn't know much more from KLINE's testimony all those years ago. "Any questions you have should be directed to them."

Vaughn frowns, disappointed perhaps. Consulting his notes, he says, "Back to my earlier question. Reports released to the press indicate over $500 billion in expenditures related to the creation and equipping of the Orbital Defense Corps. I don't doubt the Corps is worth every penny of it. What I'm wondering is how our neighbors can hope to keep up with us."

To this, Kara's not sure how to respond. She cocks her head questioningly, and Vaughn obliges.

"Are you aware, for example, that the U.S. military budget is roughly equal to the rest of the world combined? The half trillion we've spent on the ODC isn't much less than we generally spend on defense in any given year, so it's hardly a non-trivial sum. But for most every nation on earth, that's an *impossible* amount of money. In fact," another look at the notes, "my research shows that the only countries who could hope to match our preparations dollar-for-dollar are France, Britain, Germany, Italy, Japan, and China." He looks up, expressionless. "So I ask again, how is the rest of the world supposed to prepare for this threat?"

The simple, obvious answer is *They can't*. It's just as clear Kara cannot allow herself to be soundbyted admitting this, not if she wants her rear end back from Peterson in one piece. Yes, the dancing is definitely over. "Until a year ago, almost no thought had been given to defending our nation against incursions on *that* border." She raises her hand to point straight up as she says this. "The United States Orbital Defense Corps is on the cutting edge of preparation for a brand-new theatre of warfare, and that means we've shouldered the expense of paving the way. I believe our nation has a policy of sharing technological advancements with our allies, and in one sense, everyone on this planet is our ally against this threat. However, those sorts of decisions really are far above my pay grade. I recommend you ask the White House or the State Department."

For a moment, it looks like Vaughn will force the issue, but after glancing at his notebook and then again at the clock, he apparently decides on a different tack. "As it happens, I do know that some sharing of technology has already taken place. I'm sure you're aware that Axmatik Limited's entertainment division recently acquired ownership of the *Rampant* video game franchise you were instrumental in developing, including all source code?"

"Yes, about a year ago I believe."

"I understand that, given the necessary haste of our military's response to the alien threat, you have relied heavily upon that video game in training your pilots and developing the V-series Destrier fighter craft?"

She pauses. "I'm really not at liberty to discuss the details—"

"No, I understand. I just wanted to point out that Nate Williams at Axmatik has now brokered deals with thirty-two foreign nations. In an effort to be fair to nations rich and poor alike, he is offering your source code on a sliding price scale: point-zero-zero-zero-zero-zero-one—that's five zeroes and a one—of the purchaser's annual gross domestic product. Basically, one millionth. That's $17 million from the EU alone, roughly $189 million total so far… though he's sitting on a treasure trove and could really demand a much higher price if he wanted. He's being called a great humanitarian."

Kara realizes her mouth is hanging open, and she snaps it shut quickly. She had, in fact, completely forgotten about Nate Williams in the year since the tournament. Of course he had the code, and of course he would seek to make money off it—he hadn't become who he was today being shy about that sort of thing. But when she really stopped and thought about it, why not? Peterson probably wouldn't be happy to learn it, assuming he didn't know already, but was it really any skin off the collective American nose if other countries could use her code to help save lives? Come to think of it, she was happy to hear they would have the chance.

"I bet you wish you retained some ownership of that source code, don't you?" Vaughn is saying.

"I'm flattered that my work is considered that valuable," she manages. Which is a response if not an answer. In any case, it's again not much of a sound byte.

"According to my information," Vaughn continues, "all of the nations I mentioned earlier—those with large military budgets—have bought into Axmatik's offer, and sources say they are among the front runners of space navy development. Oddly enough, it looks as though China has jumped out ahead of the pack and is already launching assets into—"

"I'm sorry to interrupt, Hayden, but it looks as though your director is very urgently tapping his watch."

Hayden Vaughn colors slightly, and Kara can see the director slap his hand to his forehead. *It was about time for that portion of the interview to be over*, she thinks.

"Um, right," Vaughn says, attempting to find his equilibrium. "I understand you would like to announce the ODC's revised schedule for delivery of personnel and equipment to low earth orbit?"

"That's correct, Hayden. In fact..." she begins, glancing at her own watch, "I am pleased to announce that the first of the Longship missions to deliver personnel into orbit will be launched *tonight* at 6:05 p.m. Or, actually, about eighty minutes from now."

Kara is even more pleased to see Vaughn caught off guard by this surprising news.

"As everyone knows," she continues in a serious tone of voice, "our nation suffered another devastating loss last month when the *Herald*'s fuel tank ruptured, killing twenty-two brave men and women. It was nothing like the 11/14 strike, of course, and yet it struck an emotional blow to all of us. Believe me when I say, I know how much hope this nation has riding on the Orbital Defense Corps."

She shakes her head. "We are not going to have a repeat of July 4th. If indeed that disaster was the result of intentional sabotage, it was because the perpetrators had months to prepare, months to find a way to prevent our launch. Tonight, we launch from a secure location, protected by the fact that only a small number of people had foreknowledge of our launch schedule. By the time this interview is released to the public, all 800 servicemen and -women of the Orbital Defense Corps will be on station in orbit, defending this land.

"And..." Kara pauses, turning to face the camera directly. It is a direct breach of interview protocol, but in that moment, neither Vaughn nor his director seem to care. "Let no one doubt our resolve. If any of my people ever saw this undertaking as a grand adventure, those days are gone. July 4th bloodied us before we were even deployed." She thinks of Anna Haynes, and her voice hardens. "And yet these brave men and women still go willingly into space, humankind's most dangerous frontier, where a momentary lapse of attention can kill you more quickly and easily than any enemy. We take on this risk knowingly, purposefully, to protect the family, friends, and country we love." She thinks of Viviane, of her father, of her many friends—their faces flitting through her mind as she speaks. "The Orbital Defense Corps will not fail. We *will* protect this great nation from attack."

She holds the camera's gaze for a long moment, feeling the moisture gathering at the corner of her eyes and refusing it permission to escape down her cheeks. Then she deliberately breaks the moment, reaching to her lapel to unfasten the tiny microphone and begin feeding it back down the inside of her uniform jacket. Her meaning is clear: this interview is over.

"So…" Vaughn begins tentatively, clearly feeling off-kilter. "Do we get to tape the launch?"

Kara smiles wryly. "Of course." She hands the mic and belt clip to one of Vaughn's people, all brisk business now. "Come with me. And bring your cameraman."

[Chapter 38]

As a teenager, Kara Dunn went through a phase in which she was absolutely fascinated by the legend of the lost city of Atlantis. She studied the story extensively, in all its many facets, reading many books on the subject; most of them were fiction, of course, but she found their various theories no less alluring. Assuming Atlantis had in fact been on the surface of a continent that had sunk into the ocean thousands of years before, she'd imagine what it would be like to come upon the ruins of that once-great city. She imagined herself a deep-sea explorer with her own personal submarine, not unlike Nero aboard the *Nautilus*, and she would be the one to find the crumbling ancient edifices emerging from the sediment along the eerily-lit ocean floor. The sense of wonder and mystery that mental image evoked in her was powerful.

Little did Kara know then that something very like her mental picture actually existed in many places around the world. No sunken buildings, of course, and certainly no fabled cities. But at hundreds of places on the ocean floor—and as the years passed, that number grew into the thousands—anyone with her own submarine could find mute and mysterious evidence of mankind's artifice. Massive cylindrical tanks standing on end, jutting out from the ocean floor and so firmly embedded as to make removal impossible. Ship's anchors the size of small automobiles and weighing eight times as much. Massive steel chains lying limp in the silt, sometimes running a mile or two, no different than the chain one might buy at a hardware store… except that each link is the size of a small child. And of course the strange pipe heads that periodically protrude some fifteen feet from the sea floor, yet run unseen a further 3,000 feet into the Earth's crust. All of these things, often clustered within a mile of each other. Spooky in the wavering light as strange and seldom-seen marine life forms drift about.

As exciting and bizarre as all this would have seemed to the fourteen-year-old Kara, it is an everyday fact of life for those in the oil drilling industry. The big tanks are known as suction piles, simple tools that use a pressure differential to pull themselves deep into the sediment, forming immoveable anchors. With the use of the long chains, the suction piles and the more traditional (albeit colossal) anchors are used to secure massive floating structures known as semi-submersible drilling platforms to a stationary point on the ocean's surface, even in depths of many thousands of feet. Engineers make all of this possible so that the rig can dig deep into the Earth's crust via those strange pipes, known as wellheads, and harvest natural resources. And when it's all over, these tools are often left where they lie to be used again on another day.

At exactly seventeen locations around the globe, anyone with her own submarine can find a phenomenon quite similar to all this, but with one rather unusual difference: at these seventeen locations, there is no wellhead.

The newest of these seventeen sites consists of three formations of piles and anchors located 47 miles northeast of Point Barrow, Alaska, at an average depth of 1,115 feet. Where two weeks before this was virgin territory, unnoticed and untouched by humankind—located at the edge of the Beaufort Sea, not far from where the continental shelf drops off into extreme arctic depths—the ocean floor is now dotted with these carefully placed stabilization devices, all within six miles of one another. These three agglomerations are known as ERATO, DYNAMENE, and PHERUSA, collectively forming the most recent incarnation of now deceased Gen. Carl J. Grant's Project Nereus.

And situated immediately above these three loci, remarkably steady despite the tumultuous sea, are three semi-submersible deep-sea platforms formerly used for drilling oil. The incredible stability they offer is an absolute necessity, because on two of these platforms, towering 400 feet above the choppy ocean surface, stands an awesome sight: an ODC Longship, mated to a massive rust-colored fuel tank, straddling solid rocket boosters, pointed at the sky and ready to fly.

When Peterson had first told her about it, that day in the car after Grant's funeral, Kara had thought he was kidding; the fact that Peterson never jests—as Kara well knows—only proves just how absurd the notion seemed to her at the time. Launch spacecraft from an *oil rig*? Not even a rig mounted on the ocean floor, but rather a rig *floating* on the ocean surface? What's the punch line? And yet the concept had proven even more outlandish as Peterson filled her in on the details.

Although Grant's name will figure prominently into the project history if and when it's declassified a hundred years from now, Project Nereus was not originally his brainchild; he simply provided the funding that made it possible, back in the days when the Prometheus coffers were overflowing. With that legendary foresight of his, however, Grant was quick to take control of the project. The idea was that a mobile platform could travel just about anywhere in the world and anchor itself firmly to the ocean floor, provided the depth wasn't too extreme. It required a day to establish a rig, maybe three at the most. The tensioning of these anchor points could then be adjusted remotely during a launch, along with the ballast in the platform's massive pontoons, to maintain a rock solid and steady surface for escaping spacecraft to push off from. With his love of Greek mythology, Grant had instituted the convention of naming each site for one of the Nereid sea nymphs.

Classical allusion aside, the idea of mobile launch platforms makes so much sense that, in the mid-90s, several big-name aeronautics firms developed a similar idea independently, for the purpose of launching commercial satellites into orbit. That development nevertheless surprised and infuriated Grant, who had hoped to keep even the idea of a seagoing mobile launch pad secret from America's enemies.

The Nereus mobile platforms, of which there have been six, are themselves nothing unusual. They came off the same assembly line as standard semi-submersible rigs, costing a hefty $800 million each, and serving with no particular distinction in the fleets of various drilling and exploration corporations. A sucker for a good deal, Grant purchased them used at a savings of several hundred million, which he then put into retrofitting them as launch pads. And so for over two decades—from the late 80s on—Nereus provided something the United States was desperate for: the ability to launch new spy satellites from mobile platforms, here today and gone tomorrow, thereby evading the notice of enemy eyes already in orbit. To date, the platforms have been used for sixty-seven clandestine launches.

The paired launch of *Harbinger* and *Hermes* the night of August 9th, 2015, will ultimately go down in the annals of history as the most famous.

Sunday afternoon
August 9, 2015

As Kara steps out of the office she and Vaughn's crew used for their interview, she shrugs into her great coat. It is a relatively warm afternoon for the Beaufort Sea, north of Point Barrow, Alaska—one of the warmest days of the year, in fact—but at a mere 34 degrees, that isn't saying much.

She makes her way along a short walkway, sidling past a man moving in the opposite direction, trailed by Vaughn and his cameraman. To either side, they pass additional offices. Below, four more levels of offices, living quarters, catwalks, and defunct drilling equipment are packed together like sardines to form a manmade labyrinth one could literally spend a whole day lost within. Unlike conventional construction, however, this structure isn't built from the bottom up—it is built from the top down, a multi-story, split-level, steel frame suspended below the main deck of a semi-submersible deep-sea oil rig. The deck itself stands some 60 feet above the waves, mounted upon four massive legs, which in turn are supported by two submerged steel pontoons.

It's the most surreal living arrangement Kara has ever known.

Reaching the end of the walk, the three figures climb two short flights of rickety stairs to reach the main deck, where Kara makes a beeline for the sidewall railing. Finally free from the visual obstruction of the deck itself, they can see for miles across the water to where *Harbinger* and the even more distant *Hermes* tower over the waves. The improved vantage comes with a price, however: a brisk wind that strikes them bodily, seldom letting up. These gusts, coming from the north, are even more bitterly cold; just a few miles away in that direction, the ocean is still frozen over. Only within about sixty miles of the coastline does it ever thaw, and even then for only two months of the year. Had Peterson chosen to launch the ODC from these mobile pads in the first place, just a month earlier, they would have needed to find a more tropical locale—this entire swath of ocean had still been frozen solid at the time.

The sun rests red and fat on the horizon. Kara's instincts tell her that sunset will come soon, and yet she knows that's not true. This far north of the Arctic Circle, actual sunset won't occur until past midnight, and even then it will never truly grow dark. The fiery orb will be back within four hours, after which it will hover over the horizon for another twenty, repeating the bizarre cycle.

The view out over the water is especially compelling tonight, however. The sun stands perfectly centered between the horizon and a bank of thick storm clouds threatening from the northwest, bathing every surface in a diffuse amber light. The hanging edges of the bruised thunderhead are limned a brilliant pink. Despite the breathtaking beauty, Kara frowns; that storm might spell trouble. With the strength of tonight's gusts, those clouds could be upon them in no time flat.

"How's this?" she asks the journalists. "We can move up to the rig floor if you need more altitude."

"Uh... gimme a minute," the cam operator drawls distractedly, already peering through his viewfinder.

Kara nods, turning to acknowledge several of her pilots lining the railing fifty yards further down the walkway from her. Willie Cobb is there with a few others, including what looks like Patrick Knott and Sarah Piosa, the two pilots who now report to him. In the end, there hadn't been enough officer transfers to fill out the entire command structure, and Willie was one of just a few new recruits who had received a promotion to first lieutenant before they'd even made it to space. Kara wishes fleetingly that she were in her ABUs like the rest of the pilots; the thin material of her dress uniform pants is doing little to shut out the cold.

"This should do," the cameraman decides. "Wish the light was better, though."

"It'll be dramatic," Vaughn assures him.

"Yeah, but I can't pick out much detail on the launchpad," the other complains. "It's all backlit."

The rig on which the threesome stands—tethered to the various anchors and suction piles at ERATO, a thousand feet below—is known simply as 'Control,' its sisters as 'Pad A' and 'Pad B.' After eighteen months of working with the military, so fond of its witty acronyms and tongue-in-cheek appellations, Kara appreciates the simplicity just this once. She also appreciates this opportunity to watch the *Harbinger*'s launch in relative quietude, rather than having to join Peterson and Potteiger on the observation deck four levels above. As cramped as that level is, and given that Kara has no real duties during the launch, Peterson agreed that she should stay with the news people for the duration. If all proceeds as planned, Kara herself will be going up a week later on the *Hermes*' second trip.

Hayden Vaughn finishes a quiet conversation he's been having with his operator. "Sorry, I guess I should be getting some voiceover for all this." He fumbles with a handheld microphone, then indicates Kara should turn her back to the wind. "General, this seems an odd place for the government to build launch pads. What can you tell us about them?"

So much for enjoying the launch in peace, Kara thinks with an internal groan. "Not much, I'm afraid," she replies. "Top secret and all that."

The redhead nods gamely. "Then can you give us some idea of where we are in the launch prep? I'm a little disappointed there isn't a voice counting down over the PA." He grins impishly. "The rest of this certainly came right out of a 1960s spy thriller."

Kara laughs genuinely, leaning toward the proffered mic. "Well, Hayden, as you know, the Longships were delivered yesterday and hoisted into position by chopper, along with their fuel tanks and SRBs. Ever since that time, the technicians have been running checks and loading last minute supplies. The Gryphens assigned to *Harbinger* for today's launch have been billeted beneath Pad A all week; they went through all of *their* last minute check-ups this morning too, then suited up, and finished filing aboard *Harbinger* about... three hours ago."

Vaughn chuckles. "I understand they had quite a hike climbing that gantry."

"Oh yes," Kara agrees, smiling wryly. "These launch facilities have none of the comforts of home... unlike the gantries at Kennedy Space Center, these don't have elevators. So some of our people had to climb all twenty stories while fully suited; those with seats near the aft airlocks didn't have as much of a climb, of course."

"And they've been onboard for three hours now? Just waiting?"

"About that," Kara responds. "And I can tell you from experience, the waiting is rough too." Her own memory of sitting and waiting at Canaveral—and the memory of what followed that wait—momentarily darkens her mood. "In any case," she continues, checking her watch, "by now the checklists are mostly complete and the fuel is all topped off, and everything else that'll happen will be controlled remotely from the observation deck on *this* rig, Control. At this point it's just a waiting game, twiddling our thumbs until that launch window opens up. A little less than an hour from now."

"And *Hermes* will launch... when?"

"An hour after *Harbinger*."

Vaughn nods. "I take it those platforms are, um, shielded to protect the lower decks when the ships go up?"

"They are," Kara confirms. "There's a flame deflection structure beneath the actual launch pad, basically four large chutes that draw the ignition exhaust down and to the sides of the platform, out to sea. It's necessary to protect all the fuel and coolant lines in the lower decks."

"Not to mention the people," Vaughn adds.

"That too," Kara says. "At this point, of course, both of those rigs are practically ghost towns. Only a few technicians remaining, plus some Marine guard details—maybe thirty people. Everyone else is onboard the Longships."

"Looks like a lot more than that," the cameraman interrupts, his tone offhand.

"I'm sorry?"

"Lots of people up there. More than thirty, for sure."

"Shouldn't be," Kara responds, "though it's possible we beefed up security at the last minute."

The camera operator doesn't respond—there's a sudden look of intense concentration on his face. "What in the—" The man straightens, leaning forward slightly, the fingers of one hand rapidly manipulating a few of the camera controls by feel.

"What is it?" Kara asks uneasily.

"Some dude just fell off."

"*What?*"

"Yeah, it was like they were fighting or somethin'. Maybe, I dunno... the lighting's so bad, it's hard to tell."

"Let me see!" she demands. The man gives her a look as if she's requested the keys to his antique car. He turns in vain to Vaughn for support, then begrudgingly settles the massive camera onto Kara's shoulder. He maintains a two-hand hold as Kara presses her face to the eyepiece.

The distant platform leaps into view before her, filling her vision. With the camera's high-dollar telephoto lens, it's as if she's just fifty yards away instead of two miles. She tries to tip back a bit for a look at the gantry, but the man steadies her. "Can we... No, just—" She shakes the camera free from the man's overprotective grip. "Just zoom me in." She focuses on the gantry and is stunned to see man-shaped silhouettes—a dozen or more—systematically passing boxes or crates up the gantry tower. That can't be right.

Feeling a sudden jolt of adrenaline, Kara thrusts the camera back at its owner and casts around in search of a nearby Marine; she'd been a little surprised when Peterson outsourced the rigs' security to the Marine Corps, but apparently they're the best at this sort of thing. There—she sees one stationed at the railing near Willie Cobb and the other pilots, recognizable precisely because of the un-embellished digital camo he's wearing. She breaks into a trot.

"Sergeant!"

"Ma'am?" The man salutes sharply as she arrives.

"I need you to radio over to Pad A. Get a sitrep from someone there."

He looks a little uncomfortable at this. He takes one look at the star on her shoulder, however, his eyes widening slightly, and nods crisply. "Yes, ma'am!" He raises his walky-talky, adjusts the frequency. "Dimock to Stadler, come in."

A long moment passes, then a staticky voice responds, *"Stadler here."*

"What's your status over there?"

"We're all battened down here, just waiting for the launch. Grape duty."

Dimock frowns at the slang. "You been hangin' out with squids or somethin', Tom?" He catches Kara's look of confusion and releases the transmit key. "Sailors, ma'am. Our people just don't talk much like that."

The sound of laughter comes from over the line, and Dimock smiles as he raises the walky to his lips; Kara places a hand over his, however. "You know this man?" she asks. "Are you *sure* that's him?"

The guard stifles his glib reply as he begins to comprehend just how serious she is. "Well..." He tugs the radio gently from Kara's hand. "Sounds good, Tom," he radios back. "You in for a hand of hold'em tonight?"

"*If I can make it.*"

"Okay, see you then," the guard responds through suddenly clenched teeth. "Dimock out." He turns slowly to Kara, only now realizing that all of the nearby pilots have pulled close to listen in. "Tom Stadler hates poker."

Heart thundering in her chest, Kara says, "Patch me through to General Peterson."

The guard complies... except this time, there's no reply.

"Try someone else—anyone here on Control," she prods him, but the result is the same, no matter whom he tries. It's as if the radio has suddenly gone dead. "Are you sure your radio's working?"

He gives her an odd look. "Ma'am, I just—" he begins, but Kara Dunn has already turned away, cursing viciously—a particularly vile expression she once heard Paul use. The vehemence in her tone actually makes a few of the pilots jump, but Kara isn't paying attention. She's thinking hard. All the facts point to enemy agents onboard Pad A, masquerading via radio as the Marine Corps personnel tasked with guarding the rig.

The question is what to *do* about it. Just over fifty minutes 'til launch. Peterson needs to be made aware of the situation, but even then, what can *he* do if the radios are down? With any luck, Potteiger's people still have remote control and can abort the launch; but either way, someone needs to get over to that rig ASAP and figure out what's actually happening. Yet Kara could easily waste ten minutes if she has to hand-deliver a message to Peterson in the control room, way up on the top level of this rig—and she's already lost precious minutes with this whole radio exchange, having not trusted her instincts when she first saw those men on the gantry.

So Kara comes to a decision on her own.

She glances quickly around the group of... five pilots, she counts, each one a brand-new recruit. "You're all armed?" she asks. It's standard procedure, after all, and they *are* on duty. They all nod, though most of them grow wide-eyed at the question. Kara picks out a particularly terrified-looking specimen. "Brasseaux! Your weapon." She accepts the Beretta 9mm, confirms it's safed, and, feeling like an absolute idiot, tucks it into her belt; her dress uniform wasn't designed to accommodate a holster. Still addressing the young woman, a Lt. Kate Brasseaux, Kara orders, "Make for the observation deck. Tell General Peterson to put the countdown on indefinite hold, on my authority—we have unauthorized personnel on Pad A. And tell him about the radios. Go!" The young woman nods and scampers away. "The rest of you, follow me. You too—Dimock?"

"Staff Sergeant Scott Dimock, yes, ma'am," the guard responds.

"Good," she nods. "Okay, let's go." Kara turns on her heel and double-times it for the nearest narrow stairwell leading down. Hayden Vaughn looks just as stunned as he did moments ago, pushing himself against the railing as Kara's hastily-recruited force sidles past, but the cameraman soaks up every image. Kara ignores them.

Shouting over her shoulder to be heard over the wind, she gives her people a quick rundown. "There appear to be enemy agents on board Pad A. I could be wrong... this could all be a misunderstanding." She doesn't believe that, of course, and she doubts anyone else does either. "But after July 4th, I'm not willing to risk it." The pilots trailing her break out into muttered conversations. "We're headed for the docks. We'll collect any personnel we find along the way, but time is too short to go looking for anyone."

Kara lets Dimock take the lead, and the man easily ferrets out the quickest path down; ridiculous as it may seem, out of the twenty-some stairways on the Control rig, only one of them is continuous from the deck to the dock, and it's on the south side of the platform. As they clomp speedily along, Kara indeed keeps her eye out for additions to their meager force; but in this warren, she could pass within twenty feet of someone and never see them.

Finally, one level up from the dock, she catches sight of three forms chatting at a railing, looking down at the rough water below. "You three." They hurry forward, but they're not guards; Kara recognizes them as belonging to her pilot cadre. Again, without exception, they are junior officers, every one of them a new recruit. "With us," she orders them tersely. That brings her party to eight wet-behind-the-ears newbies plus one Marine who *presumably* has some idea how to handle himself in an actual face-to-face combat situation; at least Dimock carries an M249 light machine gun in addition to his Beretta. "Lieutenant Cobb, fill them in."

Their group finally reaches the floating dock, a series of walkways held afloat on pontoons, each joint bucking violently in the ocean chop. Running out to where the rigid inflatables are tied up, one hand sliding securely along each of the walkway's railings, a grateful Kara finds the dock security detail: a foursome of soldiers armed with LMGs like Dimock's. "Have you spoken with Control recently?"

"Just a minute ago, ma'am. Why?"

Kara's eyebrows shoot up in surprise. "You did? Raise them now!"

One of the guards tries and fails, and confusion spreads across all four faces.

Kara whirls on her pilots, their faces barely discernable with those brilliant ruby rays at their backs. She evaluates what she sees in these men and women: not their nearly invisible expressions, but the set of their shoulders, the confidence showing in their stance. It will have to be enough.

She gives the guard detail a quick rundown, then addresses the entire group of thirteen. "We'll go in three launches. Cobb, take your people plus Dimock and make for the southeast corner of the rig," she instructs, doing her best to remember her tour of Pad A from two days before. "There's an access there that should get you inside the caisson. Everyone else in two rafts with me; we'll land at the dock and go up through the understructure. Move!"

"Um, ma'am?" an embarrassed Patrick Knott asks tentatively. "What's a caisson?"

"The legs of the rig, Knott." She points out across the water—"That one, right there. Now go!"

She catches Willie's shoulder before he can climb aboard. "Willie..." she begins, then realizes she doesn't know what to say. They have no idea what they'll find when they arrive, no idea how to handle the situation. She simply has to trust him. Trust herself. "Just... use your brain," she says for both their benefits. "My team will probably come under fire, but maybe you can get through with a smaller group." She shrugs, and Willie nods in response, then focuses on someone over her shoulder. She turns into the sun again.

"Kara?" an outlined figure says in a familiar voice.

"Kevin?" she asks, straightening. A warm feeling floods her chest. "Oh, thank God."

"What's going on down here?"

"We've got problems on Pad A."

"What—some error codes again?"

"No, looks like unauthorized personnel," Kara explains, summarizing the situation quickly. "And the radios are out—we can't get *anyone*, Peterson included. So I'm taking matters into my own hands."

Kevin Smith falls into a stunned silence. Then, quietly, he asks, "What do you need me to do?"

Kara bites her lip, thinking quick. As much as she would love to have him by her side through this ordeal, it makes more sense to split their leadership between the two squads. "You lead our bigger team in those two rafts"—she points—"and make for the Pad A dock. I'll follow with Cobb and go a different route. The last we knew, there were people inside the gantry structure, doing who knows what. Whatever it is, we've got to make sure our people on *Harbinger* stay safe."

"How close are we to launch?"

She checks her watch. "Forty-one minutes."

"What!" Peterson cries in surprise. Standing at the wide north-facing window, his back to the control room staff, he's the first to see the trio of rafts dart out from beneath the rig. He jerks a handheld radio to his mouth. "Dock detail, report!" he barks.

Silence.

"Dock detail!" Pause. "Sub-level 5? Sub-level 4!" Suddenly sure this is all a mistake, he checks the radio to be sure it's working, but the signal light is steady. "Any detachment, report!"

Again, nothing.

Peterson turns to face the room, which is actually the bridge of the massive mobile platform, complete with two sweeping banks of 1970s-blue computer console desks in a nested 'U' configuration, the computers themselves cutting-edge modern. From amidst the thirty-some Air Force and NASA techs manning these stations, Peterson's comm specialist preempts his question distractedly. "I don't know, sir... I just ran a quick diagnostic, and it says everything's fine."

At that moment, a young woman in ABUs bursts into the room, a Marine's hand clasped around her upper arm. "What?" Peterson demands.

"She wouldn't stop long enough for me to radio ahead, sir," the guard responds. The woman, one of Peterson's pilots, rips her arm free and doubles over, breathing heavily.

Peterson frowns, addressing the man. "Try to raise me now."

"Sir?" the guard asks.

"On the radio!"

"Um... Sergeant Filson to General Peterson, come in..." he trails off in bewilderment, realizing his message isn't relaying over Peterson's unit. Peterson simply turns back to his comms man, a Pvt. Thomson.

"*Fascinating*," the man whispers quietly. "The log shows all of our transmissions being routed through the system and delivered, but they're clearly *not*.

"And?"

"Sir," the young pilot interrupts, still breathing heavily. "That's what I came— to tell you... General Dunn— she says— to stop the— stop the countdown." She straightens, placing her hands behind her head to open up her lungs.

"Why?" Peterson asks, beginning to tire of his own one-word questions. Andrew Potteiger, the NASA flight director, drifts over to hear her answer.

Huge lungful. "Dunn just saw something." Heaving breaths every few words, she relays the conversation between Dimock and the man answering to the name of Tom Stadler. "And then the radios went down," she concludes.

"Was that Dunn who just took off in those rafts?" Peterson demands, pointing out the window towards the shrinking watercraft.

The woman shrugs. "Um, I guess?"

Peterson clenches his teeth, turning back to the window and slamming a hand flat against it. America can't afford this, not now, not *again*. Not this far into August. "Talk to me, Thomson. What's going on here?"

The specialist lets out his breath in a low whistle. "I think we've caught some sort of virus."

"*What?*"

"Yessir. Just on the secure comms, though—it's an isolated system."

"So I can't get through to anyone?"

"I... don't really know."

Tentatively, Peterson raises his walky to his lips. "Control to Pad A. Dock security, do you read?"

"*Five by five, sir.*"

He nods slowly, thinking about the fact that someone had already—apparently—impersonated a Marine guard over the radio. "What's your status, Dock?"

"*Maintaining our established patrol, sir.*"

As casually as he can, knowing the subterfuge is wasted, he says, "Dock, I have 0207 GMT. Tango Alpha Whiskey, respond." Ever conscious of security, Peterson had instituted a brand-new comms cipher just for tonight, a simple three-character rotation to be used for radio authentication.

There's a long pause. The response, when it comes, is suffering from significant interference. "*—say—copy? I repeat—*"

"Like *hell*," Peterson announces to the room at large, not the least taken in by the other party's sudden radio difficulties. "Dunn was right, we've been compromised. Thomson, reestablish comms with our air support via unsecured frequencies—best we can do, but be sure to authenticate verbally. I want fly-bys of A and B. Filson! And you—whatever your name is." Filson and Kate Brasseaux, the pilot who relayed Kara's message, step forward as Peterson scribbles a radio frequency on two slips of paper. "Run this around to all the guard details and have them switch over. And Filson, prepare a team—I want you on our dock and ready to go ASAP. Keep me posted. Go!"

"Sir!" Thomson calls. "You need to hear this." He slaps a button on his board and rips off his headset. The rhythmic thrum of chopper rotors sounds over a speaker, and a crackly voice joins it. *"Sir? General?"*

"Speak!" he commands the pilot.

"Sir, Echo One here. I was at the north end of my patrol and thought I saw something out on the ice. I went out to—"

"Just tell me," Peterson cuts in impatiently.

"Five snowcats, sir. Big ones, parked a hundred yards from the edge. Just sitting there."

Peterson feels a chill. "You think they're empty?"

"No exhaust. But they can't've been there long, 'cause there's no drifts piled up around 'em."

"How big are we talking here?"

There's a moment of silence but for the rotors. *"Big enough for a dozen men each, I wager. And sir—"* Another pause. *"They're about as close to us as they could get on the ice. Maybe fifteen miles across the water to Pad B."*

Peterson squeezes his eyes shut, growling in frustration. Looking out across the water again, he can easily make out *Harbinger*'s silhouette against the rapidly darkening brown and blue sky, low-hanging clouds now beginning to obscure the sun beyond. *Hermes*, four miles distant, is growing fuzzy. Looks like it'll be one monster of a storm.

He turns to consult Andrew Potteiger. "How easy is it to stop and start the launch sequence?" he asks quietly.

The bespectacled man eyes him for a moment, and his response is equally quiet. "We can hold the launch, but only for a few minutes—our launch window is too tight to accommodate more than a few minutes' delay. Once that window passes, the next available will be... about twelve hours from now."

Peterson nods. "Okay then. For the time being, continue under the assumption that we're launching today, and we'll—"

"*General!*" a new voice, also scratchy from radio transmission, cuts into their conversation. "*Sir, this is Echo Three. I'm seeing what looks like muzzle flash at the water level, under Pad A!*"

Kara clambers aboard the second raft right behind Willie Cobb, only belatedly realizing she has no idea how to operate an outboard motor. Knott's already on it, however, and Kara barely has time to bury her handgun more securely in her belt and twist her hands around the grab ropes ringing the craft's inflatable hull.

As the three inflatable boats zip out from under the massive deck, Kara can once again make out her companions' faces in the dying amber light. She realizes immediately just how much darker it's grown in the last ten minutes, the storm front having already overtaken Pad A and *Harbinger*. "Open it up!" she yells back to Patrick Knott. He shakes his head but does as she says. They are riding directly into the crest of each wave, which makes for a rollercoaster ride, but does not, at least, threaten to overturn them. Each wave brings a fine spray of saltwater in their faces, water that is quite literally freezing. Wave after wave after wave crashes into their bow, where Willie crouches, taking the brunt of the spray but keeping the craft's nose down. In the midst of the swells, it's hard to gauge their progress. One moment the rig is visible, looming larger, the next it's replaced by a massive gray wall, and after that Kara is desperately rubbing saltwater from her eyes one-handed. There comes a cry of horror, and she looks back in time to see Sarah Piosa go over the side after a particularly savage jounce; Patrick Knott throws an arm around her as she falls past, hauling his squad mate back in but pulling the outboard to that side in the process. Their tiny boat nearly rolls in the precious seconds it takes him to turn back into the swells.

And then they're there, their boat bumping against the immense cylindrical shaft of Pad A's southeast leg, sliding up and down its outside edge with each passing wave. The hellish trip seemed an eternity but only cost three minutes.

Knott cuts the motor, and they do their best to hand-maneuver the tiny craft around the massive caisson's 65-foot circumference. Kara blinks away more freezing saltwater as she grunts with effort, looking down into the depths where the steel shaft quickly disappears. She knows it only runs about twenty feet down before meeting one of Pad A's two pontoons—submerged 300-foot-long steel hulls capable of being partially flooded to maintain optimal platform stability.

It feels safer within the shadow of the platform, and Kara quickly locates the set of steel hand- and footholds running up fifteen feet to a landing. Shucking her water-heavy greatcoat and uniform jacket, she begins climbing as quickly as possible in the icy conditions.

And that's when the shooting starts.

She ducks instinctively before realizing the sound is coming from some remove. Peering into the gloom, she tries to make out shapes. The dock structure here is similar to the one at Control, an articulated series of floating walkways designed to accommodate twenty or so small watercraft. The whole network is situated beneath the west side of the rig, with only a single stair access up into the understructure. And that's where the gun battle has begun, some 400 feet across the water from her.

Shaking her head, Kara forces herself to continue moving. That was the point of splitting up. Either Kevin's superior manpower would be enough to punch through the enemy's defense, or they would provide enough distraction that Kara's smaller team could sneak up via a less predictable route. With any luck, both groups would make it.

She reaches the small landing and her team quickly joins her, Knott having tied off the raft below. Dimock readies his light machine gun, and Kara spins the wheel on the ovoid hatch leading into the interior of the platform's immense leg. The door gives with a rusty squeal.

The interior is brightly lit, bright enough to illuminate the faces of two very shocked men pointing combat shotguns over a railing to shoot below. Dimock unloads his M249's magazine into them as he steps over the lintel, then takes an unexpected shotgun blast to the side from a third shooter he didn't see. As the Marine crumples, falling down the stairs, Patrick Knott shoulders past Kara and dives through the entrance, rolling onto his back and firing his Beretta back towards the hidden gunman. There are overlapping shouts and general confusion, and Knott spasms as the edge of another shotgun blast shreds his upper arm.

Kara enters as the shooting lapses, confirming three enemies down and trying to look everywhere else at once. Only slowly does she accept that—for the moment, at least—there's no one else firing at them. Willie and Sarah quickly join them on the interior landing, Sarah kneeling at Knott's side and inspecting his wounds as Willie descends a flight of steps to check on Dimock, who's rolled into a fetal position. "Whoa-whoa! Whoa!" The large man suddenly yells. "Same team! Same team!"

"State your name," a hard, unfamiliar voice demands, and Kara carefully eases over the guardrail to look below. Two figures in digital camo crouch on the next landing down, sharing the limited protection of the steel cylinder that runs up the very center of the massive platform's hollow leg. One of the men has his LMG trained on Willie Cobb; the other is aiming menacingly in Kara's direction.

"I'm General Dunn," Kara cuts in before Willie can answer, hoping that her well-known face is visible enough to the Marines below.

Apparently it is, because they step out of cover after a momentary inspection. "Ma'am!" one of them enthuses. "You have no idea how happy we are to see you."

"What happened here?" she asks as the men quickly climb the stairs, one of them stopping to kneel with Willie beside Dimock, who is groaning softly.

"There was no warning, ma'am," the guard continues. His name patch reads Brady. "We was stationed on Sub 3, at the hatch. All of a sudden, Wilson and Blanton—the rest of our team—they're down, and we fell back into the shaft. They've been pushing us down ever since. We took down one of 'em ourselves, but they had the high ground. And our radios are out!"

A third man suddenly appears from below, and Kara's gun twitches before Brady throws up his hands in a placating gesture. "That's just Hodges, one of the techs."

Hodges' eyes are wide as saucers as he slowly lowers his own hands, which had leapt up in the universal gesture for 'I surrender!'

Kara returns her attention to Brady. "And you've had no contact with anyone since then?"

"No, ma'am."

Willie and the other guard—Moore, by his patch—hoist Dimock back up to the landing. His torso is a bloody mess, but he's conscious, just the glimmer of a smile on his pale face. He coughs, but there's no blood.

Moore catches Kara's amazed look. "The third shooter was halfway up to the next level. The blast was pretty diffuse before it took him. Still..." He trails off, and Kara takes his meaning. Scott Dimock may survive the evening, but he's out of the fight. She turns to find Patrick Knott back on his feet, torn strips of Sarah Piosa's undershirt wrapped around his bicep and already soaked a deep red. The arm—his shooting arm—lies limply at his side.

All seven of them, even Dimock, look at her expectantly.

Kara wills herself to ignore the pain showing in two of those faces. She singles out the mousy technician. "You're with Nereus?"

"Yes, um, ma'am," he squeaks uncertainly.

"Obviously the enemy is trying to sabotage the launch. How would they do that? Can they sink this platform?"

The man shakes his head, a bit more confidently. "No ma'am, not without some serious explosives."

"Not even by punching holes in those pontoons?" she clarifies, pointing down below.

"These pontoons—this entire rig, it's specifically designed to be unsinkable. There are so many redundant systems and failsafes... even if we hulled a pontoon, the system would compensate, closing off some chambers, flooding others—"

"Okay," Kara cuts him off, impatient. "So the rig's unsinkable. How would *you* sabotage the launch?"

The man swallows hard. "Um, well... easiest way would be explosives up top somewhere. On the spaceship itself, or maybe up the tower. Er, the gantry."

Kara nods. "And we know they've got people on the gantry." She checks her watch and curses. "Only thirty-five minutes left. We need to get up there."

The sad group begins moving up the stairs, Brady and Kara at their head. At their tail, Willie Cobb supports Dimock, the man's M249 slung over the pilot's shoulder. Willie calls up to Kara, "They'll abort the launch. I'm sure Kate got the word through."

"Yes," Kara agrees, "but whatever these guys are planning"—she waves her free hand to indicate the saboteurs onboard—"I'm sure it'll go off before the scheduled launch time. Which could mean *any* time now."

A massive thunderclap sounds from outside, sending an odd echo down the shaft and a vibration through the stairs they climb. And then another clang echoes down from above, followed by the overlapping percussion of multiple booted feet descending.

Kara grits her teeth, and Brady shakes his head emphatically—they can't risk another firefight here. They've just reached the access out onto sublevel 2, and the guard waves them urgently towards it. As he throws open the hatch with another rusty squeal, the clomping boots pause momentarily… and then continue at a much quicker tempo.

"Move!" Kara hisses, waving her people through the open door. The first gunman appears from above just as Willie clears the lintel with Dimock in tow, and Kara and Brady loose several shots before diving through after them.

Moore pulls the hatch shut and twists the wheel. "There's no way to lock it!"

They all stand in disbelief for a moment before Knott pushes forward. "You guys go ahead," he says softly, threading his good arm through the wheel and leaning hard on it as someone begins trying to spin it open from the other side. "I can't shoot now anyway."

"Leave me too," a raspy voice sounds. Dimock. "I'll just slow you down."

Willie's questioning eyes meet Kara's, and she nods through sudden tears. It's the only thing that makes sense. He props the wounded man against a stanchion and helps him draw his pistol.

"Keep the cannon," the Marine grinds out with a weak smile, indicating the M249 LMG slung over Willie's shoulder.

Kara turns to Hodges, the technician, forcing herself to focus on their mission. "Okay, lead the way."

The man blinks. "What—me?"

"*Yes*, you," she responds, suddenly testy. "We need to get up to the rig floor, and you're the one who knows this rig."

If possible, the man grows even paler. "Um, well, actually... I only just joined Nereus. I've been here about as long as you have."

Slowly, Kara takes in the veritable maze around them, and her stomach sinks.

The President of the United States leans back in his chair, chuckling along with his dinner guests at the punch line of one of his trademark jokes. Seated beside him at the rich mahogany table, the Premier of the People's Republic of China even cracks a smile. Despite this evening's momentous—albeit clandestine—Orbital Defense Corps launches, the duties of state still call. The President knows he will still be here late into the night, he and his opposite number jockeying unofficially for position in the trade talks to open the following morning. He has, however, granted Jim Maccabee permission to poke his head in with a thumbs-up once both Longships have reached orbit.

"Excuse me, sir," comes a muttered apology.

The President turns to regard Maccabee in the flesh, blinking in surprise. He pulls back the sleeve of his tuxedo jacket, reassuring himself that it's only 9 p.m. "What is it?"

"Sir, I'm sorry to interrupt, but..." he trails off. The President's chief of staff is uncharacteristically nervous. "You've got an important phone call in the Oval Office."

The President narrows his eyes. "Who is it?"

"The Ambassador, sir."

"*Which* ambassador, Jim, we have—"

"Sir, *the* Ambassador," he emphasizes. And then the President gets it.

"He... a *phone* call, you say?"

"Yessir."

"Very well." He rises swiftly from his seat, smiling with a politician's ease despite the butterflies flitting in his stomach. "Please excuse me, your Excellency. I have something of vital importance I must attend to."

As Kara's team pushes steadily deeper into the warren of dimly-lit walkways, enclosures, and branching pipes, she revises her estimate upwards: a person could easily spend *three* days lost down here, even maintaining Kara's jogging pace. But then, she *is* lost, so she can't help but feel overwhelmed.

"I'm *sorry*," Christian Hodges whines again from her side. "I've worked rigs all my life, but they're all different.

She waves a hand to shush him. Ahead, Brady leads the way with his bigger gun, occasionally sending a nervous glance back towards Willie, who cradles his borrowed M249 right behind him. Kara can imagine the guard's unease—Willie has hardly been checked out on any weapon that powerful. There's not much call for pilots to fire machine guns. Not the handheld variety, at any rate.

Catching Hodges' eye, she forces an encouraging smile. She can't blame him; the evidence is obvious. For one thing, the structure really is massive. At first, a 300-foot-square footprint doesn't seem that big, but a quick mental calculation convinces her that Pad A's floor space must measure close to a *million* square feet. But even then, the massive structure doesn't follow any sort of orderly floor plan. The very concept of numbered floors—levels 1 and 2 above the main deck, with the rig floor up top; sublevels 1 through 5 below—is misleading. In truth, there are any number of distinct levels mish-mashed together as needed to accommodate various pieces of once-vital drilling equipment. And as Kara's people quickly discover, certain other areas of sublevel 2 are inaccessible to them without going up or down a level. And that requires finding a staircase, ladder, or even just a space large enough to crawl through—Kara's hardly picky at this point.

Unfortunately, the ability to move quickly was apparently not a priority for whoever designed this monstrosity; in fact, Kara realizes, with all of the retrofits this rig has probably been through, even before it was converted into a mobile launch pad, there's probably much about its layout that *doesn't* make sense.

Up ahead, Brady curses and turns back to face Kara. "Another dead end. Some sorta control room. I dunno." And so the human train inverts itself, backtracks to the last intersection, climbs three short steps, and continues down the next unexplored walkway. At this rate, they'll never make it. That's five more minutes gone, less than half an hour remaining until scheduled launch... and again, they won't have even that much time unless the terrorists are going for something dramatic, like an explosion at the moment of liftoff. In truth, the people aboard *Harbinger* might die at any moment... they might *already* be dead.

Kara begins to despair.

This level is almost entirely composed of old drilling equipment, and Hodges occasionally volunteers an explanation for one thing or another. Kara listens with only half an ear. It's her other senses that demand her attention right now. Even in the dark, her surroundings are a riot of color. Yellow guardrails, orange stair steps, red fire extinguishers. Mighty silver fluid tanks, and the occasional blue metal desk. Some enclosures—be they offices, control rooms, or storage spaces—appear to be nothing more than randomly-placed shipping containers, garishly-painted 20-foot-long metal boxes like one would see on a train or on the deck of a cargo ship.

And of course everywhere, pipes. Bundles lying lengthwise along a corridor. Vertical singletons appearing right out of the floor and disappearing into the ceiling. Junctures and branches of every configuration running every which way. Whites, reds, browns, blues, greens. As wide as an arm, or as wide as a man. Undoubtedly, many are no longer used, but those that have been retasked as part of launch prep are sure to be high-temp or high-pressure, and sometimes both, according to Hodges. Fuel lines, supply lines, even frigid salt water pumped up from below to be used as coolant post-launch.

These are the surroundings Kara's eyes are showing her despite the poor lighting, and her brain interprets that to mean she's inside. And yet she can feel the cold, even feel wisps of wind that squeeze through cracks too small for a human. Except for some enclosures, the whole of this structure is open to the outside. Kara wishes now she'd not been so eager to dispose of her top two layers, though they were soaking wet.

And yes, there are other sounds as well, in addition to Hodges' whispered explanations. Mostly distant, the rapid clacking of automatic gunfire, the occasional cry of pain. And then, every once in a while, the multiple ping of ricocheting bullets that sound entirely too close. It's impossible to tell just how close, and that doesn't help anyone's nerves. Even as the six of them long to find a way out, knowing a way out will only lead to more gunfire and death, they fear each corner and what surprises it may hide. Kara can only hope that Kevin's team is having a better time of it than hers.

They come to another dead end, Brady growling softly, but Hodges gives out a cry of recognition. "I think I know where we are!"

"You've been here before?" Brady asks.

"No... but this," the tech raps his knuckles against the wall standing in their way. It gives back a hollow echo. "*This* is a reservoir for drilling fluids, 20,000 gallons or so. Which means we're right below the east pit room, and I came through that room earlier today." He turns slowly, getting his bearings, then sets off.

The team moves with renewed vigor now, which is good since the small technician is setting quite a pace. Without conscious intention, Kara runs in the posture she's seen so often in movies, hunched over with gun drawn and pointed at the ground. It's absurd, because she doesn't have a clue what she's doing. Marksmanship citation or not, she hasn't been trained for small arms engagements in close quarters like this. But at this point, she hardly has a choice. She pushes back her fear and pushes on, trotting lightly along one walkway after another, twisting and turning, following Hodges' lead as he seeks the stairs.

He finds them. It's an actual spiral staircase, bright yellow. Taking the steps two at a time, Hodges guides them up a level, down another short corridor, and into the pit room. In terms of variety, color, and sheer quantity of pipes, this room outdoes anything Kara has seen until now. Literally hundreds of pipes and flex hoses run every direction, making it impossible to move more than fifteen feet without having to duck, turn, or climb carefully over something.

Oh, and the room also happens to be occupied.

Hodges stares in shock at the two gunmen, who open fire almost immediately despite their own surprise. The Nereus tech is saved only by Willie Cobb's tackle, and Brady's return fire quickly pushes the enemy shooters back to find cover of their own. In fact, in that moment, *everyone* is scrambling to put something between themselves and the enemy, but the mostly thin pipes are about as reassuring as hiding behind toothpicks.

And just that quickly, Kara's team is again stuck in a firefight. "We don't have time for this!" she yells, even as Hodges shouts, "Stop shooting or we'll all die!" There's a lapse in gunfire, and Hodges explains, "These pipes are under pressure! We could set off an explosion in *here!*"

At which point the mercenaries promptly begin shooting again, even more recklessly than before. Unlike the men Kara's team encountered before, these guys are armed with carbines, their *rat-tat-tat* three-round bursts echoing impossibly loud in the enclosed space. Bullets *ping* and *clink* and *zing* as they ricochet three, four, even five times off the closely-packed pipelines.

By luck or providence, Willie Cobb lies atop Christian Hodges behind the best cover available, a three-foot diameter length of white pipe running horizontally across the floor. He pops his head over the rim for a reconnoiter, then consults the technician. "What's in those flex ducts? The big orange ones?"

The little man is lying with his arms wrapped protectively around his head, as if that will stop a bullet. "I don't know! Seawater, I think—for coolant."

"So they won't blow up?"

"No, but they *are* under—"

Willie doesn't wait for more explanation. He simply draws his pistol, steadies his aim over the rim of the big pipe, and squeezes off three careful shots. From his vantage, it's hard to even see the enemy gunmen, much less shoot them, but he *does* have a clear shot at a big orange hose suspended a few feet above the men's heads.

The soft material rips open with a thundering sound as Willie's aim proves true. One man screams as a jet of water drills him in the back, knocking him face first to the floor; the other simply loses his footing amidst the sudden deluge. Diving forward, Brady climbs recklessly over several pipelines in order to silence the struggling figures from point blank range.

Willie jumps to his feet, and Hodges follows more slowly. "—under pressure," the tech finishes dumbly. In point of fact, those water lines are under much less pressure than most of the pipelines running through the room, but they can still release fluids at more than 3,000psi if punctured, powerful enough to cut a man's skin or throw him off-balance.

"Sir, you got hit!" Sarah calls in surprise as Willie rises from cover.

Only belatedly realizing she's talking about him, the man checks himself over and finds a bullet hole high in his chest. He probably sustained the wound when he first brought Hodges down, but with the adrenaline pumping through his system, he hadn't even felt it until now.

"Looks like the bullet passed straight through," Moore reports. "Very little blood."

"I'll be okay," Willie assures them quietly.

Kara addresses Hodges. "What now?"

"Well..." The man thinks.

"We can't afford to keep getting caught like this. There's no time!"

"The moon pool then," Hodges replies firmly. "It's wide open—we'll be able to see up several levels, see if there's any bad guys around, plot out the safest way up."

"It'll be more exposed," Brady warns. "If we can see them, they can probably see us."

Kara gives it just a moment of thought. "Okay, let's do it."

As the six move out, Brady and Hodges again at their head, Sarah calls out. "Um... can someone tell me what a moon pool is?"

∞

"It's no good!" Ramon Coe reports as he drops into a crouch beside Kevin Smith, squinting amidst flying bits of paper and the haze of gunpowder trapped in an enclosed space. Ramon is the sergeant in charge of the former Control dock guard detail. He swaps out his LMG's magazine and jams the new one home. "They're holding both stairwells!"

Kevin's crew of five pilots and four Marines had landed with minimal resistance and made it two levels up the south shaft—the only stairs accessing the floating dock, and the only stairs running continuously all the way to main deck—before encountering a significant enemy force coming the opposite direction. In that moment, Kevin proved he was a pilot and not a troop leader when he ordered his people to retreat into the interior of the rig; his plan had been to circle around and access a different stairwell, never considering how many variables this environment presented. In point of fact, this section of sublevel 4 is relatively isolated from most of the passageways supposedly sharing the same level. Since the area is filled mostly with barracks-style living quarters, the architect—if there ever was such a thing—probably saw no need for quick access elsewhere. There are actually two stairways leading up within close proximity, but as Coe ascertained, they are both in enemy hands. Unlike Kevin's and Kara's teams, the enemy squads are clearly in radio contact with one another.

Kevin's crew is already down by three, and they've lost much hope of reconnecting with the guards originally stationed here; there haven't been many bodies, but they've come across a lot of blood. If there are any still alive, they must be elsewhere in the labyrinthine structure of the mobile rig.

How did I get us into this mess? Kevin berates himself morosely.

"It's okay, sir!" Allan Shannon, one of the pilots, yells encouragingly, seeing the look on Kevin's face. "The general took a different route to the top. By keeping these guys occupied, we're helping her!" He speaks with such simple faith.

Coe moves to a nearby window, knocks out the glass, and empties half a clip through the opening before retreating again. It's just the three of them in here, backs to the wall in one of the long, squat residential structures slung beneath supports on sublevel 4; the accommodation resembles nothing more closely than a trailer home. Kevin's other three surviving team members are in the next building down. Together, they've been trying, without success, to create an effective crossfire on the entrenched gunmen's position.

A long barrage assaults the other side of Kevin's wall, the percussive repetition of automatic fire punctuated by the booming of shotguns—Benelli Super 90 combat shotguns, to be precise. Several of the more powerful shot blasts, from such short range, succeed in punching through the wall's flimsy material. Above, one of the long fluorescent bulbs is knocked free and explodes into a fine white mist of shrapnel as it hits the ground, forcing the men to retreat to a corner.

Things are definitely shaping up for a prolonged firefight, and Kevin can't have that. "I can't be tied down here!" he shouts to Allan and Coe.

"Sir?" Allan responds in puzzlement.

"Kara needs my help up top!"

"But how—"

"I'll find a way, but you have to keep these guys busy—just like you said." Kevin is an experienced climber, and he hopes to be able to shimmy his way up some of the pipelines if nothing else. He has little other choice. "Lieutenant, you've just been promoted. Hold out as best you can, and be on the lookout for anyone trying to flank you from the other stair access."

Me? the young Allan Shannon mouths the word, stunned. But Col. Kevin Smith is already kicking his way out the building's back door.

Sarah Piosa's jaw drops. "*This* is a moon pool?" She stands at a railing looking out into a great open space. It reminds her of a high-rise hotel in which she once stayed, with rooms and interior balconies placed around the rim of the structure, allowing people on any floor to look down at the lobby way below, or up through the glass roof high above.

Except in this case, there's neither a floor nor a roof. Four levels of railings stretch uniformly around the opening beneath

Sarah's level, below which is nothing but open sea, the dark waves crashing spectacularly. Just three more levels run around the opening above her head, beyond which the thunderhead is visible, roiling and writhing, lit a now umber twilight. Staring too long in either direction leaves the young woman vertiginous, though at least when she's looking down, she's not being pelted in the eye with massive dollops of sleet.

Hodges is in full explanation mode. "We use this area for lifting or lowering large pieces of equipment." He points out several massive winches that he explains are used for exactly this purpose. The man is apparently quite taken with the pretty pilot despite the danger they face. Or maybe *because* of the danger… Kara's read about such infatuations springing up in the midst of perilous situations.

"Keep moving," she orders, an edge to her voice, though she keeps the volume down. "And keep quiet."

Hodges was, of course, entirely correct. In this open environment, it's much easier to determine the best path to the top. They can all see where the stairways intersect catwalks at various levels, and Brady makes a beeline for the most accessible. Up one level and they've reached the main deck. Up another, and they're now just one story removed from the open upper level of the platform, the so-called rig floor.

It would have been too easy for them to make it that far without another encounter with the enemy.

The shot comes out of nowhere, the distinctive three-round-burst of an M4 carbine, at least one round of which finds Brady's knee. Crying out in agony, the man stumbles forward, reflexively grabbing hold of the bright yellow guardrail to keep himself up. That reflex proves the death of him as several more rounds rip into his body, throwing him back against the bulkhead on the other side of the passage. One look is all it takes Kara to know that the man is dead, a bullet through his head.

"Run!" Moore screams from his rear guard position. "Spread out!"

With Willie, Sarah, and Hodges bunched up in front of her, Kara immediately reverses direction and begins running counter-clockwise around the open space. Moore drops behind limited cover as she passes, but Kara keeps going. The guard is right—by spreading out, they force the shooter to choose his shots rather than just open up in their general direction. It may have been accuracy that took down Brady, but it was more likely a lucky shot directed at the group of them, which had been clustering entirely too close together.

Rounding the corner, she sees muzzle flash two levels below. The shooter is hunched within the opening to a branching passage, hard to pick out in the shadows. Kara levels her Beretta and puts a few shots within twenty feet of the man, not bothering to slow her sprint. It's enough to make the man duck and back further away from the edge.

Another *rat-tat-tat* sounds from across the way, and this time it's followed by two metallic clangs from the railing beside her and a whistle right past her ear. Kara's been running on adrenaline for so long now, it seems, that she doesn't expect the additional flare that comes in the bullet's wake, making her every extremity feel suddenly *alive* at the close call. Rather than drop to the deck, she pushes herself harder, looking right to see that Moore is pouring fire into a position one level below, forcing a mercenary's head down. So that means there're at least two shooters below… and since they're in radio contact with the rest, they'll probably multiply quickly.

Kara reaches the opposite stairwell and throws herself up three steps at a time. Reaching the top, now fully exposed to the elements, she glances quickly around, but her view of the rest of the rig floor is hampered by a number of long shipping containers forming a horseshoe around three sides of the moon pool opening. The unimpeded side is across from her, and as Kara watches, Willie emerges onto the deck on that side and immediately throws himself against the end of one container before peering around.

Trusting that Willie will watch her back, Kara returns to the same corner she just rounded—one level higher now—flattening herself and ascertaining that she has line of sight on both gunmen. Almost directly below her position, Moore is keeping up a steady stream of gunfire, swinging back and forth between the two mercenaries to keep them from doing any damage. Kara can only imagine just how many extra magazines the Marines carry in their numerous pockets.

She waits for a break in the man's firing, then yells, "Moore! I'll cover you!" The guard's fire does not resume, but he gains several precious seconds before the gunman to the southeast proves bold enough to show himself again. This time, Kara puts a bullet within five feet of the man's head, forcing him back down. She immediately swings her aim back to the man hiding in the shadowed passage... but he's gone. It's enough, however. Moore scrambles up on deck and takes up position opposite Willie, Sarah, and Hodges, peering in the other direction.

Sending one more bullet in the merc's direction to cover her own retreat, Kara rolls away from the edge of the open pit and sprints across the exposed space toward Moore's position. The rapid-fire sting of icy needles on her back, her arms, even the top of her head is agonizing, but she ignores it, dropping and sliding the last few feet to the Marine on the slick steel surface. Feeling some degree of elation that they've finally reached the open surface of the platform, Kara peeks over the man's shoulder.

To find that they're effectively surrounded.

The recognition comes like a kick to the stomach. There are two directions her people can run to escape this metal box canyon. Just twenty yards from where Kara crouches, the entrance to the gantry yawns invitingly... except for the squad of gunmen hiding behind crates directly between Kara and her goal. Willie Cobb, meanwhile, would have easy access to the ramp leading up to the launch pad proper if not for a similar blockade. While Kara and her people were dodging bullets below, the enemy had clearly taken the opportunity to box them in.

But it's worse than that. Very soon, there will be additional troops emerging from the moon pool behind them, and at that point, Kara's team will be totally exposed.

"This is Echo Three," the scratchy voice declares over the radio to the spellbound control room. *"Pad A is crawling with hostiles. I've seen a few squads head down below, but there are still plenty on top. And up the gantry, too—there's a guy on top waving us off."*

"Waving at *you*?" Peterson asks, clarifying.

"*Yeah, he's got something in his hand. I can hardly tell from here, but he's acting like it's some sort of detonator.*"

Everyone in the room groans as Peterson raises a pair of binoculars to his eyes. In the midst of the storm, everything is now a dark brown, the sun completely masked by the low-lying cloudbank. Even with the magnification, Peterson can't make out anything meaningful through the haze.

"Do you see any evidence of explosives?" he asks.

"*No sir, but I can't really get a good look. Visibility's nil with all this rain, and we come under fire if we get too close.*"

"Can you land your men?"

"*Not a chance, sir. There's no room to put down, and between the gusts and those shooters, rappelling would be suicide.*"

Peterson slams his fist onto the desk in frustration. "What about our people? Any sign of them?" He's not even sure who Kara took with her, or how many.

"*Hard to tell, 'cause everyone's in camo down there. But I doubt it—only shooting I've seen has been at* us."

"Fine, hold position."

"*You don't want us to engage?*" the pilot asks in surprise. After all, they have heavy machine guns mounted at each side door.

"Negative, Captain," Peterson responds. "Too much risk of damaging the launch vehicle. Just keep yourself out of range."

"*Copy.*"

Peterson turns to Thomson, who's been monitoring Filson's channel. "Any news?"

Finger to one ear, Thomson nods. "Yessir. One of Filson's squads has gained the dock with no resistance encountered. There are so many craft tied up they're having to cut some free just to land everyone else." It was an overwhelming force that Peterson sent with Filson to retake Pad A.

"Okay, keep me posted." Peterson jabs a button on his own console. "Echo One, report."

"*We circled B as close we can, but ain't no sign of nothin' wrong,*" the other pilot responds immediately.

Peterson finds it hard to believe the hostiles would bypass Pad B in favor of the more distant A, though it's possible. *Harbinger*'s launch from A is the sooner of the two. "No movement at all? We should still have thirty-four men stationed there, though they'd all be down below."

"*I don't know, sir—but no movement.*"

"Go ahead and land your men; have them ascertain whether our guards are still active, otherwise do a quick sweep for explosives. I want a sitrep in five minutes. Note that there's already another assault team headed there by boat, but they'll be coming in from below and time is tight."

"*Yessir,*" the pilot responds.

"*Sir, Echo Three!*" the pilot stationed over Pad A cuts back into the conversation. "*I think we've identified some of our own people! I don't know what you call it, but there's a big square hole running all the way down to the water, and they just came out of it.*"

Next to Peterson, a spotter stands peering out at Pad A through his own set of binocs. "That would be the moon pool, sir," he says softly.

"What's their status?" Peterson demands.

"*They're pinned in, sir! I doubt they'll last long there.*"

The thrill of hope Peterson was just beginning to feel wavers. "Okay, forget what I just said. I need you to give those people a chance. Come in close, draw some fire, whatever you have to do—but create a distraction down there."

"General," Thomson calls, "I've got Echo One for you again. Here he is."

"*Uh... sir?*" the pilot calls. "*I've got a paddle out here on the helipad. He's waving me in.*"

Pause. "Well, at least we know there's still someone onboard B," Peterson mumbles. By 'paddle,' the pilot is referring to a landing signal officer who uses colored paddles to direct incoming aircraft. It's a largely obsolete role, especially with choppers capable of landing without assistance; but in this weather, with radios down—Peterson had never been able to raise anyone on Pad B—it makes some sense that one of his people might be out there trying to assist Echo One's landing. Still...

"Echo One, I don't want you putting all the way down. Have your men rappel."

"*Yessir.*"

In the distance, through his high-powered binoculars, Peterson can just barely make out the movement of the helicopter hovering above the eastern edge of Pad B. It's impossible to make out more than that through this pea soup, but—

"*Nooo—*" the pilot screams briefly before his voice cuts out suddenly. Peterson hasn't even had time to react to the sound before he sees a sudden fireball replace the hovering chopper at the center of his enhanced view.

Grasping the horror of the situation immediately, Peterson whips around and yells, "Echo Three! Watch out for RPGs. I repeat, watch out for rocket-propelled gren—"

"Sir, we have another launch!" his spotter calls from the window. "Pad A! It's a miss. RPG for sure!"

The damage is done, however. A horrendous cacophony of sound arises from Thomson's radio speaker, before the pilot of Echo Three makes his final transmission: "*I've lost control! We're going down!*"

Peeking out from behind cover, Willie can't help but be amazed at the view. The Longship *Harbinger* towers majestically over the surface of the old deep-sea drilling platform, caught dramatically between a pair of spotlights. And the launch pad proper, what was originally the locus of the oil derrick, reminds Willie strongly of the Mayan temples that have always fascinated him. It looks very much like a miniature ziggurat, three levels of buildings, containers, walkways, and ramps forming a jagged, stepped pyramid, at the apex of which stands the launch vehicle in all its glory.

He turns back to smile at Sarah Piosa and Christian Hodges; neither smile in return.

Hodges is on his knees, sobbing, having finally grasped just how desperate their situation is. Sarah is in better control of her emotions, but she's clearly struggling as well. "It's hopeless, isn't it?" she asks softly.

Willie shakes his head gently. "No," he tells his subordinate, "there's always hope." He faces front once more, returning his attention to the squad of mercenaries standing between him and the base of the ramp leading up to the launch vehicle. According to Hodges, the two easiest methods of sabotaging the launch would be explosives on the launch vehicle itself—obviously that would be effective—or a detonation to bring the gantry tower down on top of the launch vehicle. If it weren't for those gunmen out there, he and Sarah could probably make their way to the base of the Longship to do a quick visual inspection; and Kara Dunn, similarly, would be able to sweep the gantry.

He squints through the pounding sleet, trying to get an accurate count of the men hiding behind the nearby barrels. Is it possible they'd be so stupid as to hide behind barrels of something combustible—like, say, gasoline? Does he dare waste what little remains of his ammunition? He's still pondering this when a new sound grabs his attention.

Over the booming of the almost constant thunder, augmented by the crashing of waves far below, Willie can make out the rhythmic chopping of rotor blades. And then, suddenly, there's a chopper *right there*, an HH-60 Pave Hawk seemingly hovering just between his and Kara's position. With each gust of wind, the chopper bucks wildly, jumping five feet, dropping three, swaying one way or the other. The pilot appears barely in control. At its open side doors, floor-mounted machine guns swing around to line up on the two squads of mercs.

"Yes, yes!" Sarah exults, and Willie feels the same sudden euphoria. Then his breath catches at another unexpected sight. Beyond that squad of suddenly terrified gunmen, popping up out of cover some thirty feet further away, a man is holding a launcher of some sort propped on his shoulder. Aimed right at that chopper.

Heedless of the danger to himself, Willie drops his machine gun and steps from cover, lining up his pistol for a more accurate shot. His bullet takes the man in the shoulder just as he launches, sending the projectile wide. Unfortunately, the Pave Hawk pilot shies to the side anyway—

Right into one of the shipping containers.

It's little more than a glancing blow, a nevertheless deafening *bang-bang-bang-bang-bang* as just the tips of his rotors clip the edge of the big metal box, but it's enough to wrest what little control the pilot had of his bird. Willie watches in horror as the listing chopper swings dangerously close to *Harbinger*.

And in the midst of it all, Kara is yelling: "Go! Willie, go! Go! Go!"

Of course, he berates himself, bending to scoop up the LMG. Within about ten seconds, it's likely that everyone for a hundred feet—himself included—is going to be killed when that doomed chopper comes down. Naturally everyone standing between him and the *Harbinger* is running and screaming, no longer paying him a lick of attention. Might as well make the best of it, on the off chance they survive the next few moments.

"Let's go, people," he tells Sarah and Hodges.

The Nereus tech just shakes his head in wordless terror, eyes riveted on the flailing Pave Hawk.

"Christian, we have to—"

In a sudden rush, the man turns on his heel and bolts back toward the moon pool, where even now Willie can see two men emerging. But Hodges doesn't bother with the stairs. He simply takes a running jump off the side, dropping straight through the wide opening to the water some hundred feet below.

Willie stares in shock. It's actually a pretty smart move, though the guy probably just panicked. He shakes his head, amazed that even in this dire moment, he can be distracted by something like that. Grabbing Sarah's arm, he puts everything he's got into reaching that ramp. The next few seconds stretch into a short eternity…

And then he's there, still alive, Sarah still at his side, the both of them pounding up the ramp. They drop down behind a barrier, and Willie looks back the way they came, just in time to see the chopper drop over the far edge of the rig, presumably to splash into the water below. Somehow that pilot held it together long enough to avoid damaging the rig or its precious spacecraft.

Pulling himself to his feet, Willie sends up a quick prayer—in gratitude, as well as for the brave people aboard that chopper. Meanwhile, he and Sarah have to get moving before the mercs regroup. There's so little time! They need to reach the pad, look for explosives, and... actually, he has no idea what they'll do if they find any. But at this point, that's just borrowing trouble. With Sarah Piosa on his heels, Willie Cobb rounds the corner for the final stretch of ramp up to the launch surface.

And finds himself looking into the barrel of a shotgun.

Lying on his back in a seated position, Col. John McLaughlin, unit commander for the ODC's Second Defense Squadron, tries to fight his boredom. He knows their launch window is opening soon, but there haven't been any updates over the cabin intercom in some time. Of course, as the ranking ODC officer onboard *Harbinger*, he could use his vacuum suit's integrated radio to contact the Longship's cockpit crew, but... He sighs. Best to just be patient.

And then he hears a rapid banging from outside the spacecraft, so loud that no one can miss it. So loud, in fact, that it must have been absolutely earsplitting outside. Along with most of the other personnel, McLaughlin turns instinctively to look out the nearest window. But of course, there *are* no windows. *Hermes*—the original prototype—has windows, but *Harbinger* was completed on the government's dime, and since the craft was no longer intended for tourists, they deemed windows an unnecessary extra expense.

Enough patience, he thinks, jabbing a gloved finger at the pad on the inside of his left wrist. "Commander," he intones, "this is Colonel McLaughlin. What was that sound?"

"*Stand by, sir.*"

And that's it. McLaughlin blinks in surprise at the terse reply. He's poised to break into the cockpit channel again, when he catches Tim Dillon smiling at him from across the aisle. Dillon is a former Navy officer—a submariner, in fact—who accepted a lateral transfer to the ODC rank of first lieutenant. "What?" he asks the man.

Dillon's smile only broadens. "Must be hard, sir. Trying not to be a backseat driver, I mean."

Kara wastes no time sprinting for the safety of the gantry. Moore slows briefly to fire his weapon at the retreating forms of several enemy agents, but Kara puts everything she has into the run. She doesn't know if or when one of the gunmen will turn and decide she's worth taking a potshot at. She doesn't know if there are other, more distant mercenaries already lining up on her. She simply knows she must make it to that gantry to confront whatever danger threatens her people in the launch vehicle. Feet pounding on the textured steel plating, sending up little splashes; sleet pelting her face, biting into her raw skin; every extremity, from nose to ears to fingers to toes, entirely numb. Kara runs, gun in hand.

With a gasp, almost of surprise, she dives through the gantry opening and lands prone on the floor. Breathing hard, scrambling back to the opening and tucking herself into the protection of a vertical beam, she peeks back around the corner to cover Moore as he arrives in similar fashion.

Catching her breath, Kara checks her clip. "I've only got one round left," she tells the him.

"Here." He hands her a fresh magazine, which she slides into place, feeling much better.

Across from her, much more exposed than Kara is, Willie Cobb and Sarah Piosa are barreling up the rampway leading to the pad beneath the launch vehicle. There's no sign of the tech, Christian Hodges. Kara straightens, back suddenly rigid, as she notices a gunman sneaking around the near edge of the platform. Willie can't see him yet, but the merc obviously knows the pilots are approaching; he raises his shotgun to unload on Willie as he comes around the corner.

Kara judges the range to be about a hundred feet. A tough shot, especially in this wind, but she doesn't let that stop her. Unlike everything else that's happened today, this is actually something she *has* trained for: shoot from standing still at a stationary target that's not shooting back. She raises her gun, sights down the iron reticule, and exhales fully to steady her aim. She gently squeezes the trigger.

Willie Cobb is just looking down the long barrel of the enemy weapon when Kara's bullet takes the man in the shoulder and spins him around. It takes Willie a moment, but he follows with a shot of his own and continues up the ramp. He throws a quick wave in the direction of the gantry, though Kara doubts she's visible amidst the shadows.

"Nice shot."

Kara turns to regard Moore, only to realize that the guard is not the one who spoke. He has his weapon up and pointing deeper into the shadows, a posture Kara quickly mimics.

Kevin Smith sighs. "It's just me, General."

"Kevin?" Kara asks in relief. "Where's your team?"

"We got caught in a firefight on sublevel 4. But I left them with Shannon—I knew you'd need me up here." He pauses briefly. "We've had at least three casualties already."

Kara shakes her head. "Not sure about us. We picked up a few survivors"—she gestures at Moore—"but we've lost a few as well." She cannot help but feel responsible for the deaths, including the ones on Kevin's team, but she can't afford to wallow in guilt. Not now, when they've finally reached the gantry. She catches sight of a tiny red LED behind Kevin. "There!" she points. It's some sort of explosive, wrapped in yellow and affixed to a beam.

"No wire..." Kevin comments. "I guess this is some sort of remote detonator."

"Can we remove it?" Kara asks. "The whole thing, I mean, just pull it off and throw it into the water?"

Kevin shrugs. "I don't know..." he says uneasily. "I don't know anything about bombs. What if there's some sort of tamper guard?"

She checks her watch—fourteen minutes! "We keep moving then. We find whoever has the trigger and keep his finger off it." She looks to Moore.

"I'd better stay here and cover your backs."

Kevin clears his throat. "General, maybe you'd better stay down here too. No point risking both of us. The hole it would leave in our leadership if we were both killed..."

Kara frowns. "Kevin, if we lose the *Harbinger*, it won't matter. Now get moving."

The Project Nereus mobile launch pad gantry stands at 250 feet above the rig floor, only an abbreviated version of what is generally used at Kennedy and other spaceports. It does not contain any special enclosures or rooms, and it does not sport an elevator. It consists mainly of forty-two half-flights of stairs and a framework for stretching various umbilical lines up the side of the spacecraft, with wider landings jutting out at intervals. A sliding bridge cross-member can be moved up and down the tower in order to deliver astronauts to the docked craft; that bridge is now locked into place near the very top of the tower, where just hours before it had provided access to *Harbinger*'s forward port airlock.

Kara takes the stairs two at a time, pushing herself into another sprint. At every landing they pass, she glances out to see more explosives fixed in seemingly random locations on the tower structure, sometimes three or more per landing; these terrorists are apparently very thorough, and she can imagine it taking them the entirety of this last hour to place all these charges. As she runs, she listens for voices above; to the best of her ability, she ignores the freezing cold and the bumps and bruises she's beginning to feel all over her body.

She has lost all count of levels by the time she nears the top, just a minute and a half later, but she can hear the voices above as they yell to each other over the wind.

"Okay, we're set!"

"About time!" comes the answer.

"If you hadn't sent all our help out on guard duty, we would've had the charges set a lot earlier!" the first voice retorts, obviously angry.

"Enough!" the second says. "Launch is in... ten minutes. Arm for eight. That should give us time."

Kara doesn't wait to hear anymore. She puts on a burst of speed, throwing herself up the stairs as quickly and quietly as she can. As she rounds the corner between the two flights and comes into view, she immediately notices the man crouched on the top step, gun pointed down the stairs. But he's not looking—he's turned to the side, yelling over his shoulder out onto the landing.

She doesn't pause, she simply reacts, firing twice into his chest as she races up and past. As she crests the final step and emerges once more under the open sky, she throws herself to the ground. The only other man on the landing follows her progress, pulling a weapon from his belt, but Kevin takes him by surprise from the stairwell as he appears a moment later.

Not even bothering to get up, Kara scrambles on hands and knees to a small control board lying next to the body of the last man. It reminds her somewhat of a soundboard, a compact version of what one would find at a rock concert, riddled with knobs and sliders and readouts. Centered prominently at the top, an amber digital display counts down from 7:37.

Kevin has run down the length of the bridge, presumably to check for more explosives or gunmen, and is now returning. He eyes the countdown clock with horror. "Kara, you've got to cancel the launch," he urges.

She shakes her head. "That's what I told them, but now—Kevin, I don't know…"

The other pilot sprints back down the bridge again, where he begins pounding on the airlock door. "Open up!" he shouts. "You have to get out!" It's questionable, however, whether the sound will carry through the craft's armored skin, or if anyone would be stupid enough to get out of his seat and open the hatch so soon before the scheduled launch.

"Kevin!" Kara cries. "Kevin, stop it! There's no *time* to evacuate. Our best bet is to go early, before the bomb goes off. Assuming there are no charges on the Longship itself—"

"What!?" he demands. "No, we need to defuse the bomb!"

That statement hangs in the air for a long moment before Kara quietly—or at least not yelling—asks, "Do you have any idea how to do that?"

He slumps, dropping slowly to his knees a few feet from her. "So after all that, we've changed nothing," he says dully. "Whether or not they delay, this bomb will go off in seven minutes, killing everyone." Very softly, he begins crying, tears slipping down his cheeks to mix with the sleet still peppering them from above.

Hopeless. After all of that, they still have no hope of stopping this catastrophe. This massacre. They never really did. Kara eyes the complexities of the small board in front of her, wondering if she shouldn't just try, flip a few switches, turn a few knobs. Maybe flip it over and look for a battery compartment. What can it hurt? There's absolutely no hope otherwi—

There, lying innocuously beside the board, is a godsend. A large gray shape, with a huge loop of antenna emerging from its top. A handheld satellite phone.

With a gasp, Kara snatches it from the ground, determines that it's got juice. "Kevin! Look!"

The man stares with disbelieving eyes. She waits in vain for a mirroring smile to stretch across his face, watching as he works through the implications of her discovery. With this phone they can contact Peterson and maybe, just maybe, get this mission off the pad before the explosion occurs. "Kevin, don't you see?" She begins punching in a number—

"Kara!" he screams in horror, snapping his gun up into firing position.

Reflexively, she drops prone to give Kevin a clear shot. It must be more hostiles coming up the stairs from behind her. She only needs a little time to get through to Peterson, to get the mission countdown clock reset. If Kevin can just keep them off her... She rolls away, turning to face the stairwell...

There's no one there. And Kevin hasn't fired a shot. Three seconds pass before she sits up, turning back to him in confusion.

Kevin Smith's red eyes meet hers over the barrel of his gun. He's not aiming for the stairwell at all; he's aiming for Kara's head.

The End of Book Two

Day 1,257 of Incarceration

K<small>LINE</small> Apartment, Bunker 18-B, Groom Lake Facility
37°14'57" N, 115°49'24" W – Elev. 4,252 feet
  (146 feet below ground)

The room is clean but cluttered. Row upon row of cinderblocks form each wall, their outlines visible from floor to ceiling despite several layers of yellow paint. At the center stands a little table with two chairs, on one side an economical kitchen, on the other a small carpeted space with loveseat and television. An analog clock set into the tiny oven marks time with a quiet cadence.

The subject occupies one of the two chairs. At peace.

Opposite the subject, a uniformed man occupies the other chair, his shoulders bearing the rank insignia of a lieutenant colonel. He leans over the table, spectacles perched on his nose, scribbling notes on a legal pad. He fills most of a page before ripping it from the pad and placing it within a manila folder. Pushing that folder aside, he begins flipping through the contents of another folder. A much thicker folder. As he flips, he speaks.

"I'm sorry I've been away so long."

"I understand. You have leads to follow."

"Yes, but… I know it's only a matter of time. Before…" *The man glances up, then back down quickly, returning to the stack.*

"Carl, I do not regret how things have turned out. If I could do it over again, but have a choice this time, I would still choose this." *The subject's arm sweeps the area around them, supposedly three rooms, but really just one. The subject's home, or most of it.* "Before I crashed—you have no idea what it was like. Pitched battles in orbit. Skirmish after skirmish. And so many deaths… If I can prevent that this time, I want to."

The man smiles, then returns to his folder. He comes to the end of it and frowns. "Where did I…" *He lifts a leather attaché case from the floor, begins riffling its contents.* "I ran down a few more names, and I really want you to take a look." *He withdraws a three-ring binder from the case, but when he opens it, something falls out and bounces across the table. A black felt jewelry box.*

The subject opens it carefully with a three fingered hand. A pair of small diamond studs glitters within. "Carl, these are beautiful." *Embarrassed, the man reaches out a hand for the case, which the subject closes and returns.* "I assume these are for your wife?"

"Yes... they're a surprise for her birthday."

"I will say nothing more about it then."

The man's face clouds. "You will... still be with us. Won't you?" *He has never been good with expressing his feelings, typically hiding his concern for others behind one excuse or another.* "I'm thinking of throwing a party this year. Since it's a special occasion, I can probably get dispensation to take you off base."

The subject sighs, almost longingly. "That would be nice. And no, I do not expect to die before August."

The man relaxes, but only slightly. "May I ask you a question?"

The subject finds this humorous. "Since when must you ask? Your questions and my answers are the entire basis of our relationship."

"You don't talk much about your life, before the crash I mean. Unless it pertains to our preparations, you gloss over it."

"My life might as well have started over when I crashed in that forest. I can never return, so there is no point in pining over what I have lost."

"I understand. But you must know I have many questions."

"So ask."

"Why did you never get married?"

The subject laughs, the sound emerging raw from damaged nasal passages and persisting for some time before trailing off. "Carl... for all our similarities, we come from very different cultures. People still marry, of course, many people. But I do not believe it means the same thing. In my world, marriage is not a binding commitment. And many people choose to love each other without marriage." *The subject shrugs.* "When I was young, marriage did not entice me."

"I think that's... sad," *the man says.* "Sorry," *he adds quickly, realizing his comment might sound pejorative.* "Anyway, I was just curious. After four years, I thought it was something I should know." *He returns to the binder.* "Ah! Here it is, right in the front pocket."

The man withdraws three ragged newspaper clippings and pushes them across the table. Back to business, the subject lifts the first cutout and begins reading, eyes flicking back and forth rapidly across the lines of tiny text, rereading several sections. Finally: "That does not sound right, but I cannot know for sure." *The man nods, accepting the clipping back, and starting a new page of notes on the pad. The subject reads through the next more quickly, with an instant verdict of* "Definitely."

"And the last one?" *the man asks with an expectant tone, looking up from his notes.*

The subject goes rigid upon reading the subtitle. "You hardly need more confirmation on this one."

The man shrugs. "I thought you would appreciate it anyway."

It isn't much more than a blurb, a small community interest piece inset in a much larger article about the most recent Space Shuttle mission. It reads:

Thursday, April 12, 1984

Little One Dreams Big

Kara Dunn of Westbrook has plans of becoming an astronaut one day. by Lana Daley

At an age when most children are learning to ride tricycles and use safety scissors, Kara Anne Dunn has already chosen her profession.

"I want to be an astronaut," the four-and-a-half year old told me when I interviewed her last week. As she explained, "Floating would be neat instead of walking."

I met little Kara and her parents at their home on Friday morning, and together we watched the liftoff of Space Shuttle Challenger. While her parents and I chatted, Kara soaked in every detail of the televised pre-launch sequence. When I asked her what she thought of the proceedings, she answered simply, "It's fascinating."

It may be too early to tell, but I think we can expect big things from this little girl. After all, she has big dreams. Maybe in twenty or thirty years, we will be watching on television as Kara Dunn lifts off into space

"That is definitely the right one," *the subject confirms in an odd tone of voice.*

"I thought so," *the man replies, holding out his hand for the clipping. After a moment, the subject returns it, and the man staples it together with several pages of handwritten notes before placing it in his thick manila folder. When he closes that folder, wrapping a rubber band around it to keep it together, the label on its front becomes visible:* RECRUITMENT.

BOOK THREE
REVELATION

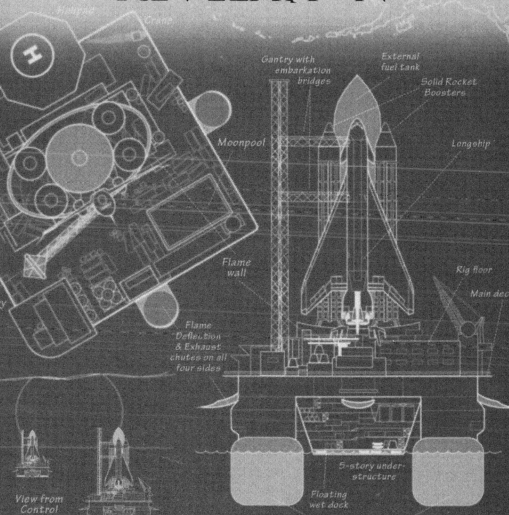

Thus, what enables the wise sovereign and the good general to strike and conquer, and achieve things beyond the reach of ordinary men, is foreknowledge.
Now this foreknowledge cannot be elicited from spirits; it cannot be obtained inductively from experience, nor by any deductive calculation. Knowledge of the enemy's dispositions can only be obtained from other men.
Hence the use of spies.

~ Sun Tzu, *The Art of War*

You know, someone wisely said that a hero isn't really braver than anyone else; he's just brave five minutes longer than anyone else. And it's because of you that America's future will be big and strong and generous and full of hope and fighting spirit.

~ Ronald Reagan
Parris Island, South Carolina
June 4, 1986

referencing Ralph Waldo Emerson

[Chapter 39]

**Sunday evening
August 9, 2015**

The President sweeps into his famous office, nervous on the inside, but nevertheless determined. Finally, *finally*, a chance to talk with this so-called Ambassador of the *K'lurans*—the call he's been anticipating for months, ever since reading the KLINE Document. He hardly expects they'll be able to chitchat and settle their differences, but he desperately needs more information. And maybe, just maybe, he can give these monsters a piece of his mind. The United States of America is *not* going to cower before their aggression. The American brand of humankind has teeth, and he'll make sure these people know it. Maybe that's all it will take to back them off.

And so the President is determined, intending to take a hard line from the outset. He seats himself behind the antique desk, pulling open a side drawer to reveal a multi-line secure phone console. "What line, Jim?"

"Uh, sir, it came in unsecured."

He pauses, then closes the drawer. "Of course."

"Line two."

"Right." He picks up the handset from atop the desk, but his finger stops short of jabbing the button. "He's actually been waiting this long for me to pick up?"

"Yessir."

"Have we traced the call?"

Another pause. "Um... yes. As far as a commercial comm satellite at least. But the call wasn't routed *through* there... it appears to actually *originate* there."

Pause. "I see. So they're hacking in somehow?"

Maccabee shrugs elaborately.

"I see," his boss repeats. He takes a deep breath, then jabs the keypad for line two. "This is the President of the United States. With whom am I speaking?"

There is a very long silence, then: *"Why?"* The voice is singsong, but even in that one word, the President knows there's something terribly unnatural about it.

"Hello? Who is this?" he demands.

"You choose death for people," the measured response comes. This time, the President can pick out why the voice sounds wrong—it's not a voice at all. It is a collection of one-word sound bytes, strung together, like the auditory version of a magazine-clipped ransom note. Except that the entire phrase flows with natural inflection. *"Why?"* the question repeats, with more emphasis.

Is this for real? the President asks himself, glancing up at Maccabee, who shrugs again from where he listens in on another handset.

"We gave you long warning. Ignored."

The President blinks. "Our people do not take kindly to threats. We—"

"No threat," the amalgamated voice interrupts, seemingly calm. The President only now begins to wonder how the creature on the other end of the line is managing this conversation. Is it some sort of automated translation function, picking recorded English words out of a massive databank on the fly? *"No threat,"* the 'voice' repeats. *"Statement of fact, fact of necessity. K'lura wish not many to die. K'lura wish not **any** to die."* The emphasis on that one word, 'any,' is communicated through a swelling crescendo. *"Restoration of Southwest Zenith came as warned. But none flee."*

Southwest Zenith? What does— Is he referring to Denver?

"Long you know. Still many cease life."

"Denver?" the President demands, enraged. "You never warned us about Denver!"

"We send K'lin'uk." The cobbled-together voices manage to convey a sense of authority with this statement. That last, unfamiliar word—Kuh-LINE-ook—is formed from a dozen different clips, rendered with an almost musical lilt.

"What?" the President asks in confusion.

"K'lin'uk," the other responds, and this time the blend of voices is subtly different. *"In your speak: first-comer, first-warner, priest of inevitable."*

The President gives a start. KLINE? "Do you mean—"

"*K'lin'uk warn today, of Restoration before. Necessity.*"

"That's a lie! You didn't send KLINE. KLINE came of his own free will, to warn us, to—"

"*Exactly.*"

"No, he warned us so we'd be *prepared*, so we could fight back!"

"*Fight?*" The syllable trills as if with humor. "*Can mortal fight gods? Can human fight inevitable?*"

The other party's constant shifting, to and from pidgin English, from full sentences to abstract concepts, is beginning to give the President a headache. "We'll never stop fighting," he assures the other forcefully. "You cannot take what is rightfully ours. We'll never give up, not as long as—"

"*Sad summary of human existence, fighting,*" the reply comes, and its drooping overtones indeed sound mournful. "*Though some enlightened, you lead to ruin.* **That** *death condemn you.*"

"We only fight to preserve life!" the President insists angrily, beginning to wonder at the point of this surreal exchange. Did this creature, this *Ambassador* call to bandy about philosophical arguments?

"*Fighting not preserves.*" Mournful again. "*We reach Northeast Zenith now. Restoration again.*" Momentary pause. "*What you preserve?*"

The strange caller falls silent, waiting, listening, as the President tries to parse out the question's meaning. According to KLINE, the *K'lurans* claim most of the continent west of the Mississippi River. Situated in the northeast of that region—

"Chicago," the President intones, voice flat as something dies within him. "You're attacking Chicago. Today." His words are not a question, simply a statement of realization.

"*Know you long,*" comes the response.

"You can't!" the President objects, suddenly overwhelmed, suddenly ready to beg, not concerned about what that will do to his negotiating position—fairly convinced he doesn't *have* a position to negotiate from anyway. "Hundreds of thousands will die!" he pleads.

"*That death condemn* ***you****. Plan to fail. How you prepare?*"

The President, one of the most powerful individuals in the world, falls silent, at a complete loss for words.

"Simple announcement all required. **But- you- make- rock- band- party**." The emphasis on each of these words is adequate to communicate the accusation within.

The President feels as if everything's turning on its head. The tangled statements coming over the earpiece seem to imply that the *K'lurans* were never the enemy, that the nuclear strike on Denver—while unavoidable—was nevertheless *not* intended as a massacre. That its actual purpose was some sort of ritual cleansing, a... what did the Ambassador call it? A Restoration? There are so many problems with this claim, including the further attacks and assassination attempts against ODC personnel, the testimony of KLINE, and yet... What does the President really know of KLINE? Was that alien forerunner's message actually so different from what he's now hearing from this Ambassador? As little as he's seen of that heavily-redacted testimony, how can the President make confident judgments about who KLINE was and what he said? Who's to say KLINE wasn't exactly as this Ambassador claims, an official envoy here to preach not resistance but acceptance of the inevitable, all in the name of saving human lives? What if that is, somehow, to some degree, the truth? It doesn't make sense, but then, miscommunication between cultures, especially when they first collide, is more the rule than the exception. Ultimately the question comes back to *him*, the President of the United States: What if, instead of releasing cutesy PSAs and attempting to entice people out of Chicago with a month-long music festival, the President had simply announced, with calm confidence, that Chicago would be the target of the next nuclear strike come August? Had he made that announcement, would the *K'lurans* have actually switched targets or not?

He shakes his head. "We couldn't tell them the truth," he insists, almost whispering, obviously unsure. There was too much uncertainty, too much risk of setting off a panic and causing even more death. Right?

"*So they die,*" the quiet amalgam responds. "*That death* **condemn** *you.*"

The President clenches his fists, angry, upset, frustrated, not even sure whether to feel guilty or ashamed.

"*You!*" the sound is joltingly loud. "***Fitless** to lead. **Careless** of people. **Our** children. **That** death condemn **you**.*"

Click.

And just like that, the conversation is over.

The President cannot stop shaking his head, and he finds that his clenched hands are now trembling. *What did that accomplish? They finally contact us, but no demands are issued. Just recriminations? Do they expect me to suddenly back down?* Even if he wanted to, the President couldn't do anything for Chicago now, not if the attack is tonight. It's the same old argument—panic, rioting, and looting would spread death and damage far beyond the unpredictable blast zone, and what would be accomplished? Would any significant number of lives be saved?

With a sense of inevitability, he slowly circles his desk to sink nerveless onto the sofa. "Jim…" he says softly. "Have Holland get in touch with FEMA." Nothing more needs to be said, and his friend and chief of staff scurries immediately out the door. The President of the United States flips the television to the latest news coverage.

[Chapter 40]

Sunday evening
August 9, 2015

"*Gryphens, this is Colonel McLaughlin,*" the recognizable voice filters over *Harbinger*'s cabin intercom, relayed from where he remains in his assigned seat. There's a pause, as if he's not sure how to impart what is to follow. Then, speaking slowly: "*I'm afraid I have some bad news. K'luran agents have seized control of this platform... and have likely sabotaged this vessel.*"

There are gasps throughout the cabin, followed immediately by a swell of murmuring.

"*Control has lost radio contact with our personnel outside, and they're frankly not sure what's happening right now. But—*" he continues over several cries of dismay. "*We know that General Dunn has led a team aboard, and they're currently assaulting the enemy positions surrounding us.*"

"What can we do?" a voice shouts out over the hubbub.

"*We,*" McLaughlin responds, "*can't do anything. We're being held in a state of readiness in case the launch goes forward. Everyone needs to remain strapped in and ready to seal your visors. All we can do is hope... and trust that General Dunn's team will handle the situation.*" He pauses again. "*I'll keep you posted on any further developments.*"

As the line clicks off again, dozens of conversations leap into existence. Seated near the very back of the craft, Shaniqua Watson just watches and listens. Two rows up, face visible from where she sits, Barrett Williams bows his head in anguish—undoubtedly reliving the horror of losing his longtime friend Anna Haynes the last time the enemy sabotaged an ODC launch. Shaniqua feels that pain, both vicariously and because Anna had been her friend too.

She tries to gauge how the others seated around her are doing. For every pilot she recognizes, there are three unfamiliar faces belonging to support and base personnel transferred from other branches of service. But everyone is scared, uneasy. It might be different if they were in a position to *do* something, but they're not. They must trust in Kara and her team.

And in all honesty, that seems like a long shot. If Kara Dunn, a pilot, is leading an assault team, it means that something has gone horribly wrong. Few of the ODC personnel have been trained for that kind of combat, and it seems unlikely they'd be capable of fighting back a determined paramilitary force.
Shaniqua recognizes the truth of this. And yet she chooses to hope anyway. To trust that Kara will defy the odds and somehow rescue them.
Though of course, it's not Kara herself she's trusting in. Shaniqua squeezes her eyes shut and begins praying very fervently for her friend.

"*Sir!*" The voice of the pilot designated Echo Four rips suddenly across the quiet Control bridge. Peterson had pulled that chopper off perimeter patrol to take up the task of monitoring Pad A. "*Sir, they've captured the gantry!*"

Several individuals stand involuntarily from their consoles, hope sweeping visibly across the control room. "Four," Peterson growls, "who is 'they'?"

"*Two people, sir, with handguns. Maybe one is a woman?*" He pauses. "*Looks like the shorter one is dressed differently. It's not camo—*"

"Could it be General Dunn? She was in full dress."

"*Maybe.*" The pilot continues his play-by-play, but Thomson whirls around in his chair.

"General!" He rips his headset off. "Report from Filson. His people have taken sublevel 4—they've joined up with some of our people who were pinned down."

"What did they have to say?"

"Apparently they were the diversion for General Dunn, sir. She went above with a smaller team."

Peterson grunts. One of his aides chooses that moment to enter, quietly passing him a slim folder. Inside are the results of a hurried census the general had ordered twenty minutes earlier. With radio communications temporarily down, an unknown number of personnel with Kara Dunn on Pad A, and some risk of enemy incursion even here on the Control rig, Peterson wanted to know exactly where he stood. The top sheet of the report lists fourteen names: five Marine guards and nine ODC pilots unaccounted for, including Kara Dunn, Kevin Smith, and Willie Cobb.

The chopper pilot is still relaying the details of goings-on atop the Pad A gantry, which seem to be tame enough after all the excitement and violence of the last half hour. Peterson finds himself wishing, not for the first time, that he was in radio contact with Kara's people, so Control knew if there were indeed explosives on that platform. Then—

"*No!*" That one word from the distant pilot, full of surprise and dismay, seizes his hope and squeezes it hard.

"What?" Potteiger gasps, unable to control himself.

"*He's... I don't understand! They're in some sort of face off. One of them's pointing a gun at the other!*"

Peterson's eyes go wide, his brain chugging furiously, tuning out the sudden bedlam so he can concentrate. He rips open that report, scanning down the names again. And there it is: Col. Smith. Col. *Kevin* Smith.

It all clicks in that moment, and Peterson could kick himself for not seeing it earlier. It was in Grant's files, the trail of logic obvious in retrospect. Grant simply identified the wrong individual. But now Peterson knows the truth.

Kevin Smith is a traitor.

Kevin Smith's red eyes meet Kara's over the barrel of his gun. *His* gun, pointing at *her*. It makes no sense. The implied threat is unmistakable, but that threat is so incompatible with their friendship, their trust, that Kara utterly fails to comprehend it.

"Kevin?" she asks.

The man looks stricken, utterly defeated, and his shoulders rise and fall in silent sobs. But the gun stays steady.

"*Kevin?*"

An explosion of white illuminates the sky from horizon to horizon, and the accompanying thunderclap sends a tremor through the deck beneath them. The sleet intensifies, like sharp needles digging into her face and bare arms as Kara lurches to her feet.

"I don't—" she tries again. "I mean, why…" Her voice is lost in the new fury of the storm.

"The Longship can't be allowed to launch, Kara!" he shouts miserably over the paroxysms of sound around them. "I'm sorry! I don't want to hurt anybody, but…"

The gun in her face wasn't enough for Kara, but this—this apology? admission? It begins to break through her shock and disbelief. And yet the idea is incomprehensible. "*Kevin?*" The emotion begins welling up within her, and her mouth falls open in horror. "*You?* You're working with them?"

"No!" He shakes his head. "Yes… not really. Kara, I don't know! I'm just trying to save lives!"

"We *can* save these lives!" she insists, meaning their friends on *Harbinger*.

He shakes his head sadly. "No. We can't save everyone, Kara. We have to make a choice."

Another peal of sound and light rips across the sky, and Kara staggers back a few steps. Kevin moves with her, his aim so steady it belies the grief in his features. "As long as we fight them, they'll keep destroying our cities!" he shouts. "The ODC isn't helping anything! You're just giving people false hope—we *can't* fight them, Kara! They're too powerful."

"*You*, Kevin!" Only now are the first stirrings of anger igniting within her, and they flare quickly. "I can't believe *you* are a traitor, Kevin. *You*, working *against* us?"

He takes an involuntary step back at the look that crosses Kara Dunn's face. "No! This isn't a *betrayal*! It's…" He fumbles for words. "Kara, this fight, it's impossible! The sooner we realize that, the sooner we begin evacuating, the more lives we save!"

"Evacuating?" she demands, the word adding a new wrinkle to her confusion.

"Yes! That's all they want—" He breaks off with a step forward, his gun now drooping just slightly in his zeal to explain. "You know what K<small>LINE</small> said! They want North America back!"

"Evacuate half the *country?*" she retorts, stunned. "That's imposs—"

"No, it *is* possible! I've run the numbers!" he insists, taking another step forward. "We have *so much* land, Kara! Why should we fight for it? Even east of the Mississippi, with 300 million people, that's only 370 every square mile! Most countries in Europe are more packed than that!"

Kara just shakes her head. "No, no, *no!* Don't you see, Kevin? You can't evacuate so many—you've said it yourself about Chicago. Millions would refuse, and there'd be violence, riots—"

"I've talked to them, Kara," he says, softer, now that he's closer—the gun still between them. "The aliens. They promise more time. We just have to show good faith, get the process—"

"Good *faith?*"

"That's what they say! And they seem reasonable, they just—"

Kara stares at him, aghast. How could he be so stupid, so easily deceived? Or is there more than what he's telling her? How much of the Kevin she knows is even real? Angry, she demands, "How long? How *long*, Kevin?"

"I don't—"

She steps forward, now pushing him back as he hurries to keep that gun locked between them. "All the times they tried to kill me, were you part of that?"

"No!"

"When they tried to kidnap me?"

"*No!*"

"When they tried to *abduct* me?"

"*Kara*, I wouldn't— They approached me after all that, right before—"

"We trusted you! We all *trusted* you! You liar... hypocrite..." She snarls viciously, barely able to see through intermingled tears and rain as she stalks forward, pushing him ever back. Looking down that barrel isn't so terrifying as she watches her words tearing wounds in the man. She is nearly insensible with rage. "Coward! You selfish, *selfish*—"

"No!" he screams. "I do this because I love my country!" He begins turning toward the *Harbinger* but catches himself. "I have friends in there too! I don't *want* them to die," he insists. "I'd rather we get them out! But you said it—there's no time. If this ship makes it to orbit, Chicago burns." He takes a ragged breath. "There's no question here. Two hundred, or two hundred *thousand*?"

"Is *that* what your masters told you?" Kara demands, comprehension dawning and incensing her in the same moment.

"If two hundred must die to save Chicago, I *know* those Gryphens give their lives willingly. It's what they signed up for!"

"So these merciful aliens agreed to spare Chicago if you killed your friends?" she bites out caustically.

Kevin cringes. "No," he replies, softer, "if I prevent the launch. This..." He waves his arm to encompass the scattered charges, the incomprehensible control board. "This wasn't supposed to happen. They gave me this software to load on the secure mainframe. They said it would just create a bogus error code—"

"They *lied*, and you *still* believe them? What about July 4th? Did they tell you no one would be hurt then either?" she snarls. "After everything they've done, how can you—"

"Kara, I'm trying to tell you—"

"How could you be so *stupid*?"

"Enough." He blinks rapidly, calming himself. Kara belatedly realizes that the storm has quieted considerably. The precipitation continues falling, actually harder and colder than before, though there's not as much ice in it. "I'm sorry I've disappointed you," Kevin continues quietly, and Kara can almost believe he's sincere. "But there's no time left for waffling. I've considered this from every direction and made my choice, and I will stand by it. I'll stand by it *here*." He swallows. "I'll be with my friends when they die—we'll die together, a sacrifice to protect our country."

Despite the man's raging emotions, Kara can see Kevin is convinced. He truly believes that what he's doing is the best option in an impossible situation. She cuts her gaze right to check the detonation countdown: 4:46. *Already?*

"Kara..." he says softly, breaking into her thoughts. "Go... just go. I don't want to hurt you... or anyone. But *you* don't have to die. Just... drop the gun, the phone, and go."

Kara Dunn is very tempted in that moment. To her shame, she realizes that's an out she's willing to take. What else can she do? What could she possibly accomplish? Gun to her head, less than five minutes on the clock. Is it even *possible* to initiate launch with so little time? Even with the phone, whom could she call? There are no other phones here in the Arctic Circle—the mobile rigs communicate solely by encrypted radio. All of which leaves her back where she started: a bomb she cannot defuse, and a gun to her head.

Kara Dunn is totally insufficient in the face of this challenge. What she always feared has been proven: she is inadequate. How did she ever get sucked into something so totally beyond her?

She actually turns to leave.

"No-no!" Kevin insists, moving another step closer. "Drop the gun and the phone."

It is not Kevin's warning that freezes her in place, however; it is a realization. A new insight that forces itself to the forefront of her thoughts, despite the tears flowing down her cheeks. Why does this realization come now, in this moment? Maybe because, for all of her insecurity, Kara Dunn is and has always been a positive person. An optimist. An encourager. Someone used to addressing others' insecurities and exposing them as lies. Maybe it's that side of her that rears its head now, demanding its say. Whatever the reason, the realization comes in this moment. Nothing actually changes. She's no more adequate now than she was the moment before... no more capable of saving the day. No, the realization is simply this: there's one thing Kara Dunn brings to the table in this situation, one thing that no one else in all the world can offer.

She's here.

Kara was never a believer in fate, but the past months have weakened her faith in her own independence. Time after time in the last eighteen months, she has been forced into roles and situations not of her choosing. And somehow, inexplicably, all of that has led her *here*, to this moment. Her alone. Whether or not she is capable of making a difference, she is the only one with the power to try.

She turns back slowly to confront Kevin Smith, his pistol now a foot from her forehead. His eyes are so tortured, conflicted, and yet he trusts in his logic. This entire argument, nothing she said could shake his confidence—not that he's doing the *right* thing, but that he's doing the *best* thing. For the first time since this surreal conversation began, Kara forces herself to be entirely rational in her thinking. Calculating, *manipulative* even. Not so she can defeat his logic, but so she can flank it. So she can riot his emotions until the man does something stupid.

Kara narrows her eyes, banishing her terror of death and demanding complete control of herself. Very deliberately, she steps forward, the gun barrel knocking hard against her head. Slowly, ever so slowly, she lifts one arm—the one holding the satphone—to point accusingly at the Longship behind him. "Before I go," she lies calmly, "I want to leave you with something to think about. John McLaughlin is on that ship. One of your closest friends. He trusts you. He *vouched* for you—you would not be standing here today if not for John." As she speaks, as she points, she keeps her eyes locked on Kevin's, refusing him permission to look away. "It was *John* who handed you this knife, and you are stabbing him in the back with it. And you are not only *murdering* your friend; because of you, he will be remembered as one of the biggest fools in history." She lays it on strong, exaggerating wildly, pulling at his emotions, using this man's overdeveloped empathy against him. "*That* is the legacy you are leaving behind for Evelyn. No husband. None of the children they dreamed of. And undying humiliation for the rest of her life."

Kara's words are shredding him inside; she can see that. If the Kevin Smith standing before her is anything like the man she thought she knew, then he's already wallowing in guilt—if anything, punishing himself more so *because* he feels this is the only choice he can make, as if atoning ahead of time for a sin he cannot avoid. If she actually gave him the chance, Kara knows he *would* ponder his treachery until the very last moment, believing himself guilty and yet not wavering from his commitment.

Forcing a sneer of utter disdain, Kara emphasizes her accusation with one more thrust of her outstretched arm at the nearby spacecraft. "Think about it," she whispers.

And then she turns her back on him.

In the wake of her accusations, finally released from her accusing eyes, feeling his undeniable culpability, and thinking that Kara has finally given up any hope of stopping him, it is only natural that Kevin would turn to regard the object of his shame.

To punish himself by gazing upon *Harbinger*, within which his friend unknowingly awaits death.

Kevin's eyes are already shifting in that direction as Kara turns away, and so she commits to seeing this rash course of action through to conclusion. Her back to Kevin, she continues her smooth motion, whirling through a full counterclockwise turn and throwing her left arm into a high block. It is a move she has practiced literally hundreds of times, intended as simple self-defense against an attacker swinging a knife overhead. As her left forearm meets Kevin's right to knock his aim off-center, her right arm naturally follows. Holding Kate Brasseaux's borrowed Beretta 9mm.

She does not pause as her pistol's iron sight appears below Kevin's shocked face... the next moment simply lasts an eternity. This is the face of a man with whom she worked closely for most of a year. A man she trusted. A man she considered a friend... and who might have become more. Most significantly, this is a living, breathing, *fragile* human life looking her in the eye as she pulls the trigger from just inches away.

Their guns discharge as one, and she remains standing just long enough to see Kevin's face crumple—something indefinable shattering within her at the same moment—and then she's spinning and falling from the force of his own bullet burying itself in her shoulder.

Lying flat on her back on the wet steel deck, Kara stares up at the roiling morass of celestial fury, its ejecta stinging her eyes. That turmoil mirrors her emotions. Her jaw slackens, a wail of horror at what she's done building within her, but no sound emerges—her throat has seized up. She retches, choking on her own gorge, and rolling over reflexively to clear her airway.

The freezing surface of the steel flat against her face sends a jolt through her, and she pulls back rapidly, sitting up. The gun drops from nerveless fingers, and the satellite phone nearly follows, but Kara tightens her grip suddenly. *The bomb!* she remembers in shock, forcing herself to focus. *Have to restart the launch!*

Kneeling on that gantry landing, at the highest level of that mobile launch platform, in the midst of a monster storm miles from land, Kara Dunn finally has the power to fix everything... but she still doesn't know who to call. In the age of cell phones and speed dial, who memorizes phone numbers anymore?

And then a number pops into her head.

"They just... Holy crap! They just shot each other!" the pilot yells over the radio, relaying events real time as they occur on the gantry above Pad A. *"Holy crap!"*

Peterson's jaw is clenched so tightly he's probably doing damage to his teeth. This whole thing is playing out like the script to a bad movie. "They shot... each other?" he asks weakly, too soft for anyone to hear. Turning back to the console with more authority, he asks, "Thomson?"

"Filson's people are still ten minutes away at best. There's a lot of resistance on the main deck."

Peterson snarls with feeling. "Echo Four, I want you to drop your people right there on that gantry—our instruments say the gusts are slowing." Indeed, on the northern horizon, patches of that massive red ball are beginning to show through once more. "Thomson, has Henry's team made it to Pad B?"

"Yes, sir. They're sweeping the lower decks."

"Patch me—"

"Wait, sir—wait!" Echo Four interrupts loudly, the tension thick in his voice. *"One of 'em's moving!"*

"What?" Peterson straightens. "Which one?"

"I don't know, sir... um, the little one?"

"What's she doing?"

"Holy crap! She's punching some sort of command into the detonator!"

[Chapter 41]

**Sunday evening
August 9, 2015**

 The dulcet tones of a marimba chime slowly, methodically, swelling with the synth strings in a barely-recognizable rendition of a 60s pop song.
 Madeline doesn't mind the music. She actually enjoys moments like this… the peace, the opportunity to think. It's not that she dislikes her job—she loves it, in fact. The rush she experiences, the power and trust she holds. But after most of an eight-hour shift, she doesn't mind a short break.
 At the next desk, Ella is telling Katie about the unusual call she received earlier—the one with the electronically-disguised voice. Madeline has heard the story twice now, but Katie only just came on duty, and she murmurs appropriate appreciation for both the uniqueness of the call and Ella's deft handling of it. Among the fourteen full-time switchboard operators at the White House, fielding over four thousand calls a day, there persists a sort of friendly competition regarding who takes the most bizarre call on a given day. At the moment, Ella Wylie is the clear winner, and she's a definite candidate for the weekly prize as well.
 Madeline's station has experienced only two minutes of disuse when it gives off a quiet tone. She fixes a pleasant smile on her face—callers can hear that sort of thing, after all—and taps a button. "Thank you for calling the White House," she says with practiced ease, pleasant but efficient. "How may I—"
 "*This is General Kara Dunn of the Orbital Defense Corps, and I need to speak with the President* now."
 There was a time when calls like this, with their name-dropping urgent demands, would start Madeline's heart racing. Nowadays, they break over her like water off a duck's back. "Of course, ma'am," she replies patiently. "May I ask what this is in reference to?"
 Precisely three seconds of silence pass. Then the unknown caller's measured but intense voice says, "*I understand that you are a gatekeeper. I understand that what I am about to say will*

not sound the least bit legitimate. But if I am not speaking with the President in fifteen seconds, the deaths that ultimately result will number in the millions. If it is even remotely *possible that I am telling the truth, you do* not *want to risk delaying me further."*

"I see," Madeline responds evenly. She flicks her computer mouse rapidly across its pad with a flurry of intermittent clicks. On her screen, she traces the call routing back through two telecom satellites to one owned by a global satphone service provider. A series of rapid-fire keystrokes follows, and she has temporarily overridden two neighboring satellites in the name of national security, requesting triangulation of the original signal. A new Internet browser window opens automatically to an online satellite mapping service, and a tiny yellow flag pops into existence in the middle of the ocean, roughly fifty miles north of Alaska. She ponders the implications for only a moment. "Please hold for the President."

She taps another button, breaking into the President's current call with his press secretary. When she speaks, only the President can hear her: "Sir, this is Madeline at the switchboard. Caller on nine claims to be Kara Dunn. I think you should take this immediately."

And with another button tap, Madeline is off the call. She glances over the summary that appears on her screen, noting in particular the length of the call, and sighs. In the next five minutes, Madeline may find herself without a job, but either way she's set an all-time White House record this evening: at thirty-four seconds, this is the quickest an unauthenticated caller has ever been connected directly with the President.

"Um, Ella? I hate to tell you, but…"

"We'll never stop fighting!" Those words, so sensible when the President spoke them just half an hour before, suddenly seem unreasonable. *"You cannot take what is rightfully ours! We'll never give up, not as long as—"*

"Sad summary of human existence, fighting." The alien response—and it truly sounds alien, with its odd combination of

voices—manages to come across both disappointed and reasonable. Not quite the inflection the President remembers. *"Though some enlightened, you lead to ruin. That death condemn you."*

"We only fight to preserve life!" comes the hysterical-sounding reply. Hysterical or not, that distinctive voice is undeniably his own.

The President groans from where he now lies flat on the couch, still watching the TV, Jim Maccabee sitting quietly nearby. At least now they know the purpose of the Ambassador's call—this news network is dutifully broadcasting it to the world for the third time in the last twenty minutes. He shakes his head... Those aliens are a lot more conniving than he'd given them credit for.

"Fighting not preserves." The Yoda-esque maxim comes across sounding like ancient wisdom from some Buddhist priest, the kind of thing people nod sagely in response to. Not good. Not good at all.

And so the subtly-retouched recording continues. Propaganda, pure propaganda. The first time it played, it simply cut across all normal broadcasting, entering tens of millions of homes unbidden. And it doesn't just contain the recording of their phone conversation; it begins with a videotaped message from the Ambassador himself.

That face is shockingly human in its expressions, the twinkle in its eyes, the arrangement of its features... and yet it is undeniably alien. The eyes are a bit too large, the forehead a bit too tall. The skin is gray with a smattering of freckles concentrated beneath the eyes. But otherwise, it could be the face of a middle-aged man, distinguished-looking, with jet black hair conservatively styled, just graying at the temples. Piercing blue eyes, with the same round shape as a Caucasian's.

The first words out of the alien's mouth are *"Good evening, We are KUH-LOO-RUH,"* and it is clear that the mouth is forming each syllable—yet they're the same piecemeal soundbytes as when the President took the Ambassador's call earlier. As if when the K'lurans learned English, presumably from American broadcast television, they memorized *the exact sound* of each word, including ambient noise. How the creatures can reproduce such sounds is a question already sparking debate. As far as the President is concerned, it's just spooky.

Video playback is a bit choppy as the Ambassador continues: "*You occupy ancestral land. We are reasonable, proud of what accomplish you since leave we. But time short.*" His face is replaced by a photo of Earth taken from orbit, centered on North America and zoomed in so the curvature of the planet is only just visible at the bottom corners of the image. A hazy yellow shape fades into existence over most of the continent, from the West Coast on the left to the Mississippi River on the right, from Guatemala in the south and tapering in the far north to cover most of the Yukon and Alaska. The mishmash voiceover says, "*Restoration of Zenith **must** continue. But **your** leadership intractable.*"

At that point in the message, 182 orange pinpricks begin blinking within the yellow section of the map; a news analyst had been on earlier to explain that all 182, which he had carefully counted, mark the positions of populous cities. More important, however, are the two bold red dots marking Denver and—at the very easternmost edge of the highlighted area—Chicago. Thanks to those two dots, and the audio recording of a hysterical President of the United States which follows immediately thereafter, the meaning of those 182 other plot points is undeniably clear.

A series of still photographs provides the backdrop for the phone recording, which starts halfway through with the discussion about fighting. Among the photos are some of the President's most embarrassing candid shots: speaking angrily to a minor foreign dignitary; wiggling his pinky deep into one ear; laughing hard and slapping his knee as a three-star Army general mimes a big explosion with outstretched hands. Incidental shots taken out of context to collectively paint a nasty picture of him: incompetent, stupid, warmongering. And then come the photos of millions of people out on a grassy lawn, laughing and enjoying themselves—that music festival outside Indianapolis—displayed in counterpoint to the Ambassador's accusation about the President's "rock band party." As if that reference isn't already obvious enough. And the *coup de grâce*—his official photo, the one calculated to build public trust and confidence, appears as his own voice whispers those six immortal words, the words that will no doubt be his legacy: *We couldn't tell them the truth.*

The retouched recording ends with the Ambassador's summary of the President as totally unfit for leading "our children," as he calls the human population of North America. The alien spin doctors even tweaked the recording at the very end, adding the sound of a phone slamming down on its hook—as if it was the *President* who terminated the call.

The Ambassador returns to the screen then to conclude his message. "*More Restoration inevitable. Flee east. KUH-LOO-RUH wish not **any** to die. But gods and mortal coexist not. KUH-LOO-RUH warn, ignore KUH-LOO-RUH. Stop ignore. Flee to live. No more warn will.*" And then the face fades, replaced momentarily by a weird silver and blue sigil, then black.

One minute and forty-five seconds of the best-planned propaganda this master of the art has ever seen. Its release perfectly timed. Its manipulations too subtle for him to make an issue of. The whole thing so ridiculously outlandish and hard to believe, hard to even *understand*, that it carries the ring of truth.

As the message—already being called the *K'luran* Manifesto—comes to a close for the third time, the network cuts to live footage from Chicago. People breaking through storefront windows to loot displays; scuffles in the street; cars loggerjammed on every expressway out of town. A scared but determined reporter interviewing random people, as others wander listlessly in the background. Protestors in front of city hall, actually organized and waving signs as they march in circles; the signs decry *him*— the President of the United States—by name, laying at his feet all the deaths in Denver and Chicago. Chicago hasn't even *happened* yet, and already they're blaming him!

The live reporting switches now to Indianapolis, where an interview takes place with a man and a woman as they sob their eyes out. "*Because of that monster, we're* here, *while our children are trapped in the city about to die.*" The reporter gently clarifies that the distraught woman is not expressing anger at the alien messenger, but rather at the President.

Burying his head in his hands, the President of the United States moans softly.

"Um, sir...?" Jim Maccabee asks quietly from his customary straight-backed chair. "Don't you think you should... draft a statement... or something?"

When the President looks up, his eyes are wet. He sighs. "Of course," he says softly. "Get me Pete."

And so it is that the President is sitting at his desk, chatting miserably with his press secretary, when the operator interrupts. *"Sir, this is Madeline at the switchboard. Caller on nine claims to be Kara Dunn. I think you should take this immediately."* The call is on an unsecured line. Again.

He taps for line nine, demanding, "Who is this?"

"Mr. President, this is Kara Du—"

"I don't know who this is, but—"

"I'm calling from the Beaufort Sea," the woman's voice cuts him off. And indeed, a howling wind seems determined to block the sound of her voice entirely.

The President sits up ramrod straight, no longer in doubt as to the caller's identity; only a few dozen people know the actual location of the new launch site; not even most of the people on those rigs know exactly where they are. "I don't understand. What's—"

"Sir, there's no time. Saboteurs again. I'm out of contact with Peterson. Is there any way, any way at all, *you could patch me through to him in mission control?"*

The President of the United States of America isn't used to feeling inadequate, but this day seems determined to give him reason after reason to feel exactly that. He doesn't need the details from Kara to understand her urgency, not today of all days. He simply doesn't know *how* to transfer a call from this outside line to the encrypted military network. He's a lifetime politician, not a tech support geek. "Kara, I'm going to have to put you on hold."

"*No!*" she shouts over the line. "*We have less than three minutes before we lose* both Longships. *We can't recover from that!*"

He swallows hard. "Right," he all but whispers. Reaching down the right side of his ornate desk, he jerks open the second drawer to access his secure phone console. The lines running out of this unit are entirely digital, 4,096-bit encrypted, with the fifteen speed-dial slots updated every morning to reflect the most important developing situations in his world. He jabs his finger onto speed dial #1—labeled "ODC Launch" in pencil—then snatches up the handset. The pause is only momentary before Peterson's gravelly voice comes across the line.

"*Yessir?*"

"General, I have Kara Dunn for you." The President now has a phone against each ear. "Kara, General Peterson." And then he simply turns the handsets opposite one another, earpiece to mouthpiece, and settles in for the duration of the conversation.

The pilot of the Pave Hawk helicopter hovering over Pad A clears his throat. "*Um, sir, I feel a little foolish saying this, but...*"

"For the love of all things holy," Peterson snarls. "This is a *combat* situation, not a chat with your girlfriend back home. Just tell me!"

"*Right, sir. Um... That detonator? Uh, I don't think it's a detonator. That person... well, she's just standing there holding it. Against her ear.*"

Peterson and Potteiger exhale simultaneously—the Air Force general in frustration, the NASA flight director in relief. The former leans over Thomson's console and slaps a key to connect him to the team now onboard Pad B, having landed via boat. "B team, report!"

"*Henry here, sir,*" comes the immediate reply. "*We've reached the surface. We didn't have time for a thorough search, so we focused on the main deck and rig floor—so far no explosives. I've got a squad heading for the gantry now.*"

"Any survivors?"

"*No sir, none that we've found. They were thorough.*"

"What about resistance?"

"*Token force, but we handled it.*"

"Very well. Keep me posted about that gantry."

"*Yessir.*"

The control room falls silent again. Dozens of men and women sit quietly around the room at their high-tech stations, monitoring the two Longships and maintaining their readiness.

But ultimately, they are all simply waiting. For what outcome, they don't yet know.

And then a unique trilling sounds from the communications station. Thomson's eyebrows shoot up. "Oh," he says simply.

Peterson crosses quickly to the man's station and pushes the rolling chair, operator included, firmly out of the way. "Yessir?" he asks, after jabbing a specially marked button.

"*General,*" the President says, "*I have Kara Dunn for you.*"

Peterson's jaw drops. "You *what?*"

"*Kara, General Peterson,*" POTUS intones.

"*General?*" Kara's voice is incredibly faint.

"Kara, is that you on the gantry?"

"*Just shut up and listen!*" she commands. "*And put me on speaker!*"

Peterson complies.

"*There's no time to explain. You have to initiate launch now, both pads. We only have two minutes before the countdown hits!*"

Potteiger meets Peterson's astonished eyes over the comm panel. "General," the flight director says, addressing Kara, "won't a launch trigger the explosives?"

"*I don't know!*" she yells over the wind. "*I just know if you don't launch, this gantry will go to pieces.*"

"Sir, Lieutenant Henry here," B team's leader shouts over a different channel. "*The gantry here is wired to blow, but it looks like remote det.*" He falls silent, waiting for orders.

"*General, we're running out of time!*" Kara shouts.

Even though Peterson has spent a lifetime making tough calls on the fly, there's just too much riding on this to make a snap decision. Too much at stake, too much unknown, too much information dumped on him all at once. He actually freezes up.

So Dr. Andrew Potteiger takes the decision out of his hands. His orders are quick but confident. "Jenny, engage *Harbinger*'s onboard automatic launch sequence."

"But sir, we have to double-check the—"

"That's all moot if the gantry topples first. *Do it.* Okay? Now reset *Hermes*' countdown to 60 seconds and engage its launch sequence at T-minus-31, as usual. And Frank, override the passenger cabin intercoms and warn them." On numerous screens set around the ceiling of the large room, two countdown graphics appear: 0:23 for Pad A, 0:53 for Pad B.

Potteiger backs quietly to where Peterson is standing. "This is asinine," he whispers. Peterson just nods in response, watching the other man's handling of the situation in shocked awe. "Those gantries are too strong to go easily," the flight director continues, "but if they so much as buckle, falling into those Longships... Easiest way to stop the launch." He shakes his head. Then suddenly his eyes go wide.

"General!" he exclaims. "You've gotta get your people off those gantries!"

Jose Morales waits quietly in his seat aboard *Hermes*, his only movement the rapid, nervous tapping of one gloved finger against the armrest. In fact, the entire cabin is largely still and silent, as if holding vigil. Just minutes ago, they had all heard the tremendous explosion of the chopper outside, and soon thereafter Col. Skylar McClinic had quietly informed them of the seriousness of their situation.

He feels a squeeze on his other hand and turns to regard Shannon Dembry, seated beside him. Holding hands through three layers isn't quite the same sensation as skin against skin, but he appreciates the contact nonetheless. He's still not sure how Shannon managed to swing seats together for them, but regardless, this was to have been the last time they'd see each other for a while. After all, they've been assigned to different units, Jose stationed on Asimov ODB, Shannon on Verne.

Now, of course, he wonders if they'll actually make it to orbit, or if they'll even survive the night.

A tense but professional voice shatters the stillness. "*Control to Hermes, stand by for liftoff in T-minus-50 seconds and counting.*"

Mouth agape, Jose meets Shannon's scared eyes. The launch, if it was to actually happen, wasn't scheduled for at least another hour!

"*T-minus-45 seconds,*" another voice cuts over the intercom, that of their mission commander in the cockpit. This voice is brisk. "*Please tighten your harnesses, return all tray tables to their upright and locked position*"—this garners a weak laugh, considering that everyone's sitting with gravity at his back—"*and lower your visors. Prepare for liftoff!*"

Jose swallows hard as he complies with the instructions. Within his now-sealed helmet, sound is muffled, but he can see the nervous motions of the personnel around him. Several rows forward, Gene Jenkins is actually turned around in his seat, pulling fretfully at an unresponsive harness strap that he'd apparently removed.

Squeezing his eyes shut, Jose blocks it all out, breathes deeply, and gets a good grip with both hands—one hand on the armrest, one hand linked with Shannon's.

"Sirrrrr," Sarah Piosa wails, crouching down as a carbine pokes its nose out from behind a nearby structure to blindly spray bullets in their direction. "I don't think they're buying it anymore!" She's been out of ammo for several minutes, but Willie had instructed her to pretend she was still shooting. It was worth something at least; in this weather, it's easy for the sound of gunfire to get lost.

A man's head pops up beside the rifle, and Sarah chucks her spent handgun at him, causing him to at least duck. With the storm abating, it's growing easier for the enemy gunmen to both see and hear everything on the rig floor.

Willie Cobb crouches behind cover a few feet away, sending a bullet flying at a different attacker. He and Sarah definitely hold the high ground at the apex of his so-called ziggurat, and it's served them well. But the enemy is growing bolder.

Upon reaching the top and dropping behind the flame deflection wall a few minutes earlier, Willie and Sarah had stepped out beneath the massive launch vehicle in stunned amazement. It was a surreal experience, standing under the yawning fifteen-foot expanse of a solid rocket booster's aft skirt, then running their hands along the trailing edge of the Longship's immense delta wing. So focused were they on the awe-inspiring sight above them, in fact, that Sarah nearly fell down one of the four gaping chutes used to safely deflect flame exhaust at liftoff. Willie caught her in time, but not before the young woman twisted an ankle on the graduated rim of the chute. The experience was enough to snap them out of their reverie, and while Sarah took the weight off her ankle, Willie performed a quick but careful search for anything obviously amiss. He checked the Longship's engines, the booster skirts, the cradle supports, the explosive bolts holding the massive vehicle in an upright position—basically everything within reach in the shallow depression of the launch pad. But nothing caught their attention. Whatever the terrorists are planning, Willie can only hope Kara has ferreted it out.

And so now he and Sarah wait, trapped at the top of the launch pad structure, though not entirely without hope. The cover afforded by the shallow depression of the basin is reasonable, provided the mercs don't try to get *too* close. At this point, Willie is down to just two pistol rounds, his LMG long since dry. It's simply a matter of waiting out reinforcements. With the launch surely canceled by now, he was hoping to maintain this position indefinitely.

Not six feet above Willie's head, a klaxon begins keening at an earsplitting volume. His wide eyes meet Sarah's.

"They're going forward with the launch?" she asks in shock, and Willie shrugs, equally stunned. Against their will, the pilots' eyes are drawn to the massive engines above them, which will incinerate them where they cower if they don't move quickly. Unfortunately, the way down from the pad is blocked by enemy gunmen, and in any case, Willie's not sure they'd be safe *anywhere* on the platform's surface when liftoff occurs.

Then a crazy idea takes form.

He forces a grin for Sarah's sake, then leaps to his feet and squeezes off his last two shots in the general direction of their attackers; with any luck, it'll force the men's heads down for a few moments. "C'mon!" he encourages his subordinate unnecessarily as he scoops her up and throws her over one shoulder. He breaks into a sprint—

Headed right for the middle of the launch pad... and the flame deflection chutes disappearing into the deck below.

Bullets begin zinging from multiple directions, and pain flares across Willie's back as he catches a few bits of diffuse shot from a distant blast. It requires ten totally exposed strides to reach those deflection channels, and Willie drops into one of the chutes without hesitation.

The short ride along the slick steel surface is as good as any theme park water slide he's ever experienced. And just before they go catapulting over the end of the chute, Willie hears a distinct triple-*whoosh* from behind him as *Harbinger*'s main engines ignite.

Kara presses the satphone harder against her ear in an attempt to hear Peterson over the sudden noise. Down on the rig floor, 250 feet below, the klaxons have begun their thirty-second warning. "—not on the—right?" the faint voice asks, cutting in and out.

"What?" she demands. Kara knows that Longship is about to blow past her with enough of a blast to cook her where she stands, but Peterson is obviously intent on communicating something.

"I *said*," the voice comes through, momentarily clear. "You're not—"

The deck suddenly begins vibrating as a triple-*whoosh* sounds from below.

"You're not still up on that gantry," Peterson finally belts out, "are you?"

With a sigh, Kara drops the phone and takes a running leap off the side of the gantry to drop over three hundred feet to the icy water below.

Two miles away, still leaning against the main deck guardrails on Control where Kara left them more than a half hour before, Hayden Vaughn and Joey the cameraman sigh in contentment. They could not have asked for a more beautiful shot.

For the first time in at least twenty minutes, the sun's rays spread across the water before them. All by itself, the reappearance of that majestic crimson orb is emotionally evocative. But even as Joey captures that exquisite scene on 8mm film, one of the two Longship-cum-fuel tanks begins inching up toward the sky. Hayden gasps, but Joey doesn't dare. He holds that camera steady.

Numerous tiny figures begin leaping from the sides of both distant platforms, like rats from a sinking ship. Flames come shooting out the sides of Pad A, then B, flaring in great gouts that draw another appreciative *oooh* from the two journalists.

Harbinger pulls free, the billowing smoke of its exhaust obscuring much of the platform. It does not, however, conceal the multiple-flash of explosions on the gantry towering over the pad. As those pinpricks of light fade, the tower folds in on itself, too late to affect *Harbinger*'s rise. Two miles further away across the orange-gilt waves, the other gantry crumples as well, and a horrible rending groan reaches them as *Hermes* rises above its platform. The second Longship lists slightly from a glancing impact with the falling gantry, but she recovers.

And the two spacecraft lift with stately grace, rolling onto their backs as they rise, disappearing into the dark cloud bank above.

"*Dude...*" Joey whispers, in awe.

Hayden Vaughn simply sits down, right there on the wet walkway, his eyes glazing over. "That right there, Joey, is a career-maker."

[Chapter 42]

About seven minutes after *Harbinger* and *Hermes'* historic dual launch late the evening of August 9th, a second nuclear weapon enters American airspace from orbit. It detonates inexplicably on the banks of Lake Michigan opposite Chicago, actually missing the city by more than seventy miles. The reported loss of life is still devastating, but not nearly as bad as it could have been.

At the same moment that nuclear weapon detonates, chopper crews are already working desperately to locate survivors in the arctic waters fifty miles northeast of Point Barrow, Alaska. They manage to rescue three ODC pilots, four Marines, and two *K'luran* agents—all in the early stages of hypothermia—but the unyielding environment has already taken the lives of the other eight floating forms they recover; among these dead is a Nereus technician by the name of Christian Hodges. Meanwhile, the strike teams onboard Pad A finish securing the labyrinthine understructure, routing out the remaining terrorists. Few allow themselves to be taken alive. At the sublevel 2 access leading out of the southeast caisson, the commandos find their way blocked because a near-catatonic Patrick Knott refuses even then to release his grip on the hatch. The bodies of Scott Dimock, John Brady, and Kevin Smith are recovered, along with more than twenty other military personnel and numerous terrorists. Many of the guards and technicians originally stationed on either platform are never found.

General Jerome Peterson makes the unilateral decision to bury any hint of Kevin Smith's duplicity. It was Smith who introduced the *K'luran* virus to the military subnet, believing it would simply cause a serious-enough error code that the NASA team would abort launch early; the virus had served a far more nefarious purpose, however, disrupting radio communications and allowing enemy agents to quietly assault Pads A and B without fear of coordinated response. Whether Kevin Smith had anything to do with *Herald*'s disaster on the Cape Canaveral tarmac the month before is less certain. What matters is that Corps morale would be crippled were the men and women to hear of a traitor in their midst… and not just anybody, but one of their squadron commanders.

Within three days, repair crews are at work on the damaged gantries of Pads A and B. By the time *Harbinger* and *Hermes* land at Post-Rogers Memorial Airport in Barrow, two days after their reentry and landing at Edwards Air Force Base, the mobile launch rigs are again ready to receive them. Kara and the remainder of the ODC personnel are catapulted into space five days later, only a week behind schedule. For once, there are no complications; but then, the weather is perfect, and security is ensured by two naval destroyers and numerous other patrols in the sky and on the ice north of the platforms.

Hayden Vaughn and Joey the cameraman release their stunning footage to great acclaim, but the beautiful images are nevertheless bittersweet, overshadowed by the most recent casualties of a *K'luran* nuclear strike. And then, just days later, another significant news bit steals attention nationwide: the U.S. House of Representatives, in answer to allegations of impeachable offenses, has launched a formal investigation into the President's handling of the *K'luran* affair.

Through it all, a very lonely Viviane Grant grieves: her father buried just weeks before; her fiancé in France indefinitely to care for his sick mom; her best friend just 200 miles away... and yet completely out of reach.

And as for Kara Dunn, adjusting to life in a zero-gravity environment, her experiences the night of August 9th, 2015 have a significant impact. She herself suffered extensive injuries, not only a gunshot wound and exposure to the elements, but also a leg broken on impact from her 300-foot fall into icy water. In light of all the lives lost that night, she can hardly bemoan her physical condition, but the emotional damage wrought by Kevin's betrayal proves harder to heal. Just as the questions he raised that night prove difficult to ignore.

With the enemy armada only nine months away, and attacks predicted to increase in the days leading up to its arrival, Kara agonizes more than ever: Is she really capable of leading humanity's defense against the *K'luran* threat?

Only time will tell.

The End of Book Three

All your questions will be answered...
Spring 2014

Keep reading for an excerpt.
For more details, visit
GRYPHENS.com

an excerpt from

PROMETHEUS
REVEALED

Wednesday, 1108 GMT
September 9, 2015

    Briefly lifting up his helmet visor's VR overlay, Lt. Trey Drogosch of the Orbital Defense Corps squeezes his eyes shut, wishing he could rub at them with his hand, the old fashioned way. He blinks a few times in the pitch dark, then pulls the overlay back down and watches the virtual displays reappear. He's barely into the second hour of his shift, but he's already having problems staying awake. He missed his morning coffee, and now that he's trapped inside his vac suit inside a Destrier for another six and a half hours, there's little he can do about it.
    Sighing, Trey pulls the virtual control board into his lap and keys for two-handed input, repositioning the yoke to his right to get it out of the way. He cycles through each of the craft in his immediate vicinity—the other nine Destriers flying outrider on Asimov ODB as it's moved on station; the four fighters flying backstop in case an emergency halt is ordered; and, most significantly, the looming, ill-proportioned shape of Asimov base itself, looking like some sort of wickedly-spiked medieval mace. The objects all appear as wireframe models rendered in varying shades of red, simply floating in otherwise pitch-black space with Trey at their center. It's all virtual, of course, slightly different images projected directly onto his retinas by his visor gear, thereby creating the illusion of three-dimensional depth and distance. As he turns his head, the Destrier's onboard computer tracks the movement to feed him appropriate images for his line of sight. Looking down past the control board in his lap, Trey can make out the other two members of his flight, apparently occupying the same space as his legs—though, of course, his legs are invisible in the dark. The only light available within the cockpit, while the ship is in operation at least, comes from inside his helmet.

Deciding to razz his wingmen, he dials the comm frequency shared by just the three of them. "Aeon Two-One calling Two Flight. Count off."

The first response is immediate and predictable: *"Aeon Two-Three reporting as ordered! Cyberbob is ready and rarin' to go, eager to whale on some alien—"*

"Thank you, Three, that's enough chatter." He can't help but smile, though.

The second response is a bit longer in coming. *"This is Two-Two."* The voice is slightly distorted.

"Nice of you to join us, Moneybags!" This from Aeon-23 before Trey can speak.

"Two..." Trey asks, "was that a *yawn* I heard?"

The sound repeats over the air, clearly a yawn this time. *"No sir, not at all."*

He smiles. "Well, keep your eyes open, boys. There's no telling when things will get exciting."

"Yessir," Aeon-22, a.k.a. "Moneybags," responds.

"On your order, Antilles!" Aeon-23 chimes in a beat later, and Trey rolls his eyes. He and his two subordinates—all of them brand new ODC recruits—had been virtually kidnapped the night before, dragged into the mess hall, and brought before a handful of more experienced pilots who had assembled to help them "choose" their new callsigns. Initially, Trey had been offered one of three options: Horseface, Splash, and Vomit. Fortunately, by surrendering his personal stockpile of quilted double-ply toilet tissue, Trey had convinced them to add 'Antilles' as a fourth possibility. He'd sacrificed a considerable amount of his limited foot locker space to bring that tissue onboard, and he would probably regret its loss the next time he was forced to use Uncle Sam's cardboard-grade single-ply, but he was nevertheless glad to have escaped 'Vomit.'

His friends hadn't been so lucky, having no bribes of value and no good way to acquire some. Rich Britt had ended up with 'Moneybags,' a rather weak pun on his name, though he didn't seem to mind. Mostly he'd seemed hurt when they laughed at his suggestion of 'Maverick.' As for Shane Ergen... well, he was so excited about getting his own "real callsign" that he didn't seem to notice just how stupid 'Cyberbob' sounded. Even *now*, the man is *still* excited. Never mind that the callsign is supposed to be more of a nickname than anything official. Notwithstanding what the movies portray, the designations aren't actually intended for use in the cockpit, since comm procedures require a more standardized identification protocol based upon flight group organization.

Still… comm traffic is more relaxed on patrol. When you're in the saddle for eight or nine hours at a go, staying alert is more important than strict comm discipline, and even casual conversations can help. Trey has already observed some of the more experienced pilots getting away with murder on duty, over open comm lines, provided it's just routine patrol. He decides to allow Shane his fun, as long as the guy keeps it within their three-ship element. In truth, Trey's already come to appreciate the other man's unflagging enthusiasm when things get dull, even if he can only boast the maturity of a six-year-old.

Then again, today *isn't* just routine patrol. Today is Moving Day.

Trey returns to studying nearby craft. As he targets each in turn, a detailed report is worked up by the radar and augmented from the squadron's shared database; the data appears to his right, in his peripheral vision, and remains there no matter which way he looks. When he attempts to focus on the blurry report, the system interprets his eye movement accordingly and brings the text front and center so he can read it properly. When he's finished, a right-left wink banishes it to the periphery again.

Drawing the IDB straw into his mouth by feel, Trey sips sparingly. The in-suit drink bag is an integrated part of his vacuum suit, providing access to roughly two liters of water through a straw suspended before his face. It's a poor substitute for coffee, but it keeps him hydrated on his long patrol. Two protein bars are also accessible hands-free within his helmet, but he quickly learned to leave those to the end of his patrol, or for emergency use. One way or another, relieving a full bladder while fully vac-suited is difficult—and humiliating—enough. Generating solid waste while on patrol is to be avoided at all costs.

Tapping the underside of his left wrist, Trey brings to life the liquid crystal display of his suit's integrated sound system. Running through the selections in his personal playlist, he selects a high-energy track, something to help keep him awake.

It's amazing, he reflects. Just a year ago, he was a computer programmer working a 9-to-5 job and playing video games late into most nights. He made decent money and enjoyed his life, even if it was generally devoid of female companionship. Since that time there have been two devastating attacks by aliens—aliens!—and he was not only recruited to become part of the defense effort, he was one of only nine new recruits to be given command of his own three-ship element. *First* Lieutenant Trey Drogosch—he likes the sound of that. And then there's the female angle. Not long after receiving his commission, he met Trudy Luckhurst on a Sunday afternoon in Houston and quickly fell under the sway of her stunning emerald eyes; she fell for him too, and he's not sure he cares how much of it was his sharp black dress uniform. And so here he is a few months later, thousands of miles outside Earth's atmosphere, flying a multi-million-dollar V-2 Destrier space superiority fighter… and after only a few days of patrols, he's bored sick.

He can't fault the equipment, though. Surprisingly similar to the setup in *Rampant*, which goes down in his list of all time favorite video games. Just like in the game, many of the Destrier's systems are customizable. Not only can he select what colors are used to display various kinds of information, he can import his own sound clips for use in place of the standard audio indicators. Trey had immediately customized his gear to match the settings from one of his favorite early-90s space combat sims. And not only because he remains a rabid fan of that franchise—with so much time invested in that particular game, the meaning of its various audio alerts and IFF color assignments have registered at a deep level, and reacting smoothly to them is second nature for him. Which is exactly why Gen. Dunn's team developed *Rampant* with that sort of customizability to begin with, to build upon each pilot's existing strengths rather than start them over at zero with a whole new system.

Humming along contentedly with his music, Trey turns his attention to the unidentified objects appearing on his scope. Even in the immediate vicinity, there are hundreds of examples of space junk, orbiting around the Earth even while Asimov and its minders mesh through on their way to higher altitude. The junk consists of anything and everything humankind has ever put into orbit, including defunct telecom satellites, spent rocket stages, detritus from explosions, and even intact satellites that just days ago were serving some vital purpose. Every contact they come across, it is the Destrier pilots' responsibility to log size and trajectory, in hopes of restoring the United States' recently-disrupted ability to track every significant object in orbit.

What makes Trey's patrol pattern unusual today is the fact that the ODC is in the process of moving its new homes—the four orbital defense bases on which most of the Gryphens live and work—into higher orbit to assume their permanent duty stations. As such, the Gryphens in the saddle today are mostly concerned with unidentified objects moving rapidly in relation to the closest ODB, because such objects represent a collision danger... or worse, they could be enemy ships. So far, the most excitement Trey's people have seen involved pulling Destriers alongside several larger contacts to carefully bump them out of the way.

Exciting or not, they've nevertheless attempted to get closer scans on anything measuring more than a square meter in profile. The process is tedious, of course. A few radar pings doesn't tell you much beyond the fact that *something* exists at a given point in space—that and its apparent size. It takes the combined efforts of multiple Destriers' radars to get a more complete 3D picture, and even then, the assistance of the distributed tactical supercomputer is necessary to stitch it all together into a cohesive wireframe model. The more environmental information the Gryphens can feed into the master database used by that computer—which was christened JCN, or "JACEN," and runs on hardware from each of the four command habs—the better capable their systems will be of predicting combat conditions and identifying types of objects they've encountered before.

Performing a general scan of the area, Trey picks out the largest unclaimed blip within two hundred miles of himself. He studies the limited superficial data available for it, deems it uninteresting, and catalogs its flight pattern and emissions signatures to the databank without seeking further detail. There's far too much garbage floating around out here, constantly in a state of flux, to do a detailed scan on everything that floats by. For the most part, what he's been trained to do is consider an object's behavior and its heat and energy emissions to establish how much of a danger it poses. Physical appearance doesn't really enter into it.

Over the next hour, he performs catalog entries for three more boring contacts before seeing something that makes him sit up straighter. He keys a request through the system, and after a few minutes, Collin Hartford of Three Flight obliges by scanning the object from a different direction. Which confirms Trey's suspicion, sending a thrill of adrenaline out to his extremities.

"Aeon Two-One to Aeon Lead, come in."

"*Go ahead, Two-One.*"

"I'm flagging a mark on your display, already in the system as Trudy-One-Zero-Three." The Gryphens are given a wide latitude in how they key their catalog records, and starting with his very first patrol, Trey had used his girlfriend's name for identifying the more distinctive entries.

"*I see it,*" his squad leader responds. "*Stable orbit. Bleeding some mild radiation, nothing unusual. What's the problem?*"

Trey smiles in anticipation. Yes, half the defunct satellites bouncing around in Earth's orbit leak radiation—the ones that were built with decaying nuclear power sources rather than solar panels. But as for Trudy-103... "Look at the timestamp, sir. I tagged this bogey yesterday at 1757—it should be about 3,500 miles *behind* us."

There's a long pause, and Trey can imagine his CO, Lt. Col. Austin Allen, pulling up the details on his databank entry. "*You're right, radiation signature is pretty close. Heat and radar could be a match, too.*"

"It's definitely One-Zero-Three, sir." There may be dozens of old satellites bleeding the same radioactive element, but the rate of emission is almost always going to be unique, based on the age of the sample. In Trudy-103's case, it's so faint as to be nearly unnoticeable. "Jacen concurs, it's the same contact."

"*Very well. Maintain your patrol pattern, but keep an eye on your girl. I'm gonna call this in.*"

Col. John McLaughlin floats briskly into the command hab aboard Asimov ODB, just swallowing his last bite of dinner. "What've we got?"

"One of the boys in Two Flight—Drogosch—may have identified an alien spacecraft," says Lt. Col. Kyle Major, base commander for Asimov. "It appears to be shadowing us. He first tagged it eighteen hours ago, and now it's suddenly *ahead* of us again."

"Have they approached it yet?"

"No, they're waiting on you."

McLaughlin pauses to think a moment. "Tell them to hold formation a little longer, and get me a secure line to General Dunn."

A minute later, Kara Dunn has been brought up to speed. *"Maybe it's one of the alien fighter craft mentioned by* KLINE. *Nymphs."*

"It's the right size, at least," McLaughlin agrees, looking at the radar data they've already captured.

"But we really won't know much until we do a higher-rez scan."

"You can pull what we have so far—Trudy-103."

A few moments pass while she does so; Kara herself is currently on patrol, leading Vulcan-One Flight. *"Yeah, not much definition here. It could be anything."*

"Except for its behavior, yeah. Pretty subtle." He bites his lower lip thoughtfully. "I'm going to send them in for a closer look—four craft, start at a distance and shrink the pyramid. No active radar until they're close-in, then ping her hard from all sides. Hopefully that'll give us the resolution we need, and if it's an enemy spacecraft, the sudden attention'll probably make her jump too."

"Sounds good. But make sure your people are clear, it's weapons-safe for now. Remember..." She trails off. *"John, are we private?"*

"Yeah," he replies, glancing around the command hab and squeezing the headphones a bit tighter over his ears. "What's up?"

"Peterson is convinced KLINE *was acting alone, but there's something he's not telling us. I don't know if we have potential allies among the K'lurans or not, or if maybe there's some other*

alien race out here, but... I just don't want to make any assumptions, okay?"

"Understood. Asimov out."

From within her own craft roughly nineteen hundred miles away, Kara uses her command override to listen in as McLaughlin explains the assignment to the pilots arrayed around Asimov base.

"And remember, what's important here is that we get information. Any of you fires on that thing, I'll have your hide, you understand?" There's a chorus of acknowledgements. *"Good. We want to know what we're up against. Get to it."*

Over the next half hour, four of Aeon's Destriers fall back and begin drifting away to investigate various objects along an entirely different trajectory from the possible Nymph. Slowly but surely they work their way through a wide loop to enclose their target in the middle of a pyramidal formation—a four point shape, each of its four sides a triangle.

"Very good," comes McLaughlin's voice. *"Now slowly close the noose. Fifteen meters per sec, max. Hold off on active radar until you're within twenty miles, but be ready if she bolts."*

They end up getting much, much closer than twenty miles, actively painting the target for more than a minute without a twitch. *"I can't believe she's holding so still,"* says Drogosch as the wireframe model in Kara's display takes on increasing detail, for it's immediately clear this is no space junk. It's a vehicle for sure—a much prettier, more streamlined design than the Destrier, sleek and sweeping like a fighter jet. In fact...

"Alpha Command, this is Vulcan Lead," Kara comms, calling out to McLaughlin. "Do those look like *wings* to you?"

"Sure do. This looks more like an airframe than a spacecraft."

A startled gasp comes across the Aeon squadron channel Kara's tapped into. *"There she goes! Man..."* Drogosch sounds surprised. *"She's moving... that's gotta be almost 300ms2!"*

Kara gulps. Three *hundred* meters per second squared? It's an incredible rate of acceleration, more than double what most of her pilots can probably handle without blacking out, enough to go from standing still to 1,000 miles per hour in less than two seconds!

"*Vulcan Lead, Asimov here. She's gone, just like that.*"

"I know, I was watching. John," she continues, momentarily forgetting comm protocol, "upgrade that Nymph to threat-priority-one and alert active patrols."

"*Will do,*" he acknowledges. "*But Kara...*" He pauses, and Kara can tell the man is a little shaken too. "*If all the K'luran craft have that sort of maneuverability, we could be in serious trouble.*"

Thinking back over what she knows from the KLINE Document, Kara finds herself agreeing with that assessment.

About the Author

R.L. Akers is a native of Florida who fled humidity and hurricanes to reside in almost-heaven West Virginia. Holder of an undergraduate degree in computer science and a master's degree in business administration, Akers has worked in software development as well as non-profit fundraising and publicity. He is a licensed foster parent who helps lead the elementary-aged children's ministry at his church, and his interests include graphic design and orchestral movie soundtracks. *Prometheus Rebound* is his first published novel.

Visit Akers online at his blog, RLAkers.com, where you can find short stories and information about upcoming novels. Make sure you also check out Gryphens.com and OrbitalDefense.com.

WITHDRAWN

MAY 1 5 2015

41144562R00299

Made in the USA
Charleston, SC
24 April 2015